birdmen

a novel

by phil williams

iUniverse, Inc.
Bloomington

birdmen
a novel

iUniverse books may be ordered through booksellers or by contacting:

iUniverse
1663 Liberty Drive
Bloomington, IN 47403
www.iuniverse.com
1-800-Authors (1-800-288-4677)

ISBN: 978-1-4502-6832-5 (sc)
ISBN: 978-1-4502-6833-2 (ebook)

Library of Congress Control Number: 2010915829

Printed in the United States of America

iUniverse rev. date: 3/22/2011

This book is dedicated to the memory of
Staff Sergeant Nathan Mudd.

To Ben, Adam, and Josh:
For the record, gentlemen, it matters very much.
With deepest respect, affection and gratitude.

And of course for Emily,
without whom nothing much would matter in the first place.

BY WAY OF INTRODUCTION

Most who read *birdmen* will understandably assume that it is autobiographic. Perhaps those who are most cynical will attempt to apply some of the more dramatic scenes in this book to my attempt at some kind of confession or exposé. And while I cannot deny that there are definite signatures here of my own experiences in Iraq and the subsequent homecoming, I can promise you those that do occur are solely a symptom of a limited imagination. Hemingway wrote that "once you write it down it is all gone," and to that extent this project has been rather cathartic, but that catharsis should not be understood as lending itself to exposure in exchange for any kind of recognition, however little it may be.

This book is a work of fiction set in an historical context. I chose the campaign in Iraq as my stage because of my belief that war serves as the most critical rendering of our human condition. In war we come to find that some of the beliefs we hold are really just silly little luxuries, and not any kind of hard truths. War telescopes our perspective of our proper place in the world—puts us back in the dirt with the animals—and reminds us just how far we are from Heaven and how near to Hell, and that the only difference between the two is a simple matter of choice. "You is sharks, sartin," preached Melville's Fleece, "but if you gobern de shark in you, why den you be angel; for all angel is not'ing more dan de shark well goberned."

What I attempt to accomplish in *birdmen* is to tell the story of a generation that has fought in a war that we do not entirely understand. And while I must be careful lest I be accused of arrogating to myself a privilege that may very well be beyond my poor talent to treat justly, nevertheless this project is an attempt at just that. The characters in *birdmen* are meant to be microcosms of the struggle between faith and despair that a generation robbed of heroes and Truth and Justice and the American Way are faced with. The Wyatt Earps and John Waynes are all dead and gone, and we are left only with their ghosts to contend with.

I don't think you can talk about my generation without also talking about Vietnam. That war left scars on our parents' generation that were passed onto us like a gene; those who did not avoid service were either killed, maimed or—if they were lucky enough to make it home in one piece—shunned, made to feel as if they had somehow betrayed their country, as if *they* were the ones who should be ashamed. The implications for who we are as a people and the value we place on selfless service are enormous in light of that blinding national blemish. Now we are forced to mythologize World War II and glean our heroes from the beaches of Normandy and the snows of Bastogne. Back when we knew who the bad guys were and why they were our enemy.

My generation went to war operating under the unspoken recognition that it was all screwed up from the get-go; there are no more absolutes and sharp delineations between the good guys and the bad. We had helped put Saddam Hussein in power in the 1970's, and now he was our enemy? We had supported and even armed the Taliban in Afghanistan in the 1980's, and now they were our enemy? While in An Najaf, Iraq, in 2003, after we had been briefed that the Sunnis were now the bad guys, I commented to a fellow platoon leader that I thought the Sunnis were the ones who had been pro-western?

Shifting alliances and fleeting truths, and something happens to a people's sense of what is real and permanent. Suddenly we find ourselves fighting a battle that may provide no sense of absolution in the end. War is truly ugly. Truth gets abstracted. Faith in anything becomes rather complicated.

Birdmen is my attempt to communicate those ideas and realizations through a fictional story. I harbor no illusions regarding my talent as a writer, nor to my right to speak for others; it may very well prove to be the case that I elevated myself to a position that I am all too ill-suited for. Still, I feel this is a story worth telling, and if it proves to be the case that I have missed the mark, I sincerely hope that someone else will pick up where I fell short. Wherever I may seem to go too far—or not go far enough—I hope those giants I fought beside will forgive me.

Before we begin, I would like to use this opportunity—by way of introduction—to relate one actual account from Iraq, if only because it illustrates a point I'd like to make before we begin.

During my second tour in Iraq, I served with the 101st Airborne Division as the Reconnaissance Platoon Leader for 1st Battalion, 327th Infantry Regiment. Having attached myself to one of our teams for a particular mission one night, we inserted into what we had expected to be an empty and abandoned building. We were surprised, to say the least, when we found a woman with her young daughter sleeping on the ground inside. Through the aid of our interpreter, "James," we discovered that they were homeless, and that the woman and the little girl "Sowsun" (which I assume is a variation of Susan) lived in the building—a library, we discovered—and "guarded" it. Evidently, in Iraq—where all the evil terrorists are—they allow their homeless and destitute to stay inside public buildings under the auspices that they guard those buildings. The fact that we were able to enter undetected in the middle of the night may testify to their security prowess.

Later, after the sun had come up, a wealthy man from the neighborhood brought by a bowl of chicken that would feed the two for over a week. All day long, as we took turns pulling security and waiting for our target, the little girl danced and sang and laughed, sharing her small world with us. I will not speak for the others, but I cannot erase her smile from my memory, though it has been five years now. Before we left later that night, the other men with me and I took up a small offering and gave it to the woman as a sort of recompense for having detained them the whole day. If I remember right, some of our offerings were rather generous, and I wonder if we were not trying to atone for something else. Just before we left, Sowsun kissed me on the forehead, offering me a warm and heartfelt "*Shukran*," and wished me a blessed Feast of Eid.

It seems to me that we in America are suffering from a lack of definition. We have forgotten that which makes us distinctly American, and I cannot help but feel that if we are to keep from losing our sense of who we are as a people, then we must re-engage in a national discussion of what exactly it means to be a citizen of our country.

I wonder if any of us today can fully appreciate what our founders accomplished so many years ago when they stood up and essentially said, "Liberty! At whatever cost, but liberty!" Can we imagine the very real consequences that such subversion to the British crown was then bound to elicit when they pledged to each other their lives, their fortunes, and their sacred honor?

Today, our demand rings slightly different, doesn't it? Something more along the lines of, "Safety! At whatever cost, but safety!"

When did we become so afraid?

When did we as a people abdicate the kind of passion for liberty that comes only at the execution of our fears? The desire for freedom is in our blood. They say that America is so diverse that trying to concoct a national identity is next to impossible. I say our identity is that which stirred men to utter treasonous words, and calls peoples from faraway lands, braving seas and scorching deserts. The American dream used to be that you were free from the oppression of others' beliefs and values, that you had certain God-given rights which no man nor instrument of man had power to sever. But somehow the American dream has since devolved into a three-car garage, 70-inch TV, and a robust 401(K).

We must reclaim the dreams of our founders, the dreams of men and women who would be free first, and safe next.

Contrary to what candidates may thunder on the campaign trail, our military is not the mechanism responsible for keeping us free. While it does provide a kind of freedom, it is a basic freedom from physical harm. Our military keeps us safe from foreign aggression, and they are very good at it. However, in a democracy, the people are the institution responsible for keeping themselves free. It is why Mr. Franklin told us that we were to have a democracy—if we can keep it.

But fear, that silent thief in the night, steals into our dreams and our natural insecurities and twists them into nightmares. Fear would replace our passion for liberty with a desire for comfort and safety, and in doing so would rob us of who we are as a people. Fear would rob us of the very thing that distinguishes Americans: that we are fanatical about our liberty. That we are a people who would rather die free than live fettered by a concern for a safe and comfortable life. We must reclaim that. It is the one thing that sets us apart from all other peoples: a scandalous insistence on the God-given rights of every man and woman to define for themselves the course their lives will take.

If I may be so bold, *that* is America. Man or woman, black, white, yellow, red or brown, gay or straight, no matter by which name you call God, if you hold to the truth that all mankind are created equal and are endowed by their Creator with certain inalienable rights, and that *among* those are life, liberty, and the pursuit of happiness, then I am happy to call you my countryman and my comrade.

America is an idea that knows no borders. Let them build their walls in the desert; freedom-starved people across the world will continue to lift their eyes to Ms. Lazarus's New Colossus, who stands in a harbor proclaiming that wall's very antithesis: This is the United States of America, and we do not build walls here. Let them pass their acts couched in patriotic rhetoric which are nothing but direct attacks upon our nation's most sacred document and a shameless exploitation of our deepest fears; nothing will stir men so deeply as the words "We the People...."

I see something happening in my generation. I hear it in conversations at night after dinner over a bottle of wine. I see it in the faces of those who are organizing our communities, teaching in our schools, serving in our wars, creating and working for non-profits, volunteering at polling stations, studying public policy, fighting disease and poverty, all serving their country, all heroes, all great patriots. I see the poison running its course, like venom from a snake-bite. The poison of self; of me and mine before my neighbor. The poison of fear.

It is high time that the true patriots of America as idea, America as incarnate hope, stand up and silence the servants of America as place and position. It is high time for a revolution—not one fought with guns and swords, but one fought with the most powerful weapon any one person was ever handed by their government: personal responsibility for their country. Our informed participation rages against the bigotry and fatalism disguised as patriotism and "American," if only we will engage.

My service in the Army exposed me to incredible people who consistently placed the welfare of their country before their own. Men and women who believe that America is capable of standing taller than she now does, and who are willing to place their lives at the alter of that more perfect union should it be asked of them, because they believe in the *idea* that is America. That America is much more than just a place; it is a goal, a process. Their sacrifice calls us to take courage and press on; their service sounds like a thunderclap in the face of our own pessimism and civic apathy.

As soldiers, we swore our lives in defense of the Constitution and charged into the fray singing, "God Bless the USA," only to come home and ask ourselves, "This is what I fought for? This?" But let me be careful lest I be accused of speaking for others.

As an American citizen-soldier, there are some things that I simply will not accept. I do not accept an environmental and energy policy that rapes our nation's natural places, poisons our soil and our water, and neglects the fact that the world is running out of oil.[1] I do not accept veterans who come home to nothing but a bottle of Jack and a street corner: those are my brothers and my sisters,[2] and I will not stand for spineless equivocations from lawmakers who never wore any kind of uniform. Who speak easily of service to nation, just so long as it involves limousines and mahogany desks. I unequivocally reject the kind of policy prioritization that gives our nation's most precious resource—our children's education—a second-class treatment in terms of resources and funds, while we spend millions of dollars a week propping up tenuous alliances. What of the implicit alliance we have with the next generation? Are they not our greatest ally?

Nowhere is the poison of fear so manifest as in our national budgets, for it is there we find where our true values find expression. Defense spending is enormous, while the monies and resources we

---

1   According to the American Petroleum Institute (API), there are 116.4 billion barrels (bbl) of Undiscovered Technically Recoverable U.S. Crude Oil Reserves. According to the API, that 116.4 bbl is enough to power "65 million cars for 60 years." (*Source*: American Petroleum Institute: *Energizing America: Facts for Addressing Energy Policy,* February 17, 2011). However, according to the Bureau of Transportation Statistics, there were over 255 million registered highway vehicles in 2008. (*Source*: Research and Innovative Technology Administration, Bureau of Transportation Statistics: *National Transportation Statistics Table 1-11: Number of U.S. Aircraft, Vehicles, Vessels, and Other Conveyances*). Simple—admittedly very simple—math shows that the U.S. has just over 15 years of oil left to run our cars. To be fair, according to the API the *world's* oil resources are much larger: 1,888.300 bbl of Undiscovered Technically Recoverable World Crude Oil Reserves. (*Source*: API: *Oil Primer: Understanding Today's Crude Oil and Products Markets,* 2006). A barrel of oil is equivalent to 42 U.S. gallons.
2   Women comprise roughly 5% of the 131,000 veterans estimated to be homeless on any given night. That's approximately 6,500 homeless women veterans, well over an entire brigade's worth. (*Source*: U.S. Department of Veterans Affairs Presentation by Mr. Pete Dougherty, Director, Homeless Veterans Program Office: *Homeless Services for Women Veterans,* July 29, 2010.)

appropriate to educating our children are paltry in comparison.[3] Let's take some of the money that we spend on increasingly expensive weapons, and pour it into our schools. Let's pay our teachers a salary that reflects their value, and at the same time place demands on them as if the future of our great nation depends upon them and their students instead of on missiles and new bombers. Our teachers are our nation's true heroes; let's start giving *them* medals and throwing *them* parades; they are the ones who communicate and preserve our national heritage, they are the ones who protect us from our own ignorance. I have a plan for a national corps of teachers that I would love to pitch to anyone who is listening.

The lack of attention we have given to education expresses itself in areas as seemingly innocuous as our prison policy. An embarrassing number of our nation's young men find their way into our prisons every year, and recidivism runs rampant in our justice system. The fact of the matter is that prison is an institution for certain populations in this country, and extricating them must become a national priority.[4] We can do that by offering them a legitimate chance at making an honest living. Education—the honest pursuit of knowledge—is the key to reversing the threat that

---

3 The Federal outlay for 2008 for National Defense was 612.4 billion dollars *(Source*: Office of Management and Budget, *Budget of the United States Government, FY 2009, Historical Tables*, Tables 8.1, 8.5), compared to 58.6 billion dollars for the Department of Education *(Source*: The Department of Education, *Budget for Fiscal Year 2008*).

4 In 2003, blacks comprised 44% of the total prison population, and one report found that "one in five black men spends part of his life in prison—seven times the rate for whites." *(Source*: CQ Researcher: *Race in America*, by Alan Greenblatt, July 11, 2003). According to a report published by the Commission on Safety and Abuse in America's Prisons, over the course of a year 13.5 million Americans spend time in jail or prison. Sixty-seven percent of those who have been incarcerated will be rearrested, and 52% will be re-incarcerated. The Commission reported that "many of those who are incarcerated come from and return to poor African-American and Latino neighborhoods, and the stability of those communities has an effect on the health and safety of whole cities and states. If there was ever a time when the public consequences of confinement did not matter, that time has long gone." *(Source*: *Confronting Confinement: A Report of The Commission on Safety and Abuse in America's Prisons, 2006*).

a growing prison population and the attendant social philosophy pose to our country.

My grandmother taught me to seek knowledge so that, among other things, I am able to "detect and confront error." Knowledge is the key to defeating the kind of religious extremism that perverts glad tidings and messages of peace. (And no, I am not thinking of Muslims.) What is truly abhorrent to me is the way our faiths have been subverted by political agendas to the point where our beliefs and our politics have become completely antithetical. The same man who goes to church on Sunday morning asking for mercy is among the first to deny 60 million of his countrymen access to healthcare that will dramatically improve their lives. Are we not called to practice more than mere mercy in the abstract? The same woman who will chain herself to a sapling will deny the enormous potential of an unborn human life on some principle. What principle, exactly? That a tree is worth more than a human life? No. Either life has value or it does not. Either we believe in mercy or we do not. There is a profound lack of integrity in our beliefs, and the dissonance and cacophony in our lives bear testament to the severance.

It is too easy to assign blame for the state of our country on our elected officials, and does a disservice to our heritage as Americans. Responsibility ultimately lies with us—We the People—in whose hands stewardship for our nation's future has been firmly entrusted.

Instead of calling us to rise above our prejudices and our fears, our leaders have exploited them in order to maintain and perpetuate their own powerbase; the great tragedy is that we have allowed them to do so. The profound lesson to be drawn from the Iraqi people in my story above is that, even in the absence of a government, *even when a foreign army had occupied their country*, they did not abdicate responsibility for each other. In a sense, they have taken the message of the American Founders to heart in a way that we seem to have forgotten—that the people are in fact the government, and that perhaps instead of relying upon a Leviathanic abstraction to provide for us, we ought to insist on our responsibility as a free people to care for our neighbor and protect our country.

But our country has gotten rather big, hasn't it? In a country of over 350 million people, it begs the question: Just who is my neighbor? It's not a new question. A man who makes quite a show of his faith asked me that once, and in answering I could not help myself: "A man was going down from Jerusalem to Jericho…." In the midst of such a huge and diverse population, it is easy to start to eye each other with suspicion. But we mustn't.

Instead we must recognize that a fundamental error has occurred in what "protecting America" has come to mean, for the only way to truly protect our country is to fight the threats to our heritage as a free and vested people. It is precisely during times such as the one we are now in that we must stubbornly insist on the perpetuation of our national values of liberty for all people, service to our neighbor, and sacrifice for the greater good. We must demonstrate the courage as a people not to act from our fear, but rather to act from our devotion to liberty and our faith in mankind. If we can accomplish that—especially now—then our country is safe from perhaps the only threat that can actually destroy her: ourselves, We the People.

The bible lying on my bedside table tells me that "where there is no vision, the people perish." Too long the vision communicated to us by our elected officials has been one of paternalism and fear. Too long we have looked out for ourselves and our narrow-minded interests first. Too long the vision for the American dream has been the accumulation of wealth at the expense of integrity and honor and service. It is time for a new vision.

It is time that we stopped asking how to advance our own selfish and often short-sighted agendas, and instead begin asking ourselves more profound questions about the legacy we will leave behind. Whether one hundred years from now our beloved country will inspire the same devotion from our great-grandchildren as she does now from ourselves is entirely up to us. How will the echo of our lives resonate with those who must follow us?

I wonder what my generation's legacy will be. Will it be fear and despair? Or will our generation take its place among those great, audacious believers in mankind who cast their lot into a future they could not see, and who spent their lives for a people they could only imagine and hope for?

This is our heritage as Americans. This is our calling. And to this end may we renew to each other our lives, our fortunes, and our sacred honor.

-Phil Williams
February 2011

And Dismay came knocking
on my door again today;
just happening by this way.

But I had nothing much to say,
so I slammed the door.

But I had nothing much to lose,
so I laced up my lucky shoes.

And I asked Dismay to dance.

- Jordan Lindsey, "One Wonderful Thing"

PROLOGUE

"You know," Randolph said softly so just the two of them could hear, "son, I don't know what you're doing in here—a young man on a Friday night—and that's none of my business, I guess. But you shouldn't be laughing at old Tom over there. Ain't nothing funny about old Tom. I suppose he doesn't dress too nice, and he talks to himself, and he drinks too much, but none of that's all that funny."

Sam grew quiet a moment, focusing on the label on his beer. "What happened to him?" he heard himself ask, as if he were asking to be forgiven for laughing at John the Baptist dressed in faded flannel.

Randolph shrugged his thin, old shoulders. "Don't know, really," he said. "Served in Vietnam. Had a name in his old unit, evidently. Called him Birdman. Was wounded twice from what I hear."

Hoping there would be a funny story behind the name that would lead them away from Randolph's lecture, Sam asked, "Why Birdman?"

But Randolph only frowned and shook his head.

BOOK I

CHAPTER 1

"Fire!" he yelled into the night and the oncoming headlights. The explosion from the machine gun next to him split the darkness, bursts of white flashes shooting out from the barrel. Through the deafening concussions, he heard other, smaller barrels firing to his right, where Olk stood by his Humvee.

The left headlight went out as the dull yellow of the remaining headlight listed to his right and started to slow. It came to a rest when it ran into the front bumper of the Humvee Olk stood behind. The young soldier peered down the smoking barrel of his rifle, into the windshield.

The noise of the machine gun fire had shot right through him; his ears rang and his head buzzed from the concussion. His vision slowly came back, though he felt stunned and unsure on his feet. Feeling drunk and somehow detached, he ran up to the passenger door.

He flipped his night vision monocle back down, casting his world into various shades of green. He saw they had fired on a small white pickup, and that it had been shot up badly. Olk quietly came up next to him, still holding the rifle ready to fire. A simple nod to Olk and he knew what to do. He stepped a little to the left, along the side of the truck so that he'd be able to see when Olk opened the car door. Out of the corner of his eye he saw steam rising from beneath the hood, and he knew that whoever was inside the cab was going to be in pretty bad shape. He prepared himself for what he knew he would see as Olk reached forward and grabbed the handle and pulled the door open, stepping out of the way so that he could see in.

And though he had tried to prepare himself for what he would see when Olk opened the door, what came falling out of the car and into his arms just before it hit the ground still surprised him. As if he had not seen it all before: big, surprised, feminine eyes and a gaping mouth, all pleading silently for help which the punctured lungs could no longer voice; a protruding stomach with several splotches of red quickly creeping outward. As he caught the quivering body and set it gently down on the ground, he felt her hands grab the back of his neck and pull his face down close to hers, her mouth closing and opening slowly, as if trying to tell him something. Terrified, paralyzed with fear as he felt the damp and warm breath from her mouth on his face, he was repulsed and resisted the urge to throw up.

He began to struggle to get away, using all of his strength to tear himself from her hold, which seemed impossibly strong. The harder he struggled, the harder it became for him to move at all, and he found that her strength was beyond that of a dying young pregnant woman, as she held his face inches from her own, her eyes, which were retreating into darkness, boring into his, pleading and accusing at the same time. He thrashed madly, yelling for help, for someone to pull him away from the woman and out of her eyes, but he suddenly realized that he was alone and that no one could help him. Where had Olk gone? The fear of suddenly finding himself alone, being drawn farther into those dying eyes, transformed into panic as he desperately tried to free himself from her grasp. He could hear gurgling noises from the blood flooding her lungs, and in his desperation he began to punch her in order to free himself.

He hit her first in her kidneys and sides, but then in her pregnant stomach, and when she still did not relax her hold, he began to strike his fists anywhere they would land, in her chest, her face, anywhere, frantically driving his fists into her flesh as he began to swear and scream at her to let him go. As he fought her, becoming exhausted with the effort and seeing that it had no effect, he watched the life in her eyes continue to fade to nothing, and the gurgling and hissing finally stopped.

Though he outweighed the young dead woman by at least fifty pounds, still he could not free himself, and suddenly the thought of being held by her for what may be the rest of his life struck him with renewed fear and panic, and he thrashed frantically about with renewed energy as he continued to scream for help.

He woke suddenly in the dark of the large warehouse, the ambient light from the approaching dawn casting the sleeping men next to him in a soft purple light. Streams of sweat ran down his face, and his heart thumped in his chest as he forced himself to believe that he was now awake and that the dead woman was a dream. Then he remembered the parts that were the nightmare and the parts that were not, and he sighed heavily, sitting up on his cot and wiping the sweat off his brow. He saw Anderson sleeping in the cot next to his, the man's back to him, his broad shoulders slowly rising and falling. He rubbed his face and eyes, trying to erase the terrifying image of the dying woman's face. He reached into his rucksack and pulled out his small bible, the pages stained with oil and dirt, and quietly walked outside into the bare, dusty courtyard where the Humvees were all parked.

The sky burned red from the fire of the yet-risen sun. A speaker crackled to life in the early morning heat, its song bouncing off the hard dry ground into the still air and over the flat rooftops of crumbling houses. A deep, guttural voice sang the words of the *salaat*, while the aging public address system popped and cracked as the words echoed across the quiet land: *"Allahu akbar...."*

At the end of the prayer, before rising, the worshippers inside the mosque each turned to the man on his left and right. *"As-salaamu 'alaykum wa rahmatullah,"* they offered to their neighbors.

One man, who but for the gleaming-white cleanliness of his *dish-dasha* looked no different than the other men in the mosque, quietly stood up and carefully began to roll up his *sajada*. He sighed as he saw the two round spots on the little rug where a lifetime of kneeling had worn it threadbare, and remembered the words his father had spoken when he had given him the prayer rug when he was just a boy. Smiling with the memory, he walked out into the street, his dark eyes sparkling with the knowledge of untold secrets as a small group of green American Humvees roared by. He smiled and waved at the gunner in the second truck, the soldier's upper torso sticking up through the roof, the baby fat on his cheeks the only part of his face showing, his eyes hidden by large, black-rimmed goggles.

The boy smiled and waved back.

Day one hundred and seventeen. It's June twenty-fifth, and I've been here for one hundred and seventeen days, Jonathon Garcia thought to himself in the quiet heat of the morning as he sat on the hood of a Humvee, his unopened bible lying next to him.

The sun was just starting to show itself over the ridge of low mountains to the east, but the air had none of the excitement typical of the mornings back home. The nights usually only cooled down to around one hundred degrees, and the ground and the Humvee that he sat on still radiated an oppressive heat. And even though it was already ninety-eight degrees that morning, it was a lot better than the 130 degree days. At least the sun wasn't up yet, and he reminded himself to be thankful at least for that, as he sat quietly on the hood of the Humvee as the sun rose much too quickly over the horizon.

He was lean—maybe 160 pounds—with sharp, strong features. His face was long, without an ounce of fat on his cheeks to match the rest of his body. His dark eyes were clear and sharp, resting underneath thick, black eyebrows, and thrust forth onto his world an innocence of accepting things at face value. When he would furrow his brow, as he was doing now, the thick eyebrows would plummet down and nearly cover his eyes. He was young, only twenty-four, and his light brown skin was dry and hard due to the life he had been living for the past five months. His whole demeanor, from the way he sat to the way he spoke, was that of constant consideration, which that particular morning was especially pronounced.

The *muezzin* in town had just finished the morning *salaat*. When he had first heard it four months ago in An Najaf, he had searched for a translation. When the battalion finally got a translator, he had asked him for the words, and had taken the time to memorize them so that when he heard the prayer, he could sing with it. As a Catholic, he wondered what Father Christopher and the folks at home may think of him whispering a muslim prayer—that he had gone native—but he thought with no small measure of satisfaction that the words were... well, catholic. So he had sung along with the *muezzin*:

"God is the greatest!
In the name of God, the Beneficient, the Merciful.
Praise be to God, Lord of the Worlds,
The Beneficient, the Merciful,
Master of the day of judgement.
You (alone) do we worship, and you (alone) we ask for help.
Show us the straight path,
The path of those You bestowed favor upon, not anger upon, and not of those who go astray.
God is the greatest!"

But the prayer didn't help with the nightmare he was still struggling to forget. Not that it ever had, or, at this point, did he really think it ever would. But still he thought it could, and so he had tried it, again. But the image was still there, the woman's dark eyes with the dilated pupils and the gaping mouth with the yellow teeth.

He sighed heavily and opened his bible and read Isaiah 48:18 again, then he moved onto Psalm 51, but words that used to—especially at this time of the day—move him, didn't really seem to do much at all anymore. Ever since Najaf and that damned pickup. Still, reading and praying whenever there was a morning like this one, where no one else was awake and he found himself alone, was a habit he had developed through the years, and he stubbornly clung to it. And even though the prayer and the verses never helped anymore, still he had believed they could. But lately his faith in these exercises had turned more into a kind of hollow hope, more like superstition than sacrament. He sighed disinterestedly and put the book down and thought that dreams were cruel things.

His thoughts trailed off. They never used to, but now they often did. He used to be able to follow a trail of thought until it was exhausted, but he had spent too much time during the past few months in meaningless thought, and his mind had grown lazy with idleness. Hours and days of staring at nothing, swatting away swarms of flies, had made his mind dull.

His memory took him to another morning, in another life when he felt as if he were another man, and another sun was coming up over another ridge of mountains as he sat by himself before everyone else was awake, holding his bible. That sun had warmed his face against the frosty air, and had filled his mind with a sense of perpetual hope and immortal youth which he was now fighting to retain. He felt the cold sting of the clean, crisp air against the back of his throat, and remembered the way the morning sunlight had shimmered off the lake spread out in front of him.

That had been a long time ago now, he thought as he relived that moment. His mind grew still again and a wave of grief flowed through him. Tears flooded his eyes. He went to wipe them away, but stopped, remembering that he was alone and would hear anyone coming up to him in plenty of time to compose himself, and let the pools rest in his eyes.

Not that anyone would bother him; it would have to be pretty important. They all knew that he liked to spend a few minutes in the morning alone, and they left him to it. Besides, the grief, he realized with surprise, was refreshing. His bored mind lunged at the realization of emotion and sank its teeth into it.

The sun, now fully exposed over the ridge, burned against his face as he raced through his own catalogue of regrets. Suddenly his mind jerked back as two flies landed on his lips, and he was back at Camp Bulldog in Makhmur, Iraq. Sweat started to bead against the light brown skin of his face from the heat of the sun. The air hinted of the smell of gasoline and human waste as a group of men burned the cans that were used as latrines. He could see the black smoke as it rose from behind the warehouse where his platoon slept.

There is nothing else quite like that smell, he thought. I don't think there's work nastier than that. He gagged as he remembered standing over the mixture, stirring in the gasoline, the black, putrid smoke rising around him.

The sound of approaching footsteps caused him to look back over his shoulder. His heart quickened from embarrassment at the apparent foolishness of sitting on the hood of a Humvee at six in the morning, staring at nothing, as Andy Walker walked toward him, his short, tussled red hair bright in the morning light.

"Hey Andy."

"Mornin' Jon."

"How'd it go last night?"

"You know how it goes. Sit out there all night, driving up and down those roads, and… nothing. I think the bad guys are all gone," Andy sighed and shook his head. "Time to pack it up and go home." They both smiled sadly.

"That'd be nice," Jonathon forced himself to say. The two grew quiet a moment.

Andy shook his head as if trying to wake himself. "Yeah. Well." He smiled and shrugged it off. "I gotta go see the CO. Take it easy brother."

"You too."

Andy hurried off, obviously aware that he had interrupted Jonathon's time alone, though Jonathon sighed when he heard more footsteps shuffling along in the dirt, and knew that his time alone was over. The men would start getting up, finally accepting the fact that it was too hot to go on pretending to sleep. He slid off the hood, reached for his bible, and walked inside the tin-sided warehouse where his platoon stayed.

"Hey sir," his platoon sergeant, Kevin Anderson, mumbled as he sat on the side of his cot, elbows on his knees, surveying the men of the platoon as they lazily got up and started to get dressed.

"Hey sar'n." Jonathon sat opposite of him on his own cot. For a couple minutes the two sat there, occasionally glancing toward the men if one of them cracked a joke or made some snide comment about the heat. There was not much for the two men to talk about.

They had spent every day together for over one hundred days, eating, sleeping, doing nearly everything together. They knew the names of each others' families, where they were from, what sports they had played in high school, favorite music, movies, and food. They had talked about God and religion and politics and the news and the weather and had beaten to death the subject of when they would go home. They had become friends of a sort, though more like brothers than friends. Jonathon knew other pairs who were closer, but the two of them were very different, and they had both accepted the balance of friendship and professionalism which they had found.

"Head out today at seventeen hundred, sir?" Anderson's gruff voice asked him from underneath the handlebar mustache he had started growing in Kuwait one hundred and sixteen days ago. The hair on his face served as a stark contrast to the clean, straight-arrow man Jonathon had known back at Fort Campbell.

When Jonathon had first noticed it growing, he had asked Anderson about it, teasing him. Anderson had stroked it affectionately, saying that it reminded him of his motorcycle back home that he had built himself. Anderson had almost knocked Jonathon down when Anderson had asked him if it was all right with him. Jonathon, flattered, asked whether he was kidding, and that of course he didn't mind. He had suggested a full goatee. Anderson had only laughed and said that he didn't think First Sergeant would let him get away with that. "Too bad, though," he had said, a mischievous twinkle in his eye. "Because I do look good with a goatee—even better than I normally do." "Even if you do say so yourself." Jonathon had laughed, and Anderson had returned it, and Jonathon was glad to have him at his side then, in the sands of Kuwait, on their way to war.

"Yeah. I'll talk to the CO today at breakfast to make sure, but I can't see why anything would've changed," Jonathon answered him.

By now they were both all too familiar with the rotation after four straight weeks. There were five platoons in Delta Company, with each platoon at about eighteen men. The company was tasked with running a Traffic Control Point about forty minutes west of

Irbil, twenty-four hours a day, as well as running a couple patrols each day. The rotation that the company commander had set up was that of a five-day rotation: day one they would pull midnight to zero-six hundred at the TCP; day two, zero-six to twelve hundred; day three, twelve to eighteen hundred; day four, eighteen hundred to midnight; and day five they would run two, four-to-six hour patrols. At the beginning, it really didn't sound like a lot, and Jonathon remembered thinking that it seemed pretty light when Captain Pham, the Delta Company Commanding Officer, had briefed it a month ago. But it was tough.

What made it so tough was not the schedule itself, but all of the "hey-you's," as they were called, that seemed to come down every day. These ranged from escorting somebody or something somewhere, to a patrol through the more remote country to maintain a presence there. It ended up averaging out to well over twelve hours a day, not including tower and gate guard, which also had to be pulled. The first week had been the hardest: the men complained the most then, and carefully crafted suggestions to the commander that it was too much. But the bottom line was that it needed to be done. So the men did it, day in and day out. They had passed the point of being tired a long time ago. Now they were just surviving. And surviving meant eating, sleeping, and going on patrol or pulling guard.

And doing whatever else it was they were told to do. Anderson also made the men do some physical exercise every day, except for Sundays. When Jonathon had questioned the logic in making the men do even more, he hadn't even budged.

"It's good for the men to get out and get the heart rate up, sir," he had insisted. "Otherwise they'll just sit and feel sorry for themselves. It's good for 'em." And that was the end of the conversation. Sergeant First Class Kevin Anderson had been in the Army for over seventeen years, and First Lieutenant Jonathon Garcia had been in just over two.

The men had dressed and shaved and were making their way across the dirt courtyard to breakfast. Jonathon picked up his rifle and followed after them, and ran into Captain Pham in the unlit hallway.

"Come see me after chow, Jon," his commander said to him.

"Yessir."

He stumbled over an empty MRE box as he walked out of the sun into the dark interior room where the headquarters element slept. Already there, eating his breakfast, was the Company First Sergeant, William Allen, a tall, lean man with dark, hard looking skin and sharp creases around narrow eyes.

"Easy there Grace, that ground'll git ya," he said.

"Mornin', First Sergeant," Jonathon said as he pulled up a full MRE box to sit on, and got out a flashlight so he could see to take notes.

The other platoon leaders came into the room; two others stumbled over the same box as they came in. The first sergeant's eyes screamed with amusement. Jonathon smiled to himself. Allen saw his smile and gave him a playful wink. Generally, as a rule, he didn't like lieutenants, but he had found that he could not help liking Lieutenant Garcia. Anderson spoke well of him.

After they had all found a seat, the commander opened his notebook. "I have some good news, guys. In about a week, we aren't gonna have to pull that TCP anymore." Andy gave an audible sigh of relief. "The Kurdish Peshmerga are going to take it over, and we will concentrate our efforts in the country, conducting our analysis on the status of water, electricity, schools, sanitation, and presence of insurgents in the AO. We've been given an area for the company and I'm in the process of assigning each platoon a sector that holds roughly the same amount of towns. There are reports that an insurgency is starting to surface, and that the enemy may be better organized than we originally thought he was. If he's out there in our AO, then we need to take the opportunity that this analysis affords us and see if we can't figure out who and where he is and how he's operating. So, just a heads up for you all, in the next few days you can expect a change of pace."

They talked about other things, the status of getting mail in and out of the country, uniform standards, and the meeting was over. Jonathon walked back across the courtyard and sat down on his cot.

The Peshmerga were Kurdistan's military. They were known to be ruthless, and the U.S. soldiers liked them for the most part. Meaning, of course, that they were the lesser of two evils. In the past couple months, Jonathon and the rest of the battalion had developed a tacit understanding of how that part of the world worked, or rather had accepted their lack of understanding.

A hazy line in the middle of nowhere marked the boundary between sovereign Iraq and Kurdistan. The Green Line divided a valley of the fertile dirt, and served as an unofficial boundary between the two countries. Of course, the United States and the United Nations could not formally recognize an autonomous, sovereign Kurdistan. To do so would have meant to take away a large portion of northeastern Iraq, and portions of northwestern Iran and southern Turkey.

Stories abounded about the atrocities the Peshmerga committed in the three nations where they fought for their independence. To travel east across the Green Line in Iraq was to move from a third-world country trapped in laziness, tyranny, and self-pity, to a world with clean water, electricity, security, schools, and a functioning quasi-democratic government. Developing a prejudice against the Arabs who lived west of that line was easy to do. Too many times Jonathon had been spoken down to, yelled at, and even—he was sure—called names by men who lived on the banks of the Tigris yet could not figure out how to get clean water, when twenty miles east, in the middle of a land with no water or rivers, there were many small Kurdish villages that had plenty of clean water.

The tension between the Arabs and Kurds could not be thicker. There were blood feuds that went so far back that neither side could even pretend to know the original cause. In the 1970s and 1980s, Saddam Hussein executed a process of Arabization, in which all the Kurdish settlers in the area were either moved, or were more likely killed, and Arab settlers were brought in to farm the fertile land for wheat. In the late 1990s, mainly due to the U.N. sanctions emplaced against Iraq, the Kurds started to move back into the area. The result was a never-ending, irresolvable claim to which piece of land belonged to whom.

It was the wild west out there. Owning a gun was an accepted part of life in the United States—a pistol for home protection, or a couple of rifles or shotguns for hunting. But gun ownership in Iraq went much further. Homes had an AK-47 machine gun for every member of the family and then some. Farmers would be stopped in the middle of reaping their wheat fields, and an AK-47 would be in the cab with them. RPGs were found in playpens. People were shot every day. There were no real boundaries and no accepted rules of what constituted ownership of anything, let alone weapons.

The Peshmerga brought with them, if not a sense of justice, at least a general sense of fear; they were ruthless, and they were good at what they did. And now they were going to run the TCP outside of Irbil—which was just fine with Jonathon.

The rest of the day passed like all the others did. Dreaming of home, planning out every dime that he had made, and thinking of all the things he wanted to do when he got home. Naps were spread out through the day, and they were a great way to kill the time, even if the men did wake up drenched in sweat.

About forty-five minutes before it was time to leave, they started to get dressed and load the equipment onto the trucks. Jonathon was always interested in the way the platoon got ready. No real orders were given; the men knew how much time they needed to get where they needed to get, and what equipment needed to be loaded. It was done quietly and deliberately, like oxen that patiently pull the plow across the earth.

Jonathon went by each truck once they were all loaded to make sure that nothing grossly important had been missed, then climbed into his truck and told his driver, Private First Class Jeremiah Olk, to go ahead. They passed through the main gate to the compound, wove their way around the sand-filled barriers to the main highway, and headed east. They passed the grainery that was the only reason the town of Makhmur existed, the two metal silos that shot up into the sky a stark contrast to the brick and cinder-block single and two-story buildings that comprised the rest of the town.

Quickly climbing out of the valley, the convoy of five Humvees made its way east toward the small ridge of mountains that separated the town of Makhmur from the TCP, about fifteen miles past the ridge. It always took about half an hour to get there, and the hot, dry wind would at first feel good as it cooled the skin from their sweat. But it would only take a few minutes until all the moisture was gone, and the wind that rushed over them became hot and dry and chafing.

On the east side of the ridge was some sort of mine where what looked like chalk was brought out in dump trucks. The white stuff covered the ground around each massive opening like some kind of gaping wound in the earth. They passed some sort of station that must have served as a radio relay tower, the chain link fence and barbed wire having been pilfered long ago.

His eyes scanned the inside of the Humvee, everything covered in a thick layer of dust. Crammed in between his two radios, he saw a folded up magazine with the headline "Untruth and Consequences," obviously alluding to the missing "WMD's." Jonathon could never quite settle his mind on how he felt about articles that questioned the war. Though in his own heart he felt sure that the elusive weapons of mass destruction would eventually be found—he remembered all too well with deep appreciation his time in May when he had sat on an abandoned Iraqi ammo dump that covered over ten square kilometers—and that such reports were nothing more than the typical and expected grandstanding of the media, he wondered to himself how he felt about what some thought was unpatriotic slander. Was it unpatriotic to question the truth? he asked himself rhetorically. But still it was not that easy, he confessed to himself, though he somehow felt it ought to be. He could certainly appreciate how certain forms of articles and news reports could appear to go too far, but should that mean they should be prohibited?

I wonder what Sam would think? he asked himself as he smiled and then quietly laughed in the chafing wind as he remembered the time after the pickup in An Najaf, when his good friend Sam

Calhoun had gotten into a lot of trouble over a reporter who had been assigned to his platoon.

Sam had been the Recon Platoon Leader at the time, and had set up a base in an old abandoned school in town, and was running his missions from there. One day, the reporter who had been imbedded with the battalion was left at his base for a couple days to take some pictures and get to interview some of his men. Sam had been flipping through the reporter's digital camera and had seen several pictures of Iraqis firing weapons at U.S. forces. When Sam had approached the reporter about it, the reporter—what was his name? Scott. Scott had tried to argue that his job was to report what was happening, and Sam had argued back that perhaps he should try to stop those who were trying to kill Americans, rather than take their picture in order to make them—and himself—famous.

The man made his real mistake when he had told Sam that it was his job to report the truth, as if he were some kind of knight in shining armor there to save the world with his photojournalistic talents. It was late at night, and Sam told him that it was his job as an officer to accomplish his mission and take care of his men, and he had no room in his perimeter for a man who was taking pictures of the very people whom Sam's soldiers were protecting him from while he peacefully slept. Sam had thrown the man's camera to the ground and had stomped on it with his boot.

When Scott had near pitched a fit about the first amendment and the right to private property, Sam had grabbed him by the collar, ordered his men to open the front gate, and had thrown him outside the perimeter, telling him to go find his friends with the RPGs in his pictures, that maybe they would give him a bed, and that, "There ain't no first amendment around here as far as I can tell, but maybe you should ask your friends about it. I'm sure they'd love to hear it." The great knight had begged Sam with tears in his eyes to let him back in. Sam had told him that if he tried to come back inside, "I swear to God—I shit you not—I will fucking kill you myself."

Scott, wandering through the streets, had been picked up by a patrol from Alpha Company later that night, and it had caused quite a stir when the battalion commander, Lieutenant Colonel Marc DaSilva, heard about it. Sam had been fired the next day.

Now, driving down this hot, brown highway, Jonathon laughed and thought that you just can't make that shit up. Not sure I would've done the same, he thought, but you gotta appreciate the irony.

Jonathon stepped out of his truck to go find David Carver, the platoon leader he was replacing at the TCP. He found him, a trace of salt on his dark face, talking to a man who was angry that his daughters were being asked to step out of the family car so that it could be searched. The daughters' eyes stared down in front of them as their father argued in broken English that it was completely inappropriate to have them stand outside and be searched. He kept saying "bad" over and over again, obviously not able to find another word in English to convey how disrespectful he felt it to be.

But David could do nothing about it, and Jonathon understood the position his friend was in. Everyone had to get out of every car so it could be searched. Those were the orders, and they made sense, because if the enemy were to figure out that the Americans were not making women get out of the cars, then they would immediately begin to use women to move their information and weapons. This was obvious to everyone, even to this middle-aged man who obviously was not an insurgent or a "non-compliant force." The man's eyes blazed, and Jonathon found himself looking away at the ground.

Right before the man relented, when he was at the peak of his indignation and obviously blaspheming David's mother and his God, Jonathon stepped beside his friend. It was all too easy, after standing in the merciless sun for six straight hours with no shade and no breeze, for a soldier to get overly hostile toward a civilian in such a situation. He was the one with the rifle, after all. So Jonathon, seeing his friend become increasingly agitated, silently stepped beside him and placed his hand on his shoulder.

"We are so sorry," Jonathon said to the man slowly and deliberately. "Please, everyone must get out," and made a gesture to the women in the car. The man paused and then muttered something, realizing that he was arguing with the wrong men; that these two young men who stood before him were not the creators of the policy, but were nonetheless obliged to enforce it. He turned and opened the doors.

"*Yalla*" he said to the girls, and they quietly, with their eyes fixed on the ground in front of them, got out of the car.

"*Shukran*," Jonathon thanked the man, who mumbled something in Arabic as he opened the trunk to allow the car to be searched.

Of course the women were not physically searched. For an American man to make an Arab woman get out of the car into the heat of the day, and then pat her down, would infuriate the men and embarrass the women long past any chance for reconciliation. After they got back into their car and drove away, Jonathon and David walked to David's truck where his men were already loaded up and eager to get back and strip out of their equipment.

David was silent until he climbed into his seat. "I need an ice cold beer," he confessed, almost pleading. Jonathon knew the feeling. One of *those* days, like so many before and so many to follow. It wasn't a beer he needed, Jonathon knew, but ice and a fridge and bare feet on a cool floor with steaks on the grill.

Jonathon patted his friend on the shoulder and said, "Well, there's no cold beer, but there's lots of warm Kool-aid. If you hurry, maybe there'll be some left." It had the desired affect: David sighed and chuckled.

"Thanks, brother," he said as the truck's engine roared to life. "Be safe."

"Yeah, you too," Jonathon answered, and the truck drove off toward the ridge of brown mountains to the west. Jonathon looked around. There was a long line of cars, just like there always was at this time of the day. He could already feel the sun beginning to heat his helmet and the Kevlar plates inside his vest. Regardless, he thought about how this was the best shift to have, because they were only in the sun for a couple of hours, yet didn't have to work all night and then try to sleep through the heat of the day. He walked over to the east side of the TCP and leaned against the sand-filled barrier next to Specialist Michael Owen, who held a machine gun pointed toward a car that was being searched by three other men.

The line of cars was long, and checking each one became repetitive and tedious. As the sun fell closer to the horizon, the line gradually became shorter. Jonathon walked from one side to the other, talking to the men, helping to pull security, checking cars, and talking in broken Arabic or Kurdish to the passengers who for the most part knew the routine well by now. They would jump out of their cars, flash a smile, open the doors, trunk, and hood, and patiently wait while the car was searched.

Just as the edge of the sun was beginning to touch the horizon, a large "bongo truck"—similar to a dump truck without a cover on the back—drove up to the western side of the TCP. Jonathon had heard them coming from some distance away, as the driver was honking the horn, and he could hear voices crying out. When the truck reached the TCP, Olk climbed up the ladder to the dusty-red cargo bed, and called Jonathon over.

"Hey sir! You need to come check this out," he called to Jonathon.

Jonathon walked over, climbed the few rungs so that he could see over the edge, and saw about a dozen men and women with a few kids all sitting around a large carpet that had been rolled up. The men were crying out, gesturing to the carpet and then to the sky, their mouths open and eyes swollen. The women were wailing—Jonathon had never actually heard the sound of wailing before, and it made him shiver despite the heat—their black *hijaab* over their heads, rocking back and forth. The driver had gotten out, and after one of Jonathon's men had searched him, had been allowed to approach Jonathon. The man, dressed in Kurdish garb, his once-white shirt tucked messily into dull blue baggy pants, patted Jonathon on the back of his leg. Jonathon looked down with a questioning look.

"*Mayyit. Mayyit...* died." He said to Jonathon, gesturing with both hands to the inside of the truck. He climbed up beside Jonathon, and hooking his arms around the high bed, pointed toward the rolled up carpet and said again, "Died, died." He then pointed to a woman in the far corner, who was completely covered in her black *abayya*, the only one not wailing and crying. She turned and Jonathon caught sight of the only portion of her face not covered.

The driver was saying "*'armala, 'armala.*" Her eyes were red, but not swollen, as she looked up toward the young American. Jonathon looked around at the rest of the group, the men patting the carpet and crying, some of the women touching it tenderly. He paused, his eyes traveling from one person to the next, and finally coming back to the woman in the corner, whose head was down, her hands folded on her lap in a quiet and firm resolve to hold her dignity.

Jonathon jumped down off the ladder, turned to Olk and told him to search the rest of the truck and the men. Jonathon eventually conveyed to the driver that the men must get out of the truck, but that the women could stay.

"You want us to search the carpet, sir?" Olk asked him.

"No. There's a body wrapped in it. Leave it alone, but search the rest of the truck and the men."

"Yessir."

Jonathon stood back and watched as the men from inside the truck climbed over the wall and down the ladder to be searched. It had taken some work to communicate to the women that they could stay inside the truck. Once everyone had been searched, the men climbed back in and the driver got back into the cab. The driver waved as the truck lurched forward, spitting black fumes from the exhaust pipes above the cab, and drove away east toward Irbil, the horn honking and its lights blinking in the dwindling light.

As it got later there was only the occasional car, and for the most part, they stood around at their positions, talking about anything—and not talking—and checking their watches for their relief. The moon was waxing as it crested the eastern horizon around ten and slowly started its climb across the sky, its reflected light casting the still and silent world into various shades of silver. Venus rose up out of the earth behind it, joining the moon in its chase after the sun through the darkness.

The air started to cool slowly, a very slight breeze stirring. They pulled the rest of the shift in relative peace, with only the occasional car to interrupt the hushed conversations of home and girlfriends and plans after they got home.

Jonathon gazed up at the night sky and thought of that staggering expanse floating above him. He had never really appreciated the presence of the moon and the stars at night before Iraq; he had never had reason to understand their phases and cycles, and appreciate the character they give the night. He felt as if the moon and stars somehow cooled the threat of darkness, and night did not seem so much like night. Thoreau was right, he thought as he looked up at the night sky. Perhaps we have settled down on earth and forgotten heaven.

Home was somehow nearer to them when the moon and stars came out, as if in their journey around the earth they carried the men to the other side of the planet, where the sun was shining on the backyard trees they used to swing from as boys. Then the world did not seem so big and they did not feel so far away, and the whole world was their home and every man their brother; and war was just a fable told by idiots as Apollo slowly drove his chariot across the sky.

* * *

Jonathon stepped out of the green Humvee into the market center of Makhmur in the late morning. He and Anderson were making a run into town with a few of the men from the platoon to get some ice, an activity they did every other day. Boys, who couldn't be any older than eight or nine, rushed at them.

"Mister, mister! Ice! One dollar!" they called out.

Jonathon smiled back at their eagerness, and found Faisal, his errand-boy whenever they came into town, walking confidently toward the truck, his hands shoved into the pockets of his jeans, as if imitating James Dean.

"Fuzzy!" Jonathon raised his hand and waved him over.

"Leftenant Jon!" Faisal beamed as Jonathon gently brushed past the half-dozen boys gathered around him and the Humvee.

Jonathon turned back to the truck, "Hey Olk, stay with the truck."

"Yessir," his driver answered him, cocking his helmet back and lighting a cigarette.

Faisal held his hand up for Jonathon to give him a high-five, and beamed at his American friend. "Ice, Leftenant Jon?"

"Yes. Four blocks of ice, please."

Faisal held four fingers out and said, *"Arba'a?"*

"Yes, *arba'a*," and handed Faisal four dollar bills. He was sure that Faisal could get the ice for much less than a dollar each, but he didn't mind.

Faisal took the money casually, and stuffed it deep into his front hip pocket. Then, forgetting his James Dean cool with a jump into the air, he turned and skipped toward a shop around the corner where he got the ice. A second later he emerged again, carrying a block of ice about three and a half feet long and half a foot square, his back arched from the weight as he cradled it as a man would cradle a stack of wood for a fire. Jonathon watched in amusement as the boy, smiling the whole while as if he had found his fortune, moved toward the truck as fast as he was able with his load.

A car honked right beside him, and Jonathon turned his head and saw a driver gesturing out his window, trying to get a group of goats to get out of the road so he could pass. The ever-present voice in the back of his head whispered for him not to become complacent, and he took a careful look around the street, touching the pistol grip of his rifle slung as his side.

"One," Faisal said.

"Waahid," Jonathon smiled and watched Faisal skip back around the corner, and resumed his scan.

The market place was sprawling with people. Two streets intersected randomly where his trucks were parked to form a large oblong circle of shops. Beat-up, old, white pickup trucks slowly moved through the crowd of people who paid no attention to the passing vehicles, off-white—almost yellow—sheep bleated as they jostled in the beds. Across the street was a shop with stacks of cages of chickens where a woman dressed in a black *abayya* pointed at two scrawny chickens to the shop owner. Groups of men squatted on the side of the road in their *dish-dasha*, their blue and white *shumagg* tossed expertly on top of their heads for the heat.

Jonathon saw the shop where he and his men used to get sandwiches of flat Arabic bread, hummus, and some kind of meat. When they had first arrived in Makhmur in May, they were relieved at the presence of local food; they had been eating MREs since they had left Kuwait in March, and so they didn't ask what kind of meat was in the sandwiches because they didn't want to know. But bouts of diarrhea and throwing up had caused them to cease their patronage of the local food stores. Jonathon looked down the street and saw chickens playing in the sewage that ran down the left side of the street in a small washout and shook his head, smiling to himself.

"Two." Faisal arrived with the second block of ice, the front of his shirt wet from the melted ice, his arms glistening from the run-off.

"*Ithnayn*," Jonathon said back and patted him on the shoulder. "You want me to help?"

"Oh no, Leftenant Jon. I do." Faisal pulled his left sleeve up to his shoulder and flexed his biceps with a smile.

Jonathon feigned impression, throwing his hands up in submission, and laughed. "Okay, Fuzzy, okay." Faisal turned and skipped back toward the corner.

At that moment, the deep resonance of prayer call swept over the market, the *muezzin* singing his melodic prayer over the town through a public address system which cracked with dust and age. If one expected that the streets would empty for every prayer call, they would discover that life continued on despite the call to prayer. Some shops closed, their owners or managers performing the *salaat* in the back of the store, but the majority of the town continued on with their day despite the call to reverence. Jonathon closed his eyes, and lifted his face toward the sound. Even though there was no music, the cadence of the prayer swept through him and lifted him with it as he recited the words he had memorized. He opened his eyes as Anderson came around.

"I'll never be able to fully describe this to folks back home," Jonathon said to him, his eyes aglow. The optimism of youth, with the delight of mystery and magic that accompany it, burst from his face.

"Yeah, it's something," Anderson muttered, squinting his eyes across the street.

But Jonathon was genuinely moved by the atmosphere and novelty of the place. He felt the heat of the sun against the back of his neck, and smelled the sewage mixed with the exhaust from passing trucks. He tasted the dust in his mouth, and listened to the sounds of market at midday, a hundred people speaking, yet he couldn't understand anything they were saying.

They waited there, standing next to the green Humvee parked next to the curb, for Faisal to bring the rest of the ice. Prayer call echoed to an end, and the magic lifted from the market. The colors that hung from the front of the stores lost their luster, the stench rose back up from the ground, and the heat settled back down on their shoulders.

"*Thalaatha.*"

Jonathon watched Faisal jog back around the corner, quickly emerging with the last block. He slid the last block into the bed of the truck with a hollow grinding of ice against fiberglass. "*Arba'a,*" he sighed with a smile and let his shoulders droop in feigned exhaustion.

"*Shukran*, my friend." Jonathon reached out and patted him on the shoulder.

"Okay, let's go boys." Anderson called out to a few of their soldiers who were looking in the local shops, surveying the odd collections of appliances, music tapes, and junk that was as good as treasure to men who hadn't seen electricity in three months. They jogged back across the street and climbed into the back, the metal of their weapons banging against the seats as they turned to face outside the truck for the quick ride back to Camp Bulldog.

"Jon, I need you to go down to Al Sharqi, which is about fifteen miles south of Makhmur, and patrol through the town and the surrounding areas," Captain Pham said, motioning Jonathon to follow him to his desk, a piece of warped plywood resting on top of empty MRE boxes. "See if you can introduce yourself to the *mukhtars, imaams*, and any schoolmasters in the area to check the status of water, sewage, electricity, schools, gasoline supply, and security. I'd like you to leave around zero-nine in the morning tomorrow. It should take about six hours.

"All in all, the total sector I'm assigning you is about 400 square kilometers. You have a network of dirt roads that run like a spider web through the area, with the main highway that leads to Irbil to your north. Your western border is a poorly maintained paved road that runs to the Little Za'ab River. Your sector's southern border is fifteen kilometers north of the river, this road here," he traced with his finger. "The main town—the capital if you will—is Al Sharqi. We haven't really gotten a chance to go down there much, so I can't tell you much about the area. So," he sighed, a smile playing on his lips, "go do stuff. Report what you find."

His commander, his finger on the map that he had used to brief off, looked at Jonathon and waited to see whether he could clarify anything. Of course, there wasn't much to clarify. Jonathon recognized the vague guidance. It certainly was not due to a lack of ability on his commander's part; the whole world was vague right now. The battalion was transitioning from offensive operations to policing operations, called Stability and Support Operations, in an area they did not know, among a people they could not relate to, who spoke a language they could not understand. Essentially, Jonathon was being told to go into an area and do something, anything.

"Sir," Jonathon said, appreciating the joke, "go do stuff, huh?" He sighed. "Yessir," he said, laughing and shaking his head as he gathered his things to leave. 'Go do stuff' was hardly a doctrinal term, hardly a specified task defined in *FM 101-5-1: Operational Terms and Graphics*, but they all got the joke: there was nothing left to fight. All that was left were things like "go do stuff."

Just as he was about to walk out the door, he heard Captain Pham's voice behind him. "Jon."

"Sir?" he stopped and turned around.

Captain Pham still stood behind his desk, the map spread out in front of him in the dull light. "Don't fuck up," he smiled, though it seemed forced.

"Yessir," he answered, not sure whether to smile back, as he turned and walked out of the room, asking himself how exactly one could possibly "fuck up" a mission like "go do stuff."

He walked back across the unlit courtyard where the dark outline of the Humvees barely showed against the gray of the walls from the moonlight. When he walked inside the warehouse, Anderson was up, reading an old letter he had gotten weeks ago from his little daughter for his birthday which had been two months ago. He laid the letter on his chest, the yellow light of the flashlight he was reading by temporarily blinding Jonathon as he sat down heavily on his cot.

"What'd the CO have to say, sir?" Anderson asked disinterestedly.

"Go do stuff," Jonathon laughed quietly and shook his head.

But Anderson was in no mood for jokes. "What the hell does that mean?"

Jonathon swallowed his levity. "Well, it looks like we've been assigned a sector around Al Sharqi, a little town about ten miles south of Makhmur. He wants us to go and conduct analysis on water, electricity, schools, all of that." He quickly related the limited information he had been given by his commander to his platoon sergeant as he unlaced his boots. "I think that we went through there once about a month ago," he said as he stripped off his boots, jerky breaths escaping him with the effort. "Do you remember that? Something makes me think that we escorted Captain Pham down there for some meeting. Remember? It had that open area in the middle, and those old men were sitting in the shade of that one building that wasn't built of mud."

"Sir, that sounds just like every other shit-hole village that we've been to here. After a while, they're all the same. Just a bunch of people living in dirt homes, with streams of shit running through the streets."

26

Jonathon let it go. His platoon sergeant was tired, and he didn't care for driving through parched fields, trying to find which dirt road was the dirt road that they needed in order to get to some small insignificant village of mud stuck out in the middle of nowhere. Jonathon focused his attention on peeling off his damp socks. Tomorrow they would deal with it, but for now his platoon sergeant just wanted to re-read his letter from his little girl. Jonathon sighed heavily and lay down on his back, spreading himself out on the cot to stay as cool as possible.

Jonathon's Humvee turned down the street that led through the market of Makhmur, and had to quickly slow down in order to let a flock of sheep pass, the shepherd nudging his sheep along with his staff. He waved to the two Americans in the green noisy truck and to the gunner whose head stuck out from the roof, his hands on the grips of a black machine gun. They slowly pushed their way through town, a line of five Humvees, winding around parked pickup trucks, chickens, dogs, and kids running up to the doors, yelling "Ice! Ice!" and "Pepsi, Pepsi!" and "Good, Bush, Good!" As the trucks cleared the middle of the market, the road narrowed to a single lane, and ahead they could see the open fields beyond the last walls of the town.

"Hold on, sir," his driver Olk said quickly as the Humvee sped up as it neared the edge of the last wall in the town. Jonathon smiled to himself. The truck hit the little canal of sewage that crossed the street with a thick thud of tires against concrete, and a sheen of dark water streamed up over the hood of the truck and onto the window. A slew of curses came from Specialist Chris MacLimore, the gunner, whose boots had found Olk's shoulder and the back of his helmet. The smell of the sewage they had just driven over filled the truck, and Jonathon stifled a gag as he thought of MacLimore being hit in the face with it.

Nazeem, Jonathon's interpreter, leaned forward from the seat behind him, and said laughing, "He does it every time!"

They were beyond the walls of the town now, traveling down a poorly maintained asphalt road that led south. To their left, a small ridgeline of dark brown mountains shot out of the ground, the dry dust in the air causing a slight haze that made them look farther away than the fifteen kilometers they really were. All around them, the bleakness of the land was a striking contrast to the richness of the soil that, two months ago, abounded with fields of green wheat stalks. Here and there, a small village of mud houses struck out of the ground, driving home the image of isolation and the constant struggle for survival that was life for these people.

About ten miles south of Makhmur, the asphalt yielded to a dirt road which kicked up choking and blinding clouds of dust behind the large trucks as they wound their way down. Through lack of care and the demand placed upon the dirt road by tractors and farming equipment, the road was littered with gashes that made travel slow and obnoxious.

Jonathon found himself longing to be stuck in traffic on the smooth surface of Interstate 99 in his old truck from high school, the windows rolled down despite the heat of a central valley summer. I'm never going to drive anywhere without the air conditioner on again, he thought. I don't care how much money gas costs. Should be cheaper after all this anyway. He smiled to himself and thought of the familiar streets of home.

Up ahead off to the right, he made out the outlines of the village of Al Sharqi resting on a slight rise in the ground. Drawing closer, spots of bright oranges and reds and yellows could be seen emerging from dark doors and from around corners. Kids running out to greet U.S. forces were always a comforting sign to the men that perhaps they could relax a bit while in that particular town. Jonathon waved through his window at the kids who tried in vain to keep pace with the trucks as they drove by. The line of trucks turned off the road in between two buildings, searching for a road to travel on that wound through the town.

How well-planned our streets and cities are, he thought, is one more of those little luxuries we enjoy in the U.S. that we take for granted. Often, while going to a town, Jonathon and his platoon found "roads" that would disappear altogether, or would lead an entire line of trucks into someone's courtyard, as the owner stared incredibly at the process of turning around five Humvees in such a small space. Depending on the perspective, it was either pure comedy or maddeningly frustrating.

Wires, loosely wrapped around gnarled branches that had been stuck into the mud structure of the houses, dangled between buildings, causing the gunners, who sat at about the height of the wires, to have to carefully raise the wires above the guns mounted to the top of the trucks to keep from tearing them down. Many times, the radio antennas, which stuck above the trucks by five or six feet, would catch a wire that was dangling too low and bring the whole thing to the ground. The men would have to try to reattach, however loosely, the wires back to their houses. Sometimes their convoy would kill the power in a whole village by doing nothing more than driving through it.

Carefully turning a corner, Jonathon saw on his left a group of men sitting in the shade next to one of the houses. He grabbed the handmike to his radio and called his lead squad leader. "Hey One. Six. Let's go say hi to those men. Eleven o'clock."

"Roger Six," Staff Sergeant Justin Hoover squawked through the speaker box.

The convoy approached, the three other trucks pushing out around the large opening in the middle of town to provide security, while Jonathon's truck slowly drove up to the group of men. He was familiar with the sight by now, one of those habits that seem peculiar to poorer societies, that of the local men gathering at a certain time of the day at a certain place to discuss the state of their world as they saw it. The men rose as Jonathon stepped out of the truck, his rifle in his left hand as he raised his right in greeting, a warm smile on his face. Nazeem followed behind him.

"*As-salaamu 'alaykum,*" Jonathon greeted, walking toward the group.

"*Wa 'alaykum as-salaam,*" a dozen men's voices greeted back. Most sat back down, their faces still on the young soldier who approached them. They were gathered around a large blue embroidered rug, some sat or leaned against pillows, their faces intently studying the white face that was still foreign to them.

One man, dressed in a long clean white *dish-dasha* motioned for him and Nazeem to take a seat on the edge of the carpet next to him. He was obviously, if not the *mukhtar*, then the senior man present, to offer him a seat at the village "council."

Whatever the men had been talking about was put aside for now, and they waited patiently for him to begin, a couple men across from him exchanging a quick conversation in hushed voices. The man who had offered him the seat looked intently at him, then looking at the rest, said something in Arabic, to which they all nodded in agreement. "What did he say?" asked Jonathon of Nazeem.

"He says you are young," said Nazeem with a slight smile, despite himself.

Jonathon fought the swell of embarrassment that rose inside and began.

"My name is Lieutenant Garcia, I am with the U.S. Army base in Makhmur."

Nazeem translated. Jonathon always found himself fighting frustration whenever he had to endure a conversation through a translator. It was yet another one of those peculiarities of being in Iraq that he had never thought of, another tormentor and reminder of how far from home they were. Conversations which were already as simple as they could be, often took three times longer then they should.

The men raised their hands and touched their chests in warm greetings, "*Salaam*" was echoed throughout.

"Welcome," Nazeem translated.

"I am here to try to see if there is anything that we can do to improve your village," said Jonathon, slowly looking around the group of men. "I would like, if you have the time and would not mind, to ask you some questions," he paused, letting Nazeem translate. "And, of course, if I can answer any of your questions, or be of help in any way, I would be happy to."

Nazeem translated and the men all nodded their heads saying, "*Na'am, na'am.*"

The man in the long white *dish-dasha* said something to Nazeem. When he had finished, Nazeem turned to Jonathon and translated.

"Of course, they are willing to help in any way they can. You are only the second U.S. officer they have seen."

"*Shukran*," Jonathon bowed his respectfully. "Well, first, let's begin with anything that we can help you with." Nazeem translated. "Schools? Roads? Water? Electricity?"

When Nazeem said "*maa*'" and "*kahrabaa*'," the men leaned forward, nodding their heads. Again, confirming that he was most likely the village leader, the man in the white *dish-dasha* spoke, his eyes shifting between Nazeem and Jonathon as he did. After he had obviously said several sentences, in fear of Nazeem not being able to remember everything that he was saying, Jonathon lightly touched Nazeem's arm and asked, "What is he saying?"

Nazeem politely signaled for the man to wait, and turned to Jonathon. "He says water is a big problem. They used to get water from a well nearby, but a group of Kurds from the village over there," at this he pointed in the general vicinity the man had, toward the ridgeline, "one night broke the pump they use to get the water, and they have not been able to fix it."

"How long ago was that?" Jonathon looked at the man. Nazeem translated, and the man answered.

"About three months," said Nazeem.

"And how have they been getting their water since then?" asked Jonathon, trying hard to keep his eyes on the man he was speaking to, and not Nazeem.

Again the exchange.

"He says they must go to a village near the river and fill... ummm... jugs? Like big barrels, you know?" said Nazeem, shrugging his shoulders.

The man spoke again. Jonathon waited while Nazeem listened. When the man finished, Nazeem said, "It seems the water in the well is also bad..." he fumbled and turned back to the man, asking for clarification. They spoke quickly to each other, the man motioning with his eyes for Nazeem to be sure to tell Jonathon what he was saying.

Finally, Nazeem turned to Jonathon. "Do you know what this man says?" Nazeem asked. Jonathon shook his head, barely able to repress a smile. How the hell would I know what he says? he asked himself. "No, what is he saying Nazeem?" he asked out loud.

"Umm... he says the water in their well is... how you say? Poison?"

"By the Kurds in the next village?" Jonathon asked, surprised.

"No." Nazeem shook his head. "The water is bad... like metal... or salt, he says. Even before the pump was broken, the water in the well would sometimes go away."

"Did the well used to dry up?" asked Jonathon, looking at the man in the white *dish-dasha*.

Nazeem translated, and the man shook his head. "*La,*" he said, shaking his head for emphasis, and speaking more to Nazeem.

"No," Nazeem said to Jonathon, "only in the past few years has the water in the well begun to go away. Before, it was always there. You understand?"

"Yes, I see," Jonathon affirmed to Nazeem.

The man touched Nazeem on the arm and continued. Again Jonathon had to interrupt so as not to lose anything in translation.

"Nazeem, I need you to translate each sentence at a time."

"I am trying, but he has much he wants to say, and will not stop," Nazeem said. Nazeem was a little man—kind of mousy, Jonathon often thought—and whenever he had to be corrected, however mildly, he looked like a dog that had just been kicked. Jonathon remembered a time several months ago when he had seen some soldiers shooting a dog for the hell of it. Part of him had wanted to stop them, but he hadn't, and it had taken him a couple weeks to get over the thing. Sometimes Nazeem looked like that dog.

"I understand that, but I need you to try to tell him to talk slower," said Jonathon, his hand on Nazeem's arm.

Nazeem translated.

"What was he saying before?" asked Jonathon.

"He was talking about the Kurds in the village over there." Nazeem pointed to the east. "They stole some wheat the farmers in this village had harvested." Jonathon stifled a sigh. He had been down this road before, and he dreaded another journey. The never ending, entangling mess that is the history of blind hatred between the two ethnic groups.

Jonathon sympathetically shrugged his shoulders with regret and said, "I am sorry for that. But there is nothing I can do about that unless you have proof."

It worked. Because, of course, there was no proof; because, of course, in fact no wheat had been stolen. The men grew silent. Jonathon followed with, "What about electricity and gas? How do you run your lights and heat your food?"

Nazeem spoke to the man.

"He says that electricity is unreliable, but it has always been like that, ever since he was a boy. But benzene is a big problem. Now, they have to drive all the way to Qayyarah, and sometimes, they are out, so they have wasted an entire day and some benzene for the journey. He says it is a big problem for all of the villages."

"Yes," Jonathon countered, "we know that gas is a big problem for this area, and we are working very hard to improve it." Though the truth was that he did not know whether anyone was working hard on it, but he had nothing else to say, and thought that he had heard of convoys of gasoline being escorted by U.S. forces throughout the country. Regardless, to appear impotent at their first meeting was not the right way to start this relationship; Jonathon had to present the image of the entire U.S. Army: that of control, knowledge, and the power to improve the way of life and provide security for the fragile country as it tried to rebuild. The answer was apparently acceptable, as the man in the white *dish-dasha* nodded and said something to the others, who nodded in agreement.

"I'm sorry, may I ask your name?" he asked, looking at the man who had carried the burden of representing the village.

"*Ma issmak?*" Nazeem asked the man, who answered.

"He says his name is Jassim Khalil," Nazeem told Jonathon.

"*Fursa sa'eeda,*" Jonathon did his best, looking at the man, who smiled, obviously accepting the attempt.

"You also," Nazeem translated to Jonathon.

"Mr. Khalil, are you the *mukhtar?*" asked Jonathon, his eyes on the man in the white dish-dash.

"*Na'am.*" His eyes danced with delight and pride and the other men nodded their agreement to his position.

Jonathon decided that he had acquired enough formal information, and decided to cement the relationship with talk of the village, family, and neighbors.

His battalion commander, Lieutenant Colonel DaSilva, had made it clear to all of his young platoon leaders that, though ranger school and their Infantry Officer Basic Course had taught them how to meet their enemy on the field of battle and kill him, the struggle they were currently in was unlike anything they had been trained for. He could not have been more right. If anyone had asked young Cadet Garcia four years earlier what he thought he would be doing during a war, it would certainly not have been sitting on a carpet in the shade of a mud hut, exchanging pleasantries with the local men of a small, insignificant village in an obscure corner of Iraq.

These thoughts and others like them often entertained Jonathon as he recalled his previous perceptions of what the war with Iraq would be like. He had envisioned bombs, and gunfire, and explosions. There had been very little of that. The large majority of what he and his generation were being asked to do was to win a war through securing key sites and interacting with the locals in order to restore stability as quickly as possible. Far from maneuvering his platoon to attack an entrenched enemy position, he was engaged in conversations about water and gasoline and electricity while his men pulled hours of mind-numbing security over a town that showed no sign of hostility. This was war, evidently.

Their conversation came to a close, marked by greater and greater intervals of awkward silence between questions. Jonathon rose to his feet, his right foot having fallen asleep from sitting on the ground in all of his equipment for so long, and made his goodbyes. He shook the hand of Mr. Khalil first, and then the hand of each man who had sat around the carpet.

Mr. Khalil walked a few steps with Jonathon toward his truck, with Nazeem between them to translate. No translation was necessary. "Leftenant Garcia," Mr. Khalil said in a thick English accent to a very surprised Nazeem and Jonathon, "when will you return?"

Jonathon recovered quickly, and looking the man directly in the eyes, said, "I will be back to visit you within a week." Nazeem backed from between them quietly.

"I look forward to talking with you again, Leftenant Garcia," said the man softly.

"Yes, as do I, Mr. Khalil." Jonathon stopped at the door of his truck, his eyes on the man in the white *dish-dasha*.

"The next time we meet, you may call me Mr. Marie," said the man, bowing his head slightly, a smile playing on his lips, his dark eyes sparkling.

"I am surprised at how well you speak English," Jonathon confessed.

"If you will continue to visit us, Leftenant, perhaps you and I both can learn many more things from each other," spoke the dancing eyes.

"I would like that, sir." Jonathon smiled, offering his hand.

"Then I look forward to seeing you again soon," said Mr. Marie as he gently nodded his head.

"*Insha'allah*," Jonathon bowed his head.

Mr. Marie smiled and echoed, "*Insha'allah*."

* * *

His eyes flashed open, and then slowly closed. The green meadow full of wildflowers resting under towering snow-capped peeks and an achingly-blue sky was gone. Those he had been walking with, shadows of people and friends from home, vanished into a sea of black. The sound of a great river roaring and crashing was swallowed up by the deafening silence of the warehouse. His mind fought to recapture the dream, desperately grasping for the fleeting images already outstripping his memory. Opening his eyes, he sighed quietly and heavily, and yielded.

A depression rose up from inside and pressed in on him like a gigantic weight that threatened to suffocate him. He did not move—he didn't want to. Moving meant being awake, and being awake meant another day. Another day in Iraq. Another worthless, wasted, wearisome day. He watched, in a silence so stifling that it threatened to wake the whole group, the slow rise and fall of Anderson's shoulders outlined in the ambient light from the moon outside. A tidal wave of envy washed over him as he watched him sleep. It didn't matter what he was dreaming. Right now, at this moment, he was not here, yet Jonathon was trapped inside this prison, clawing at the walls not knowing for what crime he was sentenced.

Jonathon lay on his side on his cot, a drop of sweat running down the side of his face, tickling him. But he did not move to wipe away the perspiration that gathered on his face from the heat of the night. He did not care. What did it matter if he was covered in sweat?

And as he lay there, the depression in him swelled and morphed into sadness and fear, or rather exposed the great sadness and the great fear that was always gnawing at him now. He accepted the grief and let it run its course. He had learned since coming to Iraq not to avoid his shame or pretend that he was not afraid. He had had to forgive himself of the sadness and the fear that nearly paralyzed him at times, like this one, when he was alone and found himself suddenly overwhelmed. Fear and sadness, he had learned, were not shameful emotions. The idea he had had in his head of great men being those who were never afraid, never distressed, he had found to be simply untrue. What had made those men great was the same thing that was forming inside him now; a willingness to accept the seasons of his emotions. That all men were afraid, that all men were grieved at times by the circumstances in their lives when they felt themselves nearly overrun, overwhelmed, surrounded on all sides by nothing but desperation and defeat. So he let this pity run its course, better now in the night than in the day anyway.

What does it matter? he thought to himself, lying there in the dark. I'm going to sweat all day anyway. Just like yesterday. How many days now? One hundred and forty? One hundred and thirty-nine? So what does it matter? Whether I'm here for a hundred days or two hundred? Two hundred is still a hundred and fifty away from home, and we're not even close to two hundred yet. Is this ever going to end? Already I've been here so long that home seems like the dream I just had. Just a dream. And the reality is here, in front of me, all around me. A hopeless, meaningless existence of survival, day in and day out. I don't want to sleep. I don't want to be awake. I just want to be home, away from this miserable place.

His mind took him back to the kitchen at his home. The light blue of the tile on the counter against the white of the grout. The light oak of the cabinets. He could see the grass that grew against the patio his dad and he had built two summers ago. That spot on the wall where he had inadvertently marked an "X" while washing off the paint from a brush when he had painted the fence. Home. There was a knick in the wall where he had bumped the new couch against it as he and a neighbor wrestled it through the narrow door. His desk, and the initials "E.F." that he had carved into the underside when he was in middle school, for the girl he'd had a crush on. He visualized his mom, bent over the counter, kneading white flour into balls for tortillas; and the taste of the warm, simple bread in his mouth as he snuck one out of the towel that kept them warm. The feel of his dog Kiowa's tail rubbing against his leg as they sat around the table for dinner, steam rising out of the bowl full of sliced carne asada....

Sleep mercifully stole him away and led him to new visions, where again shadows and ghosts of people he knew met him and walked with him in strange but comfortable places.

Jonathon awoke with Anderson tapping his foot. "Chow, sir."

He sat up and swung his feet off his cot onto the warm concrete. Pulling on his stiff black socks formed in the shape of his foot, he felt the weight that had pressed upon him so heavily just a few hours ago leaving him. Only the aftertaste remained, and some food would rid him of even that. Emerging from the warehouse where they slept, the brightness and heat of the sun punched him hard in the face. He squinted and looked at his watch and thought how it was only eight in the morning. Gonna be a hot one today. He looked at his watch again. July eighteenth. So that makes it day one hundred and forty, he thought. He sighed heavily and shook his head and tried to laugh it off.

He ran into Captain Pham at breakfast. "Hey Jon, how are you?" His commander affectionately patted him on the shoulder, smiling through the heat of the early morning.

"I'm all right, sir, how're you doing?" Jonathon asked, squinting his eyes in the bright light.

"You know, another day," he sighed.

"Yep. Another day, sir." And that feeling that had attacked him in the morning surged and rose up inside of him again.

"Are the boys all through?" Captain Pham asked him.

"The last few are in line now, sir."

"Good. Let's go get some chow." Captain Pham placed his hand gently but firmly on his young platoon leader's shoulder, obliging Jonathon to move into line for breakfast.

The two men got their plates and shuffled past the plastic tables that bent and threatened to come toppling down from the weight of the green containers that held the food. The few men who were serving piled up the spongy yellow "eggs" onto their plates, heaped a generous portion of shriveled sausage, and stacked several stiff and stale pancakes to finish off the breakfast. Jonathon looked down with indifference at his food; he wasn't even hungry, but he had enough food on his plate for two men.

He and Captain Pham wandered over to a portion in the small courtyard where the sun's rays had not yet heated the concrete to stovetop temperature. The dust from the long-dead garden rose lazily from the movement of the men, and gently settled back down. There was no breeze, only the stifling heat of the morning from which even the shade could not protect them.

"How are things going, Jon?" his commander asked him after they had each had a few bites.

"All right, sir," Jonathon managed after he had washed down a bite of the cold sausage with some of the warm orange juice.

"Hmm," Captain Pham acknowledged, his mouth full. Once he had swallowed, he continued, "You know, yesterday, as I was sitting at the desk, I started thinking about home. You know how it is, home is always on your mind here, but you know how there are those moments when you really think of home? Like the details? I was thinking of my wife Kim working in her garden, and my boy Matthew squealing his head off as he rode his four-wheeler around and around our cul-de-sac." He paused, a smile playing on his lips, as he allowed himself a brief moment to live in that memory. "I always miss them, but when I think of specific things like that, it's harder than it normally is." He shot his young platoon leader an inquiring look, one that Jonathon missed.

"How're your folks doing? Have you heard from them lately?" Captain Pham pursued.

Jonathon swallowed a forkful of eggs. "Yessir. I got a letter from them about a week ago. Of course, it was over a month old. But they seem to be doing fine."

"Well, I'm sure they miss you. You're an only child, right?"

"Yessir."

"Must be hard on your mom, especially."

"She's not too thrilled with this whole thing, sir." He forced an insincere laugh.

His mind shot back to an image of his mom kneading tortillas on the kitchen counter as he stood in the kitchen with her. It was the last weekend he was home before he had left. His dad was in the living room, drinking a cup of coffee and reading through the Sunday paper. His mom, already in her church dress, the apron over her to keep the dough off, turned her face as he walked into the kitchen. Her shoulders betrayed her, though. Jonathon walked up and placed his hands on her shoulders and reached over and kissed her gently on the cheek.

"Buenos dias, mama."

"Buenos dias, mijo," she choked out, struggling to maintain her composure.

"Mama, it will be all right. Please don't cry."

"Then you will come home safely?"

"Of course I will, mama," he said gently.

She turned abruptly, holding up her hands, covered in white flour. Her face was only inches from his, her eyes were red and her pupils strained and bore into his. He looked away, past her, to the counter. "Look at me, Jonathon."

He obeyed, and his eyes met hers. They stood there like that for only a few seconds. Then she wrapped her arms around his neck, and pulled him down and close to her so that her head rested on his shoulders. She was crying now; Jonathon could hear her nose running.

"Of course, I know that you must go. This is what you men feel you have to do, to fight in these wars," she managed to say, between quiet sobs. Jonathon could feel the slight coolness of her tears as they fell onto his shirt. "But you must come home safe to me. I am so proud of you, a grown man now. But you are always my little boy." She stopped abruptly, and squeezed him tighter. "It is you who puts these gray hairs on my head," she said as she pulled back and feigned a smile and turned back to the counter.

Fighting back the lump that swelled in his throat, he turned away, and saw his dad standing in the doorway to the kitchen, his empty white mug in his hand.

Captain Pham smacked his lips. "Now you can't beat that kind of a breakfast, can you?"

Jonathon smiled, "No sir. It's hard to beat sponge eggs, cold sausage, stale pancakes, and warm orange juice. Again." They both forced a chuckle.

"Hey Jon," Captain Pham said to him, his face suddenly becoming very sincere. "Being here is hard. It's hard for every one. But you and I, we have to lead our men; that is our duty, both to God and to our country. You and Andrew and Dave and the others, man, you're having to do more at a younger age than any of us older men had to. You're doing a great job too, Jon, you really are. The 'Colonel has asked me about you, asked how you were doing the other day. I told him that you were one of the best platoon leaders I've seen." He paused. Then, patting Jonathon on the shoulder, he stood up with empty plate in hand, "Keep it up, Jon. I know it's hard, but keep up the good work."

Jonathon, slightly embarrassed by the open compliments of his commander, looked down at the ground. "Thanks, sir, will do."

"All right. What're you up to today?" he asked, looking down at Jonathon.

"I'm going to Al Sharqi to revisit the town at about fourteen hundred, sir," Jonathon held up his right hand to shield the sun from his eyes.

"All right. Come see me when you get back. I'm interested in that man you talked with last time—what was his name?" Captain Pham asked.

"Jassim Khalil. He told me to call him Mr. Marie," he added.

"Mr. Marie. Hmm. Strange," Captain Pham mused.

"Yessir, it is a little strange. Out there in the middle of nowhere, this man speaks English as well as you and me," Jonathon said, shaking his head pensively.

"You and I," offered Captain Pham, smiling.

Jonathon laughed, "Right sir, you and I; well, point made."

Captain Pham laughed, "All right. Well, come and see me when you get back."

"Will do, sir."

Jonathan watched as his commander walked away from him, saying hello and making quick jokes with the men who were still milling about after breakfast. As he watched him walk away, he felt relieved of the weight that had plagued him all morning. Perhaps the day was redeemable after all.

He was sitting on his cot, his hands folded in front of him, staring at the ground, when Sam Calhoun walked in from behind him.

"What's up, man?" Sam asked with a friendly smile and a pat on the shoulder as he plopped down on Anderson's vacant cot across from Jonathon.

Jonathon looked across at his friend. His jet-black hair was sloppily parted to the side, and his dark sideburns jutted down his face much longer than the regulations called for. Square-jawed, broad shouldered, at six-one, he was an imposing looking man, and had the personality to match it. Plus, he was older than the other lieutenants—Jonathon thought he was either twenty-eight or twenty-nine. Jonathon had first really gotten to know Sam when his platoon had been attached to Charlie Company during An Najaf. Sam had been the scout platoon leader at the time, and Jonathon had immediately felt a friendly attachment to Sam's bold abrasiveness.

Sam had the reputation of speaking his mind perhaps a bit too clearly, which always put him a little at odds with his superiors. There was that incident in An Najaf with the reporter, and he'd been moved to Charlie shortly after. Then there was also the story of a time when he was out with 'Colonel DaSilva and had to set up a landing zone for a couple helicopters that were coming in. Things had somehow gotten mixed up, and Sam, not realizing that he was speaking into the battalion radio frequency, had said that if 'Colonel DaSilva could give clear directions none of it would have happened. Of course it wasn't an accurate statement, 'Colonel DaSilva was a great commander and well loved by all of the officers in the battalion, but that was just Sam, all passion. When he realized what he had done, he walked over, took his scolding, apologized, and then moved on.

"Hey Sam. What's up?" Jonathon asked with a weak smile.

"Nothing," Sam shrugged. "How you livin'?"

"All right." Jonathon struggled away from his thoughts, reluctant for conversation right now, even from so good of a friend. "You go out last night?"

"Yeah, I went out with first platoon to the TCP last night until midnight."

"That's the best shift to have," offered Jonathon.

"Yeah, but that ain't saying much."

Jonathon smiled. "No, sure isn't."

"Hey, have you heard about what happened while we were out there?" Sam said with a smile, his eyes beaming.

"No. What happened?" Jonathon leaned forward in his cot, his interest piqued.

"It was crazy, man, I'm telling you. Never in a million years would I have thought of something like this," Sam said, obviously getting excited as he prepared to tell his story. Jonathon smiled as he thought about how Sam was one of the best storytellers he'd ever known.

"What happened?" Jonathon repeated, now entirely curious in what Sam had to say. "Did you guys find something?"

"Did we ever!" he slapped his knee. Sam was from Louisiana, Jonathon remembered, and whenever he said things like "Did we ever!" his southern accent really came out. Then, gathering himself and taking a deep breath, he began. "So the sun was just going down, and I was just thinking to myself that there were only a few more hours of just standing out there in the dark—because you know how there are almost no cars after about twenty-one hundred."

"Yeah."

"Well, traffic had kind of settled down, and like I said, the sun was just going down, when this big orange truck with a blue cab— you know the type I'm talking about, with the Christmas lights in the windows and everything?" Sam asked.

"Yeah—a bongo truck."

"Yeah. Well, this truck comes up to the TCP, and we could all hear it from a couple clicks away laying on its horn. Well, the truck pulls up to the TCP, and I could hear all this wailing and crying coming from the back of the truck, in the bed. So I jump up and climb on up the ladder to take a look at what was going on, and I see all these women and some men, all crying and carrying on. And in the center of all of them, is this huge carpet all rolled up. And they're all crying and wailing and beating the carpet."

"Same thing happened to me about two weeks ago," offered Jonathon.

"Really, did you find weapons too?" Sam asked.

Jonathon raised his eyebrows. "Weapons?" he asked. "No."

"Hmm," Sam continued, too involved in his story to linger long. "So I hop down, and tell the guys to check the drivers and the folks up front, and to check all the men from the back. You know, the normal thing."

"Yeah?"

"Well, so the men all get out, and they got tears rolling down their faces. The boys check them, and they have nothing, just like always. Nothing in the cab, either, just like always, right?" he shrugged.

"Yeah." Jonathon leaned back a little on his cot.

"Well, then I get this idea. And Jon, man, I swear I have no idea where this idea came to me," Sam held his palms out toward Jonathon. "But I tell a couple guys to have all of the women come on out of the back of the truck, and to check the rolled up carpet."

"Did you find anything?" Jonathon's heart beat faster.

But Sam wasn't ready to deliver his punch line yet. "Well, this guy must have understood what I wanted the boys to do, because he jumps up to me, tears running down his face, telling me there's a dead old man in the carpet, and asking me to leave it alone."

"Did you still unroll it?" Jonathon asked.

"Hell yes, we did," he exclaimed. "You never know with these people."

"Did you find anything?" Jonathon asked again though he knew the answer already.

"We sure did," Sam answered, letting the moment build.

Jonathon swallowed hard. "What?"

"Ten loaded RPG's, three PKMs, and a whole shit-pot of ammunition," he said with a huge smile.

Jonathon's heart sank. His face turned pale and his heart pounded violently against his chest. He suddenly felt sick. "Then what happened?"

"They all freaked out, of course, swearing that they didn't know shit about the weapons, crying—for real, this time—and begging us to believe them. We detained every last one of them," he paused. "Andy Walker showed up with his platoon about an hour later and took them all to the detention cell at Brigade."

"Where's that?" Jonathon asked absently, thinking of the widow in his bongo truck sitting in the corner, rocking back and forth.

"Q-West. It's this old airfield about forty-five minutes away from here to the west. Rumor is that we're going to finally settle down a bit and make a home somewhere," Sam said.

"I hadn't heard about it," Jonathon mumbled, still thinking of the widow with her dead weapons all rolled up in a carpet, grieving for her loss and laughing at his naïveté.

"Well, anyway, so we end up rolling up nine men and six women and all those weapons they had in the back. Isn't that incredible? That they would pretend to be going to a funeral, but really transporting weapons? These people, I tell you. But you gotta respect that," Sam nodded his head. "An idea like that takes some imagination. Because who would think, or would want, to check a carpet all rolled up with a dead guy in it? You know? It's a pretty damned good idea. Makes you wonder what else they're doing that we don't know about yet. What else they're doing right in front of our eyes, but we can't see."

"Yeah." Jonathon was terrified.

"Incredible. These people. One minute you think they're no better than the dogs that shit in the street, and the next you find out that they're pretty damned tricky. But we caught 'em this time. They won't do that again." He finished his story of triumph with a smile from ear to ear.

Jonathon smiled back at his friend. "Well, great job man. I never would've thought they'd do something like that."

There was a quick moment of silence that followed, and the air grew heavy between the two friends as Sam finally stopped long enough to realize Jonathon's position. He sat there a quiet minute, all the air gone out of his story. Then he shrugged his shoulders, stood up slowly, picked up his rifle, and looked down at Jonathon. "Hey Jon, you have no idea if the truck you stopped a while back was doing the same ours was. You had no way of knowing, brother. We just got lucky, that's all."

"You don't have to apologize, Sam, you were right. I know," Jonathon looked down at his hands. "You're right."

"Yeah?" Sam asked.

Jonathon looked up, "Yeah."

"All right. Hey, when you headed back out?"

"In a couple hours," Jonathon answered.

"Well, I'll see you later then."

"Yeah, take it easy, Sam."

*   *   *

A cloud of dust enveloped them as the truck came to a stop in front of the meeting place. The group of men seated on the blue rug stared with eyes fixed as the young American stepped out of the truck, followed by a small man dressed in blue jeans and a long-sleeved light blue shirt and another American with a radio on his back.

"*As- salaamu 'alaykum*," greeted Jonathon with a friendly smile.

"*Salaam.*" "Hallo," came a dozen replies.

Jonathon's eyes found Mr. Marie as he stood up to shake his hand and usher him toward a pillow on the ground next to him. "Please Leftenant, sit."

I guess we're starting with English today, thought Jonathon as he clumsily flopped down onto the ground in all his equipment with a stifled sigh.

Once he was settled, he let himself take a long look at the stranger sitting next to him. Mr. Marie's skin was the first thing that he noticed. He looked as if he had never shaved in his life, the skin on his face was smooth and shone a healthy light brown. Like all of the people of the area, he had jet-black hair, but he lacked the unwashed look that the other villagers all sported. His face was small and well-organized, without a trace of wasted flesh. Every feature of the man's face moved toward another feature. His clear, bright eyes were punctuated sharply by the black pupils that seemed to be forever dancing, and sat between a sharp nose that curved down almost like a beak. His mouth was small with thin lips, but revealed a surprisingly white smile when the man laughed. His jaw line was sharp and met at the man's slightly pointed chin. The face bespoke of a ruthless efficiency, and Jonathon found himself wondering at the rather strange anomaly that seemed to have landed there by accident, without purpose or explanation, in the middle of Nowhere, Iraq.

There was a brief silence while he got comfortable—not an easy thing to do, sitting cross-legged on the ground in all of his equipment. Soon his right leg would fall asleep, and he would spend the rest of the conversation changing positions to try to bring feeling back. It was what always happened.

"Leftenant, have you eaten?" asked Mr. Marie.

"No," Jonathon lied.

"Please. Stay and eat with us."

There was no other response possible other than gracious acceptance, though Jonathon knew the fare that was to be prepared, and he was not that excited about it. It was not as if the home-cooked food did not have its perks: after four months MREs and mermites, fresh-cooked food was a blessing. But the food was always followed by an inevitable bout of diarrhea that by now he knew would hit him sometime the following day.

Ours not to reason why, he thought, and said out loud with a smile, "Thank you very much."

There was the awkward—but by now familiar and expected—period of silence where the men who were gathered around the rug waited to see what the American would say, and while the American figured out how to start a conversation that was mostly devoid of any meaning. Finally, he started.

"Mr. Marie?" he asked.

"Yes, Leftenant," Mr. Marie turned his head from the group of men with a warm smile.

"I am sorry it has taken me a week to get back here," he offered, trying to start the conversation.

Mr. Marie answered, shrugging his shoulders and showing his palms, "It is not a problem, Leftenant, we know you are very busy."

Jonathon nodded, thanking him. "How are things going since we last talked?"

"How are things? Things are good. Though the electricity is bad. And the water... very bad," he said, brushing his hands together as if he were knocking the dust off them. "And we have only one truck to get benzene... gas, for cooking, you see."

"So things are not so good," Jonathon quipped with a faint smile.

Mr. Marie responded, "No. But they are not so bad," with a smile of his own.

"So how often do you have electricity?"

"Sometimes it is on, and sometimes it is off," Mr. Marie shrugged.

"About how many hours is it on every day?" Jonathon pursued.

Mr. Marie turned to the dozen or so men that were gathered around the rug in the shade who were bored with the unintelligible conversation, and had begun small discussions of their own. He said something to them in Arabic, which caused general soft laughter. Jonathon shot Nazeem an inquiring look, but a small boy who had brought a treasured item to him to show off had distracted Nazeem.

"Nazeem," Jonathon shot out quickly, and made a nod with his head for the translator to come sit next to him and tell him what was being said.

"I am sorry Lieutenant Garcia," Nazeem apologized.

By the time Nazeem had time to turn his ears to the conversation, Mr. Marie was turning back to Jonathon. "We think that there is electricity for three to four hours each day. Though you understand, that there are some days where there is no electricity, and some days when there is much more. Very bad."

"Yes, that is bad," agreed Jonathon.

"Because without the electricity, we have no lights, and we cannot see at night," Mr. Marie explained.

"Yes, I understand," Jonathon assured him.

"Jassim," called one man from across the rug, and spoke some words in Arabic.

"He says something about the Kurds in the next village," Nazeem quietly translated for Jonathon.

Mr. Marie turned to Jonathon. "Leftenant... did you understand what this man said?"

"Would you please tell me?" Jonathon asked.

"Of course. He says that Kurds in the village over there," to which Mr. Marie pointed to a village hidden by both distance and the mud houses in the town, "came and stole some of his wheat during the harvest."

Jonathon fought to hide the surge of frustration that swelled inside of him. Again with the endless, unsubstantiated charges. He feigned interest. "Really? How long ago?" He could feel Mr. Marie's eyes on him as he took out his pen and scribbled notes onto his small notepad for recording information.

"He says that it happens every year, but this year was the worst."

"It happens every year?" Jonathon asked.

"Oh yes." Mr. Marie nodded emphatically.

"Do other people in your village complain of the same thing? Do they have similar problems with the Kurds in neighboring villages?" Jonathon questioned.

"Yes, we all do. It is very bad. They come and harvest their wheat and they harvest more than is on their land. They harvest our wheat as well." Mr. Marie explained.

"And what is this man's name, who told you about his wheat being stolen?" asked Jonathon, nodding to the man who had spoken.

"His name is Mohammed Hazan," said Mr. Marie slowly so that Jonathon would understand the annunciation.

"Mohammed Hazan?" Jonathon repeated slowly, and then wrote the name in his notebook. Looking back up, and finding Mr. Marie's eyes directly on his, he asked, "Mr. Marie, is there a way that the people here mark their property? Do they have stakes or rocks that they use to say what is their land?"

Mr. Marie's eyes danced with amusement, and there was a slight smile on his lips. "This is a very western thing to do, Leftenant, and the Arab people do not do this. Every man knows what is his property and what is not his property, ignorance is not an excuse. If a man takes your wheat, it is not because he did not know he was on your land. It is because he is stealing your wheat."

"I see," said Jonathon.

A woman's voice called from behind Jonathon across the empty square in the middle of the village. Mr. Marie's eyelids raised, "Ah, it is time to eat. Please, come this way," and stood up with the group of men.

Jonathon clumsily raised himself off the ground, aware that he was not exactly painting the picture of the fierce, lithe, American soldier, as he grunted with the effort of standing up. His right leg had fallen asleep, and he was a bit unsteady as he put his weight on it. Following the group of men across the open square, Jonathon ushered Olk over with a wave of his hand and said with a smile, "Olk, you want to come in to eat?"

"Sir, no. I really don't," Olk answered.

"Well, you're going to anyway," Jonathon said with a playful smile and hard pat on the shoulder.

Olk's face fell when he recognized the sincerity of his platoon leader's words. "Sir, their food makes me want to hurl. Please don't make me."

"Look man, eating with these people is how we do this. It's how we establish that connection," Jonathon explained, a smile on his face.

"So why can't you be the one who establishes the connection, and let me just stand outside with the radio?" Olk asked.

"Because you're my RTO, and you go where I go. And if I'm going in to eat, then it just wouldn't be right for me to leave you standing outside in the heat. You see? You see how I take care of you?" Jonathon said with a laugh.

"Yeah. Thanks sir," Olk said as his face fell. He then muttered, "But if they serve the milk, I'm not drinking any."

"Oh really?" asked Jonathon in mock severity. "Olk, you'll drink and eat everything they put in front of you."

"Seriously sir?"

"Absolutely. I don't want you to miss out on this experience." He smiled an exaggerated smile at Olk, whose eyes teared up in frustrated anger.

"Sir, I'm being serious," he said. "You're not really going to make me drink the milk, are you?" Olk pleaded with his eyes to Jonathon, recognizing his habit of having some fun with the authority he wielded.

"Not if they don't put any in front of you," Jonathon offered.

"All right sir."

It was a sad exchange for Olk, but Jonathon was smiling and laughing the whole time as they stepped inside a large mud-walled room with a bright-red embroidered rug in the middle on the floor. There were pillows arranged all around, and Mr. Marie ushered Jonathon and his party to take a seat next to him on the ground.

Sitting down, Jonathon crossed his legs and took off his helmet and laid it next to him, leaning his rifle against the wall. He wiped at his wet forehead with his hand and tried to shake off the heat, which, though less in the shade of the building, still clung to him. In the middle of the room on the rug large bowls were placed which were full of steaming rice and soup, as well as plates full of Arabic flat bread, and other dishes of yellow and red vegetables. His mouth watered despite itself at the sight of freshly prepared food.

A barefoot man from the group walked to the center and picked up a big bowl and a pitcher of water. Starting with Jonathon, he walked around and poured a little water over everyone's hands, holding the bowl underneath to catch the runoff. After he had done this for everyone, he grabbed a stack of bowls from the center, and starting with Jonathon again, placed one in front of each man. He then brought over the bowl of rice, and spooned huge spoonfuls of it into his bowl, the hot steam rising to the air.

"*Shukran*," said Jonathon, as the aroma filled his nose. The rice was good. It was the best part of these meals, because there was never—or mostly never—a surprise associated with it, it was just rice. The man went around and filled each man's bowl, then placed the large bowl back in the center of the room and squatted next to the food, waiting to serve the next course.

Jonathon ignored the bits of dried food that were left on the dull and dented spoon that had been given him, and being careful to use just his teeth to remove the food, he devoured his bowl of rice. There was casual conversation between some men in the room, but mostly the room was filled with the sounds of spoons scraping against bowls and the sound of men eating. Setting his bowl down, he glanced at his small opaque plastic cup that sat empty in front of him. He pulled his eyes away quickly, hoping the server had not noticed. But he had, and approached Jonathon with a pitcher of water.

"*La*," Jonathon said apologetically, "*shukran*." He turned to Mr. Marie, "I am sorry, thank you very much, but I will get sick if I drink your water. Do you understand?"

Mr. Marie smiled sympathetically. "Of course. You are not used to our water. Do not worry, Leftenant."

"I do not want you to think me rude," Jonathon offered sincerely, "the food is delicious."

He said this even as the server brought over the main dish, a soup made from the caudal fold on a sheep. The rear flap was cut off early in America to promote the storage of fat in the rest of the animal. But in Iraq they kept the rear flap, and the result was what was considered a delicacy in the Middle East, what the Americans had dubbed "ass-flap-de-la-sheep soup."

As the man ladled the soup into his bowl, Jonathon examined each spoonful, assessing how much of the actual fat he would have to choke down. Much to his chagrin, the man searched around until he was sure he had found the largest piece, and laid it delicately into Jonathon's bowl. His stomach turned, though he had to appreciate the graciousness of the server, giving him what was to the men in the room the best piece in the soup.

"*Shukran*," he said, mustering as much sincerity as he could to the server, who replied with a warm smile of missing and brown teeth. Jonathon turned to Mr. Marie, waiting for the rest of the men to be served, "You are very generous to offer us such an amazing meal. Thank you." Jonathon shot Nazeem a quick look, who translated what he had said to the entire group of men, who nodded and smiled in approval.

"You are welcome, they say," Nazeem translated.

Once he could see that the server had filled every man's bowl, he lifted it up graciously and nodded his thanks. The broth really didn't taste bad, in fact it had the pleasant flavor of meat and oil and spices. But once he had practically exhausted the broth, in the middle of his bowl sat a ball of gristle and fat the size of a baseball, all of which was—apparently—edible. He deliberately cut away small pieces of the mass with the edge of his spoon and practically swallowed them whole.

To his left, Olk was having a half-conversation with a man who was interested in his rifle. As Olk was pointing out specific things to the man and saying their English name, the server came around with a pitcher of milk, in which was set a huge block of brown-opaque ice to cool it. He poured Jonathon a glass, who offered a weak "*Shukran*" as he battled a tough piece of gristle that had been caught in his teeth, and then poured some milk into Olk's cup before he noticed.

Turning his head just as the man topped off his glass, Olk pleaded, "No, *la, shukran, la.*" But it was too late.

Jonathon laughed despite himself.

"Sir?" Olk's eyes pleaded.

"Oh yeah. Drink up, brother."

"Sir, really?!"

"Yeah man, really," Jonathon said. "I'm barely getting down a piece of ass fat that's clinging to every crack between my teeth. I need to share some of this love that I'm feeling right now." He leaned over to Olk with a genuine smile.

"Sir, I'm not drinking that milk," Olk said.

"The hell you aren't," Jonathon said as he raised his eyebrows with a smile. "Drink it. You will eat and drink everything they put in front of you." The smile was gone now, and though it was entertaining for him, he let his young RTO know that he was unfortunately not kidding.

"Really, sir?" Olk pleaded one last time.

"Really really. Drink up," Jonathon ordered.

Olk reached over and brought the glass up to him to look at. There were white and opaque chunks floating on top, as he gently swirled it around, examining the glass.

"Don't look at it man, just drink it," Jonathon said sympathetically.

Olk raised the glass to his mouth and drained it in seconds, and barely hid the shudder that raced down his spine as he set the empty glass down. Mr. Marie, overhearing the conversation between the two men above the gathering noise of several Arabic conversations being held at once, asked Jonathon, "He does not like the milk?"

Jonathon's eyes danced with laughter, "No, he is not used to your milk. Me though, I love it." And raised the glass to his mouth and drank half the glass while his stomach did a summersault. Swallowing hard, he finished the glass with a smile. "Thank you very much, Mr. Marie, that was very good."

The server, noticing Jonathon's apparent enthusiasm for the milk, hurried over, and poured another glass before Jonathon could refuse. Olk, sitting beside him, laughed quietly. "Drink up, sir."

"Yeah," replied Jonathon with a smile, "that figures," and finished the second glass, waving off the server when he offered him a third.

Most of the food had been cleared away, and all that was left were a few plates of the Arabic flat bread which each man tore at and lazily sopped up the remainders of the soup with. The whole meal had taken about an hour, and the men were now sitting comfortably, either leaning against the pillows or the cool mud walls. The same sporadic conversations in Arabic between men in the room continued to carry on.

Nazeem tried to interpret the general meaning of the conversations, whispering key points to Jonathon in order to keep him informed, while Olk sat lazily against the wall, playing with his hands. Jonathon's mind buzzed heavily from the heat and the meal, and he struggled to maintain interest in the conversations as he fought sleepiness.

"Leftenant," broke in Mr. Marie. He hadn't said a word in over fifteen minutes, and the sudden intent in his tone yanked Jonathon's mind back into gear.

"Yes, Mr. Marie?" Jonathon asked, leaning forward.

"Did you enjoy the meal?" Mr. Marie asked him.

"Oh yes, it was very good," Jonathon nodded, yawning. "Thank you very much. We do not get to eat home-cooked food here, and it is very nice. Thank you very much for your generous hospitality," he offered again, this time to the group as a whole. Nazeem translated his thanks.

"*Ahlan wa sahlan,*" Mr. Marie tilted his head with a smile. "It is our pleasure."

Jonathon nodded his thanks, and said politely, "*Shukran.*"

There was a brief pause as Mr. Marie pursed his lips and lowered his eyebrows in thought. Then, "Leftenant?" he asked.

"Yes?" Jonathon swore at himself and told himself to wake up when he yawned again.

"Leftenant, what is it you are doing here?"

CHAPTER 2

The direct tone of the question surprised him.

Jonathon, guessing the true intent of the question, decided to carefully sidestep. "Well," Jonathon started, "we are here to check on critical aspects of quality of life for the local population in our area. To ensure that you have clean water, electricity, access to gasoline, and are free from harassment."

Mr. Marie's sparkled like black diamonds. He smiled. "No, Leftenant, I do not mean what are you doing in our village. What are you doing here, in Iraq?"

"We are here to secure Iraq, and to help provide stability while we help to repair the infrastructure that is necessary for Iraq and her people to be free." Jonathon shifted his legs.

Mr. Marie gestured out the door. "Leftenant, look around you. We *are* free, insomuch that our only real oppressor is what you would call our relative poverty."

Jonathon swallowed hard. This is gonna be a real conversation, he thought, then said aloud, "Well, sir, you are right. Looking around, I would not think that you or your village were oppressed in any overt sense. But Saddam and his Ba'athist Party were brutal in the way they treated their detractors. They killed political opponents, silenced any voice of opposition to their ideals, and wiped out entire villages that were even suspected of resistance."

"Yes, this is true. But these things are happening all over the world. In Sudan, in Pakistan, and in China... in many other countries as well. Tell me, why doesn't the United States invade China?" He asked with his eyes lighting up in delight.

"China is not a threat to world stability."

"And Iraq is?"

"Saddam Hussein was."

"Based upon intelligence?"

"Yes. Secretary of State Powell went to the United Nations with details of intelligence that we had gathered in reference to missile launch sites and factories suspected of producing weapons of mass destruction," said Jonathon, shifting again.

"And who could we hurt with such weapons? The United States?" Mr. Marie said, raising his dark eyebrows and wrinkling his brown forehead.

"No. Not us. But Israel, even your neighbors, like Iran. Europe."

"If Saddam was such a threat to world stability, then why did the United States have so much trouble getting a resolution from the members of the U.N. to invade Iraq?"

"Well, it's important to note that most countries are with us here in Iraq, and the countries that you are referring to are few," said Jonathon.

"Really?" asked the dark eyes.

"Yes."

"Then why do you think that there is such opposition?"

"I heard that some were buying the oil that flows up your main pipeline into Turkey—against UN sanctions," said Jonathon, shrugging his shoulders.

"Ah. So you do not believe that they disagreed on principle?"

"What principle?" asked Jonathon.

"That the United States should not be allowed to invade whichever country it sees fit whenever it chooses?" Mr. Marie asked, though it was more like an accusation than a question.

Jonathon raised his eyebrows. Mr. Marie's English was steadily improving. He paused briefly. "Yes, I believe that it is possible to

---

disagree on principle, but I do not believe that that is the case with those countries when it comes to Iraq."

Mr. Marie nodded his head thoughtfully for a moment before he spoke again. "Tell me, Leftenant, have you found any weapons of mass destruction since you have come here?"

"No. But we have only been here about five months." And to himself he thought, Five months! It's been one hundred and forty days… give me a few minutes and I'll tell you how many hours I've been here.

"So you think that you will find them?"

"Yes, I believe it is only a matter of time until we do."

"Hmm." Mr. Marie nodded and grew quiet again, mulling over what they were talking about, before he spoke again. "Tell me, why did you join the army?"

Jonathon paused as his mom's tear-streaked face flung itself up in his memory. She, too, had asked him. It had been hard for him to answer her; he found that he was embarrassed by his boyish sense of patriotism in her presence. But the answer came easily in front of this strange man. "I wanted to serve my country." And a surge of pride rose in him because he realized suddenly that that was what he was doing and that he had earned the right to say that proudly to any man who asked.

"And you believed that by joining the army you would be able to do that?"

"Yes. I believe that we have many gifts in America. That we are free beyond our capacity to understand fully the life that we enjoy. But I believe that we are free because men are willing to serve in time of war." Jonathon twirled the silver spoon from dinner in his right hand.

"But didn't Locke say that man has a divine right to life and liberty? If it is a divine right, then why must it be protected with guns?" Mr. Marie challenged with a smile.

Jonathon frowned. "Because Locke is dead. And all men do have that right, but that does not protect us from those who would want to take it from us," he paused, thinking, his brow wrinkling as he sighed. Was he really having a discussion on the rights of man in a small hut made of deteriorating cinder block in the middle of Iraq? he asked himself. You just cannot make this shit up, he thought, marveling at how many times he had thought that to himself in the past five months. The air was warm and stifling in the small room, and the weight of his body armor vest was becoming oppressive and heavy on his shoulders. "But freedom is not the only thing we fight for. War is the oldest struggle in the history of man. And it is always about resources, whether it be food, water, hunting grounds—"

"Oil?" Mr. Marie raised his eyebrows.

"Perhaps," he acknowledged, shrugging his shoulders. "But I don't think the answer is that simple."

There was a quiet pause. Some of the men near the two of them were watching intently, though obviously not understanding the conversation. Olk was listening while watching an interaction between two men across the room who, from their gesticulations, were discussing something of apparent importance.

"Leftenant, tell me, you are from Mexico, yes?"

"Yes. Well… no, not really. But I know what you mean. My parents came to the United States before I was born, and settled in the Central Valley in California. I was born two years after they came to America. My dad works as a foreman for an almond farmer and my mom works as a house cleaner for wealthy people in our town."

"So you grew up poor?" Mr. Marie asked, the smile gone.

"I guess, though my parents worked very hard." Jonathon shrugged, adding, "We had plenty."

"And you went to college, yes? That is how you became an officer in the army?"

"Yes, I was accepted to the United States Military Academy, and was commissioned as an officer when I graduated."

"West Point." Mr. Marie's eyes lit up with approval. "And your parents?"

"They still live in Fresno," remembering the intense heat of the Central Valley sun.

"It is a good story. The son of immigrants who goes to West Point to become an officer in the United States Army, and then goes to fight in a war for his country." Mr. Marie nodded his approval, a smile playing on his lips.

Jonathon laughed, shaking his head.

"Do you think it is a good story, Leftenant?"

"I guess. But that's not why I was laughing."

"Why were you laughing?"

"Because your English has significantly improved throughout our conversation."

The eyes danced again with delight, hiding volumes behind the dark pupils.

"Mr. Marie, how did you learn to speak English so well?" Jonathon asked, his eyes on the spoon in his hands.

"I was educated in Paris. That is how I got my name that you call me by, Mr. Marie. The name Jassim Khalil does not fit in with Parisian life so well; they are so arrogant about their language there. So I chose a name that I thought would help me get along better while I was in Paris. And the name followed me back here to my village." He shrugged and smiled. Jonathon smiled back, enjoying the irony of a Paris-educated man living in a village made of mud in the middle of war-torn Iraq. "But we have not finished what we started our conversation with."

Jonathon looked up from his spoon to Mr. Marie. "How did we start our conversation?" he asked.

"I asked you what you were doing here."

"I thought we answered that."

"Yes, we did, though I believe that there is much more to talk about relative to that topic."

"Like what?" Jonathon tilted his head toward the man, and shifted his right leg, which had once again fallen asleep. He proceeded to make a fist with his toes inside his boot to get the blood flowing back down his leg.

Mr. Marie leaned forward and asked, "What do you think that you will do once you have overthrown the government and caught Saddam?"

"Well, we have already overthrown the Ba'athist government, and it is just a matter of time until we catch Saddam."

"This is true," Mr. Marie acknowledged, nodding his head. "So what will you do once you have accomplished your goals? Again I ask you Leftenant, what are you doing here?"

Jonathon shrugged. "I suppose that we will help build a government that is a representation of the people of Iraq."

"Like you have in America?"

"Perhaps similar to it, though I think that it will be more like the Westminster model of democracy than the American. Which may not be a bad thing," he added with a smile.

"So you think the people of Iraq want a democracy?"

"Why wouldn't they? Would they prefer a dictator who randomly imprisons them and has absolute power to do whatever he chooses, with little to no accountability?" asked Jonathon, lightly tapping his spoon against the edge of his plastic bowl.

"I can agree that such a dictator, who does not look out for the good of his people, is not good. But I have studied democracy in America, and do you try to tell me that the politics that are practiced there are what the framers had in mind when they wrote your Constitution?"

"Perhaps it's not exactly what they had in mind, though there's no way that they could have anticipated all the issues that would arise in trying to govern a nation."

"Perhaps, yes," the man frowned as if annoyed, and then sighed quietly. "But let us talk plainly. Tell me, I will give you two situations, and you tell me which is the better of the two," Mr. Marie said, drawing himself up on his pillow.

"All right," Jonathon squinted his eyes in attention, shifting under the weight of this vest and the heat.

"In our first situation, you have a country whose leader is a monarch. And the monarch, from the day he is born, is taught and trained in how to govern a nation. He gets to watch his predecessor in his successes and his failures, and gains the benefit of his experience. In this way, he is groomed from the very first day in how to govern a country, which you must agree is not something that just any man can do well. When he finally does take the throne, he will rule for around twenty to twenty-five years, when he will either die or abdicate the throne to his successor, who had all the benefits of teaching, training, grooming, and experience that he had himself.

"In our second situation, you have a country whose leader is chosen by the people in a vote, such as in many western parts of the world. There are obviously great benefits to this situation, as the leader is the voice of the people, and it is therefore assumed that he will govern in the best interest of the people of his country rather than in his own interests. This is, no doubt, what the framers of your Constitution had in mind when they endowed men with certain inalienable rights—"

"God did that," Jonathon interrupted politely, "not Thomas Jefferson."

Mr. Marie smiled. "Of course. I am sorry. So, this system seems best, as it is the one that reflects the will of the people governed. But the question is—"

"Are the people in fact better fit to govern?"

"Exactly!"

"It's a good question, and yes, I have read my *Republic*, but history has taught us that all monarchies have disintegrated into selfish, repressive governments who extort the people under their power, and that democracy is the highest form of government. Not perfect, but the best we may be able to do," Jonathon added.

"That is because your American education stops with Hegel, and you have misunderstood Nietzsche," Mr. Marie cautioned.

Joke's on you, Jonathon thought, I haven't even read Hegel. But Mr. Marie continued.

"Is not the present only showing us what one of your framers called 'the tyranny of the masses?' And did not one of your English writers say that all tyrannies are only tired democracies? That in times of fear and uncertainty, men will give up their rights and freedoms in exchange for security?"

"How so?" Jonathon asked, sincerely impressed with the apparent knowledge that Mr. Marie had of political theory and history and his allusions to authors whom Jonathon knew nothing about.

"The men who run for the office of your president are hardly able to present clear and intelligent opinions on important national issues. This is both because they know that your media will not cover long and boring arguments on the state of welfare or public schools, but also because they have to present themselves to the masses in order for them to be elected or to pass a piece of legislation. And the masses themselves, were they even presented with the full content of each issue, would simply be bored and turn off the television or put down the newspaper. In short, do not the American people demand a right that they have shown only half-hearted enthusiasm and even capacity for?"

Jonathon was silent for a moment while he thought of what this Arab man, sitting in a mud village in the middle of Northern Iraq, had said about the validity of American democracy. "You raise some interesting points. But I would still have to maintain that—even if things were so bleak as you paint them to be—even that would be better than to have all power resting in the hands of a single individual who was accountable to no one."

"But you said you had read Plato's *Republic*?"

"Yes," nodded Jonathon.

"So you disagree with his Philosopher King?"

"Not in theory," said Jonathon. "But in practice, yes. Emphatically yes. It's the same with communism in the Soviet Union. To read Marx's *Manifesto* and the ideas of justice, equality, and provision for all is a very moving idea. His response to Hegel that democracy would ultimately fail is even compelling. On paper. But the whole world found, and the Soviet Union experienced, that some ideas are only great on paper. When they're applied to our human condition, they become oppressive and destructive."

"A monarchy is how we got Marcus Aurelius."

"That's true." Jonathon nodded. "But it also gave us Commodus."

Mr. Marie nodded his head silently while he played with some strands from the carpet they sat on. Without looking up, but still intent upon the carpet, he asked, "Tell me, Leftenant, are you a Christian?"

The question took Jonathon by surprise, "Uh, yes. I am."

"Can you see, then, how your Christianity and your philosophy on government are connected?"

"I'm not sure that I do, no." Jonathon shook his head slowly.

"Well, you believe that Jesus Christ was the Son of God, who became a man."

"Yes," Jonathon said carefully, wary and not sure where the man was going.

"In so doing, in the act of God becoming man, can you see how that validates the existence of every man? Doesn't that speak of the apparent importance of every human life, once God himself has deemed man worthy to bear his essence? And, furthermore, don't you believe that Jesus Christ would have died for just one of his children?"

"Yes, though I have to tell you that I do not think that is explicitly stated in the bible," Jonathon said, raising his spoon as if it were a pointer. Then he added, "But you make a very good point. I have never thought of it that way," he nodded, sincerely appreciating the connection between his faith and his politics that the man had drawn for him.

Mr. Marie continued. "So you can see how men who believe that God has deemed each individual worthy of his death, would therefore decide that each man ought to have a voice in deciding the course his nation should take?"

"Yes I can see that." Jonathon nodded expectantly.

"So what kind of government do you have if men do not believe that God became man to save the world from their sins? You see? In Islam, the stress is not placed on the individual, but on the whole." At this, Mr. Marie gestured with a sweep of his arm to the group of men gathered in the room. "It is an effort that all should sacrifice so that the community can reflect Allah's intent for our world. A world of brotherhood and justice. So you see that perhaps our systems of preferred government are chosen by deeper beliefs that certain groups of people hold regarding the status of the individual and the community toward their god? And can you see how we, as Muslims, may reject your democracy, which to us seems to be steeped in Christian principles?"

"I can see that," Jonathon nodded. "That makes a lot of sense. Though I must, respectfully, bring up a point that you raised just now about Allah's intent for the world," Jonathon said, setting his spoon down in the bowl.

"Yes?"

"The problem that many in the world see, is that it is the nations who have either Islam as the state religion, or have a strong Islamic base inside that country, which are our world's biggest obstacles to security and peace," Jonathon said carefully, telling himself to tread softly.

Mr. Marie's eyes lit up again. "Yes, it is true," he nodded. "It seems that most of the problems in our world today have extremist Muslims involved somehow. At least the ones we hear about on the television and newspapers. I cannot argue that point. But tell me, what is the difference between the Palestinian who blows up a café in Jerusalem, and the Baptist who blows up an abortion clinic in Kansas? Do you see? So, perhaps we can change our argument to mean that religious extremism, in any form, is a danger to security and a free society."

"I can agree with that for the most part. But I'd have to say it would seem on the practical side that Islamic extremism has proven more destructive than Christian extremism," said Jonathon defensively. "What practical comparison is there between flying planes into buildings, killing thousands of innocent people, and a sick man who runs into an empty clinic on a weekend? Christian extremism seems like a kitten compared to Islamic jihadists."

"How so? The Crusades—all seven of them—the Spanish Inquisition, even modern Ireland, where both sides are Christian! Your American memory is so selective," he said, shaking his head. "But the rest of the world, well do we remember the sins that you so easily seem to forget. Can we not agree that the specific threat to world peace is whenever man's idea of god, instead of being used as a symbol for self-reflection and repentance, is used to elevate our own prejudices and give them a holy sanction?"

Jonathon shook his head, tapping his spoon on his boot. "But it was partly due to the sense of empowerment that God had given to Christians, in becoming a man himself as you spoke of before, that Christian societies and culture have proved the more fruitful, liberal, and progressive. I do not deny what you say. Yet it seems to me that democracy, whether it is Christian or not, is a better answer for government than a monarchy or theocracy," said Jonathon.

"How can you be so sure, as a Christian democratic nation, that your way of government is really what is best for our Islamic world?" Mr. Marie shook his head, a shadow of a frown on his face.

"It's a product of our country's arrogance, for sure," nodded Jonathon. "But does that negate the possibility that we are here, perhaps, for the right reasons?"

"*La*," Mr. Marie shook his head. "History has always shown that there are no right reasons. There is only survival, whether it be political, economic, or actual."

"So say the conspiracy theorists, but there are those who choose to believe that men do things for the right reasons, and not every action of ours must be steeped in ulterior and selfish motives. There are those who do things simply because they are good and right and just." Jonathon, his eyes throughout most of the long conversation focused down on the rug, following the intricate patterns of the yarn, brought his eyes level with Mr. Marie's, whose eyes continued their shining dance.

"So you choose to believe?" His dark eyebrows raised as he nodded his head emphatically. "I think that is good. It is good to believe. But, Leftenant, will you still believe when you do not find your weapons of mass destruction? Or when the people of Iraq reject your Christian ideal of democracy? What will you believe in then?"

The ride back to Camp Bulldog was a short one for Jonathon. He was lost in thought as the small convoy of trucks bumped up the dusty road back toward Makhmur. Getting out of the truck, stripping off his body armor and letting it fall to the ground with a thud, he grabbed a bottle of water and drained half of it in one gulp. Wiping his mouth and closing the bottle, he headed across the courtyard to report to Captain Pham.

He and Captain Pham had a brief discussion about the meeting with Mr. Marie. Captain Pham had been out the whole night before on a joint patrol with Andy's platoon and had just returned, and was tired and soaked in sweat. Jonathon, likewise, was exhausted and hot and in no mood for a drawn-out report. He thankfully left the small room after only a few minutes and headed down the hall to Sam's room.

It took a minute for his eyes to adjust as he came into the dark room, a poncho hung over the window in a vain attempt to block out the sun's vicious heat. He saw Sam over in a corner, laid out on his cot, his shirt off and his boots unlaced. He was reading a letter, one hand holding it on his chest, and his other arm propping up his head.

"Hey Jon," he said, putting down the letter and sitting up on the cot. "Come on in."

"Hey Sam, I didn't want to interrupt."

"Nah, don't worry about it. It's like the third or fourth time I've read it."

"From your folks?" asked Jonathon.

"No. Rachel."

"Oh yeah?" Jonathon said with a smile, "How's she doing?"

"She's fine. Claire's getting big. She was only one year old when we left. Now look at her, man." Sam offered a picture from behind the letter. It was of a young woman with long, wavy light brown hair in a light blue sundress sitting on a patchwork quilt laid on a green lawn. Sitting next to her was a little girl in a bright pink outfit with a white hat, her right hand pointing toward the camera, while she stuffed the fist of her other hand into her mouth.

"I didn't know Claire had red hair."

"Yeah. She got that from her dad," Sam said quickly.

"Well, you have two beautiful girls there, Sam."

"Thanks Jon."

"Well, I'll let you get back to it. Just wanted to stop in and say hey," he said, standing up and heading for the door. "See you later."

"Yeah, take it easy."

As Jonathon walked into the warehouse, his soldiers were slowly getting up off their cots and lazily putting on their blouses for dinner. Large U-shaped outlines of salt traced down the backs of their shirts, the collars brown from the oil of their skin and the countless gallons they had sweated.

Hot. Always hot, Jonathon thought as he watched them get dressed for dinner chow. I feel like we've done nothing but sweat since we stepped off the plane in Kuwait. And he saw the little red buses sitting on the runway that had whisked them away in the dark from Kuwaiti International Airport to Camp Pennsylvania. Though only March, the desert heat had been a rude change from the frosty winter temperatures of Fort Campbell. Even then the heat had seemed unbearable, though only in the low nineties. At night the temperature would drop, and mornings would find the men shivering as they stood in formation for PT. Now it's just sweat, all the time. Sweat during the day out on a mission or pulling guard, sweat at night lying on your cot. I'd kill for snow right now. To be cold, to put on a sweatshirt and a pair of jeans. His stiff, salt-encrusted collar rubbed against his neck, chafing against the hairs that had grown since his last haircut two months ago.

"Hey sir," Olk said as he passed by.

"What's up, Olk?" Jonathon said back. "Gonna get some milk with dinner today?" Jonathon asked, teasing. The others that were with him laughed and slapped and pushed him playfully. Shipley's from Florida, Melton, Des Moines, Stufflet…somewhere in Texas… Jonathon drilled himself as they walked past him. He sat down on his cot while Anderson finished lacing up his boots.

"Make sure you hold onto your plate tonight, LT," Staff Sergeant Cline ribbed him as he walked by with a smile. Cline was from Phoenix… wife's name is Lisah… two girls… what are their names?

"Yeah," was all Jonathon could say, thinking of the time that he had knocked over the entire company's breakfast one morning when he accidentally kicked out one of the precarious table legs where all the food was stacked. It was one of those "lieutenant" moments that he knew he would never be allowed to live down. Jonathon watched him, Staff Sergeant Hoover, Washington, Fleet, Sergeant Cheney, Mathis, Jedzeniak, and MacLimore all walk out as he and Anderson followed behind across the courtyard to dinner.

The whole company was there. Captain Pham was joking with some new privates who had just gotten to the unit a few weeks ago. First Sergeant Allen was, as always, berating the servers for not serving quickly enough, and berating the soldiers in line for not moving fast enough. Jonathon saw Andy Walker and his platoon sergeant, Tom Merideth, standing back under the broken shade of a dying tree. Jonathon and Anderson walked over and heard Merideth talking about the new base over at Q-West.

"… and they have showers, not like real showers, but a tent with hot water—"

"Hot water's the last thing I want," interrupted Anderson with a smile. "I could go polar-bearing right now."

"Hey guys," said Jonathon.

"Hey," Andy returned.

"Yeah, but—hey, have you two been over to Q- West yet?" Merideth asked.

"Nope," answered Anderson, with a hint of pride.

"Man, they have showers—"

"Yeah, you already talked about that part," teased Anderson. Anderson would always joke with Jonathon about how if you ever wanted to know anything that had to do with comfort—phones, internet, showers, chow, cots, etc.—that Merideth was the man to ask, because he always knew all that stuff. "Rangers don't need all that shit," Anderson would always tell Jonathon. "Makes you weak."

"You gonna let me finish?" asked Merideth.

"Go ahead, go ahead, tell your story," said Anderson, gently mocking the man.

"So anyway…." but Merideth had lost his train of thought. "What have you guys heard about us going over there?"

"Have you heard anything, Jon?" Asked Andy, his white face and bright red hair practically glowing in the harsh sunlight.

"Damn sir, you should wear a mask or something. You're gonna blind people out here with that white skin of yours," teased Anderson. Jonathon looked at his platoon sergeant with a smile and a questioning eye. He's in a particularly good mood today, he thought. Anderson loved to give people a hard time, especially officers, and especially young lieutenants.

Andy's face blushed pink. "All right, sar'n," he said with a sheepish smile.

"I heard something about us moving some of the battalion back in a couple weeks," Jonathon swooped in. "Maybe start some kind of company rotation out here. I don't know, that's what I heard."

"I heard First Sergeant say that in early August, Bravo and Charlie Company along with two Delta platoons are moving back to run missions from there, while everybody else stays. He said that they're talking about two weeks at Q-West, and two out here. Sounds good to me. It'll be a nice break. Make the time go faster," Anderson said with an air of finality. And Jonathon accepted what he said as fact. He had learned that the NCO chain of communication was often dead-on when it came to certain information.

I wonder who Captain Pham will rotate out first, he thought as they started moving toward the serving table.

"Who do you think that Captain Pham will move first, Jon?" asked Andy. The two platoon sergeants went on ahead as the two young officers stopped to talk.

"I really don't know, Andy. I wouldn't mind staying a couple more weeks. Besides, once you know that there's an end in sight, it's not so bad. It's being here and not knowing how long you're gonna be here that kills you."

"You're right, though I'm pretty sure that Sergeant Meredith is going to do some heavy lobbying to get us in first."

Jonathon laughed. "How's he doing?"

"Sergeant Meredith? Oh he's fine. Makes me laugh. Always talking about how we don't have any nice comforts here. I wonder what he expected."

"Yeah."

"He does a good job, though, I'll say that," Andy nodded. "I've learned a lot from him."

"Who're your two section leaders? Barrier and Gregson?" Jonathon asked.

"Gregory. Gregson's with Bravo," Andy corrected him.

"Oh yeah." Jonathon nodded his head. "How're they?"

"Great, man. You know, you get pretty close with these guys over here," he nodded his head slowly. "How're your boys?" It was the kind of question that they asked each other by way of checking to see how the other was doing without coming out and asking.

"Oh fine. I mean, you know, this isn't the sexiest stuff in the world, but they're doing a great job I think," Jonathon said as they started toward the table and each picked up a styrofoam plate and plastic-wrapped set of utensils. The soldiers on the other end piled food up on their plates as they moved down the table.

"Hey Fleet, what's up? How'd you get stuck with serving?" he asked as Fleet plopped a spoonful of green beans onto his plate from behind the table.

"Second Platoon said they needed some help, so I volunteered, sir."

"All right, make sure you hold onto that food, in case I kick the table over again," Jonathon said with a smile.

Fleet laughed, "Yessir. But if you do it again, they'll probably make you stick to MREs."

"I don't know, that may be an upgrade," Jonathon said with a smile as he filled his cup full of bright red juice and walked over to two empty five-gallon tan water cans and sat down, resting his plate on his lap. Andy followed and sat on the other one next to him.

They talked about how they thought the company and the battalion were doing, about their soldiers, about meetings they had had with locals, and about the area in general. With drops of sweat tickling their brows, they hurriedly ate their chow, and stood up.

"Are you going out tonight?" asked Andy.

"Nope, we went out this morning. We've got the TCP from zero-six to noon tomorrow."

"That shouldn't be too bad."

"No, it's not that bad. That noon to eighteen hundred is the bad one. But still, I like getting out in the AO. Pulling that TCP is just boring," said Jonathon, dreading the six-hour shift of heat and lines of cars.

"And hot as a motherfucker," Andy added, articulating the syllables.

Jonathon laughed. "You got that right."

They dropped their plates into the trashcans and walked back inside the main hallway of the building. "How'd your mission go today?" Andy asked.

"Good, man. I'm telling you, there's this *mukhtar* out in my main town, Al Sharqi, and there's something about him that... I don't know," he stopped. "Today we talked about God and democracy and all kinds of things. It was the strangest thing. I still don't get it. Anyway," Jonathon said, shaking his head, a hint of a smile on his lips.

"Is that that Marie guy I've heard about?" Andy said, stopping outside of the doorway that led to a dark room filled with cots and bags. A musky smell flowed out of the room and tickled Jonathon's nose.

"Yeah, Mr. Marie. Speaks perfect English. Weird. Just weird. I don't know what to make of him."

"Yeah, well, if you ask me, he's no good. What's a guy doing out there in the middle of nowhere that speaks perfect English?" Andy asked.

Jonathon shrugged his shoulders. "I don't know." He paused and thought. "I really don't know what to make of it. But we had a great talk today, and I can't wait to get back out there to talk to him again."

"Hmm," Andy grunted. "Oh hey, did Sam talk to you about the big catch?"

"Yeah, he did," said Jonathon, hoping they weren't going to talk about it.

"So he told you about how my platoon showed up to escort the detainees back to Q-West, right?" he asked, not pausing long enough for Jonathon to answer. "Well, while we were there I saw Amber Gibson—have you seen her, man?"

"Yeah, I know her... the trauma PL out of Charlie Med, right? She's pretty," he nodded his head.

"Jon, sunsets are pretty—she's hot, and not like five-months-in-Iraq hot, either," he said with a laugh. "Like *really* hot."

Jonathon laughed and nodded. "So she's at Q-West, huh?"

"Yeah, there is a God after all, my friend." Andy shook his head and said with a smile. "All right. Hey brother, I'm gonna hit the rack. We were out all night last night. And you can't sleep for shit during the day here."

"All right man. Good talking to you."

"See ya, Jon."

"Take it easy, Andy," and Jonathon continued down the hall into the blinding sunlight of the courtyard, and passed into the warehouse.

The men were settling back down after chow, taking off their dirty blouses and tossing them on their cots. A few of them had picked up the soccer ball and were playing some round robin with the netless basketball hoop Anderson had somehow found and rigged up. Some of the others were sprawled out on their cots, the combination of the heavy food and the heat practically putting them into a coma. Except for the sound of the ball being bounced against the slick concrete floor, there was not much noise in the warehouse as the sun slowly climbed back down out of the sky.

At about seven, Anderson called Hoover and Cline over to his cot so that he and Jonathon could talk to them about the next morning, making sure that nothing would be forgotten. Hoover sat next to Jonathon on his cot as the four men talked. In order for them to get out to the TCP by six, it would be an early morning wake up call. Anderson made first call for four-thirty, giving the men about a half hour once they woke up to get dressed, shave and brush their teeth, and load up the trucks. Since the trip took about forty-five minutes, if they left by five, then they'd get there in time to touch base with Fourth Platoon before their shift was up. The best way to piss off a sister platoon was to be late to that shift change, and

Anderson, true to form, was adamant that his platoon not earn a name for being late. When he had finished what he had to say, he turned to Jonathon and asked, "Anything else, sir?"

Jonathon nodded. "Yeah. Look, I know that we drive this road all the time, but we need to make sure that we don't get lazy. How many trucks are we taking tomorrow?" Jonathon asked Anderson.

"All five," he answered.

"Okay. Look, my main concern is the top of the first ridge out of town. Nowhere to go if you get hit there, and the way that the road is surrounded by high ground, it's a textbook ambush site. Order of movement will be the same as normal: Hoover in his truck in the lead, and I'll be behind him. Sar'n Anderson, you keep Sergeant Cline's section with you, and keep about half a click behind us. Our section will travel through that canyon first, and then call you when it's all clear, okay?"

"Sounds good, sir. You want to travel that way the whole way there?" asked Sergeant Cline.

"Yeah. Just keep your section about half a click back," said Jonathon.

"Too easy, sir," said Sergeant Cline.

"Is that it, sir?" asked Anderson.

"Yeah," nodded Jonathon.

"All right. Make sure the men go to sleep at a decent time, no playing card games until zero-two, and then they're all beat tomorrow. Any questions?" Anderson growled from beneath his mustache, looking at the two section leaders sitting on the cots.

"No sar'n," Hoover shook his head.

"Nope," answered Cline.

"All right," said Anderson with a nod of his head that meant, "Get outta here."

The two men got up and walked over to their respective areas where all their men's cots were next to each other, and called their men around them to relay the following day's plan.

Anderson swung his feet back onto the cot, and stretched out lazily. Jonathon could see through the broken windows that the sun was starting to set, the sky having changed color from the day's blinding white to a soft gold. Jonathon stood up and turned to go outside, but before he got to the open doorway, he turned back around and went back to his cot. Opening the top flap of his rucksack, he reached inside and pulled out his small bible, and with just a touch of embarrassment, held it so that his body was between it and Anderson as he walked out. Anderson's eyes followed his young platoon leader until he disappeared around the corner.

Sitting down on the white plastic chair that sat under the shade of an olive tree whose scrawny branches and sparse leaves attested to its struggle to survive in that parched world, he thumbed through his bible. Jonathon flipped through the thin pages until he reached Isaiah. He then thumbed through the pages, looking at the chapters, trying to figure out where he had read last.

When was the last time I read? I can't even remember. At least a week, he thought to himself in the quiet light of dusk. Then, remembering what he had read last, he started at Isaiah 52, and read quietly, his elbows resting on his knees. He quickly read through the chapter, and then closed the book absentmindedly. Slouching deep in the chair in order to get his head to rest on the back, he sat looking up into the sky as it slowly darkened from gold to orange to red to purple. When the shadows were gone, telling him that the sun had set, he walked back inside, setting his bible on his cot, and changed into his PT's. Lacing up his shoes, Anderson asked him what he was going to run.

"I think just a few laps around the compound, nothing big. You want me to wait for you?" Jonathon asked, turning around and facing Anderson.

"No sir, go ahead. Thanks though."

"All right," said Jonathon, and walked back out into the still darkness of the night. The moon was almost full and already high in the sky as he stepped out of the warehouse into the open air. Stretching quickly, he started off along the choppy paved road that followed the southern fence, jogging slowly. He had no intent of running too hard; he just wanted to get the blood flowing. And the promised quiet of the next twenty or so minutes sounded inviting. He ran along the fence, fluorescent lights shining through the open windows of the houses from the town nearby. He passed by the main part of the large building that housed most of the battalion, the sound of the generators violating the otherwise pleasantly quiet night as they powered the computers and swamp coolers inside.

His little road bent to the left, and he followed it as it traced the fence on the eastern perimeter. It was only a minute until he had to cut off to the left again, as the road he was on would take him out the main gate and onto the highway that ran along the northern perimeter of the compound. The soft dirt he was on splashed up onto his legs like fine powder. He could feel the dust settling on his already sweaty legs. Running along the fence, he passed two towers, the men inside quietly watching outside the compound. He finally reached the western edge and hit pavement again. This area of the compound was not being used by the battalion, and as such had not been cleaned up. Bent pieces of metal, broken glass, plastic bags, a torn down light pole, were all things Jonathon had to maneuver his way over and around on this leg of his run. Then, his road bent left again, and he found himself approaching the warehouse where his platoon was. As he passed by, he saw Stufflet sitting outside by himself, his hands folded in his lap, facing toward where the sun had set.

"Hey sir," called out Stufflet.

"Hey Stufflet," Jonathon spat out, surprised at how out of breath he was, and continued on. Barely a quarter mile, he thought. I'm in terrible shape. Gonna have to start doing this more often, he thought to himself as the noise of the generators approached again. A figure stepped out of one of the open doorways that led into the battalion Tactical Operations Center. It was 'Colonel DaSilva.

"Hey there Jon," he said with a wave, a friendly smile on his slightly round face.

"Hey sir," Jonathon said, slowing his steps down in case he was called over, but then saw that he was just headed out to the latrines.

"Little run?" he asked as Jonathon ran by.

"I feel like my heart is going to explode, sir," Jonathon said, turning around and slowly running backwards.

'Colonel DaSilva laughed, "Hooah. Keep it up, Jon."

"Yessir," said Jonathon, spinning back around and heading toward the western fence again.

Fifteen minutes later, the world now only lit by the silver light of the waning moon, Jonathon stopped at the entrance to the warehouse, sweat running down his face. Stripping off his wet shirt, he felt the initial slight cool of the small breeze against his skin. Walking over to his cot, he unlaced his shoes and pulled off his soaked socks and hung them over the side of his cot to dry. Then, grabbing a water can, he walked outside and slowly poured the water over him. The instant cool of the water felt great, and the memory of swimming as a boy at his friend Steve's house came to mind as the water rushed over his head and down his body. Water always did that to him and he didn't really know why. When the can was empty, he set it down and stood still, catching the slightest stirring of the air and relishing in it. He stood there until he was dry and the heat returned.

Having dried off, he walked back into the warehouse. Most of the men were still awake, either reading, writing, or playing cards. Activities once the sun went down were limited to whatever battery-powered flashlights they had. Jonathon stretched silently and slowly, and then stretched out onto his cot and drifted off to sleep.

Jonathon awoke in the dark with a start. His stomach was in knots, and beads of sweat formed on his forehead from the pressure inside him. He sat up and almost lost control of his bowels. He reached over and grabbed his flashlight and dug for his toilet paper and carefully stood up, trying not to upset his fragile stomach any more than was necessary to move. His insides lurched, and he walked quickly and deliberately into the night, bent slightly at the waist. Walking down the sidewalk to the building where the latrines were kept, his stomach gurgled and lurched and screamed at him. He felt his insides liquefy, and he knew he wasn't going to make it. He got to a dead bush six feet off the sidewalk and pulled his shorts down only just in time. He felt sick, and cursed the soup from earlier that day. Cleaning up, and spreading some dirt over his waste, he pulled his shorts back up and looked at his watch as the sweat popped and ran down his forehead.

birdmen

Zero-three, the nineteenth, he thought. Day one hundred and forty-one.

* * *

Jonathon walked in and saw Sam sitting on his cot, lazily flipping through a magazine with a picture of a woman in a small swimsuit on the cover. He glanced up as Jonathon walked in and cast a weak smile at him.

"Hey Jon."

"Hey," Jonathon said as he pulled up a chair and sat down near Sam.

"You hear about Staff Sergeant Gregson?"

"Yeah," Jonathon nodded slowly.

"Roadside bomb, right?" Sam asked, putting down the magazine and sitting up on his cot, his elbows resting on his knees.

"That's what I heard," Jonathon nodded. "Blew up right next to him. Practically cut the Humvee in half."

"Sonofabitch," Sam said in a half whisper.

"Yeah," Jonathon sighed heavily, slowly shaking his head.

"Did you know him?"

"Yeah. Well, yeah. I don't want to seem all dramatic or anything. We weren't best friends—"

"That's because you and me are best friends," Sam said with a dry smile.

Jonathon smiled and nodded solemnly, "Yeah."

"Didn't you work a lot with his squad in Najaf?" Sam asked.

"Yeah. Good man. Great leader. Just amazing. Ruthless, exacting. But he wasn't mean about it, you know? He cared. He just loved his guys, you could tell. And they knew it, you could tell by the way they interacted with him." Jonathon paused, remembering. "He was a good man."

"I heard good things about him," Sam nodded his head slowly.

"Yeah. You know he shouldn't even have come here?" Jonathon asked, looking up at his friend.

"What do you mean?"

"Well, when he was in Vicenza, he broke his back on a jump," Jonathon said.

"No shit?" Sam's eyebrows rose in disbelief.

"Yeah, and it never really healed up. He'd just had surgery three months before the deployment."

"How did he even qualify for deployment?" Sam asked.

"His original profile from the doctor expired like two weeks before, and he just stayed away from the hospital," Jonathon shrugged.

Sam shook his head. "Wow, I didn't know that. He didn't walk like—"

"He popped percocet like candy," Jonathon said. "Two, three, four a day."

"Not really?" Sam was impressed.

"Yeah man, I saw it," Jonathon nodded, remembering. "We'd be getting ready to go out on a patrol through the city, and I'd see him pop a pill into his mouth. Then he'd pop another when we got back. Didn't find out until we'd been working together for a couple weeks what they were or why he took them."

"Where'd he get the pills from?" asked Sam.

"He had a bunch from the surgery still. But I think that the docs were taking care of him, too," said Jonathon.

"No kidding," Sam said, slowly shaking his head.

"Yeah." Jonathon looked intently down toward the ground. "Four kids, too."

"Jesus," Sam muttered quietly.

"Yeah, and you know what? His youngest, his daughter... Alexa, I think... was born two months before we left."

Sam shook his head slowly, looking at the ground.

Jonathon continued. "It's just... terrible, you know? Like... I don't know... It's just ugly." He shook his head.

"Goddamn. Yeah, it's too bad."

Jonathon's eyes shot toward his friend at his last remark, searching for sincerity. But he could see that Sam, staring at his hands, which he kept rubbing together slowly over and over, was truly affected by the news. The two young men sat in the silent heat for a few minutes, nothing but the sound of the whir of the oscillating pink fan Sam had bought in the market disrupting the stifling quiet. The green light from the poncho in the window added to the room's silent heaviness.

"What are we doing here, Sam?" Jonathon asked quietly, looking up from the floor to his friend's face, which was still fixated on his hands.

"What do you mean?" Sam shrugged his broad shoulders.

"I mean, what are we doing here? Just what the hell are we doing here?" His voice carried a quiet and wild desperation though he didn't mean it to.

"What do you mean?" Sam repeated.

"I don't know anymore," Jonathon sighed and shrugged his shoulders. "I used to know exactly why I was here... but now, man, I just don't know anymore. All I can think about right now is Alexa growing up, never knowing her dad, except that he was killed on some God-forsaken road in the middle of nowhere. And for what? Some ambiguous threat to American freedom? Man, you've seen the same places I have. Have you seen one man here capable of attacking the 'American way of life?'" Sam watched as Jonathon sat up, his eyes wide, his head slowly moving from side to side.

Sam was quiet a moment before he spoke. "When are you ever gonna learn, man? Come on, 'God and Country?' Really? Is that why you're here?" Sam asked, shaking his head.

"What?" Jonathon stared at his friend.

"You really believe in all that, don't you? Life and liberty and honor and glory and right and wrong and justice... Don't you?" Sam's eyes bore into Jonathon's.

"Well... you don't?" stammered Jonathon.

"Yeah, I believe in them. But that's not why I'm here. It's never that simple, Jon. Maybe it used to be, I don't know. Maybe once there were wars that really were fought for freedom and everything. But I don't know... maybe not," Sam shrugged. "And the longer I'm here, the more I see what war—or at least this war—is like, the less convinced I become of all the stories you hear."

"So if we're not here to defend our country's freedom, then why the hell did Sergeant Gregson die? What is Alexa going to have to hold on to so that she can live her life without her daddy?" There was still a quiet desperation in Jonathon's voice.

"That's your problem, Jon."

"What's that?" Jonathon asked.

"Yeah. Everything has to be *about* something. Everything has to be right or wrong, or about justice and freedom. But it's not always like that. Sometimes it just *is*."

"And what's wrong with that? With believing?" asked Jonathon.

"Nothing man, nothing's wrong with that. But you're trying to live in a world that simply doesn't exist," Sam said, shaking his head.

"What kind of world do you live in, then?" Jonathon spat back.

"The real world, Jon. And it isn't about freedom or justice. It's about who's in power and who's not, and how to use whatever leverage you have to get to the top and stay there as long as you can."

"So why are you here, if that's how you believe the world is? Why would you want to be just another pawn in some fucked up game of chess?" Sam's eyes shot up toward Jonathon; it was the first time he thought he'd ever heard him swear like that.

"I don't know," Sam shrugged. "They said I'd get to blow things up. Jump out of airplanes. Sounded like a lot of fun."

Jonathon smiled faintly, "You don't really believe that."

"No, not entirely," Sam shook his head. "Look, I'm a patriot, same as every other man here. I just don't choose to fool myself into thinking that everything we do in this uniform is about freedom and defending our country. Sometimes it's about other things, things that don't sit too well with folks back home, but need to be done anyway. And I'm okay with that. Because you know Jon, I don't give a damn about God and country and nine-eleven and all that other garbage. I'm not here to defend some punk's spoiled ass who never has—and never will—do a goddamned thing for anyone but himself. What do I care about his freedom? Does he even deserve it? No," Sam shook his head. "And he sure as hell isn't worth Sergeant

Gregson's life, or the torment that Alexa is going to have for the rest of hers."

"So how do you do this, then? Keep doing this every day?" Jonathon's eyes were wide.

"Because I'm here for the men I serve with. Because when haji steps around a corner with an RPG pointed at you and your boys… man, America and the Constitution don't mean a goddamned thing. Then it's just you and him. And it's not glorious and honorable and magnanimous. It's personal. He's trying to kill you. It's the oldest struggle there is. So you kill him before he kills you or one of your boys. And that's it," Sam clapped his hands once. "That's all there is."

"Kinda bleak, don't you think?" Jonathon said softly.

Sam shook his head. "No. It may not sound as high and mighty as 'defending the American way of life,' but it's still something holy. Men who believe in something, who really believe in service and sacrifice. Who come together and bond and fight together. This is the only aristocracy as far as I'm concerned. The rest of them can all go to hell. I'm here for the man down the hall."

"But there's gotta be something more than that, Sam. Why else would you join in the first place? That all sounds well and good once you're here, but you didn't know this was coming when you signed up—none of us did."

"Yeah, you're right. I guess I just believe that I have to do my time. Besides, I hit a point in my life where it was either the army or dead." He paused. "You know about my divorce and all that, right?" he asked.

Jonathon said carefully, "I know that you used to be married. In Colorado, right?"

Sam smiled. "Park City. Utah. I went there the fall after I graduated from Tulane. I don't know what I was thinking. I think I was trying to hold on to something, I don't know. Anyway, I took off to Park City and got this job bussing tables at one of the local bars. The No-Name Saloon," he said, remembering. "I did that for about eight months, then I got hooked up with some wild-land firefighters and quit the bar for the summer to fight fire in the Rockies."

"That must have been awesome," Jonathon interjected.

"It was man. Hard work and long days. But the pay was real good, and it was good work." He paused. "Well, the fire season ended, and I somehow landed this job as a ski instructor at one of the resorts."

"Do a lot of snow skiing down in Louisiana, did you?" Jonathon asked with a smile.

Sam laughed, "No man, but there are only three things people do who live up in Park City: ski, drink, and work so they can afford to ski and drink. I already had the drinking part down, and it didn't take me long to get the skiing part figured out. So anyway, I got a job as a ski instructor during the winter, and I fought fire during the summer. I did that for three years up there."

"Sounds like a blast. I never got to do anything like that," said Jonathon.

"Yeah, it was, Jon." Sam stopped and reached around into his rucksack and produced a can of dip. Packing the can a few times, he opened it and stuffed a pinch behind his lower lip. He offered it to Jonathon, who shook his head. Sam put the can back in his ruck and continued. "Stephanie was an instructor for the kids at the same resort I worked at. We dated for a year and then got married. A little over a year after our wedding, she came home and found me in bed with a local barkeeper. She threw me out and we got divorced. Twenty-six years old and divorced."

Sam picked up an empty bottle on the floor, and spit carefully into it. Jonathon listened silently as Sam continued. "It's like my whole world came crashing down. I started drinking; and I mean like, *drinking.* I'd drink myself blind, go home with whatever girl I could, only to wake up, get dressed and show up to the slopes still drunk and reeking of booze. That lasted about three months. Then—in February I think—my boss fired me. Said that I was a wreck. And Jon, for the crowd up there in Park City, that's saying something, let me tell you." He laughed half-heartedly to himself, shaking his head.

"So I was out of work, almost broke, and hadn't talked to anyone from home for months. My mom would call all the time, worried about me and asking me to call her. I sobered up enough once to finally call her when she threatened to fly up there. Well, that drunken haze lasted about two months, until the beginning of April 2000. Then I was really broke. I had five credit cards that were maxed out, and I had *no* money. None. I got evicted from my apartment, and stumbled over to a friend's. He gave me money for a bus ticket home and told me to get out of Park City. Listening to him was the smartest thing I did in the whole three-and-a-half years I was up there. I bought a ticket on Greyhound and went home."

Jonathon leaned forward in his chair. "What happened when you got home?" he asked.

"My dad met me at the front door." A smile played on his face. "He told me I had some nerve not calling home for six months, drinking myself stupid, and then just showing up on the doorstep expecting to be taken in."

"Did he let you in?" Jonathon asked.

"Yeah, of course. My parents, Jon, they're saints. But he told me that I couldn't just live there. He told me to go do something. Well, one day I was walking downtown, and passed by the Army recruiter's station. The sergeant there said that I could do OCS easy, no problem. So I signed up," he sighed, clapping his hands together. Then, spreading his arms out, gesturing to the room, he said with a wry smile, "And now, here I am!"

"That's incredible," Jonathon chuckled, amazed at the story. "But why the Army?"

Sam shrugged, spitting into the water bottle. "Guess I needed to do something that would literally force me to behave. I knew enough to know that I needed some kind of wake up call, some kind of shock. I needed something that could literally keep me from destroying myself," he said.

"Did it work?" Jonathon asked with a smile.

"Until I graduated ranger school." He laughed again—kind of sadly, Jonathon thought.

Jonathon laughed with him, more delighted with the story than the joke. When they quieted down, he asked, "Yeah, but why the Army?"

"Guess I felt like I had to pull my weight before I could go live the rest of my life. I'd lived such a selfless, meaningless existence, I felt I had to earn the right to life and liberty and so forth and so on. Guess I don't believe it should be that easy. You shouldn't just get to be free, you know? You should have to prove that you're worthy of it, that you won't waste it."

"I guess I can understand that. That's kinda like me, I guess."

"Yeah?" Sam asked, surprise in his voice.

Jonathon paused, blinking fast, lost in thought as he decided whether to say what he felt swell up inside him. Sam waited patiently, not knowing whether he was going to get an answer or not. Jonathon swung his head to Sam, locked eyes with him, and stared straight into him.

"Do you know what it's like to be treated like a second-class citizen? I don't look American, Sam; I look like a Mexican." Sam looked back down at the ground as Jonathon continued. "All my life, my mom cleaned up after rich white people. And my dad worked out in the fields for a man who treated his workers like shit. All my life I watched them. I watched them sweat and bent over with the weight of the choice they had made to come to America for a better life. But you know what? It wasn't their lives that they came to make better. It was mine. I wasn't even born yet, but they came to America so that my life could be better. And all their lives, even in the land of the free, where the Statue of Liberty beckons to the world to 'bring me your tired and your weak,' they have suffered and existed in a country that did not want to acknowledge their right to be called citizens of the United States.

"My parents' English is spoken with a strong Mexican accent; they still speak Spanish better than English. We live in the poor area of Fresno, where all the other immigrants live. But I'm an American, Sam. I'm a citizen, born and raised. I have as much of a right to claim the benefits of an American citizen as anyone else. But still, all my life I've felt like I had to prove it. For some reason, I was made to feel guilty about my background, as if the white kid on the other side of town who was born in the same hospital I was had a more righteous brand of citizenship than I did. Kids in elementary school and junior high used to make fun of me because I didn't speak English well. And that's how I've felt my entire life.

"So if I wasn't going to be given my full rights as a citizen, with all the respect and dignity it involves, then I decided that I'd earn it. I'd put on the uniform of my country. And I'd do what that white kid on the other end of town thought was beneath him; I'd serve my country. I'd prove to everyone that I'm worthy of being an American, and to be treated like an equal, like a man. I'd take an oath to support the Constitution that that white kid takes for granted because he knows nothing else. But I know better. I know the depth to which our country can fall. But she can rise up just as far as she can fall down. And I'll be one of the ones that help her rise, Sam. She can stand on my coffin to reach the next step if it takes that. Because America is my country, and I love her. For all her faults, with all her narrow-mindedness and short-sightedness and bigotry and arrogance, I love her," Jonathon finished, almost in a wild whisper.

Sam looked up and saw that Jonathon's eyes were glazed over. Sincerity was carved into the narrow brown face of his young friend. Sam could see the muscles on his jaw bulge, a slight hue of red spreading over his face as he continued to stare hard at the ground.

"But you're wrong, you know," Jonathon added, looking up at Sam in the dark room.

"Impossible," Sam shook his head, trying to lighten the mood. When he saw that Jonathon didn't respond, he sobered up and asked, "About what?"

"You *should* just get to be free, Sam. You shouldn't have to earn it," Jonathon said, slowly shaking his head. "No kind of freedom is a waste."

The two men sat quietly in the silent heat for a few minutes.

"Wow, Jon, I didn't know all that. I mean, I knew you were Mexican…" said Sam with a shrug and a gentle chuckle. Jonathon laughed under his breath and shook his head. "But I didn't know—I never thought of all that," Sam offered.

"Yeah, well, like you said, we all have our reasons," he said with a modest smile.

"Yeah, but I'm just trying to keep myself out of the gutter; you want to save the world," Sam said with a smile. "These people can go to hell for all I care."

Jonathon just sat there, the red slowly leaving his face as he laughed quietly at his friend's abrasiveness. "You just think that some people aren't worth saving, and I think they are, that's all. I'm no big fan of these people, especially when I think of Sergeant Gregson, but I still believe that they can be saved. I think they can be taught to solve their problems with dialogue rather than with guns and bombs."

"Yeah, but guns and bombs sure would be a hell of a lot easier," Sam said.

"Yeah," Jonathon sighed. "That's what the army is supposed to do. That's what we've always done. God knows neither of us went through all that training so we could sit and talk with our enemy, but that's the way it is now. The world is different now. September eleventh changed everything."

"Tell me about it. You can't even call a bad guy a bad guy anymore. He's a 'non-compliant force.' What a bunch of bullshit," Sam said between his teeth, shaking his head and suddenly becoming angry. "If we started rounding up all the people in this country who we even thought were bad, flew them away, locked them in a tiny little room, and gave them a month to think about it, I bet we'd get a whole lot more answers with a whole lot less casualties. Or even better, just kill them right then and there."

"We've done pretty well so far," Jonathon offered. "We haven't taken that many casualties. I think we're going about this the right way. Doing what you said would only breed more enemies, and we'd only take more casualties in the long run."

"Yeah, I know that that's what they all say. And I know that at some point, operations have to switch from combat to stability and support, but I wonder if we didn't do it a little too soon, that's all. You watch, give it a year," Sam nodded his head. "With the tempo that we've set across this country, there's going to be a huge insurgency because we made the switch too soon. We pulled back on the reigns too soon, and it's given them all the time in the world to go underground and reorganize. You watch. We're about to get our asses kicked by a bunch of third world Arabs who have barely figured out sewage. The United States Army is going to get hammered by a bunch of people who still shit in the street," Sam said, his face coloring slightly as he shook his head slowly. "Again."

Jonathon felt a surge of arguments rise against Sam's apparent impatience. He thought that we had learned from Vietnam, and that is why the Army was doing things the way it was doing them this time around, because it had learned the last time that all-out war against an insurgency cannot win. The insurgent population will outlast the occupying power every time. We can't kill them all, it's impossible. We have to attack their political and social systems, change those, suffocate the passion from the insurgents by producing systems that will not tolerate an insurgency and all of the repercussions that come with it. That that is how we have learned to beat an insurgency. But Jonathon saw that his friend was in no mood to hear high theories. He was consumed by what was around him, and he had a right to be angry.

"The problem is that the folks back home just don't have the stomach—" Sam stopped short. "But that's not their job. Just don't pretend to tell us how to—you know what? Fuck it. What difference does it make, anyway? Let's just go home and drink ourselves blind." He looked at Jonathon with a smile. "Blind and stupid, my friend," he said with a laugh, shaking his head. "When we get back, you need to come on down to New Orleans with me, and we'll hit up Bourbon Street. We'll get back just in time for Mardi Gras. Girls, beer, what else does a man need?"

"Is Rachel gonna come too?" Jonathon said with a laugh.

"We'll just tell her we're going camping or something," Sam said with a mischievous smile and a wink.

Jonathon laughed. "There you go again. But you got a deal. Sounds good to me."

"All right then. Now all we have to do is survive." They both laughed and then the dark room grew quiet as they sat there together for a few minutes, neither saying anything to the other.

"Well, man," said Jonathon standing up, "I gotta get going. Thanks for the talk."

"Yeah, I'll see ya Jon," said Sam, reaching back for the magazine he had laid aside. Jonathon walked out into the lit-up hallway and disappeared around the corner. Sam set the magazine back down on the floor after Jonathon left, and then stretched out on his cot with his hands behind his head as he stared at the dark ceiling. Absently, he reached for the oil-stained letter from Rachel and read it again, trying to make it like the first time.

* * *

"Back off a little bit, Olk," shouted Jon over the roar of the truck's engine.

Olk slowed down, and the cloud of dust that they had been enveloped in moved in front of them. "I had it, sir."

"Oh you did, huh?" Jonathon said with a smile. "You have x-ray vision or something?"

"No sir," said Olk sullenly, his round face staring straight ahead.

"Look man, you have to pay attention to what you're doing," Jonathon said, his smile fading. "You hit something, the truck in front of us or something in the road, and Mac up in the gun is gonna to get screwed up. You understand?"

"Yessir."

"It's not all fun and games, Olk. People get killed over here for no other reason than just plain stupidity," said Jonathon, a bit parochially.

"But you gotta have some fun, sir."

"Not if fun gets one my men killed, I don't."

Olk's head jerked off the road to his platoon leader, his eyebrows furrowed in consternation. But there was no hint of the usual teasing in Jonathon's face; Jonathon was dead serious and communicated that through the stern look he gave his driver. Olk slowed the truck even more. Jonathon smiled and blew a kiss at him, and Olk quickly turned his head back to the road as Jonathon laughed to himself.

The road they were on was just one in a spider web of dirt roads that networked across the brown arid land, joining one small mud village to another. The sun had only been up for a few hours, but already the air was hot and chafing. It was going to be a long, hot, and dusty day, traveling from one village to another. Jonathon wanted to visit eight villages in the southern-most part of his area, which took them close to the Little Za'ab River. He was hoping that they would be able to get close enough to the river to justify a little stop and enjoy some greenery, maybe even let the men take a swim to cool off. Just the thought of running water and some green trees comforted him. The whole world seemed to have been lost in a sea of brown, and the chance of getting to see something pretty and colorful, even if only relatively speaking, sounded promising.

Of course, getting to the villages, much less the river itself, would prove quite a feat. The map he had did not reflect all the criss-crossing dirt roads they came across, and they often found they were on a road taking them away from a village that they thought the road would lead them right to. It was a hot and frustrating process, only compounded by the fact that he did not have Nazeem with him today; Captain Pham had taken him with Second Platoon up north near the town of Al Guwar.

At their last stop, and their third attempt to find someone who could read the translated questionnaire about water, electricity, schools, presence of police, gas, etc, Jonathon was starting to doubt whether their patrol was going to produce anything useful at all. The trouble was, of course, that though they would sometimes find a person in one of these small, insignificant villages who spoke English or who could read Arabic, most of the interactions turned into a game of charades. Jonathon, partly out of frustration and partly in the interest of getting the men involved in the patrol, would sometimes call one of the men over and have him try to get the locals to answer the questions on the answer sheet. Most of them enjoyed it, but then again, they only had to do it every now and then.

As he stepped out of the truck, three men dressed in Kurdish garb approached from the shade of a house, waving a greeting. Traveling in this area from town to town required a knowledge of rudimentary greetings and key words in both Arabic and Kurdish, as he never knew which he would need at the town he was going to talk to next. This town was Kurdish, as the men wore loose fitting pants, which the men had called 'Iraqi hammer pants,' and their headdresses were wound tightly around their heads, not loose like the Arabs wore their *shumagg*. Jonathon looked around the town as he took off his helmet and rested it next to his clipboard on the scorching-hot hood of the truck.

"About how many houses, you think, Mac?" He asked his gunner.

"Umm, about twenty, sir," MacLimore answered, looking around from the top of the truck.

Okay, twenty houses, he thought, about ten people per house… we'll call it an even two hundred people. And he noted '200' in the column next to 'Population' on his sheet.

The three men came up and stood around Jonathon, smiling friendly smiles, their hands crossed in front of them expectantly. Jonathon smiled back at them and raised his hand in greeting, "*Marhaba*." Holy shit, it is *hot*, he thought to himself behind the smile he forced through the heat.

"Hallo," "*Salaam*," "*Marhaba*," were all echoed back by the three of them.

Jonathon put his hand on his chest and said, "Lieutenant— *mulaazim*—Garcia" to which the men's eyebrows raised— impressed—and slightly bowed their heads. Jonathon continued, pointing in the direction of the two silver silos just barely visible on the horizon, "Makhmur." The men nodded their understanding. Wiping his forehead with his hand, he sighed heavily. Ushering them closer, he slid the clipboard with the survey over, pointing at it and offering his pen. The men, refusing the pen, stared hard at the piece of paper, obviously not able to understand it.

The first time he had come to a Kurdish village to conduct one of these surveys, Battalion had just recently had the surveys translated, and was very excited about the new product. But the translation had been in Arabic, and Jonathon had spent two hours in the heat of the day playing cross-culture charades, trying to get a census on water, which he had poured out of his canteen, exaggerating the shrug of his shoulders, or of electricity, which he had eventually communicated by using the wires in the truck as props. There had been many other subjects on the survey, and he eventually got through all of them, though not without much patience and broiling frustration. When he finally got back to the base, he told Captain Pham that there had to be a better way to conduct those surveys. Nazeem had showed up a few days later.

Looking at the men, who had turned and yelled "Naqib!" toward the homes, he realized he now faced the problem of them not being able to read the Kurdish writing on the paper, which had been written by one of the battalion's interpreters. He only hoped that Naqib would be able to understand enough of what he was reading to circle the right answers. A small man with large eyes came jogging out of the dark entrances to one of the buildings and came their way, obviously proud that he had been publicly recognized as the one who could communicate with the Americans. Reaching the truck, Naqib, a young man in his late teens or early twenties, smiled warmly to Jonathon.

"Hallo, mister," the young man smiled.

"Hello, Naqib," Jonathon smiled back, relieved at the man's apparent understanding of at least rudimentary English. We might get home sometime today after all, he thought to himself. "*Cho-nee?*" he asked in Kurdish.

"*Zor-bash!*" Naqib exclaimed with a brown smile as he took the pen Jonathon offered to him, and read through the survey. Turning to Jonathon, he gestured with the pen toward the paper.

"Yes," Jonathon said, slightly relieved, pointing at the pen in his hand and to the paper, "I want you to write the answers. *Aow? Kutab-khana?*" he asked as he pointed to "water" and "school" on the paper. "Circle," he instructed, drawing a circle with his finger around one of the offered answers.

The young man's eyes lit up with understanding, and he eagerly attacked the questions put to him. A small crowd had gathered around the truck by now, and several kids, dressed in tight blue jeans and old t-shirts, stood staring at the foreign spectacle that stood before them. A couple of the kids had walked around to Olk, who was sitting in the truck behind the steering wheel, leaning into the truck to stay out of the sun as much as possible.

"Mister, mister, mister," Jonathon could hear them say to Olk, as he sat quietly ignoring them. Jonathon chuckled, as he could sense the impatience rising in his young soldier. After what could very well have been the hundredth "mister," finally exasperated, Olk gasped, "What?! Jesus Christ! GO AW-AY! *Imshi!*"

Jonathon laughed, partly at Olk, but mostly because he was feeling the exact same way at the moment.

One kid pointed at the pen that was clipped onto his vest. "*La*," said Olk. Another pointed at the rifle on his lap, the barrel pointed out of the truck. "*La*," he said again.

Jonathon turned his attention back to Naqib and the men gathered around the hood of the truck, their eyes flitting from the paper he was reading to Jonathon, to MacLimore behind the machine gun on the roof. Jonathon could feel the sweat pouring out of him, soaking his clothes underneath his vest. The sweat practically poured in a stream down his legs as he waited while Naqib completed the survey. It took him some time to get through each question, though each was only a line long, and Jonathon wondered whether he was not just milking the moment for all it was worth. Between that and the crowd's insistence on being involved in the process, it was taking quite a long time to answer ten very simple questions. There was no breeze, and the crowd that continued to build around him and the truck, the ceaseless "misters" from the kids who had tired of Olk and moved back around to investigate Jonathon's potential for a handout, were all adding to Jonathon's rapidly escalating impatience. He reached around for his canteen, unscrewed the cap, took a long, slow drink of warm water, and a long, deep breath, and patiently waited for Naqib to finish.

He eventually did, after many revisions and quick, animated conversations with some of the men in the crowd. Handing Jonathon the sweat-marked piece of paper with a smile of triumph, Jonathon stuck it behind the empty ones remaining on the clipboard.

Jonathon tossed the clipboard in the truck and paused, thinking that he ought to say something poetic and inspiring. But he didn't feel particularly poetic or inspired at that moment, and told himself that there was no point since he could not speak much Kurdish anyway, and they would most likely not understand whatever he said in English. At this point, he had pretty much decided that Naqib, for all of his celebrated bilingual talents, was not too sure himself exactly what he had just filled out, or whether it was very accurate of the conditions in the town. But, with the sun beating on his head, and with five or six more towns to go, all of which promised more of the same, he decided that he really didn't give a shit and offered a quick goodbye.

Leaning into the truck and putting his helmet back on, he told Olk to call the other trucks, each of which by now had their own crowd of admirers, and tell them to get ready to go. Olk turned the ignition on and the Humvee came to life with a roar, and Jonathon smiled and held up his hand to the men gathered around him. "*Sur-pas, hwa-ha-fees,*" he offered over the engine, and shook the mud-caked hands offered him.

Climbing into the truck and pulling the door closed, he turned to Olk with a tired smile. "All right," he sighed, shaking his head slowly. "Well, that's one more down."

"How many more towns do we have to hit today, sir?" Olk asked as he fell in behind Hoover's Humvee and weaved his way slowly around a house back to the dirt road that led out of town.

"Only like ten more man," Jonathon said as he watched the chickens run from in front of the truck and a group of dogs in his rearview mirror, their teeth bared, chase after the small convoy until it was away from the farthest home.

They bounced along the dirt road, Jonathon staring hard at his map and the GPS in his hand, trying to keep track of the direction and distance they had to go to get to the next town. The heat and the dust and all of the equipment he had on always made him nauseous, as he tried to keep them on course in the bouncing Humvee.

"Sir?" asked Olk, after several minutes of silence.

"Yeah?" Jonathon said, his eyes still on his map.

"Do we really have ten more towns to hit today?" Olk asked, turning his head toward his platoon leader.

Jonathon smiled, "No man, we only have like five or six more, that's all. Don't worry."

Olk paused. "That's not cool sir," he finally said, turning his head back to the road.

Jonathon smiled. "I was cool for years, man. I'm done being cool."

Olk looked at his PL, Jonathon smiling an exaggerated smile back at him, baring all his white teeth. A stark Olk just shook his head and stared at the brown road in front of them. After a few minutes of silent riding down the bumpy dirt road, Olk turned back toward Jonathon.

"Sir, you know, this heat's got me thinkin' about my truck back home that I used to have," he said, slouching slightly in his seat, a cigarette hanging loosely from his lips as he draped his right hand over the steering wheel.

"Oh yeah?" Jonathon asked absently, his head down looking at the map in his lap.

Olk continued on. It didn't matter whether anyone heard his story, he just felt like telling it. "Yessir. It was this old eighty-nine Ford Ranger that I bought for eight hundred bucks from some guy in my hometown. Red, but the paint was all chipped and faded in places. I took her home and worked on her all summer before my senior year. Put on a six-inch lift, cleaned up the engine, slapped on some big ole' thirty-fives. She was awesome." Olk looked over to Jonathon, but his head was still down in his map. "Anyway, I got her all fixed up before school came along. Back home the thing to have was a raised up truck. One day after school, me and my buddies were all hanging out in my garage, drinking beer and talking about our trucks. We got to thinking about how hot it was, and what a pain in the ass it was to have to hold a beer when you were driving and all."

"Huh?" Jonathon's head looked up from its map, an incredulous smile on his face. Olk smiled to himself, knowing that now he had Jonathon's full attention.

"Yessir. So I came up with this idea, and yanked the windshield washer fluid tank out, cleaned it up, and ran a tube from it to inside the truck." He could see Jonathon shaking his head in disbelief. "It was perfect. You could just drive down the road, and you had all the beer you could want for a drive. 'Course you had to turn the windshield wipers on."

"Well, of course," Jonathon teased.

"Yessir," continued Olk, taking a long pull of his cigarette and holding it in the hand draped over the steering wheel, quite pleased with himself. "And you had to drink it all pretty fast, because the engine would start to heat it up pretty quick."

"Well yeah, sure. I mean, warm beer is absolutely unacceptable." Jonathon laughed contentedly at the story, which he figured probably wasn't true, but was a good story nonetheless.

A few more hot dusty minutes passed while Olk finished his cigarette and tossed the butt out the door, lost in memories of home. Jonathon returned to his map, sure that Olk would tell another story soon. He always did on these long patrols, and Jonathon made a point to humor him. He knew that driving along these roads was hard enough on him, but for his guys who spent the day in a seemingly pointless tour of worthless towns, it was even worse. Olk's way of escaping the boredom and frustration of the heat and the dust and the jostling Humvee was to tell stories from home, and Jonathon found that he had come to enjoy hearing them.

Olk lit another cigarette and started another story. "Hey sir, so there was this hill back in my hometown. Wilson Hill. Well, every so often in the early spring everybody'd get together at Wilson Hill, and see whose truck could get to the top. It would be so covered with snow and ice, and all tore up from everybody trying to get up it, that nobody ever could." Olk turned toward Jonathon with a smile of triumph. "My truck was the only one to ever get to the top."

"No kidding? That's great man. Has anyone gotten up since you left?" Jonathon asked.

"Nope. I'm still the only one," said Olk, a smile on his lips.

"Do you still have your truck? Turn left here," Jonathon said, pointing at the up-coming intersection.

"Roger sir," said Olk as he slowed the truck and spun the wheel counterclockwise hard with both arms. "Sir, I think something's wrong with the power-steering. I'm having to work awful hard to turn. I checked the fluid today, and it was good. Maybe something came loose with all this bumping around."

"We'll have Chief look at it when we get back," Jonathon said. Olk took an abnormal amount of pride in the fact that his—and the Platoon Leader's—Humvee was always running right, a fact that Jonathon had come to greatly appreciate. Olk took good care of him, Jonathon thought right then, and he was lucky to have him as his driver. He felt a strong affection rise up for the young man seated next to him, his half-finished cigarette dangling from his lips and his helmet cocked back revealing a burst of light, tangled hair underneath.

"Roger sir. What'd you ask me? Oh yeah. No sir, I had to sell her. But I was just thinking about trying to find her when we get home. You were probably wondering what got me started on talking about all that."

"I'll admit I'm a little curious."

"I was just thinking about how much better my truck would drive out here than these Humvees, they're so heavy. And a cold beer sure would be good right now, wouldn't it, sir?" Olk asked, his eyebrows raised.

"It sure would. I'd probably even take a beer from the windshield washer fluid tank," Jonathon said with a laugh.

"I'm telling you sir, it was awesome," Olk insisted with a great big, innocent smile, the end of his sentence trailing off as Jonathon imagined his mind traveling back home to Wilson Hill and beer in the engine. Jonathon's own mind started to trail off until he saw the town they were headed for ahead to the right.

"Hey Olk, take this next right. That town to our two o'clock is the one we want."

"Roger sir."

The convoy of Humvees, with a long brown tail of dust behind them, pulled slowly up to the small group of houses. Children stuck their heads from behind doorways and windows. A group of men, dressed in long, dark *dish-dasha*, casually approached the trucks.

Jonathon smiled at Olk. "Well man, here we go again."

"This town's Arab, sir," Olk offered.

Setting his helmet down on the fiery-hot hood of the Humvee, Jonathon sighed heavily and leaned back into the truck as the men approached. "Hey Olk, maybe when we get home, after you find your truck, we'll take it out to the back forty or something."

"Yeah," said Olk with a smile and a nod. "That sounds good, sir."

"All right," said Jonathon, tapping the door lightly and leaning back out into the heat. "Hey Mac, how many houses you think?"

* * *

It was midday in late July as Jonathon and Anderson stepped out of the cargo Humvee into the noise and clatter of the Makhmur market place. The same noises, the same smells, the same indiscernible faces passing by. Jonathon stepped onto the rough sidewalk with large chunks of missing asphalt and black pools of stagnant water scattered throughout. A short man with a round and unshaven face stepped out of his store and attempted, in Kurdish, to convince Jonathon to buy a large piece of purple fabric that hung from outside his window. Jonathon offered a weak smile and moved down the sidewalk, stepping over the dark pools.

Ahead he saw a group of kids running toward him, obviously having figured out by now that the Americans always came into town at about this time in order to buy ice and other things. He spotted his ice boy, Fuzzy, in the back of the crowd of racing children, obviously not worried—Jonathon had always ignored the others and given him the business.

It happened in an instant; there was no warning, nothing. It felt as if the world split. An explosion shot through the air, the concussion hitting him like a train. The sun disappeared behind the dust and the world was dark. His ears rang.

What happened? he asked himself through his pounding head.

He strained his eyes to see through the cloud of dust and smoke. His head ringing, he felt his way forward, his hands finding the hood of his truck. The dust started to clear.

A bomb, he thought to himself.

His mind raced. His eyes found Anderson, who had found the two others who had come with them, and was yelling at them to follow him. He disappeared into the dust and smoke. Instinctively, against his will, Jonathon followed.

Women screamed and people staggered out of the cloud with their hands to their heads, covering what were mostly superficial wounds or cuts on the arms, though one woman had had her left arm blown off just below the elbow. He saw the little body of Faisal, all twisted and charred and splayed on the ground, and he knew that he was dead. Jonathon spat and cursed the whole goddamned world for all of its indiscriminate barbarity, but caught himself and kept walking. Later. Not now, he told himself. Think about that one later.

Men yelled and dogs barked. Car horns blared a warning.

Just on the other side of the street, he found the origin of the explosion. There was a crater just under a foot deep, the concrete of the street cracked around the hole from the force, the surrounding area charred black. Against the wall of one of the shops by the sidewalk there was a young girl, her body propped against the wall as if she were reclining against it. Her head rested on her right shoulder, a small stream of red ran down from the corner of her mouth, down her chin and neck, and disappeared under her dress. Her dress was a light blue, with yellow and pink outlines of flowers adorning it. Her black hair was a tangled mess, some clinging to the cracks of the wall that her head lay against. Her arms rested loosely at her sides, one charred palm facing up. A fine layer of dust had settled all over her skin and her dress, dulling the brightness of the cloth.

Jonathon instinctively rushed toward her and knelt beside her limp body. He reached out and grabbed her arm with one hand to try to wake her, and put two fingers against her neck with the other hand. Out of the corner of his eye he saw Anderson moving from one body to another. He could not tell, but it looked like at least half a dozen bodies were strewn around the site. All little bodies, no big ones. Dresses of blue and yellow, shirts with soccer balls and cartoon characters on them. As he watched Anderson, the girl at his side moved her head and moaned weakly.

"She's alive!" he shouted, motioning Anderson to hurry over to him. Anderson knelt beside her and the two of them moved her delicately so that she was flat on the ground. The street, which had emptied in a flash, was slowly filling back up with people. A few men started to wander into the blast zone, and saw what Jonathon's men had already determined: dead little bodies. All but her. Her eyes half open, face pocked with black, she moaned incoherently.

"She's bleeding. Her back." Anderson, with his experience, had run his hands underneath her to determine whether there were any injuries that they could not see, and when he pulled his hands away, they were both covered in blood, telling the two men that the little girl had catastrophic injuries. Jonathon ripped off his body armor vest, which landed on the sidewalk with a dull thud, and pulled his blouse over his head. The two wrapped the little girl in the blouse, the ends of her little legs jutting from underneath. The light brown of the blouse quickly showed spots of red that grew outward from the center. Jonathon, seeing the spots multiply quickly, without thinking scooped up the little girl, who moaned even more weakly at the movement, and started back toward the Humvee. Anderson, sensing Jonathon's intent, grabbed his vest off the ground and yelled at the two men who were checking on other bodies to go to the truck.

Halfway across the street, a woman, dressed hastily in her black *abayya*, her face uncovered, screamed as she ran toward Jonathon. She reached him as he was climbing into the Humvee, his arms holding his bundled blouse. Her hands pulled away the blouse that covered the little face and saw the little eyes closed, and the mother exuded a sound that came from somewhere between the pains of childbirth and death. Jonathon slid into the front seat, the woman pleading with him in hysterical Arabic words he understood completely. He motioned with his head for her to get into the back of the truck as Anderson and the men climbed in. Anderson, sliding into the front seat and turning over the truck said, "Sir, you know that she can't—"

"Just go."

The truck started up and took off down the narrow—now empty—street.

As the truck drove through the front gate, Jonathon yelled at the men holding up their palms in an effort to slow the truck down to get out of the way, and for added emphasis held up the bloody bundle that he cradled in his arms. The men stepped out of the way, and once the truck had entered through the gate, he told Anderson to stop. Anderson, knowing what he needed to do, got out and went around the back of the truck to tell the woman that she had to get out, she would have to be searched. Jonathon, as soon as the truck had lurched to a stop, stepped out and started to run toward the aid station, yelling "Medic!"

Two medics reached him before he got to the front of the aid tent. The head medic, Allan Naeve, folding back a corner of the blouse to see the face, frowned with eyes that understood immediately the tragedy of what lay before him, and gently took the bundle from Jonathon.

"I got her, sir," he said, and disappeared into the fluorescent white light of the tent, leaving Jonathon standing alone outside.

Jonathon stood there, his hands at his sides, staring into the tent but unable to see anything other than the flap that covered the interior entrance. His mind did not race; it barely moved. No thoughts came into his head; there was no panic, no rush, no musical score. All was silent. A car drove by on the highway that ran next to the fence of the compound. Two men, with nothing on but black shorts and brown t-shirts, emerged from one of the buildings on the far side of the courtyard. Silence.

He turned and started to walk back to the truck without realizing he had done so. Shipley and Melton—the two who had been in town with him—walked toward him with the girl's mother between them. She had to be escorted to see her daughter, and they needed to be checked out. The mother's eyes widened in silent horror at the sight of Jonathon. She stopped feet from him, her mouth dropped and her hands covered her face as she fell onto Jonathon's chest, clutching the shirt that had been dyed red by the blood of her little girl. She sobbed silently, as if the sounds that tore from her were not meant to be heard by men.

"It's okay," he lied, and put his hands on her shoulders in a mockery of effort to give comfort. "It's okay," he lied again and made an effort to gently push her away. It was the only thing he could muster the courage to say at the moment. He cast a look at Melton, who gently took the woman by the arm to lead her to the aid station tent. "Are you two all right?" he reflexively asked.

"Yessir," said Shipley.

"We're good, sir," said Melton.

Okay. Good. She needs to go to the tent. I can't look at her right now. Thoughts were beginning to form again in Jonathon's mind as he wandered toward the warehouse where the platoon stayed. Anderson had already parked the truck and had just taken off his gear to go check on the two men who went to the aid station with the mother when Jonathon walked in. The men in the platoon jumped to their feet at the sight of him, but fortunately Anderson got to him first.

"Leave the LT alone, guys. Go on, get outta here." Wide-eyed, the men turned and headed back to their various time-killing activities. Anderson stood in front of Jonathon with his back to the men, his arms crossed in front of him. He was squinting hard, his leathery brow wrinkled, as he growled from underneath his mustache, "You all right, sir?"

"Yeah, I'm fine." Jonathon looked back at him with expressionless eyes.

"You need to get cleaned up, sir," Anderson ordered softly.

"Huh?"

"You're covered in blood, sir. You need to get cleaned up," he repeated, articulating the words more carefully this time.

Jonathon looked down at his shirt. The whole front had been soaked with blood. He walked over to his cot, sat down, and rested his elbows on his knees. Rubbing his hands together, he glanced at them absently. His hands, virtually covered in the dried blood of the little girl, caused him to start.

I'm sure that will affect me later, he thought solemnly. Out, out, damned spot, he quoted as he got up. He quietly grabbed a water bottle and walked outside. He twisted the blue plastic top off the bottle and carefully poured the lukewarm water over his hands. Rubbing them together, he noticed his arms were also painted a light shade of red. His hands clean, he poured the water down his arms, but the farther up his arms he looked, the farther the light red kept going, until it disappeared under the short sleeves of his t-shirt, also dyed red. Putting the water bottle down, he pulled his shirt off over his head, the wet shirt feeling sticky against his face. He shuddered slightly. This cleaning process was going to take more time than he thought. He noticed his pants, also, were splotched with blood where he had cradled the little bundle on the ride into the base. His boots had red patches also. He was covered, he realized.

He sat down on the chair underneath the gnarled olive tree, and began to unlace his boots. Pulling them off, he set them beside his seat. He then stood up and undid his belt and dropped his pants, casting them in a heap beside his boots. He would not even bother trying to clean them. He could barely bring himself to look at them, and only with deliberate effort did he reach back into them to pull his effects out of the pockets, only to leave them in a heap on the gray concrete. Now, completely stripped except for his socks, which he yanked off and tossed onto his pants even though they were by every means salvageable, he stood up and carefully poured the water over his whole body, slowly and conservatively at first, but then realizing that in order to get the dried blood off his skin, he needed more water than just the liter.

The bottle emptied, he stepped back into the entrance of the warehouse, and picked up a five-gallon tan water can. Anderson saw, from the corner of his eye, the light brown skin of his naked young platoon leader walk back out of the warehouse, leaning to one side from the weight of the water, and disappear outside around the corner. Jonathon unscrewed the top from the hard plastic can, and heaved it above his head. Tilting the can so that the water came cascading over him, it splashed off his head, ran down his face and shoulders, and down the rest of his body where it spread out in a thin pool around his feet. Conserving half of the can, he set it down and rubbed his body all over with his hands until he was satisfied. Then lifting the rest of the can, he rinsed himself off. When the water was all gone, he stood there naked and soaking wet with the empty can in one hand, while the water dripped off him onto the warm concrete at his feet.

He saw Sam walking slowly toward him across the dusty courtyard. Stopping short of the pile of stained clothes and the shallow pool of water, Sam squinted his eyes as he stood next to him, staring beyond the fence toward the highway that ran by the compound. Jonathon remained as he was, naked, looking toward the ground, watching the drops that ran off his nose and chin fall softly into the pool around his feet.

"I heard what happened Jon," Sam said quietly. "You all right brother?"

Jonathon was quiet for a few seconds. "Yeah," he said, nodding his head slowly.

"Okay," Sam nodded, searching for words. "Well, I'm glad to hear it."

"Thanks."

Sam turned and started to walk away when he heard Jonathon say his name in a half whisper. Sam turned toward his friend, the water quickly evaporating off his smooth, light-brown skin, his eyes still staring at the ground beneath him. "Sam, what kind of a world do we live in?" he asked desperately.

"I don't know, Jon," he said and began to slowly turn away, but then stopped and looked back at Jonathon. "But I love ya, and that's gotta count for something." Jonathon looked up at him and knew that he meant it, and he smiled and nodded his head as Sam turned back and walked across the empty courtyard.

It was the middle of the day. No one was outside due to the heat. But Jonathon, finding himself in the shade of the dying olive tree and dripping wet, found the temperature comfortable as the water evaporated off him. He remained there until he was completely dry and the oppression of the heat returned.

He was quite a sight when he walked back in, naked accept in one hand carrying his boots. No heads turned toward him, but every man's eyes were fixed on him as he walked over to his cot. Dropping the boots with a light thud, he picked up his black shorts and put them on. No one spoke a word; Anderson, next to him, tried to look absorbed in what he was reading. Jonathon stretched his body the length of the cot. Then, folding his hands over his chest, he closed his eyes and feigned sleep.

Only when the men felt that he was asleep, did conversation slowly start to pick up again. Every now and then the noise would rise to a level Anderson felt to be too loud, and he would shoot a sharp look toward the violator, and the noise would abruptly cease, and day one hundred and fifty-one finally ended for Jonathon.

* * *

The truck rolled to a smooth stop, and a cloud of dust enveloped them as Jonathon opened his door and smiled at the group of men who sat in their usual place on the blue rug in the shade of the mud house. The men waved a friendly greeting as they stood to receive their guest.

Jonathon saw a flash of light blue to his right, and turned his head to see a little dress in bare feet disappear around a corner. He heard the sound of children laughing. It had been two days since the explosion. Good thing I don't believe in ghosts, he thought, as he stared toward the corner that the apparition had fled behind.

"Lieutenant Garcia?" He heard Nazeem's voice call softly to him, halfway between the truck and the group of men.

"Coming Nazeem," he called out as he grabbed his notebook from the truck and walked over to the carpet. His rifle slung over his shoulder, he shook hands warmly with faces he did not recognize. Smiling weakly, he said, "Good morning. It is good to see you again."

Nazeem translated to the group, who all replied with the typical "*Salaam.*" Looking around, Jonathon did not see Mr. Marie, but figured the man would appear once he heard Jonathon was there. After being invited to take a seat on the rug, he took off his helmet and laid it next to him, carefully leaning his rifle against it. Olk leaned against a low wall that was still in the shade of the building, the handmike from his radio shoved between his helmet's chinstrap and his ear, and his right hand on the grip of his rifle. Jonathon felt a wave of warmth rise in him as he saw in his young soldier's posture a desire to provide security for his PL.

The morning before, and a day after the bombing in Mahkmur, as they were getting ready to go out on a patrol, Olk had confronted Jonathon about the bombing.

"Sir," Olk had said as he climbed into the truck.

"Yeah?" Jonathon answered distractedly, studying the open map in his lap.

But Olk was serious and he wanted Jonathon's full attention. "Sir," he had said sharply, and Jonathon's head jerked up, confused by the tone. "Sir," Olk continued, smoothing his voice down appropriately, "about yesterday."

"Don't worry about yesterday."

"Well sir, I'm your RTO," Olk continued. "And I'm supposed to look after you."

"You do a great job for me too, Olk, you really do," Jonathon had said.

But Olk shot him a look which said to cut out the bullshit and not interrupt him, that what he had to say was important and Jonathon needed to listen to him. "Sir, I don't want you going anywhere from now on without me. Like I said, I'm your RTO, and I gotta look out for you. 'Cause the way I see it sir, is that if you go down, then we're all in a heap of trouble. So from now on sir, I go wherever you go."

Jonathon was smiling and was glad that he had sunglasses on because his eyes had welled up a bit. He had nodded his compliance, still smiling, which Olk evidently mistook for Jonathon laughing at him.

"I'm fucking serious, sir. I'm not kidding. It's dangerous over here, and I don't want you going anywhere—"

"Okay, Olk. All right," Jonathon had cut him off, erasing the smile and plastering a sincere and grave countenance upon his face to match the tone in Olk's voice. "You got it, I won't go anywhere without you from now on. I promise." He nodded for emphasis, though inside he was about to burst.

Olk had nodded once emphatically, obviously pleased with himself and his new role as the Grand Protector of Lieutenant Garcia, and had turned the engine over with a roar.

Now, sitting on the big blue carpet in the shade with the strange men, Jonathon heard from behind him, from the corner where the bare footed dress had gone, the sound of children laughing. His mind flashed back to a dozen small bodies running down the street, laughing and tagging each other as they raced to the Americans. Jonathon started at the sound of a crash. A man, carrying a large aluminum tray, had tripped over a corner of the carpet and dropped the empty tray with the hollow clang of aluminum. Jonathon recovered, shaking his head. Come on, Jon, he said to himself. Pull yourself together, brother.

Looking around, he gathered himself for conversation. "I am sorry it has taken me so long to get back out to you." He looked at Nazeem to translate.

The men nodded their understanding, one speaking to Nazeem in Arabic.

"He says they know you are a busy man, and they are always glad to see you, whenever you can come," he said softly to Jonathon, Jonathon's eyes on the speaker, a man with a round, unshaven face, who sat across the rug from Jonathon.

"*Shukran.* I enjoy visiting with you," Jonathon said, nodding his head. The men nodded their approval at his compliment expressed through Nazeem. Silence followed, all the men looking at Jonathon expectantly. He could not help the apathy and frustration that rose inside him, and sighed slowly. The man with the unshaven face spoke again to Nazeem.

"He would like to know if you would like something to eat," Nazeem said.

Jonathon looked at his watch. It was only nine o'clock in the morning. They had eaten at eight before they left, and he was still full. He smiled and bowed his head slightly in thanks and said, "Thank you very much for the offer, but we have just eaten." As Nazeem translated, he could swear that he heard Olk sigh with relief off to his left. The man said something back to Nazeem.

Nazeem leaned in, "Would you like some chai?"

Jonathon winced inside, unable to refuse two offers even though he was in no mood for hot tea. "Yes," he smiled graciously, "chai would be very good. Thank you."

They always served the chai piping hot in small two-ounce sized glasses. With all the sugar the Iraqis put into the tea, it could have been boiled water straight from the Tigris—which it may very well have been—and still would have tasted sweet. Jonathon turned to his left and asked Olk, "Olk, want some chai?"

Olk leaned forward off his little perch, "Yessir." Jonathon smiled. Olk never turned down chai; he was often even a little forward when visiting towns in asking them whether they had any. Jonathon's sense of propriety and manners revolted at this, and he was constantly chiding Olk for his rudeness. The last time he had corrected him, Olk turned to him and said with a smile, "But sir, I'm building a rapport," recalling Jonathon's own words to him. That had been four or five days ago, and Jonathon smiled now as he had then at his young soldier's sense of humor.

The same man who had dropped the aluminum tray now reappeared again, this time with the tray full of little clear glasses sitting on porcelain dishes. A large white porcelain pitcher with steam rising from the top sat on the tray as the man set the tray in the middle of the carpet. He poured the hot liquid into each glass, dropping several spoonfuls of sugar into each. Jonathon recognized the man's brown and toothless smile as the same server from his last meal with Mr. Marie. Despite the shade, the heat was already unbearable, and drinking a piping-hot drink did not seem to make much sense to Jonathon. But the sweet tea tasted good, even though he had to wait for it to cool, stirring it slowly with the small spoon he had been provided.

Stirring the chai, trying to dissolve the sugar into the tea, he heard the sound of laughter again, this time from off to his right. His mind took him back to the morning before. He was sitting under the old olive tree in the white plastic chair, his unopened bible in his hands. The sound of footsteps down the sidewalk caused him to look to see who was coming, his face flushing at the approaching _*a novel*_

company. It was Naeve, the medic who had taken the little girl from him the day before. He was in black shorts and a brown shirt, wearing flip-flops that shuffled along the pavement. He was holding a roll of toilet paper, on his way to the latrine. Jonathon saw his face turn sullen as he said good morning.

"Morning, Doc," Jonathon returned.

"How you doing, sir?" Naeve had stopped and asked.

Jonathon slowly nodded his head, his bible in one hand on his lap. "All right. I hear she didn't make it," though he hadn't been thinking about the girl—not really, anyway, but kind of—and he wanted to tell Doc about Faisal and about how he should be in school right now, learning how to find the area of a triangle instead of being laid to rest in the dirt, and what a fucking waste the whole goddamn thing was.

"No sir, she didn't. She was dead when you handed her to me," Naeve said quietly. He then added, "But she died from the concussion of the explosion and from loss of blood, sir. It wasn't anything you—there wasn't anything anybody could've done."

Jonathon nodded his head and gave a soft grunt of affirmation. The quiet stillness of the early morning enveloped the two.

"All right sir," said Naeve, "I'll see you around."

"Yeah, I'll see you, Doc," Jonathon said, forcing a friendly smile. Naeve continued down the sidewalk, the sound of his shuffling growing more and more faint. Alone in the quiet, a single tear had rolled down Jonathon's cheek.

His chai glass empty, and drops of sweat beading on his forehead which he wiped away with his hand, he grew impatient for the arrival of Mr. Marie. Deciding that he had better just move the meeting along despite his absence, Jonathon picked up his notebook and addressed the group.

"I know when I was here a couple weeks ago, Mr. Hazan spoke about his wheat being stolen from the Kurds in a nearby village." Nazeem translated. "Is Mr. Hazan here?" Jonathon asked.

A man to his right raised his hand with a yellow open mouthed smile, "Hallo!"

Jonathon bowed his head slightly toward the man. "*Salaam*," he said. "Have you had any trouble this week with your wheat?" he asked.

"*La*," the man said, slapping his hands together, "*Dhahaba*," shrugging his shoulders.

"All of his wheat is gone. He has finished harvesting," Nazeem interpreted the gestures.

"Oh yeah," said Jonathon, remembering now what he had noticed on his drive down to Al Sharqi. The landscape had changed dramatically in the past few weeks. The rolling fields of endless golden wheat stalks were gone, replaced by the dusty-brown earth, chewed up from the combines. The harvest had begun in July that year, and had finally ended. Despite the blazing heat, the sense of life the fields had brought had provided some comfort, some relief. Now all that was left was dry, brown dirt that the sun would bake mercilessly for the next few months until the first rains came in October. Jonathon wrinkled his brow at the thought of the coming months and the inevitable heat they would bring.

"Lieutenant Garcia?" he heard Nazeem say softly.

"Oh, I'm sorry," he said, focusing back on the conversation, "how was the harvest this year?"

The men around the circle shrugged their shoulders and said in a neutral tone, "Good."

Nazeem leaned in, "They say that it was—"

"Nazeem," Jonathon laughed softly, "I understand what 'good' means." He patted Nazeem affectionately on the shoulder.

Nazeem smiled sheepishly, "I am sorry sir."

"No Nazeem, it's okay. You are doing a great job," Jonathon reassured him, thinking back a few days to his last survey patrol, and the endless charades and broken conversations that he had had to endure. Turning back to the group of men, he held up his survey for them to see. "I did not get a chance to talk to you all about some questions we have about things like water, electricity, and schools last time. I would like to see if there is anything that we can help with."

Nazeem translated. One of the men said something, and Nazeem leaned in, "He says that you did ask them about these things last time, and that they answered."

Jonathon smiled. He remembered that he *had* briefly talked to them about these things in his last visit. Smiling and looking around at them, he recovered and said, "Yes, but now we have these new forms that I must fill out," he said, holding the piece of paper for them to see. "Would you mind talking about these things again?" he asked them as Nazeem translated. The survey was not new, but Jonathon had to keep coming back to villages and asking them the same questions in order to monitor any progress. He wondered whether anyone was doing anything to actually improve the things that he was asking about, or whether he was just conducting these surveys because they didn't have anything else for him to do.

"*Na'am*," was the consensus.

"*Shukran*," said Jonathon, as he took out his pen and quickly went over the items on the survey. For the sake of simplicity, he offered them three possible answers, "Good, okay, and bad."

The survey took a while to complete. The sun was now upon them, and sweat poured out from Jonathon as he hastily wrote the answers on the survey. It seemed as if the men wanted to discuss every question, but Jonathon was in no mood for getting drawn into a long discussion on whether the one "school"—nothing but a mud hut packed with rickety old desks—in the town was "good" or just "okay," or whether the electricity was "okay" or "bad." After he had all the answers he needed, he folded up the survey and placed it inside his green notebook. Looking around, he paused a moment in thought. He was trying to decide whether he wanted to get into asking where Mr. Marie was. Sighing, his curiosity overcame his impatience.

"Excuse me, but before I go, is Mr. Marie here today?" he asked.

"*La*," the men shook their heads.

Jonathon was surprised, though he did not know why. He could be any number of places. "Do you know where he is? Will he be back soon?"

"Baghdad," the man with the round, unshaven face pointed over his shoulder.

Baghdad? What's in Baghdad? Well, I'll just have to catch him next time, he thought to himself, feeling both sorry to have missed him and glad that the meeting could now end. Standing up clumsily, shaking his right leg which had again fallen asleep as he sat cross-legged on the floor, he picked up his rifle and slung it around his shoulder and put his helmet back on his head. The group of men also stood up, aware that the meeting was now over and the American was leaving.

Raising his right hand and smiling, he offered a warm, "*Shukran, ma'salaama*" and shook the hands that were offered to him. Offering a warm, "*Shukran*" one last time, he smiled and turned toward the truck, which Olk was already standing by, waiting for him to give the signal to start it up. Jonathon called out to him, "All right, Olk, let's go," as he held up his right index finger and twirled it in the air to signal to the rest of the Humvees, which were all dispersed around the center of the town, to start up.

Climbing back in, he turned around and waited for Nazeem to get in. "Ready, Nazeem?" he asked over the roar of the truck.

"Ready, Lieutenant Garcia," Nazeem answered, pulling his seatbelt across and buckling it in.

"Okay, Olk, let's go," he said as he grabbed the handmike and, depressing the talk button on the side, said, "All right Seven, we're done, let's go."

"Is that it, sir?" the radio box squawked back, "Any other villages you wanna hit?" he heard Anderson ask through the radio.

He thought a moment. He had blocked off four hours to spend at Al Sharqi alone, and it was the only town that he wanted to hit today. The thought of bouncing along in the midday heat on the dusty, winding roads, getting lost and sick as he tried to follow their route on the map in his lap, was not something he felt up to that day. He looked at his watch. It was already ten o'clock. It would take a half-hour to get back, if they drove slowly. That put their patrol at two hours, a respectable length for a single town visit. I'll explain to

Captain Pham when we get back, he thought as he pressed the talk button on his handmike and said, "Nope, let's go home."

"Roger that!" came the enthusiastic response from Hoover over the radio.

"Hey One, take the lead," Jonathon told Hoover through the radio. "I'll follow, then you Seven, and Two will bring up the rear."

"Two likes it in the rear," he heard Hoover say through the speaker.

"All right," Jonathon smiled, "let's go. No hurry back, boys," he said as he hooked the handmike onto the speaker and Olk turned the truck out of the town and onto the main road leading north to Makhmur, the two silos barely visible on the horizon.

That evening, Jonathon sat on the hood of one of his Humvees, watching the golden sun sink toward the horizon, casting the sky into shades of red and purple. The heat of the day was far from gone, and the hood he sat on was still hot from the sun. Drops of sweat formed on his brow as he leaned against the windshield, a small pack of cookies he had recently received in a care package from home in his hand. Traffic on the highway that ran alongside the compound had dwindled, with only the occasional passerby. The world was settling down for the day. The sound of dogs barking reached his ears, punctuating the silence of the rest of the world. He put a cookie in his mouth and chewed slowly. His unopened bible lay next to him on the hood, the edge of its pages brown from the oil of his hands. For a moment a slight breeze picked up, and his eyes closed as he relished in it. When it passed and he opened his eyes, he heard the soft sound of footsteps coming from behind him. He recognized the sound of Sam's gait. Turning his body so he could see over his shoulder, he saw his friend, the dark hair long and unkept, his face unshaven.

"Hey Sam," Jonathon said, turning back around toward the sun.

"Hey Jon," said Sam as he walked to the front of the Humvee and leaned against the bumper, looking toward the sunset. Except for the occasional crunch of Jonathon's cookies, the two remained quiet, as the sun, its light distorted by the heat waves rising from the earth, gently touched the horizon, its color deepening to a warm red.

"You want a cookie?" asked Jonathon quietly when the sun was halfway down, leaning forward, extending the bag toward Sam with his hand.

Sam looked casually over his shoulder. "Yeah, thanks," and reached into the small bag. Jonathon leaned back against the windshield, and the muffled chewing of cookies resumed. The sun disappeared behind the horizon, and the sky started to darken. There were no clouds, and toward the east, pinpoints of light were already showing against the dark blue sky. Sam reached into his pocket and produced a green soda can. Turning around, he offered it to Jonathon silently as he cast a wary eye at the bible lying next to him.

"Thanks," said Jonathon as he leaned forward to accept. His dark eyebrows raised in surprise when he grabbed it. "Cold," he said with a smile. "Thanks," and rubbed the can over his forehead, his eyes closed. Sam turned back around toward the now-gone sun, and leaned against the bumper of the truck. He pulled another green can out of his pocket, and the silence of the night was broken by the crack and splash of him opening his soda. Raising it to his mouth, he took a long draught, then burped silently. Jonathon's can also opened in the still night.

Still facing the same direction, Sam asked, "How you doin', Jon?"

Jonathon's munching stopped, and Sam heard a long sigh from behind him. "I'm livin'," Jonathon replied.

"Yeah," said Sam, his head tilting down toward his feet and he shifted the dirt on the ground.

"I'm having a hard time," Jonathon's voice spoke into the growing night, his words spoken deliberately, "reconciling what I believe with the world I see around me. I used to be so convinced about things, certain that there were some things in this world that were true and permanent. Tangible, like you could feel them in your hands."

Sam, unsure of what to say or how to respond, only nodded his head slightly without turning around.

In the continuing stillness, Jonathon said softly, "I keep having the same nightmare. From Najaf," he added in order to clarify, slightly ashamed at the confession, but feeling a strong need that night to talk.

Sam turned around silently and leaned his arms against the warm hood of the truck, his eyes darting back and forth between Jonathon and the bible next to him. Jonathon was looking toward the sunset, his eyes calmly searching the horizon. With that faraway look in his eyes, and the solemn, honest expression painted on his face, he could have been talking to himself. The sky was quickly growing darker, but his smooth brown skin still reflected the deep red light from the west. Taking a slow drink, he shook his head, "I'm all out of faith, Sam. I don't think I believe in anything anymore." He stopped, looking down into his lap, the green can cradled in both his hands. Sam saw his eyes shoot toward the unopened bible beside him. Jonathon sighed slowly. Looking back up, he said, "All I have left are platitudes and religion."

Sam waited a moment before he spoke, the growing quiet of the night surrounding them. "Jon," Sam finally said slowly, "this is the worst kind of place," he looked down and slowly shook his head. Looking back up, he said, "I don't mean Iraq—I think we can agree this place is a goddamn shithole—I mean the thing itself, war. War is man at his worst." He shrugged. "It's hard for anyone to have faith in anything in the middle of something like this."

Jonathon, a smile slowly forming on his lips, tilted his head toward Sam. Sam looked up during the silence and saw Jonathon staring at him. "What?" Sam asked, shrugging his shoulders.

Still shaking his head, his smile growing, Jonathon asked, "Where...? What....?" then his smile grew to a laugh.

Sam returned the laugh and then in mock offense said, "Hey, I wasn't always a reprobate, you know. I used to be a good church boy like you."

"I'm sorry Sam," said Jonathon, still shaking his head and smiling, his eyes sparkling, "I don't mean it that way. It's just that... you never cease to surprise me, that's all." The two young men laughed contentedly in the dark, and then grew quiet as the sky above them slowly filled with stars. Sam jumped up on the hood and sat down next to Jonathon, his long legs crossed out in front of him, his boots unlaced. The two sat there quietly for a few minutes, watching the millions of stars that form the Milky Way hover against the dark sky like a cloud of white smoke.

"Incredible, isn't it?" asked Jonathon quietly.

"Yeah, sure is. I think this is the one redeeming quality of being here. I've never seen stars like this," replied Sam.

"Not even in Park City?" asked Jonathon, a bit surprised, and glad for the change in conversation.

"Stars were good there, too," Sam nodded, "but there's something about the ones here that makes them feel different. Like…"

"Like we're really not so far from home after all."

"Yeah," Sam nodded.

"Yeah," Jonathon said as he leaned his head back and gazed up at the sky. A few minutes of silence passed, broken only by the faraway sound of a dog barking.

"There was this girl," Jonathon spoke suddenly. "Rebecca Shultz. She was that girl, you know?" Jonathon asked. Sam grunted and nodded his head, smiling. He continued, "I came home for about six weeks the summer between sophomore and junior year at West Point. We ended up running into each other at a friend's party and spent the rest of the summer together. Sam," he shook his head, "she was beautiful. I was totally in love with her." He paused, looking down at his soda. "She was my first."

"Really?" asked Sam, surprise in his voice.

"Yeah," said Jonathon, nodding his head, a bit embarrassed. "Anyway, we spent the summer together, and then I went back to New York and she went back to Stockton for school, and it just… ended," he said, shrugging his shoulders. He took one long, last drink from his soda and said, "But man, it was big for me. I've never loved anyone like that. Ever. The past couple days since the bomb, I haven't been able to get her out of my mind. I don't know why," his words trailed into the still night.

Sam finished his soda, the empty can clanking against the fiberglass hood of the Humvee as he set it down. He reached into his cargo pocket and produced a can of dip. Packing the can several times with a flick of his wrist, he opened it and pinched out a healthy dose. The by now familiar and not unpleasant odor of the tobacco hovered around the two men as Sam placed the pinch behind his lower lip. He wiped the excess tobacco that clung to his fingers off on the side of his pants, and picked up the empty soda can he had set down and spit carefully into the opening. Setting the can back down, he reached to put the dip back into his pocket. Stopping, he offered the can to Jonathon with a smile.

"Want some?" he asked, dark bits of long cut clinging to his lips, his lower lip bulging from the size of the pinch behind it.

Without looking, Jonathon shook his head silently. His head leaned back against the windshield, his eyes on the patchwork of stars that multiplied by the second. Whole minutes passed and entire constellations stabbed their way through the darkness, the two sitting silently in the fading light, Jonathon's eyes to the sky and Sam occasionally spitting into his soda can. Jonathon's mind took him back to a scene four years ago. He was remembering the weekend that he and Rebecca had gone camping in Yosemite together. He had borrowed his family's camping gear, and they had loaded up her car for the weekend. It was early August and he was leaving to go back to West Point that week, and they were going to go down swinging. The trip had that air of one last desperate struggle against the inevitable, like the mortally wounded lion that waits in the grass to pounce at the hunter when he appears.

They had arrived late on Friday night and had set up the tent in the dark. It was cold, the icy air sweeping down from the mountains into the valley, and he could still hear her teeth chattering as they pitched their tent by the headlights of her car. He started a fire while she unloaded the necessary items for the night. As the fire crackled to life, she came to him with a blanket wrapped over her shoulders, and offered him a cup of hot chocolate. Wrapped warmly in her blanket, they talked together as the pitch from the pine popped and cracked in the fire. He heard her yawn as she laid her head against his shoulder. He could smell her hair, the quiet scent of peaches, and his heart beat faster in anticipation.

The fire slowly died to warm red embers that pulsed like a heart in the darkness of the night. She crawled into the tent as he stared at the beating hot redness there against the black ground, and he thought it looked like what they want you to believe Hell looks like. He poured water and dirt over the fire, a slight smile on his face as he watched all the embers go out. When he crawled into the tent, he found that she had zipped the two bags together. He heard her voice ask him softly if he was ready for bed, and he answered with a nervous laugh. As he layed down, he felt her come close to him, her warm breath soft against his cold cheek. He ran his fingers along her face, tracing the contours of her nose and lips, and then his mouth found hers somehow in the dark, her strong tongue pushing against his. He felt her roll over on top of him and straddle him, her long dark hair, invisible to him in the dark, tickling his face.

Sam spit into his can, and Jonathon drew a long, quiet breath. "What're you thinking about?" Sam asked.

"Huh? Oh, nothing," he said casually, then added, "Rebecca."

"Hmmph," Sam grunted.

"You ever been in love, Sam?" Jonathon asked.

Sam laughed to himself, setting the can down. "Yeah. Twenty-seven times, I think." Both of them laughed. "How about you? How many times?"

"Just that once," Jonathon said slowly, shaking his head, "Only her."

The two sat quietly talking as their conversation gradually turned to stories about home. Jonathon told Sam about the yearly camping trip that his family went on up to Kings Canyon every summer, and how, once he was old enough, he would bring his best friend and they would go off by themselves to camp one night away from his folks. When they got older they would hike all the way up to a place called Rae Lakes. He said that King's Canyon was like a second home to him, and how, the first chance they got, he was going to go back up there for a few days to camp and hike and fish.

"I've never been to the Sierras," Sam said.

"You should go, Sam, you really should," offered Jonathon, still sitting beside an alpine lake in his mind. "Everyone should. Did you ever backpack or hike in Park City?"

Sam grunted, nodding his head. He talked about the backpacking trips he had gone on with old friends of his from there, and weekend trips to Grand Teton National Park and Bryce Canyon. He started a story about a weekend up at a lake called Fish Lake where he and Stephanie had gone, but stopped halfway through it and Jonathon chose not to pry.

Changing subjects quickly if not subtly, Sam talked about weekend trips to a house on False River in Louisiana that he and his family used to go on. He told Jonathon about catching basket loads of perch, and how they would catch catfish and his granddaddy would clean and fry it fresh right there while they fished off the pier. He said he could still taste the warm breading in his mouth, and swore that there was nothing better than fresh fried catfish on a warm southern evening while the fireflies danced on the lawn.

Jonathon was laughing at Sam's story about the time when he had hurt his ankle one night while he was out drinking with friends on Bourbon Street in New Orleans. Finally deciding that there was something wrong with his ankle, he had walked the two miles to the hospital and had burst into the emergency room, shouting and demanding that an x-ray be taken on his ankle, that—goddamnit—he knew what was wrong with it and didn't need a goddamned doctor to tell him, he just needed a goddamned x-ray. Sam was quite a storyteller, and despite his earlier sobriety, or perhaps because of it, Jonathon found himself laughing out loud, tears running down his face.

Anderson approached them out of the darkness, and told Jonathon that Captain Pham wanted to talk to all the platoon leaders. Jonathon wiped the tears from his eyes and looked at his watch. It was past ten o'clock. Sam jumped off the hood, dug his index finger into his mouth, and pulled out the wad of tobacco from behind his lower lip and flung it on the ground. Jonathon stepped off the hood.

"Take it easy, Sam," Jonathon said with a smile. "Thanks."

"I'll see you, brother," Sam said, patting Jonathon once hard on the shoulder.

"Yeah, thanks."

A week had passed since Sam and Jonathon had talked on the hood of the Humvee. A week of hot, dry, dusty roads with broken conversations and games of charades with men with dirty faces, and kids who constantly poked and prodded and asked for money or other items. A week of growing dissatisfaction from the locals in his area with the lack of progress and the redundant surveys. A week with hours of mind-numbing guard duty for the men, of latrine duty, and of sheer boredom.

But it was a new month. The good news was that it was not yesterday anymore. Jonathon came walking across the hot courtyard in the middle of the day when Shipley passed him with a roll of toilet paper in his hand and his other hand on his stomach.

"You all right, Ship?" Jonathon asked with a smile.

"I got the Pesh, sir," moaned Shipley, as he waddled toward the latrines.

'The Pesh' was what the men had dubbed the cyclic bouts of diarrhea and nausea that everyone seemed to come down with at some point; 'pesh' coming from the name of Kurdish army, the Peshmerga, which meant, 'those who face death.' Jonathon laughed to himself and thought how one of the endearing qualities of the military life was how the men seemed to find a way to laugh at everything, regardless of the circumstances.

Jonathon knew it was a life and a perspective that many people back home would call barbaric or immature. They would no doubt gasp in shock—horrified—at what they believed to be a lack of respect for life in the military community. But Jonathon thought they missed the point. He had learned a great secret while in Iraq: that it was not the quantity of a man's years that gave his life meaning, but the quality of the years, and the manner in which he spent them. And he had come to understand that he was doomed to die, that there was no way around it, and that the only question left that remained to be answered was the manner in which he would die. At some point while in Iraq, though he was not sure when, Jonathon had settled his own mind on actually facing his death as if it could happen at any moment, instead of fooling himself into believing that he had a right to live to the age of eighty-five.

He saw that modern man had taken a truth, that all life was precious, and had extended it into an error by assigning life a value in and of itself. What was to be cherished above all was simply to live. Whether in that life any manifestation of mercy or honor or courage could be found was irrelevant, just so long as there was life. And so he thought that people were losing their sense of that which gave their lives purpose, that which separated their lives from the animals'. A man who cherished above all his own breath, and forfeited his responsibility as a human to struggle—in whatever form, but to struggle—against the powers of oppression and injustice and evil that permeated the world, was lost; he was empty, a shadow, and his life was worthless to all but himself.

For Jonathon and those he served with, this new philosophy was more than an abstraction, it was a truth that informed their existence. For the soldier—for the warrior, the man who fought—he must have accepted at some point that he was dead already, that the question was not whether he will die, but how and when. Clinging to his own life may lead him to cowardice, and therefore a betrayal of the brotherhood of arms.

And if he would approach that precipice and fling his hopes of a future happiness into the abyss below, then he would find the life left to him stronger and more solid than the specter he had cast away. And so long as he was willing to live on that precipice, he would find that the new life would not grow less sweet, nor would his dance with death be the destruction that he feared it would be. Instead he would discover the truth that suffering and death are not the worst of evils, but that both in their proper nature are a fire that purifies, even though they may scald.

Jonathon felt these truths forming inside him, though on that day he was as yet unable to recognize and express them in words. He had crossed a threshold—they all had—and none of them were to be the same again.

When the survivors returned home, they would find their homes different than they were before and their loved ones a kind of stranger. And when they would try to share their new knowledge with their families and friends, those whom they used to know so well would not understand and would think that something tragic must have happened to make them think this new way, and they would call it shell-shock or PTSD or combat fatigue to ease their own minds that the world was still as they thought it was. But those gentle giants returned home would know that they knew a great secret, one that cannot be told but must be lived, and they would find they were content to be thought mad. It put them in good company.

*   *   *

"Hey sir, has Hoover come talk to you yet?" asked Anderson in the waning light of the day, the world cast into the shades of purple that dusk brought.

Jonathon looked up from his book and shook his head. "No. What about?"

"Evidently his wife left him."

Jonathon leaned against the front tire on the shady side of his truck. "Heather?" he asked, putting down his book and standing up. "When did this happen?"

Anderson shrugged. "He just got the letter today before we headed out. You may want to go talk to him, he's pretty tore up about it."

"Yeah," Jonathon sighed. "I'll go talk to him," Jonathon said sadly, his heart breaking for his squad leader and his friend. "Is he out by his truck?"

"I just saw him there a few minutes ago," Anderson answered.

"Yeah, okay," Jonathon sighed, stomping off over the rough mounds of broken dirt that made up the ground of their patrol base.

The day before, Captain Pham had called Jonathon in and told him about a weapons cache site that had been found in the southeastern corner of his sector, tucked up in the foothills near the Little Za'ab. Since it was in Jonathon's sector, Captain Pham assigned his platoon to go secure it until engineers could get there to blow it. He gave Jonathon an eight digit grid, and pointed his finger on the map in the general area where the cache was reported to be. When Jonathon asked him how long they were going to have to be out there, Captain Pham had said with a dry smile that if the engineers had still not shown up after four days he would send David Carver's platoon out to relieve him. These types of caches were starting to pop up all over the place, and the engineers found themselves in very high demand.

When they finally arrived at the site, after hours of searching along dusty trails and performing endless u-turns, they found a sizable store of RPGs, three surface-to-air missiles, a pile of 100 mm and 120 mm artillery rounds, and a couple dozen AK-47's, PKM's, and RPK's, with several boxes full of ammunition. The site was in a draw, tucked up against a rock wall that shielded the weapons from the harsh sun. The river was only about half a mile away, a few green trees clinging to life on its banks through the merciless heat of the summer.

Hoover sat on the hood of his truck, facing the river to the south, with what was obviously the letter from Heather in his hands. He heard Jonathon come up from behind the truck and turned to look over his shoulder. Folding up the letter and stuffing it into his cargo pocket, he smiled faintly as Jonathon leaned up against the hood. A few brief moments passed, neither sure of what to say or how to say it.

Finally Jonathon broke the uneasy silence. "Sar'n Anderson told me about Heather," he said, looking up and at the side of Hoover's face, which he stubbornly fixed toward the river, his eyes shining in the fading light. Overhead, the stars began to come out. It would be another beautiful night spent sleeping under a blanket of stars. "I'm so sorry, Justin." Hoover turned his face quickly toward Jonathon, surprise written on his face that he had used his first name. It may have been the first time; Hoover had not even thought that Jonathon knew his first name. But his sorrow and desperation quickly overcame his surprise, and he turned his face back to the river with indifference. A few more silent minutes passed by, the world now almost covered in night. Jonathon pushed himself up off the hood with a quiet sigh. He honestly did not know what to do or what to say, and was frustrated with his lack of ability to comfort a man whom he considered a friend. "Hey," he said, "I don't know what to say, man. I'm just sorry. I don't wanna... I'm just sorry," he stammered, his mind racing to find the right words. "What happened?" he asked, and then was immediately sorry. He recovered. "We don't have to talk about it."

He could see Hoover's large frame in the silver light of the stars. He was a big man, strong and solid. Dark-skinned with thick dark hair, he had shown that he could be incredibly intimidating when he wanted to be. But now, on the hood, the huge man whom Jonathon had gotten to know in the past year looked as if the slightest breeze that came down from the mountains might blow him away like dust. Jonathon yielded to his frustration and was about to excuse himself when Hoover spoke.

"She took the girls with her," he said deliberately, not addressing Jonathon directly. He stared down toward the outline of trees where the river was. Jonathon, having stood up to leave, now leaned his back against the truck, his back to Hoover as he spoke. "The car. Even the dogs," he continued, a quick rush of air escaping from him in disbelief. "She said in her letter that she was in love with him."

Jonathon's head snapped around. He hadn't heard anything about another man, and his heart pounded in his chest. "Who?" escaped him before he could stop it.

Hoover answered quickly and indifferently that he was a reservist on base.

Jonathon was literally stunned, rooted to the spot where he stood, his eyes fixed on the man in front of him. His mind raced. How? What kind of a man does that? he asked himself. What kind of a woman does that? He found himself becoming angry and checked himself. His mind searched wildly for words, but he had nothing to say. Several quiet minutes passed as the two men dealt with their own internal questions, one searching for comforting words and seething in anger, and the other trying to figure out what his new life would look like.

Jonathon finally relented, realizing that there was nothing he could do or say that would comfort Hoover or bring his wife back. He offered a quiet and sincere condolence, and walked away.

The night passed quickly. Jonathon had kicked out Cline's section at about midnight to do a two-hour defensive patrol around the area. Jonathon stayed up and pulled radio guard until they returned. When he got back, Cline came up and reported that nothing was out there, all was quiet. Jonathon told him to keep someone up on each of his two guns, and to put the rest of the men down for the night.

After Cline left, Jonathon walked over to where Olk was lying on the ground, and tapped him on the foot. He woke him up and told him it was his turn for radio guard. Olk got up slowly, strung out from being yanked out of sleep in the middle of the night. He stumbled over to Jonathon's seat where both the radios were as Jonathon stretched out on the hood and went to sleep.

He awoke to the sound of distant voices, and could already feel the heat of the barely-risen sun. It was just past six in the morning, and it was going to be a long, hot, boring day. Sitting up and wiping the sleep from his face, he looked around. Four of his trucks were spread out in a kind of box-shaped perimeter, with about one hundred meters between each. Anderson's truck, the only cargo truck in the platoon, was in the middle of the perimeter, and he could see Anderson and his driver, Shipley, moving around the truck, getting ready for the day. Jonathon jumped down, and almost landed on Olk, who was lying on the ground next to the truck. MacLimore was now in the seat pulling radio guard, and said good morning to Jonathon.

"Morning Mac," Jonathon said with a tired smile. "Hear anything?"

"No sir," MacLimore quietly.

"All right, well, folks are up now, so you can leave the radios," Jonathon said.

"Roger sir," MacLimore said, and moved around to the back of the truck where he had tied off his rucksack to the back hatch.

Jonathon dug through his ruck and found his hygiene kit. He told MacLimore that he was headed over to Sergeant Anderson's truck, and to keep an ear on the radios.

"Roger sir," MacLimore said quickly.

Jonathon traipsed across the short distance between the two trucks, and said good morning to Anderson.

"Mornin' sir," Anderson growled.

Jonathon set his hygiene kit on the hood, and rotated the side-view mirror around so that he could see himself. Going around to the back, he lifted a five-gallon water can from the bed, and carefully poured water into his tin canteen cup. Walking back over to the mirror, he set the cup down. Dipping his hand into the cup, he splashed some water on his face, and after lathering his face with shaving cream, began shaving. His ritual every morning of gathering his things on the hood of a Humvee and shaving his face using the side mirror had become second nature to him. His daily shaving was the closest thing that he came to a shower most days, and his face always felt fresh and clean afterwards.

When he had finished and washed away the left-over shaving cream on his face and inspected himself, he walked back around to the back of the Humvee and saw Anderson making his coffee. The first time he had seen him doing it, Jonathon had expressed some concern. Anderson had made a friend of one of the engineers attached to the battalion, and had thus procured for himself—and for the platoon should they ever need it—several blocks of C4 explosive. Anderson had shown Jonathon that by cutting about an inch of the one-pound block and lighting it with a match, he could bring an entire canteen cup of water to a boil in less than thirty seconds.

When Jonathon had asked him if it was safe, Anderson laughed the way veterans do to rookies, and told him that C4 would only explode with heat and compression. "So," he had said with a playful smile, "just don't stomp on it to try to put the fire out, and you won't blow your leg off, sir." Anderson always kept about three blocks of C4 in his assault pack, for times just like those. When the water started boiling, he ripped open three of the instant coffee packets that came inside the MREs, and poured their contents into the hot water. Mixing the coffee to dissolve all the crystals, he raised his canteen cup and took a gracious sip. With a smile he said, "It's the simple things, sir."

Jonathon chuckled to himself and thought of how Anderson used the same cup to shave with. Reaching into a box in the back of the truck, Jonathon pulled out an MRE and walked back to the spot on the hood where he had shaved. He ripped open the bag, laying out the contents and preparing his breakfast, which would be the only thing he ate until that night when the sun went down and things had cooled off a bit. Anderson walked up to him and sat down in the seat next to where Jonathon stood. A few quiet minutes passed, Jonathon munching on a cracker and some peanut butter from his MRE and Anderson sipping deliberately on his steaming cup of coffee. The sun burned hot, and they both squinted in the fierce light.

"Damn shame about Hoover," Anderson said shaking his head slowly, blowing the steam off his coffee.

Jonathon continued chewing softly, Anderson expressing what Jonathon was thinking. Jonathon slowly nodded his head, his eyes squinting hard in the harsh light of the morning. "Yeah," he managed between chews. He took a couple more bites in silence. "What makes a person do something like that? I mean, I guess it's one thing if she had written him saying that she wanted a divorce. But there was something, I don't know, *mean* about the way she did it."

Anderson sipped on his coffee. "Yeah, sir. Some of the women these guys marry, it's crazy. There's no way you can't know a woman is capable of something like that before you marry her. He's talked to me before, saying that she'd been going out to the clubs in town, hiring baby sitters, and not coming home until the next morning."

"Really?" Jonathon asked, ashamed that he didn't know that, and jealous that Hoover had told Anderson and not him.

"Deployments can do crazy things to people, sir. And not just us, though I'm sure we'll all have our own crap when we get home." He took another careful sip. "It's hard on the families. Hard on the wives. And some of these guys marry so young. Nineteen some of them. Married with a kid." Anderson shook his head.

"Yeah, but Hoover and Heather had been married for like seven or eight years." Jonathon shook his head. "They had a family together, two little girls. They weren't a couple of newlyweds. I just don't get it."

Anderson took a good, long look at his young platoon leader. Jonathon knew that look, and knew he was about to get a little lecture.

"What?" he asked.

"Sir," Anderson said slowly, "these men are not your friends, they—"

"I know that."

Anderson drew a breath. "No you don't. Calling them by their first names, the way you talk to them sometimes. How're you ever gonna tell Sergeant Hoover to charge a machine gun nest when you're thinking about his little girls, huh? It's not your job to be their friend; you have to be their leader. What they need from you is a man who's willing to order them to kill, or to be killed, not give them a shoulder to cry on." He paused, never much for words. "The men love you, sir. Maybe too much. Especially Olk. You need to be careful."

Jonathon listened to his platoon sergeant patiently. The man did not speak much, but Jonathon had learned that when he did, he had better listen carefully.

Jonathon thought about the last time—and the first time—he had seen Hoover's wife and their two girls, Ashley and Jennifer. It was the night they had left. It was the last day of February, and the air was cold and biting as the men milled around outside the company area in the parking lot, wives clinging to their hands, children with their arms wrapped around daddy's legs.

Jonathon had had a friend who was a Blackhawk pilot in 5/101, who was not leaving for another few days, drop him off. He had helped him carry his bags inside, and then Jonathon had walked back out with him through the crowds of sad and resolute faces. They had shook hands warmly, each wishing the other the best of luck. Tears had rushed into Jonathon's eyes as he turned away and walked back to the crowd of people.

Everywhere he looked, there were women in baggy jeans and sweatshirts, and kids in pajamas. Daddies held babies with one arm, and held the hand of another child with the other. Jonathon passed by one woman whose eyes were set hard, angry and sad and full of despair all at the same time.

He made sure to say hi to all his men, clapping them gently on the back with a warm smile, and saying hello to their wives and kids. He had spent the week before memorizing all of their names. Inside is where he had met Heather. She was standing up against a wall outside the platoon's office. Both her girls stood next to her, all three studying Hoover's every move. Jonathon had walked up to Hoover, who was at a desk checking serial numbers on weapons one last time before the final draw, and asked if those were his wife and daughters outside. Hoover had smiled and looked at them, and nodded his head. He asked Jonathon if he wanted to meet them, and Jonathon followed him out. The introduction was brief and forced, as there was not much else to talk about except what nobody wanted to talk about.

An hour passed like that. An hour of people standing around, looking at each other, holding hands. Finally, First Sergeant Allen had come out and given the word that it was time to say goodbye, formation would be in ten minutes. When he had told all the leaders the day before that everybody would have to say goodbye at the formation, he had said that he hated to do it, but that it was the only way anything could get done. And there was a lot that had to be done. The barracks where most of the men stayed had to be inspected and locked up and the men would have to turn in their keys. Duffel bags would have to be loaded and moved over to the airfield. All the weapons and equipment from the arms room would have to be issued out and accounted for, and then closed. Finally, the company building itself would have to be inspected and signed over to the rear-detachment commander.

The first sergeant's announcement of formation almost came as a relief. A kind of relief that stabbed and burned at the same time. Everyone was tired, exhausted both from lack of sleep and also from the emotional strain of the past few days. Wives had stayed awake, and children had fallen asleep in their dad's arms, solely out of a stubborn insistence not to be cheated of every last minute they had together. To leave early made them feel shallow, like cowards, despite the apparent absurdity of standing around together in the dark, not talking. The announcement of the formation relieved them of all that. They could go. They had to. Not because they didn't care, not because they didn't love their daddies and husbands and sons, not because they were afraid; it was time to say goodbye because the circumstances demanded it. And they relented, relieved and grief-stricken and terrified all at the same time. Children screamed for daddy as moms with tear-streaked faces pulled them out of his arms. Grown men cried, shamelessly kissing their loved ones goodbye one final time.

Outside, at the edge of the parking lot, Jonathon passed an older couple he had seen standing with Olk. They recognized him as their son's platoon leader. Mr. Olk had reached out and warmly shook Jonathon's hand and wished him luck. He held Jonathon's hand in his just longer than necessary, and Jonathon saw that the man's eyes were heavy and sad. "Yessir," Jonathon answered. Mrs. Olk, a short, thin woman whose face was red and puffed from crying, attempted to say something, but lost her voice and instead threw her arms around Jonathon's neck. She managed a "Be good," as she affectionately patted his chest. Jonathon forced a smile and choked down the tears that sprung into his eyes. He told them quickly that Jeremiah would be fine, and then spun around to hide the tears.

He stopped in a dark shadow to gather himself. Catching his breath and checking to make sure the moment had passed him, he walked back into the lit parking lot and waited for his men to form up.

Hoover came up from behind him in the dark and stood next to him behind the men, his large frame dwarfing Jonathon. Hoover's hands shook as he took out a cigarette and lit it, taking long, hard pulls. Jonathon could see in the street light that his eyes were red and swollen. Hoover felt Jonathon looking at him, and said with a weak smile that that was the worst, most goddamned thing he'd ever done.

"I wouldn't wish that on anybody," Jonathon had said, and patted him warmly on the shoulder. Hoover quickly rubbed his face to liven it up, then stepped into his place in the formation.

Anderson walked up to Jonathon and told him that everybody was there. "All right, sar'n," Jonathon said, mustering more enthusiasm than he felt. "Let's go."

The steam rose more slowly from Anderson's cup when be broke into Jonathon's thoughts. He evidently wanted to move past his lecture and get on with the business of the day. "What're you thinking for today, sir?" he asked between sips.

Jonathon paused thoughtfully and then smiled. "I was thinking about ordering you to charge a machine gun nest." They both laughed, and Jonathon continued. "Look, I'm not really worried about getting hit out here. I was thinking of sending each section out once sometime today for a couple hours each. I'd like to see if we can walk up a bit and take a look from a little higher elevation. Not sure that we can get the trucks up there, so I may just grab a team to go take a look."

Anderson nodded and sipped on his coffee.

"What do you think?" asked Jonathon, aware by his face that Anderson had something on his mind.

"Well, I think that we should have stayed away, maybe put a team in to watch to see who came to get this stuff, and then killed them when they did," he said matter-of-factly.

"Yeah," Jonathon sighed, "but all the sniper teams were out doing other things, and I don't think that they felt they had the time to go into the kind of planning that that would involve."

"Hmph, we could've done it."

"Yeah, but Captain Pham said not to, to just come out here and sit on it," said Jonathon with a little frustration.

"No reason we couldn't have done it anyway," said Anderson. "I don't know what the hell is wrong with those people. It's like they can't think outside the fucking box."

Jonathon was silent for a moment, a swell of embarrassment and frustration rising in him. Then he chuckled softly to himself and took another bite of his cracker.

"What's so funny, sir?" asked Anderson.

"You're just such a joy in the mornings, sar'n, that's all," Jonathon said with a smile. "Like a little ray of sunshine." He laughed, his mouth full of peanut butter.

"Shit," Anderson cursed and laughed to himself, taking a self-contented draught of coffee.

* * *

It had been a couple days since Jonathon and his platoon had left to secure the cache site. Sam was sitting in his room, alone in the dark green light, surrounded by cots and bags. He looked intently at the white envelope that sat on his chair next to his cot. He could recognize Rachel's handwriting, and thought it significant that this letter from her was in a plain envelope. Every letter that she had sent so far had been in a card stuffed inside some kind of brightly colored envelope. This one was different, he knew it without reading it, and he had been thinking about reading it since he had received it a few days ago. But every time he did, he imagined what he knew must be inside, and found something else to do. Like read a magazine again.

Sam had had the letter for two days now though, and his curiosity and the need for some contact from home finally overcame his reluctance. Using his knife, he slit open the envelope and pulled out the letter. His first thought as he unfolded it was that it was only one piece of paper, with no writing on the back.

"Short and sweet," he sighed. In the top right corner, she had written the date, June 25, 2003. Over six weeks ago now. He began to read:

Dear Sam,

I just got your letter today. It's late... past eleven o'clock and I have class early tomorrow morning and all I've been doing all day is thinking about what you said in your letter. At first I was angry, but I got over that, and then I was just sad. And I'm still so sad, but I'm also frustrated.

I don't know how I'm supposed to respond to what you said. Especially since you're so far away, and I know this letter will take a long time to get to you, if I even send it. And that frustrates me, because I want to be able to sit with you and make you talk to me. You probably think I don't understand why you want to break things off. But I do. I know you. You have this need to feel free, and you think that loving me and Claire traps you somehow, makes you less than what you want. But I think there's another side that's just afraid. Afraid that you'll screw it up like you did with Stephanie and I'll walk away from you. But I'm not going to do that. I'm not, and I think that deep down you know that, but are afraid of taking that step again.

And it's not because I need you. I'm not some poor girl who needs a man to help her raise her child. I don't want anyone's pity. And I don't judge you either, Sam. I don't know why I just wrote that, but it's true, I don't. God knows that I'm no one to be judging what anyone else does. So I don't need you, or judge you. I only love you... that's all I have.

Sam, this is what I would tell you if I could make you sit down and talk with me right now: I love you. And I know what love is when I see it. And I know that you love me. I do. And the part that makes me angry Sam is that you're not breaking up with me because you don't love me anymore, but that you're doing it because you're afraid. And that makes me think that you're a coward when I know you're not. But you're afraid of growing up and you're afraid of hurting someone you love again. Well, you are growing up, and getting hurt is part of life. Wasting your life trying to avoid that is childish. You forget that I know heartache, too. That I was left by someone I loved. But he also left me Claire, and Claire is my daily reminder that God can work in the midst of our brokenness if only we'll let Him. I've been hurt before Sam, but I've made the decision not to be afraid to love again.

I'm so sad right now. I want you to be far away from there, safe with me. And I want to cry and have you hold me. I pray for you every night. I love you.

Love, Rachel

When he had finished reading the letter, he sighed and then read through it again. Her handwriting was always very artsy, on words like 'love' and 'need' and 'pity,' the letters were so big that she always took up two lines. He noticed the second time through that at the end she signed her letter as she had all her others, a large heart in the middle with 'Love, Rachel' inside it. He folded up the letter and held it in his hands, lost in thought.

He was a little taken aback. It was not the response he had expected from her. In fact, he had expected no response except silence; that her letters would abruptly cease, signifying that she had received his letter wanting to end their relationship. But now he was left in a fog of uncertainty. He was unsure of what was going on. He didn't understand. He had written her that he thought they should break up, and she had responded by saying that she loved him and that she knew he loved her. All true, he knew. She was right: he did in fact still love her.

But a relationship with a woman who was on the other side of the world, who had a child already, when he was twenty-nine years old, did not fit the image of the life he had envisioned for himself. The problem, of course, was that now virtually nothing fit that vision. He had realized that a couple months ago, and it had led him to write that letter. And when he had sent it, he had accepted as a foregone conclusion that he and Rachel were over, and thus he had let go of her in his heart.

Or he had tried to. He told himself that you can't stay in love with someone you never see. It was impossible, and he had hoped that one day he would just fall out of love with her. So when he had received the plain white envelope with her return address on it, he had assumed that it was to be the last communication from her. His reluctance to open the letter had betrayed his true feelings. But now, he realized with shock, there would be no long silence. She still loved him, and he had no idea what to do with that.

The next day Jonathon and his platoon returned to Camp Bulldog. The engineers had showed up early that morning, and had spent four hours stacking the various munitions in the proper place, using blocks of explosive and rolls of detonation cord to ensure that everything was destroyed. Anderson managed to get his hands on a couple more blocks of C4. "You never know when you'll need to blow something up, sir," he said with a smile underneath the mustache, which by this time had grown into what looked like a push broom perched under his nose.

The engineers rigged the explosives with a remote detonation device, and moved with Jonathon's platoon back two kilometers from the blast site. Once they had all pulled back, despite orders to the men from Hoover and Cline to keep security, all eyes were fixed on the area where the munitions were piled, hidden by a slight rise in the brown earth. One of the men asked if they would be able to see the explosion from this far. The man holding the detonator, an old staff sergeant who squinted hard in the harsh sunlight, who had creases permanently cut in the leather-like skin around his eyes, replied with a dry smile that yes, they would indeed be able to see the explosion from here.

He did a final systems check on the remote initiator, and began to count down from five. He pressed the detonator with a metallic click, and for a solid second there was total silence. Then a large black mushroom cloud rose quietly into the sky. A couple seconds passed in thick silence, the men craning their necks, waiting for the concussion. They could feel it come before they heard it, rumbling through the earth. It blew through them as if it had a mass of its own. The men gasped and swore, smiles on every face. The old staff sergeant, pleased with the reaction of his audience, told Jonathon that he had to go back up to make sure everything blew, and then they could all get going.

"We'll be right here, sar'n," he said.

"Shouldn't take longer than a half hour, sir," the old staff sergeant said as he jumped in his truck, and his three trucks wound toward the blast site. The large black cloud of smoke continued to rise into the air, and slowly started to dissipate in the sky. One of the men muttered something about hoping that they would hurry up.

Anderson turned around and found Melton. "What, you miss your nice comfy cot?" he asked with a smile, shaking his head.

Melton smiled, embarrassed. "No, sar'n," he muttered.

"He misses his teddy bear," Stufflet chimed in, and the men all chuckled contentedly.

Jonathon thought how it was strange that he felt such excitement to return to a place that he would expect to feel no attachment toward. Literally the only difference was that back at the compound he had a cot to sleep on and a tin roof over his head. Hardly home, but home had become wherever the platoon based out of, and they had gotten so used to this transient lifestyle that the idea of a solid structure with couches and a TV and different rooms for cooking and eating and sleeping seemed almost absurd, like silly luxuries. Running hot water? Who needed that? They had water cans and canteen cups to shave and drink out of.

The engineers returned, and the convoy of trucks started its way down the long, dusty road that led north to Makhmur.

When he got in and took off his gear, he made his way across the courtyard to go catch up with Captain Pham. His CO stood up and greeted him with a smile and Allen nodded a cold hello as he walked into the dark room of the company's CP. They sat and talked for about an hour, Jonathon reporting the specific number of munitions and materiel by type, and providing his assessment of its intended use. Captain Pham listened attentively, asking questions occasionally. At the end, Jonathon handed him the oil- and sweat-stained piece of paper that he had used to take the inventory, and headed back out the door. As he was leaving, Captain Pham asked, "When are you planning on going out to Al Sharqi again, Jon?"

Jonathon paused and shrugged his shoulders. "We could easily head out tomorrow, if you want us to, sir." He shook his head. "I don't have anything planned out yet."

"Yeah, that sounds good. Go get cleaned up and come see me sometime tonight about some things I need you to talk to Khalil about."

"Will do, sir," Jonathon responded, and headed back to the warehouse.

The dust cloud enveloped their Humvee as Olk stopped the truck next to the group of men who stood up from their places in the shade to greet Jonathon as he stepped out. Olk laughed contentedly to himself as they coughed and waved away the dust that surrounded them. Jonathon shot back at Olk with a disapproving look and a smile, shaking his head.

Turning back, he saw Mr. Marie and offered his hand to the sparkling eyes. Mr. Marie put his hand on his shoulder and led him to the blue carpet where they sat down. The man with the toothless grin came out shortly with little glass and porcelain cups of steaming chai and went around to each man, starting with Mr. Marie and Jonathon.

They talked about the weather and the life of the village. One of the men in the village had been robbed one night by a group of Kurds from the village to the east—the same village with the wheat harvest allegations.

"Is everyone all right?" Jonathon asked.

"Oh yes, yes," Mr. Marie nodded. "It is a small matter, it does not concern you."

A few moments of silence passed until a thin, wiry man at the other end of the circle asked Mr. Marie a question Jonathon could not understand. The man was indicating with his hand toward Jonathon and his men, and Jonathon waited expectantly for Mr. Marie's translation.

"He says that he has a family member who has a very bad cut on her leg, and wants to know if you have a doctor who can look at it. Do you have a doctor, Leftenant?" Mr. Marie asked.

Jonathon shook his head slowly. "No, we do not have a doctor, but we do have some basic medical supplies that may be able to help." He turned over his shoulder toward Olk, who was leaning in the shade against an old rusted metal box. "Hey Olk," Jonathon said, "call up Sar'n Anderson and have him bring the CLS bag."

"Roger sir," said Olk, and called Anderson over the radio. "Seven, Six Romeo. Six wants you to bring the CLS bag, over."

Jonathon had often talked to Anderson about how he should come to the meetings and did not have to stay out with the trucks in the heat the whole time. But Anderson had shrugged his shoulders and said that sitting through long boring meetings held in another language didn't sound all too inviting, that he'd rather stay out with the trucks and keep an eye on things. Jonathon had acquiesced, realizing that Anderson was a fighter, an old soldier who had spent over a decade honing fighting skills and tactics to fight and kill the enemy, only to find himself in the middle of Iraq, sitting down and having tea with men he in fact considered to be the enemy. Tea, of all things to be drinking.

"Mr. Marie, can you have the woman come to us? We may be able to help," Jonathon said as he saw Anderson walking toward them with Shipley and the aid bag. Mr. Marie said something to the thin, wiry man, who got up and disappeared around the corner. He reappeared a few minutes later with a woman wrapped in her black *abayya*, her face and head uncovered. Jonathon noticed that she favored her right leg. Anderson walked up to her and had Shipley open the bag. Mr. Marie and Jonathon walked over to where she sat, and Mr. Marie told her to show the American her wound. Hesitantly, she lifted her *abayya* and showed a deep wound on her calf, which was red and obviously infected, with blue and green hues around the edges. Anderson put on a pair of latex gloves and inspected the area. The area around the wound was tender, and the woman winced quietly with his touch, soft though it was. He asked Shipley for some hydrogen peroxide, which he used to clean around the wound.

The group of men who had been on the carpet were all now gathered around the woman and Anderson, watching him gently clean around the wound. Jonathon stood next to him, with Olk standing outside the crowd. Anderson turned to Jonathon and said that the best thing he could do was to clean and dress it a bit, but that it was infected and she needed to get some antibiotics, which their little aid bag did not have. Mr. Marie nodded his understanding and translated to the crowd, who smiled and nodded their approval.

The woman's leg bound with the strip of gauze, Anderson handed her husband a few packets of peroxide wipes, attempting in loud and broken English to tell him how to best use them. It was a funny exchange, the thin man shrinking from the large American who slowly yelled at him—in words he could not understand— instructions on how to care for the wound. The man took his wife away, and after all the men had made a point to shake hands with Anderson, they made their way back to their places on the rug. Jonathon noticed that Anderson lingered a little longer than he had expected him to before heading back to the trucks. Shipley, having handed Anderson the combat life-saver bag, elected to stay behind, taking up a position next to Olk against the old metal box.

Once they had sat down, Jonathon wiped away the sweat from his face and decided that now was the best time to get down to the business Captain Pham had spoken to him about the night before.

"Mr. Marie," Jonathon started, "I have something that I would like to discuss with you."

"Yes Leftenant?" Mr. Marie leaned forward, his dark eyes dancing in expectation.

"There is a council of leaders that is being formed in Makhmur for the province. I have been asked to come here to see if you would consider a seat on that council, to represent Al Sharqi and the surrounding villages." Jonathon waited eagerly as Mr. Marie sat up straight, surprised by his offer.

After a few moments of silence from the man, the rest of the group waiting for some sign of the business that was being discussed, Mr. Marie translated Jonathon's offer to them. They all smiled and clapped their hands in agreement to the offer. Jonathon noticed a shadow of concern pass over Mr. Marie's countenance amid the affirmations.

Jonathon leaned in to him. "Do you have reservations, Mr. Marie? I can assure you that not only will the meetings be very safe, but that you will have an opportunity to make a great contribution to your province."

Mr. Marie smiled, the cloud having left his face. "Yes, I accept your offer, of course," he said quickly.

Jonathon, worried that he would refuse, relaxed and leaned back in his seat. "Good. I am glad to see that you will be a part of the council. I believe that you have a lot to offer the Makhmur province."

Mr. Marie bowed his head graciously, his eyes sparkling and a smile on his face. The next half hour passed with much talk that Jonathon could not understand, but which he assumed from the mannerisms and gesticulations was all centered around Mr. Marie's new capacity as an official for the province. There were many smiles, much loud talk, and every now and then a man would leave his place to shake Mr. Marie's hand.

When talk had died down, and an impending awkward silence threatened itself, Jonathon leaned into Mr. Marie and addressed a question which he had had since he saw the cloud of doubt pass over his face.

Mr. Marie smiled warmly at Jonathon's question. "It is a very dangerous thing during this time to be seen as a leader working with the Americans. Many men who step into these positions will be killed. I have a family that I must think about, you understand?"

"Yessir," Jonathon answered. "And I understand whatever reservations you may have, but I want to assure you that we are determined to support this process in Makhmur. Think of what could happen, Mr. Marie," Jonathon said. "This is the start of a great thing for Iraq."

Mr. Marie seemed hesitant. He took a long breath and smiled. "Leftenant, there are still many things that you do not understand about our country or her people. This process of democracy will be a very long and painful one, and few of us who see it started will see its completion."

"Mr. Marie, you were asked to be a part of this council because of your obvious influence and respect in the area. I can think of no one other than you who is ready or capable to help start this process. Think of what it will be like. It may be that your name in Iraq will be as well remembered as Jefferson or Franklin in mine."

Mr. Marie, however, was not pierced with the same patriotic fervor that had struck Jonathon. He was grateful for the nomination, and conveyed that sincerely to Jonathon, yet Jonathon could tell that he was still hesitant. This hesitancy produced in Jonathon only deeper conviction that Mr. Marie was the perfect candidate for a seat at the council. It reminded him of Plato's Philosopher King. Jonathon was convinced that his obvious humility and reluctance to grasp for the position, coupled with his knowledge, experience, and respect throughout the area, would prove to be invaluable to the fledgling council. A warm and sincere affection for the man formed itself in Jonathon's heart.

Their talk revolved around the progress being made in the province, and the hope that lay ahead. Mr. Marie always seemed to choose the side of caution and skepticism, though Jonathon asked him how it could possibly turn out any other way.

Mr. Marie shook his head slowly. "Leftenant, I have told you that things in Iraq are not as they are in America."

"Yes, but they can be. This is the time when your country can begin to grow and develop and become a serious player on the international stage." Jonathon beamed with hope and pride.

"Leftenant," Mr. Marie shook his head, "you know only what you have experienced in your own country. Rebellions and insurgencies are only things that you have read about. Here, they are concrete realities. You speak of a free and independent Iraq as a foregone conclusion because you have no appreciation for the complexities that allow peace to exist." He paused, sighing. "We can all only believe what we have been taught. And your world is full of a false and shallow hope that is not grounded in the reality of this world. You think that you can sweep into Iraq, crush its government, and set up a freely elected one within one short year? And suddenly we will have SUVs and big screen TVs, yes? *La.*" He shook his head. "It is not so easy as that. It saddens me to say to you that many more people will die in this undertaking. Men who do not share your enthusiasm will stop at nothing to ensure that you do not succeed."

"That *we* do not succeed," Jonathon interjected with a warm smile of comraderie.

Mr. Marie smiled back weakly. "Yes. We." His thoughts seemed to trail away.

Jonathon was quiet for a minute before speaking again. This time the joyous passion that had driven him had settled down, and he could think and speak more intently and directly. "Mr. Marie," he said, touching the man on the arm and looking him in the eye, "I believe that this is going to be a great success. I do. I believe that."

His sincerity did not illicit the response Jonathon had hoped it would. The man's face still seemed uncertain. "I cannot blame you for this belief, Leftenant. A man can only believe what he has been taught, what he has been introduced to. And you do not know the things that I speak of, therefore you cannot believe in the things that I speak of. Have you ever stopped to ask yourself if the things that you believe are right? Have you ever experienced anything other than what you were raised to believe? I have traveled to western Europe and have seen and heard what the West believes, and still I am not sure."

Here the man paused, unsure of whether to continue. Finally, he spoke again. "A man must have the courage to determine for himself what he believes. I spoke to you before of how our politics are closely tied to our religion. Every man believes that God is on his side, that God has consecrated his task with divine authority. How could he be or do otherwise? For his god can be no more or less than what he has experienced and been taught to believe. It takes a great man to step out of that condition and face the world as it truly is with eyes that, for the first time, are not colored by his own prejudice."

This last monologue knocked the fire out of Jonathon's gut, and left him incapable of continuing the conversation. He resorted to the small talk of the weather and the village and Mr. Marie's family before announcing that he must be going. The men, who had all been involved in their own conversations, stood up gratefully and said goodbye. Olk had the truck started by the time Jonathon reached it, Mr. Marie by his side. Jonathon turned to say goodbye to Mr. Marie, and saw that the dance in his eyes had stopped. Replaced was a piercing resolve, of what Jonathon could only guess. But he could not hold the gaze, and quickly shook his hand and wished him well.

When Jonathon got back after the long quiet ride back to Makhmur, he stripped off his gear and found that he had received a package from home. Momentarily forgetting the weight Mr. Marie's last comments had burdened him with, he broke into the box as if it were a Christmas present. Inside, his mom had written a letter and included cookies, baby wipes, and some razors that he had asked for in a letter that he could not remember writing.

Pulling the last item out, his heart sank as Mr. Marie's words echoed inside him. In his hand he held the blue, leather-bound bible of his childhood. His mother had attached a sticky-note to the cover. It read, "So you don't lose your way."

CHAPTER 3

It had been too easy. There had been pockets of respectable resistance during the initial invasion, but the thing as a whole had been too easy. And the men could feel it in their bones. Though they were extraordinarily relieved at the lack of fighting the organized Iraqi units had shown themselves capable of, there was something that echoed deep inside all of them: it had been too easy.

In March 2003, the Army's Third Infantry Division had literally raced the Marine's First Expeditionary Unit north, running right through the poorly organized and poorly equipped Iraqi units, chewing up huge chunks of land. While the 3rd ID and 1st MEU crushed whatever organized resistance they met, the 101st Airborne Division was tasked with what essentially became a mop-up operation, charged with cleaning up whatever fighters were left in the wake of the two spearhead units.

The apparent blow that the "shock and awe" campaign had dealt to the Iraqi Army—in effect crippling it—led President Bush to announce in the middle of April the end of combat operations in Iraq, to the end of the war. But perhaps what the U.S. failed to realize was that its definition of war was outdated; September 11th had forever changed the face and nature of war.

Before that morning, an act of war had always been defined as an act committed by an organized group or a nation that flew under a unified flag. Individuals could commit acts of terror, but they could not wage *war*. But September 11th had all of the trappings and devastation of an act of war. The comparison to Pearl Harbor was easy, with one glaring exception: September 11th had been executed by a handful of ordinary men, not a nation's military. The flag that they fought under was a common ideology. They wore no uniforms and carried no standard issue weapons or equipment. They were financed by individuals spread out all over the world, some who were leaders in nations, and others who were simply citizens who sympathized with their passion.

The United States felt that an act of war had been committed, but could find no nation which was singly responsible. No prime minister or king or emperor had taken responsibility for the attack. An act of war had been committed outside of the understanding of the rules of war, and for a while the U.S. floundered around like a stunned boxer, searching to find where its enemy lay hidden. When its vision cleared, it found a concentration of sympathizers and supporters for the attack all together in the Middle East, and so it struck there. Afghanistan had never declared open war with the United States, but neither had Iraq or Iran or Syria or Saudi Arabia. The United States struck the countries it held responsible because it did not know how to wage war on individuals, only on nations. Those countries, and the people in them, had learned that they could never win a conventional war against the military machine of the United States. So they changed how they would wage their war. Knowing that they could not win by operating within the established rules of war, they changed the rules to fight a different type of war.

Korea and Vietnam and the war between Afghanistan and the USSR in the 1980s demonstrated that the one place where the superpowers' large and deadly militaries were vulnerable was in their ability to combat a decentralized enemy. The definition of war for these superpowers had caused them to build a military that could fight according to that definition's inherent rules and restrictions. The dominant rule was simple enough: the nation that could bring to bear the largest and most lethal force would win.

On September 11th, however, the rules of war changed.

Saddam Hussein, sitting in his palaces with his generals as the Americans and their Coalition friends massed on their southern border in the sands of Kuwait, understood this. He knew that to wage a conventional war was an effort in futility; he had learned that lesson easily enough in the Gulf War of 1991. But he also knew that the American Coalition expected to meet his Republican Guard Brigades echeloned in a defense in depth, forcing the Americans to bleed their way to Baghdad. But the rules had changed.

This war would be fought in the cities and the towns, along the roads and in the mountain passes. It would be fought in the market places, among throngs of innocent people. While the Americans wore uniforms and moved in large convoys that stood out in sharp contrast to the people and environment in which they operated, the insurgent force would live and fight among the population. Mao had said that the guerilla is the fish that swims among the people: from them he finds his resources, his supplies, and his camouflage. In order for your enemy to therefore find you, he must be willing to become a fish as well. But to become a fish violated an American rule of war. They were men, and they would fight like men. They would also therefore die like men.

Establishing rules of conduct in how wars ought to be waged seemed a noble and necessary thing on the surface, but it betrayed the true intent of the actors involved. The boxer in the ring abides by rules of conduct because, at the end of the day, it's just business. But the man backed into the corner of a dark alley by men who intend to do him harm knows of no rules. He will kick and bite and scratch, because he is fighting for his life. As a sovereign body, the Iraqi government was in a fight for its life, and it knew it. The American Coalition was in a boxing match, and fought like it.

The plan was simple enough. Saddam and his leaders knew that the Americans had targeted them, and that soon they would all be captured or killed. The same fate awaited their Republican Guard Brigades. They could place no hope in a conventional victory, so they planned an insurgency, assigning leaders unrecognized by the Americans and scattering them throughout the country. There was to be no coordination, no unifying effort, no nesting of task and purpose.

The mission given to each was simple: kill Americans and their Coalition partners. Kill them one at a time in the market places, on the open roads, and in the cities. Never stand to fight them, but strike quickly and lethally, and then disappear back into the faceless crowds. Large stores of munitions were spread throughout the country, which if left undiscovered, could feed the insurgency for years. There was no wall they could build capable of stopping the overwhelming tidal wave of American force that was soon to come crashing down on them. But they could build a reef just under the surface of the water, innocuous enough to be underestimated, but which would rob the wave of its energy and reduce it to a ripple before it delivered its catastrophic power. So long as every day one Coalition soldier died, even if it was just one in a sea of thousands, eventually the enthusiasm and pathos would bleed out of the invaders. This truth had been demonstrated in Korea, in Vietnam, and in Afghanistan twenty years earlier, and was to show itself again in Iraq: you cannot defeat an insurgency. Insurgency may represent the pinnacle in the evolution of warfare.

War had changed. It was true: it had been too easy. The hard part was just beginning.

Eight days after he had last seen Mr. Marie, Jonathon headed out again for a meeting. But this time, Captain Pham and Lieutenant Colonel DaSilva were coming along. Jonathon's CO had talked to him several days ago about setting up a time when Mr. Marie would be available to meet with the Battalion Commander. Jonathon had traveled out four days prior, and had a quick visit with Mr. Marie while on his way out on a presence patrol on the southern sector of the AO. When Jonathon told Mr. Marie about the meeting, and asked when would be a good time for him, Mr. Marie's eyes had flashed in brilliance and he had said that four days from then, at eleven o'clock, would be a good time.

"Would they like to eat with us, do you think, Leftenant?" Mr. Marie had asked as he walked Jonathon back to the truck.

Jonathon had told him that he thought that it would be very gracious of him to offer a meal for the meeting, and that his commanders would be honored to dine with him.

Now, as the long line of trucks pulled into the small square in the middle of the village, there were people all around. The village had a distinct difference to all the other times that Jonathon had visited. The idleness seemed to have been shaken out of it, and everywhere men were dressed in fine blue and black *dish-dasha*. Children ran around, the energy of the village expressed through their shouts and screams. The mood was practically festive.

As Jonathon stepped out, he smiled as he saw Mr. Marie approach, dressed in what must have been his finest *dish-dasha*. It was the first time he had seen him in anything other than his white one, and the regal attire of the deep gray fabric, trimmed with gold thread, reminded Jonathon that Marie was a successful and well-educated man. Mr. Marie shook hands warmly with Jonathon, the sparkle in his eyes threatening to consume the entire village. Though the men were by now past formalities, there was something in the air and in the dress that caused Jonathon to resort to more formal language.

"*As-salaama 'alaykum*, Mr. Marie," Jonathon said as he shook Mr. Marie's outstretched hand.

"*Wa 'alaykum as- salaama*," returned Mr. Marie, bowing his head warmly.

"Let me introduce you to my commanders," Jonathon said, walking with the man a few trucks down the line. "Mr. Khalil, this is my Company Commander, Captain Pham. Sir, this is Jassim Khalil."

Captain Pham shook the hand that was offered him and exchanged greetings in Arabic. Nazeem stood behind Captain Pham, bowing his head slightly as he greeted Mr. Marie. Lieutenant Colonel DaSilva approached the small crowd. At only five feet, nine inches, he was not a large man, and the amount of equipment he carried on his vest only furthered to reduce his apparent height. Jonathon introduced him to Mr. Marie, and the two men exchanged formal greetings in Arabic.

Jonathon had assumed they would all gather on the same blue carpet where he had spent countless hours discussing the business of the village and the surrounding area with Mr. Marie and the other men. He realized as they walked toward the building where he had had his first meal with Mr. Marie that of course the current circumstances demanded a more formal setting. As they walked into the room, Jonathon noticed initially that it had been cleaned and decorated. The large red rug that covered the entire floor of the room had been swept clean, and showed beautiful intricacies of weaving he had not noticed before. Tapestries of blues and greens and reds and purples adorned the gray walls of the room. Pillows and cushions of as many varying colors rested against the walls for sitting on and reclining against. 'Colonel DaSilva and Captain Pham had already begun speaking with Mr. Marie, and Jonathon realized that he would not be invited into the general conversation. His role today was as preparer and introducer, and he settled down comfortably on a pillow, with Olk at his side with the radio.

Jonathon noticed first that the men were not speaking English. Instead, Nazeem sat on the left side of 'Colonel DaSilva, while Mr. Marie sat on his right. Captain Pham sat on the other side of Nazeem, easily able to hear the conversation, and asked Nazeem for interpretations or clarification. Jonathon found himself on the adjacent wall to the left of the men, close enough to hear most of what was said, but far enough away to be uninvolved in the conversation. He sighed and placated himself with the thought that at least he would get a meal out of the trip, even if his ego was to come out slightly bruised. This was his village, after all.

The meal was similar to the one that he had been served before, but with greater attention to detail and presentation. The same man with the missing teeth served as the waiter, though he had cleaned up for the occasion. The men that were gathered in the room all listened attentively to the conversation which, it being in Arabic, they were able to follow. Jonathon was able to see, through hearing bits from Nazeem as he translated back and forth, that the bulk of the conversation revolved around the area surrounding the village and the upcoming inauguration of the provincial council.

Jonathon paid close attention to the conversation which proceeded without his active participation. At one point, while the men discussed the progress of electricity in the town of Al Sharqi and the surrounding area, Jonathon interjected that there had been no significant improvements. His sudden interruption from off to their left triggered a surprised silence as the four men all stopped abruptly to look at him. Captain Pham's look clearly communicated to Jonathon that though this was his town, his presence in the conversation was not needed. Jonathon's face flushed in embarrassment at his own rashness. He swore to himself, and picked up the fork from his meal and began to move the food around in his plate until he was sure all eyes were off him. He then contented himself with hearing whatever bits he could. The remainder of the conversation passed efficiently, centering almost entirely on business and the inauguration of the Makhmur provincial council that Mr. Marie was to be a part of.

Two hours later, the meal finished and talk having come to a close, it was time to go. 'Colonel DaSilva walked with Mr. Marie while the Americans headed back to their trucks. The men who had been contending with crowds of people and the incessant begging of the children scampered thankfully into their trucks as they saw them approach. Olk started up the truck as Jonathon climbed in and waited for Captain Pham to tell him they were ready to go. He watched in his rear view mirror as Captain Pham and 'Colonel DaSilva expressed pleasant wishes and goodbyes in English with Mr. Marie. Jonathon thought dejectedly that he was not even going to get a friendly wave goodbye from Mr. Marie. He was sinking further and further into self pity and resentment when Mr. Marie walked by his window and waved goodbye with a warm smile, the sparkling eyes in an instant wiping away any trace of anger in Jonathon. He returned the wave and opened his door as Captain Pham's voice came over the radio telling him they were ready to go.

"I will see you soon, Mr. Marie," Jonathon called out with a smile and a wave.

"*Insha'allah*," Mr. Marie smiled back as Jonathon shut his door and his truck drove out of town back to the main road leading north and to Makhmur.

a novel

Later that night, Anderson came walking into the warehouse from a meeting with First Sergeant Allen. As he sat down heavily on his cot, Jonathon asked him how it went. Anderson pulled out his notebook and went down a short list of things they had talked about in the meeting, mostly pertaining to guard shift uniforms, enforcing standards in the guard towers, chow rotations, and burning the latrines. Closing his small green notebook, he added that it looked like the entire battalion was pulling out of Makhmur in a week.

"Who's going to replace us?" Jonathon asked, surprised.

"He thinks it's 2-17 Cav."

"How's an aviation unit going to cover this area?" Jonathon asked as much to himself as to Anderson. Anderson just shrugged his shoulders, indicating that it was not in his area of interest what unit was replacing them, or their capacity to do so. He was already thinking about where the platoon was moving to, and how he was going to get there. Reading his thoughts, Jonathon asked him if he knew where they were going next.

"First Sergeant says we're moving to Q-West, that the company has an area already marked out over there, a bunker per platoon, and that the company will start to operate along the Tigris."

"Over by Qayyarah?" Jonathon asked.

"Yessir," Anderson said. "Oh yeah, the CO said that he wanted to see you."

Jonathon sighed and thought about the look Captain Pham had given him earlier that day, and he was sure that he was about to get a lecture on when it was and when it was not appropriate for a platoon leader to interrupt the Battalion Commander. So it was with reluctance that he headed across the dark courtyard, and found his way down the long dark hallway that led to the Company CP.

He knocked as he entered. "Hey sir, you wanted to see me?" he asked as he walked in. First Sergeant Allen sat on a stool, flipping through a magazine by the light of a small lamp he had found and made work. The soft yellow light of the bare bulb cast a warm light in the room, and accentuated every crack in the walls and the roof.

Captain Pham sat behind his desk, and looked up with a smile and waved Jonathon over.

"Hey Jon. Yeah, come on in," he said, waving Jonathon toward a chair near him. He cast a look at First Sergeant Allen, who got up and left the room. The warm reception that had sparked some relief in Jonathon was extinguished as First Sergeant smiled sympathetically at him as he left the room and closed the door behind him. Jonathon's heart beat faster. What's going on? he thought, feeling that though he may have stepped over the line earlier that day, surely it could not have been this serious.

"What's up, sir?" he said with some worry in his voice as he sat down adjacent to Captain Pham.

Captain Pham leaned back in his chair and crossed his hands behind his head. He looked at Jonathon for a full ten seconds before answering.

"Jon, there's something that I need to talk to you about." His voice carried the warmth in it that he had when he had spoken to Jonathon weeks ago over breakfast when they had talked about home.

"Yessir?" Jonathon asked hesitantly, his mind racing over the possibilities of things that could warrant this meeting.

"Jon, it's about Khalil," Captain Pham sighed quickly and leaned forward, resting his arms on the desk. The light from the bulb hid the right side of his face as he looked at Jonathon and told him that Jassim Khalil was not who Jonathon thought he was. "Jassim Khalil—or Mr. Marie, as you know him by—is not who he says he is. The S-2 has been getting reports on him for a while now which implicate him as the leader of the insurgent cell in Makhmur. His real name is Abdul Yousif Mahmoud. He used to be a Colonel in one of Saddam's Republican Guard Divisions. We think that he was told to come up here knowing that the Republican Guard would be destroyed in the invasion, and that his talents would be better used in the insurgency. The 'Colonel wanted to speak with him today so that he could put his own eyes on the man and be certain that he is who we think he is. Now we're certain that the man who you know as Mr. Marie is the Division's High Value Individual Number Three."

Captain Pham paused as Jonathon sat in his chair stunned. He became angry as he realized that the man whom he had begun to trust and think of as a teacher was in fact his enemy. He tried to argue against it, but he found that his own mind produced evidence that convinced him quickly that Captain Pham was right. Mr. Marie's English, his trips to Baghdad, all things which earlier today Jonathon had been able to easily explain away as part of life's random unpredictability, now came crashing down as undeniable proof that Mr. Marie was an insurgent and that he, Jonathon, was a fool. There was one thing, though, that he could not quite understand.

"Sir, if we knew that he is an insurgent, then why did we offer him a position in the council?" Jonathon asked, looking directly at his CO. He offered the question not searching for a proof as to Mr. Marie's innocence, but rather as a curiosity.

"Sun Tzu say: keep your friends close," began Captain Pham.

"And your enemies closer," finished Jonathon, agreeing with a silent nod. A few minutes of silence in the warm light of the room followed. Questions began to form in Jonathon's mind, and he struggled to find his own understanding of their answers, and to separate the ones that were pertinent from those that were not.

"You must have questions, Jon," Captain Pham offered. "I may be able to answer a few of them."

"Am I still going to get to work with him?" he asked. "Sar'n Anderson just came in and told me that we're moving this week out of Makhmur and to Q-West?"

"Yeah, the battalion is getting moved to work along the Tigris, where there is a heavier concentration of insurgent activity and attacks against friendly forces. As we pull out, our company will take up exclusive operation of the TCP outside Irbil until the battalion closes at Q-West. But things need to seem normal for Mahmoud, so you will go out to see him again same as always. This man is very dangerous." Captain Pham paused and then added, "He was responsible for the attack that killed Sergeant Gregson."

"But sir, other than that, we really haven't been attacked at all," Jonathon thought out loud, curiosity having now replaced the embarrassed anger he had felt earlier. "If he's a cell leader, then what's he doing out here?"

"He's basically here to start a civil war. Once we toppled the Iraqi government, the Kurds were in a position to secede from the country, something they've been fighting for forever. Our battalion was sent up here as a force that could react in case the Kurds tried just that. Mahmoud's job is to try to force that event, to ignite the powderkeg. By stirring up enough conflict between the Arabs and Kurds in this region, he could have caused a distraction strong enough to divert American resources away from key areas of influence such as Baghdad and Mosul and Kirkuk. The kidnappings, the murders, the thefts, all of them came from his cell. All of which were an effort to ignite a civil war on the eastern border of the country. And," Captain Pham added dryly, "in his free time, kill whatever Americans he could. That cache you sat on last week? That was his. God only knows how many more there are like that spread throughout this whole area."

Jonathon nodded his understanding. "He was a shaping effort."

Captain Pham smiled. "Exactly, Jon. Not a key player as far as the direct insurgency is concerned, but he has the opportunity up here to cause significant problems in our efforts to maintain a stable environment in the rest of the country. Can you imagine the mess it would cause if the Kurds and Arabs up here started a civil war? Our entire brigade would get involved, maybe the division. Then the story becomes how the American Coalition is unable to keep the peace in Iraq. You see?"

Jonathon's eyes were wide. "Brilliant," he said, shaking his head.

"Yeah, it was," Captain Pham agreed. "But now it's over," he said with a smile.

Jonathon jerked himself out of his admiration for the plan and asked, "Sir, why don't we just go scoop him up tonight?" His anger resurfaced. He swore to himself. When are you gonna stop being so goddamned naïve? He heard Sam ask him, When are you ever gonna learn? Not again, he thought as he remembered the bongo truck with the rolled carpet in Sam's story. Never again.

"I can understand why you want to do that, Jon, I really do. But that's not the plan. We have him right where we want him. We know that our sources are accurate now, and we want to be able to see where and who else he can lead us to," Captain Pham said as he leaned back in his chair with his hands folded in his lap, his gaze intent on Jonathon's shadowed face, only partially lit in the soft light. "No, nothing changes. No sudden clues that may tip him off. You were going to see him again in a couple days, right?"

Jonathon swallowed. "Yessir."

Captain Pham nodded. "Good. We're heading out in a week, so this next time will probably be the last. Jon," he paused for emphasis. "This is very important. We cannot tip our hand on this one. Got it?"

"Roger sir, I got it."

Walking back across the empty courtyard, the moon barely a sliver on the western horizon, Jonathon tripped over a rock, sending himself tumbling to the ground, his weapon clattering on the dry dirt. All else was quiet, and he swore as he stood back up and swiped the dirt off his pants. He took a long, slow breath then as he stared up at the night sky, the Milky Way hovering over him like a cloud. And he told himself with tears in his eyes that he would not let fall that those dots of light up there were only burning balls of gas, that there was nothing beautiful in them after all; they were just a chain of autocatalytic nuclear explosions and there was no purpose or poetry to them. Just clouds of exploding gas, and our vain attempts to assign them patterns and names only hid the ugly truth and were perhaps the cruelest sort of fable.

* * *

A little over a week later, Jonathon and the rest of the battalion had relocated to Q-West and had started operating along the banks of the Tigris River. Qayyarah was a small city that sat on a corner just north of Route Chevy, about thirty kilometers east of Q-West, and on the west bank of the Tigris. Small towns and villages spread north and south from Qayyarah like a third-world version of urban sprawl, nestled along both banks of the river. Two main roads traced the river on either bank, connected by a large bridge that crossed the river at Qayyarah. It was the nearest bridge for over fifty kilometers in either direction, and therefore served as a vital funnel, both for the economy of Iraq and for the American military. By controlling the bridge, the Americans could severely restrict the free movement of insurgents and their materiel. The bridge also served as a vital commercial link from Irbil and eastern Iraq to Highway 1, the main national highway that ran north-south outside of Q-West.

The battalion, after it had moved out of Makhmur and relocated to Q-West, began patrolling the area and the towns surrounding Qayyarah. Delta Company was assigned the eastern banks of the Tigris, tasked with the security of the area as well as denying insurgent freedom of maneuver. One of its platoons was always tasked to either Alpha or Charlie Company in order to provide mounted support and to serve as a quick reaction force along the western bank. Bravo Company had been tasked with securing the main pipeline that ran north-south along Highway 1 and which pumped Iraq's oil out and up to Turkey to the north and down to Al Basra to the south. The insurgents had recently began attacking the oil pipeline in an effort to show the lack of security that the American Coalition was capable of providing.

While the Americans laughed and shook their heads at the thought process—or lack thereof—that led the Iraqis to destroy their own oil pipeline and therefore their main source of revenue, they also understood the impact it could have on the national economy and therefore on the infant insurgency. Reluctantly, and with an appreciation for the irony, the Americans set up a series of observation posts that covered the entire pipeline from north to south, protecting the Iraqi pipeline from the Iraqi people. This move dedicated all of Bravo to cover a little over fifty kilometers of the pipeline. Every month promises were made and rumors were passed around that Bravo was coming off the pipeline and that a British company had bought the contract to secure it; yet Bravo was not taken off the pipeline security mission until the battalion redeployed back to Kuwait in January 2004.

Alpha and Charlie were tasked with securing and facilitating the rebuilding of the oil refinery in Qayyarah and with providing security along the western banks of the Tigris. Every two weeks, the two companies would switch from operating from Q-West, where they performed refit, training, and force protection such as gate or tower guard, to Qayyarah, where they ran their operations from the oil refinery. While at the oil refinery, the company responsible for those two weeks was charged with overseeing its reconstruction as well as multiple other civic projects throughout the area. Life at Qayyarah was good and the men enjoyed not only the way that time passed faster while they were out at the oil refinery, but also the break from life on Q-West.

As what always happened whenever a large group of military personnel lived in a common area, in the interest of discipline and order, rules had to be implemented and enforced, and Q-West proved no exception. Thus, Jonathon and his men, after months of operating out of the backs of their humvees or from old bunkers, living out of their rucksacks and doing the best with what was available, found themselves speechless when a first sergeant from another unit approached them and ordered them out of the line for chow and told them to go clean up. Enraged and embarrassed, the men got out of line, and as they walked away wondered aloud where he had had his uniform starched. Anderson called him a worthless sack of shit just loud enough for the first sergeant to hear him; for a moment Jonathon thought he was going to lose his platoon sergeant. But, either out of shame or out of fear, the first sergeant must have pretended he had not heard him.

The men knew that the world they had been yanked out of and thrown into at Q-West was one in which they did not belong, and which seemed out of place with the fact that right outside the wire there were men who wanted to kill them. Inside the fenced-off airfield that the Americans had taken over and called Q-West, every effort was made to imitate life at Fort Campbell. Jonathon was incredulous. Stop signs appeared on corners. Speed limits were posted, and soldiers who evidently had nothing to contribute to the actual war itself stood on the side of the road and wrote out tickets for soldiers not wearing their seatbelts.

Jonathon and his men looked around and saw their brothers in Bravo sitting in the middle of nowhere for days at a time, staring at a mound of dirt underneath which ran an oil pipeline, and at the new life that surrounded them at Q-West, and he realized that the Army had decided to stop waging war. That regardless of how many roadside bombs went off—now termed Improvised Explosive Devices—or how many times they were shot at by an invisible enemy, that the war was over. The emphasis was no longer on finding and killing the enemy, but on security and safety. The men laughed at the irony of getting shot at while on patrol, only to return to base and be handed a ticket for going twenty-one in a twenty mile per hour zone.

Not that Q-West didn't have its benefits, Jonathon had to admit. The new dining facility being built was larger than a football field, and the food was excellent, prepared by Pakistani workers drawn to the job for the pay. There was a gym that had three employees who spent all day cleaning the small structure. Several locals had been allowed to come onto base and open stores, which the men referred to as "haji-shops." There was electricity—most of the time—and phones and computers and a sense of permanence. TVs appeared everywhere. Days passed and routines developed. Life became normal—misleadingly so—for the men, and they counted down the days until the year would be up and they could go home. With the apparent changes in intent, and the routinization of life at Q-West, the men began to believe that they were going to survive, and they took a welcomed step back from the precipice upon which they had lived for the past six months.

It was early September, and as hot as it ever had been, but it was no longer hot all the time the way it had been at Makhmur or near Al Hatra or in An Najaf or at Camp Pennsylvania. The phone and Internet centers, the haji-shops, and a sense of finally being somewhere semi-permanent, seemed somehow to relieve the men from the constant oppression of the heat.

Just over two weeks after the conversation with Captain Pham when he had been told the true identity of Mr. Marie, and one week after they had moved back Q-West, Jonathon found himself conducting a patrol on Route Tahoe, the road that ran north-south on the eastern bank of the river. The sun had set over five hours ago, the moon now nothing more than a sliver that was slipping down to the west.

Jonathon had stopped at the oil refinery in Qayyarah before sunset to coordinate with the Charlie Company Commander, Captain Brent Daniels, for his patrol. He had walked into the main building and found Captain Daniels sitting with Sam in a small room that served as the company's command post. When Sam saw Jonathon walk in, he jumped up in the middle of Captain Daniel's sentence and bounded over to him with a warm handshake and a large smile. Charlie Company had been at the oil refinery for ten days, and he and Jonathon had not seen each other since the day before Charlie had left Makhmur over two weeks ago.

"How are you Jon?" Sam asked as he stood there looking at him, his white smile fading to a warm grin.

"Good Sam, how're things here?" Jonathon asked as he and Sam sat down around the table where Sam and Captain Daniels had been talking. "Hey sir," Jonathon greeted Captain Daniels with a nod and shook the hand offered him.

"Jon," Captain Daniels offered warmly.

A moment of silence followed, Jonathon obviously having interrupted a conversation between the two that had now left both searching for a new subject.

Jonathon felt slightly awkward and said, "Sir, I'm sorry if I interrupted. I'll be working Route Tahoe tonight, and I just wanted to come and touch base with you."

"Great!" exclaimed Sam, his face smiling and his dark hair tussled from lack of a haircut.

"Hey XO," cut in Captain Daniels with a smile, "I think that Jon wants to talk to the company commander, not the executive officer. Is that okay with you?"

"Yeah, I guess so sir," said Sam with a wink to Jonathon, who just shook his head at Sam's blatant disregard.

Captain Daniels brought his attention back to Jonathon and asked, "How long are you going to be out?"

"Well sir," answered Jonathon, laying his map board on the table. "I'd like to spend about six hours out there once the sun goes down, then come back in here to get a few hours of rack, and get out there again to cover the couple hours before sunrise."

Captain Daniels nodded his head approvingly. "All right, sounds good," he said, and then proceeded to ask the requisite questions about radio frequencies and number of personnel, and told Jonathon where his units would be that night. Paul Batsakis's platoon would be operating on the other side of the river adjacent to Jonathon that night, on Route Corvette. The conversation was quick and formal, and ended with Captain Daniels telling Jonathon to give them a call if they needed anything.

"Will do, sir," Jonathon had said, and stood to go. Sam stood up with him to walk him out.

"Hey XO," called Captain Daniels, still seated behind the table. "Where are you going?"

Sam smiled back and ran a hand through his long dark hair. "I wanted to go talk to Jon before he left. Chow's here anyway, sir, and we've been at that shit for two hours now. Time for a break," he headed out the door, not waiting for a reply.

Jonathon laughed to himself as Sam stepped beside him and the two headed for the line of trucks. They talked for about a half hour, catching up and seeing what they each thought of the new AO. Sam asked how the new dining facility was coming along, and Jonathon told him that they almost had it finished. Jonathon asked how Rachel and Claire were and noticed a quick hesitation in Sam before he answered.

Jonathon shook his head, smiling despite himself, and asked, "Sam, what'd you do?"

Sam shrugged his shoulders, "What? Nothing. She's fine. Both of them are. I got a letter from her a couple days ago, in fact."

"All right," Jonathon said skeptically.

"What?" Sam pursued.

"Nothing, man. I just thought for a minute there you'd done something stupid."

"Who? Me?" said Sam with mock offense and the two laughed.

Jonathon looked at his watch and said that he had to go.

"Good to see you, Jon. Take care of yourself," said Sam as they shook hands.

"Yeah, I'll see you when you get back to Q-West," said Jonathon as he climbed into the truck and drove out the gate.

The world was now dark as Jonathon and his trucks slowly moved north along Route Tahoe, the only paved two-lane road in the area. Their movement was slow and deliberate. Two trucks would move ahead about half a kilometer and pause while the remaining trucks would leap frog ahead of them another half kilometer, and so forth and so on. Occasionally, Jonathon would call out to his platoon to set up a quick traffic control point, and the trucks would conduct immediate drills that would section off about one hundred meters of the road, with two trucks on either side, waiting for a car to come through. They would sit there in the dark quietly, and then flash their lights if a car happened to approach to warn it of the check point, and check the car and its occupants. They never stayed longer than a half hour, when at a word from Jonathon the men would scoop up the various signs and accoutrement, and in a moment continue their long and slow movement up the road. It was a tedious technique, but hard to argue against from a tactical standpoint.

About fifteen kilometers north of where Route Chevy crossed the river, the road took a gentle and long bend to the right, and then dropped into a large *wadi* that filled with water during the rainy season. About two hundred meters later, the road climbed out and passed through a small village whose buildings sat perched against the far bank. The bare and exposed fluorescent lights of the houses were bright against the darkness of the night as the line of trucks descended into the empty streambed.

Jonathon's truck, moving with Hoover's in the lead, passed Anderson and Cline in the two other trucks as they sat on the high ground watching while Jonathon and Hoover passed through the low ground.

Suddenly, the darkness was split by a flash of light and an explosion off to their right. Olk swore as a shapeless roaring scream passed right in front of their windshield; the trail of smoke that followed told them the RPG had only barely missed their truck. Jonathon heard Anderson call over the radio, "Contact right," and heard MacLimore up in his gun swear as tracer fire swept over and around the two trucks that were totally exposed on the open road in the low ground.

Olk had stopped the truck in all the noise and confusion, and Jonathon heard himself yelling "Go, Go, Go! Get out! Get outta the kill zone!" Olk responded quickly, floored his gas pedal, and followed right behind Hoover's truck. Up in the gun, MacLimore was attempting to return fire, but the quick, jerky movements of the truck on the poorly paved road caused his fire to spray wildly anywhere but where the ambushers might be hiding. Jonathon saw the red tracer rounds of his .50 cal shooting off into the dark sky. The two trucks left the low ground and reached the opposite bank. The enemy had ceased firing, but MacLimore was still shooting, and Jonathon had to yell at him a few times to get him to stop.

Grabbing the handmike, Jonathon asked whether anyone had seen the ambushers. Anderson came back over the radio and said they hadn't been able to see exactly where they had fired from.

"Okay," said Jonathon into the radio. "One, let's push a little farther up and see if we can outflank them."

"Roger Six," came Hoover's reply as the truck in front of them pushed up the road to the edge of the town. Jonathon had Hoover push off the road about one hundred meters, screening the northern edge of the town.

Jonathon swore and said into the radio, "Is everyone all right? Check your guys and give me a report. Seven, you and Two go ahead and bound across, we'll cover you from here."

"Roger Six, Seven is good," Anderson called back, letting Jonathon know that everyone in his truck was all right.

As Jonathon spoke, Olk asked MacLimore if he was okay, reaching back with his right hand in the dark to feel for any signs of injuries or blood. He found none, and MacLimore called down that he was fine and to stop grabbing at him. "We're good, sir," Olk told Jonathon.

"Two's good," he heard Cline call in.

"One's up," called in Hoover.

Jonathon could feel his heart pounding, and his voice shook despite his efforts to calm his nerves as he told MacLimore to keep an eye on the other two trucks as they moved across the *wadi* to catch up.

Over the radio to the Charlie Company frequency, he could hear Captain Daniel's voice calling him. Jonathon reached over in the dark and grabbed the other handmike. Holding his platoon handmike in his right ear and the company one in his left, he gave instructions to his platoon to try to surround the town as best they could while he reported what had happened to Captain Daniels.

Jonathon reported that they had been ambushed by coordinated RPG and machine gun fire to the east of their position on Route Tahoe by about three to four men, who had then broken contact to the east, and that Jonathon now had his trucks postured outside of the small village where he believed the men had gone into. Captain Daniels told him that his quick reaction force would be there in ten minutes, and not to move into the village until they arrived.

"Roger sir," Jonathon said as he felt his heart slow down. He relayed to his trucks to try to get into the best positions they could to prevent anyone from leaving the village. The quiet of the night had returned as quickly as it had been violated by the gunfire; it was obvious that the brief fight was over.

Olk turned to Jonathon, his eyes wide. "Sir," he said in disbelief, "did you see that?"

"See what?" asked Jonathon, turning to him.

"That fucking RPG bounced off of our hood!" Olk gasped.

"No," Jonathon said in disbelief, a smile playing on his lips. "Really?" he said, as he opened his door to take a look at the truck. Looking at the hood in the faint light, he saw a slight scrape on the fiberglass of the hood and a trail of char where the heat from the round had burned the hood as it skipped over. Touching the scrape with his hand, Jonathon laughed to himself and swore. "Well," he said, "that was close."

"A little too close, if you ask me, sir," called down MacLimore from the gun, never taking his eyes off the surrounding area as he scanned from behind his machine gun.

"Yeah, me too, Mac," replied Jonathon. "Great job returning fire. We may need to work on your aim a bit, though," said Jonathon, teasing him, trying to get his gunner to ease his grip on the trigger.

"Sir, I was just pulling the trigger and trying to keep the gun pointed in the general direction where I thought they were. It ain't easy the way Olk drives, sir," he added, still scanning. Mac was proud of his title as the best gunner in the platoon.

Jonathon laughed. "I know, it's tough. Good job. You sure you're all right?"

"I'm good, sir," he said, his pride still wounded. "Just want another shot at 'em, sir."

"All right. How about you Olk, you good?" Jonathon asked his driver.

"Other than the fact that I almost shit myself, yeah, I'm good sir. Jesus, fuck! Bounced off our hood! Can you believe it, sir?"

"No," Jonathon shook his head as he climbed back into the truck and reached for both of the handmikes in the dark, and held them to his ears.

A few minutes passed and the night was quiet as people from the village, awakened by the noise of the brief firefight, walked out of their houses. Jonathon could see Anderson off to his right talking to a man dressed in a long white *dish-dasha* waving his arms wildly. He could hear the man yelling in Arabic and see Anderson standing firmly in front of him, unmoved by the display.

"Hey Seven, is everything all right?" he asked and heard Shipley come back over the radio.

"We're good sir, this man's all pissed that we woke him up, I guess," he said, and then added, "I think Seven is about to punch him, though."

"Seven Romeo, tell Seven to just stay calm; Cobra Six will be here in a few minutes, and we'll have enough men to search through the village," Jonathon instructed Shipley over the radio.

"Roger Six," Shipley's voice responded.

In the minutes that passed, more and more people came out of their houses, attracted more by the lingering presence of the American trucks than by the firefight that had passed now over fifteen minutes ago. By the time Jonathon saw the line of trucks from Charlie Company round the bend and drop into the far side of the *wadi*, it seemed as if the whole town were awake. Clumps of men stood around talking, casting glances at the trucks that had surrounded their village in a half circle, with the bank to the south completing the perimeter.

Jonathon climbed out of his truck as Charlie Company arrived, men jumping out and shouting orders. He recognized Captain Daniels, and headed over to talk to him, calling over his shoulder for Olk to stay with the truck and watch the radios.

"Hey sir," Jonathon said as he came up to Captain Daniels in the dark.

"Hey Jon, everybody all right?"

"We're good sir. Nobody hurt, no damage except my hood's a little scratched," Jonathon shrugged.

"Okay," said Captain Daniels and started to lay out the plan for how the village was going to be searched, asking Jonathon if he had any idea where the ambushers may have gone off to.

"No idea, sir, there's no way I could've sent men down there to take a look, too risky with what I had. The trucks would've gotten stuck," Jonathon explained, half apologizing.

"No, you were right to wait for us," Captain Daniels nodded. "You did exactly the right thing. They broke contact, and you didn't let yourself get sucked into anything. You chasing after them in that *wadi* may have been exactly what they wanted. I'll send a dismounted platoon down there to take a look."

"Sir, there's no way the people in this town don't know who these guys are or where they went to. There isn't another village around here for five clicks," Jonathon offered.

"Yeah, you're right, Jon," Captain Daniels sighed. "But finding something that will prove that is an entirely different story. We're gonna search through every single house, and see what we can find, but…"

"I know, it's a long shot, sir," said Jonathon.

"Do you think you hit any of them?" Captain Daniels asked him.

"Honestly sir, it happened pretty fast, and—"

"Don't worry about it, we'll see if we find any of them," interrupted Captain Daniels, who then moved onto the business at hand. "Okay, you have four trucks, right? And they're all in position around the village?"

Jonathon was pointing out to him his trucks' positions when he felt a large hand clap him on the shoulder. When he turned, he saw Sam with his rifle in his right hand and a friendly smile on his face.

"I saw your hood Jon," said Sam, "I guess goin' to church all those years paid off, huh?"

Jonathon chuckled and shook his head, "I guess so Sam. It's good to see you."

"You too, brother," Sam returned warmly and then turned to Captain Daniels. "Hey sir, I'm gonna go over with Paul's platoon to search that *wadi*."

"Okay, give me a call if you find anything. Let me know if you can see any tracks," Captain Daniels ordered.

"Too easy, sir," Sam said as he clapped Jonathon on the back and bounded off into the darkness.

It took the company over four hours to search the village. It was not a very big village, but the process of methodically searching every person and every structure was a long and tedious task. Sam had come back reporting that the tracks went off to the east, where they climbed up the bank of the *wadi*, and then disappeared. They had found the firing positions, he reported. With a smile, he held out a handful of spent PKM machine gun shells. He handed one to Jonathon with a laugh. "Here you go brother, a little souvenir from your trip to Iraq," he said. Jonathon took it from him and shoved it down into his pocket.

During the search, the village *mukhtar* and *imaam* came out and found Captain Daniels, demanding to speak to the man in charge of the search. Captain Daniels, through the aid of his interpreter Ahmed, was able to communicate to them why they were searching their village, and asked them if they knew anything about the attack. Of course neither of them knew, and of course both of them swore that they were friends of the Americans. Captain Daniels knew that neither was true, but the operation had turned from a combat one into an investigation, and if no evidence could be found to contradict their stories or the stories of the local people in the village, then there was little that could be done.

Once the town had been searched, the inevitable report came back that nothing significant had been found. They had amassed quite a collection of AK-47s and ammunition, none of which showed any signs of being fired recently. No RPGs or PKM machine guns, the weapons that had been used in the attack, had been found in the village, however. The result of a full night of work, therefore, was only sweat-drenched and frustrated men as they climbed back into their trucks as the sun peaked over the eastern horizon.

Captain Daniels had one last talk with the two leaders of the village, communicating to them that the men responsible for the attack would be found. Sam had stood by Jonathon and Captain Daniels during this last exchange, Sam's huge frame and scowling face threatening the men with their lives. When he had finished, Captain Daniels turned away and told everyone that they were leaving and to get in the trucks.

As Jonathon drove away, a couple kids from the village ran alongside his truck, waving their hands and smiling. He heard MacLimore from up in the gun swear at them and they stopped abruptly, the smiles wiped off their faces as the trucks left them behind in a trail of dust reflected in the light of the early morning sun. And Jonathon tilted his head back in his seat and thought about that RPG and gave thanks as day one hundred and eighty-six began.

* * *

A couple days later, Jonathon sat in the large, unfinished dining facility at night after the dinner crowd had passed. He was thinking about the last time he had talked to Marie, when he had gone on his last patrol through his old sector before being moved back to Q West. The old man rose to greet him the same as he always had, but there was a difference in the way his narrow face was set. The dark eyes still sparkled, but above them the brow wrinkled slightly where the eyebrows met. Jonathon could feel his heart pounding as he shook the man's hand, trying hard to remember exactly how he had always shaken the hand and suddenly finding it impossible to remember every little detail of their past meetings so he could recreate it now. He swallowed.

"Good morning, Mr. Marie," Jonathon forced his rigid lips to bend and his heavy cheeks to relax as he shook the soft brown hand.

"Good morning, Leftenant," Marie acknowledged back with a nod and Jonathon could not help but think that the man seemed to be rehearsing the same as he was. The two stood there for two infinitely long seconds, both seeming to insist to the other with their phony smiles that they were perfectly comfortable and everything was as it had always been. Finally turning, Marie welcomed Jonathon to sit in the shade on the carpet, "Please, join us? Perhaps some chai?"

Jonathon saw Olk step forward at the offer and asked himself how Olk would feel about the chai if he knew this man was all too willing to kill them both and the rest of the platoon. That this man was their enemy. He caught himself wetting his lips, and thanked him. "Chai would be very nice, thank you." Marie turned to the toothless man who always brought the chai and the man stepped inside the building beside them and disappeared into the shadows.

They sat down beside each other, Jonathon taking off his helmet and laying it down bottom up and balancing the barrel of his rifle in the bowl it created. He dragged his left sleeve across his wet forehead and could feel the stiffness of the cloth where the salt from his sweat had starched it. Two men in the corner spoke quickly and quietly back and forth while the others waited patiently for the conversation to begin.

Jonathon had pulled Anderson aside after his talk with Captain Pham and had told him about Marie. Anderson had just nodded his head as if he had expected it all along.

Jonathon had spent a lot of time thinking about how to handle this last meeting. He had spent so much time trying to create a normal reason for him to go back out that he found that none of the reasons seemed normal anymore and he wondered whether he had not already thought the thing too far. Finally frustrated and confounded, he had asked Anderson, who had answered with the same reliable common sense that had always served them so well.

"Why don't you just whip out another one of them surveys, sir?" he had growled from beneath the mustache.

But it couldn't be that easy. "But don't you think it's a little hard to buy the fact that we are really going out there to collect the same information when we know that nothing has changed?"

Anderson waited a moment, his eyes resting on his young platoon leader before he spoke. "Well, yeah. But I don't see why that should stop us at this point, sir."

In the end, Jonathon took his platoon sergeant's advice, and had brought the survey with him. But he had decided to lead with the meeting with 'Colonel DaSilva.

"'Colonel DaSilva told me that he was excited to hear that you would be joining the provincial council in Makhmur." He waited for Nazeem to translate for the benefit of the group, who all nodded their heads. But Marie was quiet a long time before he spoke, and in that silence grew a knowledge that became more and more undeniable with every passing second. Marie knew. The sonofabitch knew.

Marie's dark sparkling eyes looked at Jonathon as if the man had been slightly insulted with the reference, as if he had been denied the post. Finally drawing a slow breath to speak, the corners of the man's mouth rose slightly and the severity left the dark pupils. "Yes," he said, "I am excited as well." He paused, as if deciding whether to say one thing or another. Jonathon's heart beat faster and he found himself questioning his own posture, his language, where he was looking and not looking, was he breathing too fast, anything out of the ordinary. "It seems strange to me that your commander would come all the way down here to our little village to offer the post to me. I am not a business man, I have no official political influence in the region. Surely there are better candidates in Makhmur and Debega for this position? Don't you think it is strange that he would think that I am a likely candidate? Based upon what criteria?" He smiled slightly and shrugged, as if mocking the game they both knew they were now playing. "I can think of none. Can you, Leftenant?"

"Um, yes," Jonathon fought to regain control of himself and form a sentence, any sentence at all.

The toothless man emerged from the doorway with the chai and Jonathon seized the distraction as an opportunity to clear his head. He quickly stirred his chai and sipped at the liquid, which scalded the tip of his tongue so that he winced. Marie noticed and offered a patronizing, "Careful Leftenant, it is hot," as if it weren't always served piping hot. Jonathon realized he was losing this dance, if he had not lost it already. Marie had asked him a question. But Marie was not the man's name. You are not Marie, Jonathon said to himself as he stirred his tea. You are Mahmoud. Jonathon looked up again, his eyes hard and accusing. Fuck it, he told himself. If the man knows, he knows.

"Yes, although you do not own a business, it is obvious that you have incredible influence, not only in Al Sharqi, but throughout the area." The rest of the men around the carpet nodded their agreement, but Mahmoud's eyes did not leave Jonathon's.

Mahmoud shrugged his shoulders again, and Jonathon thought for the first time that maybe the man was not as confident as Jonathon gave him credit for. That maybe the man was still just a man and afraid that the Americans knew who he was. Then why didn't he run?

"*Insh'alla*," Mahmoud said, "what is done is done, and I am pleased to be a part of the council." The last part was obviously for the other men around the carpet, and Jonathon thought the first part was for the both of them. God willing. What is done is done. Mahmoud would stay. Better if he would run. That would somehow confirm his malevolence, if he ran. But to stand in the face of his enemy and rest on the will of God was something else entirely. It made the man more than just a two-dimensional target, and suddenly Jonathon saw the whole thing turned on its head and Mahmoud was the good guy and he, Jonathon, was the bad guy in the story. And he saw that the world's stories get told by the winners. That Mahmoud was the enemy only because Jonathon's side owned all the printing presses, nothing more. But it could easily be told the other way, and doubtless it was being told the other way around in homes all over the country.

Jonathon took out the survey and held it up. "I have a survey I need to ask you about, if you would not mind," speaking to the group and leaving time for Nazeem to translate.

The men nodded disinterestedly. "Ah, another survey," Mahmoud said aloud. "Of course."

Jonathon shot him a look that betrayed the secret, as if it were not already known.

"How is the water?" Jonathon asked, pulling the cap off his pen with his teeth.

The men around the carpet nodded.

He heard Mahmoud say, "The same. Of course." Jonathon made a point not to acknowledge his answer.

"Electricity?"

"It is the same, Leftenant," Mahmoud said louder this time, such that some of the men, unable to understand and only concerned by his tone, did not answer but only glanced uneasily between the two men.

Jonathon continued. "Schools."

"The same."

"Police."

"The same," stronger now, more forceful, and Jonathon's heart started to race.

"Gasoline."

"The same! Always the same!"

Jonathon looked up into the eyes of the man who had been his friend and hated him. He glared at him as he felt the oppressive stares of the men around the carpet. Olk had circled behind Mahmoud and Jonathon could see his finger in the trigger well, obviously unaware of what was happening, but daring Mahmoud to make a move. He heard a Humvee door shut behind him. He took a long breath and stood to go. Mahmoud remained seated, his eyes to the floor, bent forward with one hand propped on a knee, the thin arm protruding out. As Jonathon put his helmet on, he heard Anderson ask behind him if everything was all right.

Without looking back he answered that it was and to get the trucks started. Anderson moved back, hollering to the trucks to start up while Jonathon told Olk to take Nazeem back to their truck. "You coming sir?" Olk asked, unsure, torn between his promise and his duty.

But Jonathon reassured him with a look and a smile, "Yeah man, go on back, I'll be right there."

When Olk had left and Jonathon had turned to go, he heard Mahmoud say from behind him, "Do what it is you are here to do, Leftenant."

Jonathon bent his head down to the ground, unsure of what it was he was there to do, what to do now, what anything was ever going to be like again after this mess, and shook his head slowly and walked off, hating everything.

"Mind if I join you, brother?" Sam's voice broke in as he slid his tray across the plastic table and sat down.

"Hey Sam, no not at all," Jonathon sat up and smiled back. "Sit down."

"This place really is something, isn't it?" asked Sam as he looked around at the enormous building. "Bigger even than a Wal-Mart. Food's pretty damn good, too," he said as he shoveled a spoonful of rice pilaf into his mouth.

Jonathon nodded silently and continued his distracted gaze at the bare metal walls of the building. Sam felt Jonathon's silence pressing upon the table, and blurted out between spoonfuls of pilaf that he had been hanging out with Amber Gibson, the trauma platoon leader out of Charlie Med. His comment did not quite have the effect he was hoping to elicit.

"What?" asked Jonathon, staring straight at Sam, his face twisted in disbelief. The weight of accusation that Jonathon conveyed in his eyes was not what Sam had had in mind; he had hoped for a chuckle from his friend with his typically mild disapproval. He discovered suddenly that Jonathon was not in the mood for shallow banter, and he averted his eyes from Jonathon's and back to his plate.

A full minute passed like that, Jonathon's suffocatingly patient gaze on Sam as Sam poured all of his attention to his plate. Finally, unable to bear the silence any longer, Sam swore and threw his spoon down in frustration. "Come on! What? You gonna say something or are you just gonna sit there and stare at me while I eat?" Jonathon's expression did not change, and his eyes remained glued to Sam. Sam realized that he was not able to hold Jonathon's gaze, and he started to get angry. "What the hell's wrong with you, man? It's not like we've done anything… We're just talking, that's all." And right when he was about to get really angry, a slight smile played on Jonathon's lips and Sam instantly relaxed and went back to his dinner.

When he was just about to shovel another spoonful of rice into his mouth, Jonathon finally spoke.

"You're a fool."

Sam was dumbstruck as he chewed slowly and searched Jonathon's face for some hint of sarcasm or sport. There was none, and Sam realized that Jonathon was looking at him in a way he never had before. Sam had always had the pleasant feeling of being like a big brother to Jonathon. He had seen it in the way Jonathon had always seemed to defer to him and in the way their friendship had developed. Jonathon had placed himself under Sam's tutelage when the two had first met in An Najaf back in April, and ever since then the two had had a strong bond, but their friendship had always had the feeling of Sam being the older and wiser. Jonathon had always deferred to Sam's seniority and laughed at his stories and his tales of conquest. But here, at a long plastic table by themselves, in a near-empty warehouse, Sam was struck with the change that he saw in his young friend. And though he had heard clearly enough the words Jonathon had spoken, he asked despite himself, "What did you say?"

Jonathon didn't flinch, though his gaze had softened from one of accusation to one of… pity, Sam realized with a shock. "You're a fool, Sam," Jonathon said in a half whisper with eyes that spoke as if seeing clearly for the first time. "What about Rachel? And Claire? Are you really gonna throw all that away for some cheap fling?"

Sam sat up and took a long slow breath, his lips pursed as he pushed his empty plate away from him. "I broke things off with Rachel almost two months ago now," he confessed. "But she still sends a letter every now and then."

Jonathon sat silently across from him at the table and shook his head, the pity in his eyes changing to genuine sadness. "That's how it is with you, Sam," Jonathon said softly. "You have this thing in you that wants to push away and destroy everything good in your life. It's like you have some need to punish yourself for something."

Sam smirked, "Maybe I should go see a shrink—"

"No," Jonathon cut him off. "That's not it at all." He caught himself and took a long breath. "I'm sorry, Sam, I didn't mean to… It's just… well, I don't know. I'm sorry, I didn't mean it." He sat back in his chair and played with the now empty plastic cup that had held his coffee.

Sam shrugged and smiled weakly, trying to ease the weight that had settled on the table between the two. "It's all right, Jon, don't worry about it. I'm not sure I understand it myself, to be honest. I think the whole idea of *her*—I've dated a lot of girls, but from the moment I met her, I knew she was different." He laughed to himself and shook his head. "She wasn't just gonna be another girl, she was going to be *the* girl, you know?"

Jonathon, his eyes staring at something far away as he played with the plastic cup, said, "You're not any different from anyone else, Sam. Sure, you've got your thing, but we've all got something. I've realized that lately." He shook his head, his eyes and mind still somewhere far away, somewhere in the mountains with a girl in a tent, far from the empty cup that he held in his hands and was slowly tearing apart. "I used to think in such strict absolutes. Everything was right or wrong, good or bad. And I was good because God was good, and America was right because freedom was right, and whatever wasn't right and good had to be wrong and bad. But Sam," he said softly, "being a Christian doesn't make me good and being an American doesn't make me any more right than anybody else. I don't know what I thought before, or how I thought it, but that's what I've learned."

Silence settled on the table before Sam spoke. "You just think the same as we've all been taught to think," he offered. "We all think we're right and that the causes we fight for are right. And we comfort ourselves in the middle of uncertain times by telling ourselves that what we believe is good because it gives us the moral courage to keep on."

Jonathon remembered what Mr. Marie—Mahmoud—had said to him what seemed like a lifetime ago. "But I don't want to believe that, Sam." Jonathon had torn himself away from the scent of peaches and his eyes bore into Sam's with a quiet rage. "I don't want to believe that it's all just a matter of perspective, that everything is relative, that everything can be spun, has an angle. I don't want to believe that my sense of patriotism has been used to advance someone else's agenda. Or that men are dying here for... nothing," he shrugged. "I don't want to believe that everything is relative, but at the same time I see now that things are not as absolute as I once believed them to be. I don't want to believe that the girl who died in my arms is in hell because she didn't know Christ." He shook his head resolutely. "I will not believe that—the God I know does not do that. But there are those back home who would hold to that, that she did not deserve to be in Heaven—as if any of us do! And the men who shot at us the other night, they feel like God has blessed their struggle and you know"—here he pointed a finger at Sam—"that they were doing exactly what you and I would do were a foreign army in our country. We'd fight until we were killed, and we would be, and we'd be okay with that. We'd feel justified by the fact that we were defending our homes and our way of life, and that God Himself had blessed our campaign to protect those we love from those we saw as a threat to our families and our country. Wouldn't we?"

"Goddamned right," Sam smiled, his eyes firing to life.

Jonathon grew quiet. "But I don't want to be an occupier, Sam," Jonathon said suddenly. "I don't want to be the bad guy. I don't mind being the bad guy's enemy, but I just don't want to be the bad guy. That's not why I joined the Army, that's not why I wanted to serve." Jonathon paused. "I had visions of grandeur, picturing myself leading my men into the mouth of the enemy, standing like Leonidas with his three hundred against Xerxes' millions, defending our country and our homes from the enemy."

"But that's not how war is anymore, Jon," Sam offered. "Maybe that's how it used to be, but it ain't anymore."

"It's still an evil thing, it always has been," injected Jonathon.

"Yeah, it is. You're right. War's a crime. But it's in the very nature of war to be an evil. And it should be that way. War should be so destructive and terrible and unbearable, that it's only waged under absolutely desperate circumstances, when there's no other option. In the book you're reading, Tolstoy says it himself, right? Let war be war, and stop all this foolish magnanimity." Sam paused again and sighed, while Jonathon sat impressed that Sam had just quoted Tolstoy.

"But now we play at war. We launch our missiles from half a world away to blow up some building that supposedly has some bad guy in it, and we call that war. Like war has degenerated into some kind of fucking video game. The man who kills another in a battle with his rifle or his bayonet, walks away with the unshakeable conviction that what he has done is a sin, regardless of the fact that he was his enemy. Folks at home try to tell us that God forgives us because we are defending our country—defending *them*. What else can they say?" he shrugged. "But to the soldier it's personal, and he lives with that—carries it inside him, for the rest of his life. But the man who punches a button and watches a screen as a missile strikes a target is relieved of that personal burden. He's spared the reality of what he's done. It matters nothing to him if he pushes the same button fifty times and fifty times over watches the same computer image. He's saved himself from the burden that you and I must carry, but as a result he's sinned against humanity and excused himself from the burden that as a man he ought to feel."

"But doesn't all that save lives?" asked Jonathon.

"Yeah," nodded Sam. "In the short term it does. But look at what it's led to. Now countries go to war for whatever reason they can think of, sometimes for no real reason at all."

Jonathon shot him a surprised look at the allusion, and then frowned. The two were quiet a moment before Jonathon spoke again. "Just what the hell are we doing here, Sam? I know as officers we're not supposed to talk about that, but will somebody please tell me what we're doing here? Where are all those WMD's, huh? Where are they?"

When Sam didn't answer, Jonathon continued. "They don't exist, Sam. We were lied to. That's the truth, isn't it? We were lied to? And men are dying because of it? Can you believe that? The fact that that's not a crime…" but he couldn't find the words to finish the sentence. "And where are the American people? We're over here bleeding for a lie, Sam. What is that? Where are they, Sam? Huh?"

Sam was quiet a moment before he spoke. "They're where they've always been, Jon. At home, in front of the TV or reading smut magazines. Shoving Big Macs into their fat faces." He paused. "They don't care, Jon—no, listen to me brother: they do not care. Well, they *care*, but like they care about starving Ethiopian babies: not really." He paused again. "Look Jon, in the sixties it was the evil communists; now it's the evil terrorists. And forty years from now our so-called leaders will think of a new 'ist' that poses some kind of obscure threat to the American way of life, and off you and I will go again. And the American people will be where they've always been: at home, holding their hands over their hearts and wiping a tear from their eye when they hear another one of us has been killed. And then they'll go back to their video games and H3's and big-screen TVs." He shook his head, both angry and sad at the same time.

"But can you blame them?"

Jon looked up at him. "What do you mean?"

"Think about it, Jon. It's not Congress's fault. Not really, anyway. If the American people really—I mean *really*—gave a shit, then guess what? Congress would do something about this. The real tragedy is that the American people are watching their neighbors and children die because they don't have the courage to claim responsibility for this bullshit. They are complicit in the crime. If the President and Congress committed us to a bullshit war—to a lie—then the American people are implicated in the lie because they let themselves be lied to. And they all know it. Think about the shame you would feel. And think about the courage it would take to stand up and say that this war is what it is, knowing that you are responsible. Knowing that, at the end of the day, it's your fault that people are over here dying for a lie." Sam sighed and the two of them grew quiet a long while, Jonathon continuing to shred his paper cup.

"Anyway," Sam shook his head and returned to his original thought. "Think about the dialogue that would be forced were two countries to know that if diplomacy failed, they were going to each experience the full devastation of actual war, Ares himself." But that subject had died and Sam dropped it.

Jonathon sat quietly. The huge room was practically vacant now, with the exception of another pair of men on the far side. Jonathon wondered what it was they were talking about, and whether their conversation was anything like the one that he and Sam were having.

Suddenly, a thought occurred to him that made him smile, so clear that he wondered how he had never before understood something so simple. Why nations waged war, and why men went to fight in them. Why men fought others they understood as their enemy and believed—perhaps rightfully so—that God had consecrated their struggle. Why Sam sought to destroy every truly good thing in his life, and why he himself struggled so hard with his realization that what he had always thought to be right and good, in fact may not be so.

Sam saw the slight smile play on Jonathon's lips and asked him what he was thinking. Jonathon finally released the tortured cup, now torn to shreds, and looked up at his friend.

"We're all fighting the same wars, Sam," Jonathon said. "You, me, our country, our world, all of us, we're all fighting the same battles. All our wars are really just expressions of the conflicts inside ourselves. People talked about World War I as the War to End All Wars. As if world war can bring about world peace. But they really thought that, you know? Can you imagine?" Sam shook his head, and Jonathon mirrored him. "How can we possibly hope for some kind of abstraction like world peace when we don't even have any peace in the day-to-day activity of our own lives?" He frowned. "There's never gonna be a war to end all wars because war is never gonna get us the thing we're really fighting for."

"What's that?" Sam asked.

Jonathon shrugged. "Freedom... some kind of redemption... a victory that constantly eludes us. All of it, all of this," he gestured with his arms, "the whole thing, is some kind of crusade to find the thing that'll relieve us of the brokenness we all know we're burdened with. It's all broken to pieces—the entire thing, from top to bottom—and each of us is just trying to find a way to get it all put back together. You're right: we're not perfect, we may not even be all that good. But we can be, Sam. No. I've looked down that dark road of disbelief and there's nothing there, Sam. Nothing there but emptiness. Maybe it's all a lie and the whole thing's some kind of cruel joke. But I won't believe that. Because I'd rather believe than not believe. If I'm gonna get it wrong, I'd rather get it wrong believing it could be right. Believing that we can be good. No Sam, listen to me, brother: we can be good; we just have to make the decision."

"I guess that depends on whether you believe it all *can* be put back together," Sam added with a shrug of his own.

Jonathon looked at his friend sitting across from him. A deep love for the man rose up in him, and he wanted to tell him that it wasn't true, what Sam thought about himself: that he didn't have the capacity for heaven. Because that was what it all boiled down to, Jonathon thought, whether we believe we are capable of choosing who we are, what kind of men we'll be. If Judas never had a choice, then that changed everything, didn't it? But if he did, if even Judas could have chosen another path, then that opened the road a little, gave the rest of us a legitimate shot, and gave Sam a damned good one. Because Sam was a good man, Jonathon saw that and he knew Rachel saw it too, and he prayed quickly with one of those prayers where a thousand words were said in a split second, yet the prayer was still complete and heard in its entirety, that Sam would see that he had the choice to be good.

And something settled inside him and told him that it would all be all right—that all will be well and all manner of things will be well—and he looked forward to meeting Rachel because he knew that if anyone could, then she was the one who would convince Sam of the potential he no longer believed he had. That maybe between the two of them they could bring him around.

And he smiled again when he thought about getting dinner back at Fort Campbell with Sam and Rachel. How they would all laugh happily and contentedly because the war would be behind them, a bitter memory made sweet by the wine and the steaks resting in front of them.

Yes, Jonathon thought, that will be a good day. That will be a very good day.

* * *

Three days later, on day one hundred and ninety-one, a man crouched on the side of Route Chevy on the backside of a berm that followed that section of the road. American convoys were constantly traveling up and down the highway, and he knew he would not have to wait long before one would come driving past him. He had been lying there for just over twenty minutes by the time he saw Jonathon's convoy materialize out of the heat waves that danced off the asphalt. He was drenched in sweat and practically frozen to the ground in fear.

Only after he had set everything up, did he realize that he had not put much thought into his plan. If an American helicopter happened to fly overhead, they may think him just slightly suspicious, lying on the side of the road, a copper wire leading from him to an artillery round covered with an old cardboard box he had only thought of at the last minute. He was not near a village. Out of fear of being found out, he had intentionally picked a place over five kilometers away from his home. This, he now realized, had spoiled him of any opportunity to vanish into a crowd. He had planned on using the system of *wadis* that ran just south of the road in order to make his getaway, but the realization that his plan had not taken into account any helicopters made him start to doubt whether this was such a good idea. He wasn't *mujahadeen*, after all. A man dressed in a gleaming-white *dish-dasha* in Qayyarah had paid him fifty dollars—American—just to detonate this roadside bomb on a U.S. convoy. Those had been his instructions. The man had not even asked for proof. All he had to do was go set up the bomb, a simple procedure once he had been shown how, and detonate it on any Americans. The man had paid up front. Fifty dollars.

He would have detonated it on the lead truck, but his shaky hands caused him to drop the wire in the sand just as he was about to touch it to the car battery in front of him. He didn't miss on the second truck. Placing the wire on the negative contact of the battery, it sent an electric current down the one hundred feet of wire to the blasting cap he had fixed to a 152 mm artillery round with some PE4 explosive.

The instant concussion of the explosion made him start. Tires screeched, and he could hear small pieces of metal clang against the road. A black cloud of smoke rose into the air. His heart raced. He did not dare to even peer over the berm to see what he had done; he could easily imagine. Sliding back on his belly, he cautiously rose, bent at the waist, and disappeared into the *wadi* that would lead back to his village.

The explosion of the round sent shrapnel tearing through the engine block of Jonathon's truck, destroying the front end completely. A piece of shrapnel, the size of a quarter, hit Jonathon just to the right of his front kevlar plate, entering at the axilla, and puncturing the pleural cavity around his right lung. The negative pressure caused it to collapse, causing tension pneumothorax.

In the dust and smoke, Olk felt blood dripping down his face, and started to panic until he felt the sting from the small split on his forehead where he had hit the steering wheel. He yelled into the dust for Jonathon, and reached back to check on MacLimore. When his hand found warm sticky flesh, he jerked it away and wiped it on his trouser leg.

"Sir!" he yelled into the cloud of smoke filling the Humvee. Out the shattered front window he could see smoke rising from where the engine block had been. "Sir! Mac's hit!" he yelled again. This time he heard Jonathon gasping to his right, trying to respond. Olk tried to climb over the middle to get to Jonathon when he felt hands grab at him from behind. He heard Shipley's voice ask him if he was all right as he was pulled out of the truck. The last he saw of Jonathon, Anderson had reached his door and was applying aid. Jonathon's head was up to the sky, his mouth and eyes wide open as he gulped for air.

Olk desperately fought the hands that were forcing him to the ground, groping and prodding. "Lieutenant Garcia and Mac are still in there!" he yelled. He heard a voice tell him to calm down, that they needed to check on him to see if he was hurt, but he knew that he was all right. He thought of Jonathon gasping for air and MacLimore's leg. "Sir!" he yelled into the smoke, his eyes welling with tears. He fought the hands holding him down. "No!" he yelled at them as he writhed on the ground. "No! Let me go! Sir! Sir!" He looked up to see Hoover and Stufflet pull MacLimore out of the truck, his right leg dangling grotesquely below the knee, his pants dyed red. Olk fought with tears in his eyes, pleading to get back to the truck, until he passed out; the hit he had taken on his head had caused a concussion.

MacLimore would wake up in the hospital at Landstuhl, Germany two days later to find his right leg amputated below the knee. A piece of shrapnel had severed his popliteal, the artery that runs behind the knee, and another piece had shattered his tibia. Hoover had saved his life by applying a tourniquet to stop the massive bleeding, but the muscle and bone damage had been so catastrophic that the doctors could not save his leg. Olk did not see MacLimore again until he stepped off the plane when the battalion returned home to Fort Campbell the following February.

Air Force Captain Ben Summers and Chaplain Tyler Babigian from Edwards Air Force Base were tasked with notifying Mr. and Mrs. Juan Garcia that their son, First Lieutenant Jonathon Alejandro-Gonzalez Garcia, had been killed in the line of duty by a roadside bomb in Northern Iraq. Neighbors had seen the dark sedan pull up to the house and the two officers approach the front door in their spotless blue uniforms. Within an hour, a crowd had gathered on the front lawn. Men with crossed arms scowled at news vans that had already set up their cameras and antennas, reporting on Fresno's lost son. Women held each other as the neighborhood boys and girls stood quietly watching on the fringes, unsure of how to behave.

After a couple hours, the news vans and neighbors still out in front of the house, Mr. Garcia left his grieving wife to go talk to the cameras. His brother and sister-in-law, who lived just three streets away, told him that he didn't have to, and his brother offered to say something for him if he wanted. He sadly shook his head and said that no, he would talk to the cameras.

Mr. Garcia walked into the bathroom and splashed cold water on his face. Drying his eyes, and rubbing his shaking, calloused hands, he opened the front door and walked out to the edge of the small lawn where the men from the neighborhood had formed a perimeter where no one had been allowed to pass except family. Mr. Garcia's brother walked out with him, and stood silently behind him as he addressed the cameras and microphones that were flung in his face. He did not have a speech planned. He said that his son was killed fighting for his country, for the greatest country ever. He pointed back to the house, referring to his wife inside.

"We," he said, pausing to choke back his tears, "are very proud of our son." He nodded once, to punctuate his sincerity, and then turned and walked back to the house.

The reporters, convinced they had gotten whatever live coverage their stations would use, packed up their vans and left; there was no story, no scandal. Perhaps if he had questioned the reason for the war, attacked the administration's strategy, or asked where the ever-elusive weapons of mass destruction were, they would have been more interested in his loss. But there is simply no story behind a grieving father who refuses to sacrifice his dignity and dishonor the death of his son in front of the cameras.

The neighborhood kids moved farther down the street to play hopscotch and tag, leaving the specter of death that surrounded the house behind them. Most of the neighbors trickled away to their kitchens, where they would produce meals for the Garcias for over a month. A few of the men stayed behind, talking in hushed tones on the edge of the lawn, until the sun had set and the kids had gone inside. Someone had fetched Father Christopher, and he sat quietly on one of the wooden chairs in the corner, praying and reading Psalm 22. In her bedroom, Mrs. Garcia finally cried herself to sleep with her sister-in-law. Mr. Garcia and his brother sat up all night in the living room, drinking coffee and not talking.

Captain Summers helped Mr. and Mrs. Garcia arrange for Jonathon's body to be brought home. His casket was flown in to the Fresno airport; a single soldier had escorted it from Dover Air Force Base. A funeral detail from Edwards Air Force Base had been provided to drape the flag over the casket and bear it from the plane to the hearse. People on the plane waited and craned their necks to see the flag-draped casket carried across the tarmac while a small group of people cried and held each other as it passed.

The memorial service was held later that day at Saint Francis Catholic Church in Fresno. Word had spread quickly, and most of Jonathon's classmates from high school who were still in Fresno came to the service. Rebecca Shultz was there with her new husband, married that summer. Father Christopher gave the eulogy and a few others spoke.

When the service ended, Jonathon's body was carried out of the church into the hearse to take him to the cemetery. A majority of those at the service elected to join the long train of cars as they wound their way down the streets of the city. A circle of people dressed in black, with family members seated next to the casket, stood around while Father Christopher gave the final blessing.

Three well-synchronized shots split the still heat of the day as the seven-man funeral detail paid their final respects. The flag was lifted off the casket, silently folded, and handed to Captain Summers, who approached Mrs. Garcia with the triangular flag held softly in his gloved hands, one underneath, and the other resting firmly on top. Taking a knee before the grieving mother, he offered the flag to her, "On behalf of a grateful nation." He then rose, slowly saluted, executed a right face, and walked away.

The circle of black melted as friends and family filed by to pay their last respects. No small number of roses' lay on the soft mahogany of the casket when they had all left. Mrs. Garcia held the flag to her chest while her husband sat quietly, his calloused hands folded in his lap. After several minutes of silence, he gently put his hand on her knee, and with tears in his eyes gave her a weak smile. She nodded once and stood up. They both stood before the casket for several more minutes, neither saying anything, until Mr. Garcia placed his hand on her back to take her away. As she walked away, Mrs. Garcia placed her hand on the casket, and patted it gently. She stopped to kiss the warm wood once, the flag still pressed against her chest, and then walked away, her husband's hand placed softly on the small of her back.

That flag would form the centerpiece of what would soon develop into a sort of shrine in Jonathon's memory in the back left corner of their living room. Mrs. Garcia had found a picture of him smiling in his gray uniform from West Point, and had had it enlarged and framed. The medals he had been awarded, including the Purple Heart and Bronze Star, rested on either side of the flag. Two American flags, like the ones handed out at parades on the fourth of July, had been hung on the wall. Letters that she received from Lieutenant Colonel DaSilva, Captain Pham, Andy Walker, and others who had served with Jonathon, expressing sorrow for their loss, were placed around the flag and picture and medals.

Mr. Garcia watched his wife grieve with a patient compassion, though the memorial that she was building, which she dusted and rearranged daily, was like a ghost that sucked the life out of the house. Friends who visited found it impossible to be cheery or to talk about anything seemingly superficial in the presence of such a monument, and some started coming over less often. It was all so sad, they would say.

It took him two years to suggest to her that perhaps it was time to take the faded flags and pictures down. His biggest fear was that she would fight him—that she would accuse him of not loving his son. But instead she nodded silently and cried tears as fresh as if he had only just died. The folded flag that Captain Summers had given them was placed in the dining room, and his picture put on a small end table next to the couch. She bound the letters they had received with a rubber band and placed them in her bedside table, which she would take out and reread every now and then for the rest of her life whenever her husband was out of the house. His dad put the medals in his top dresser drawer. The two parade flags she took down and threw away, though she cried all over again when she did.

One cool fall evening, shortly after they had taken down the flags and pictures, Mr. Garcia sat out on the front steps with his brother, and spoke to him about Jonathon for the first time. He had never been one for many words, and in the two years since Jonathon died, had never once spoken openly to anyone about his son's death.

"I did not say that we should take down the pictures because I do not love Jonathon or do not miss him," he said half apologetically while his brother listened silently. "I do love my son, I miss him very much. I hope that she understands that. I understand her need to keep him alive with the flags and medals and all the letters. She is his mother. I cannot know the bond a mother feels for her son." He paused. "Did you know that she wrote to our congressman?" he asked. "She wanted to know if there was anything that could be done to prevent other young men from being killed by these IEDs. Sometimes she gets angry, and looks for anything and anyone to blame. But there is no one to blame."

He paused again and gazed silently across the street with eyes that glistened as he rubbed the arthritis out of his fingers and studied his calloused hands, the hairs starting to show flecks of gray. "Fathers should not bury their sons," he said. "But it's sons that are killed in wars, not the old men. The old men stay home with the old women and envy the passion that the young still feel and wonder when the world stole theirs. Some content themselves with the thought that war is a noble calling. Some try to ease their own conscience by saying that all war is a waste." He laughed quietly to himself and shook his head. "Who knows? But Jonathon knew the life that he chose. And even though he is my son, and I love him and miss him very much, it was still his life to choose what he wanted. As a man, I respect his decision to give his life for his country. He was a man—even though he will always be my little boy—and it was his life to choose. And what else can I do with that, as a man myself and as his father, but honor that choice and thank him for the freedom he purchased for me?" Tears filled his eyes as his brother grunted a soft affirmation and the two finished their beer.

On day one hundred and ninety-five, Jonathon's memorial ceremony was held in a dry field across from where the battalion had set up its headquarters at Q-West. Most of the battalion had formed up by companies. In front of the formation was a single rifle, the bayonet on the end of the barrel had been driven vertically into a sandbag, and a helmet rested carefully on the rifle's butt stock. A pair of dog tags hung from the pistol grip, and a pair of boots, conspicuously new, sat on the ground in front of the sandbags and the rifle.

It was the middle of the day, and it was hot. Faces glowed with sweat, and the men shifted slowly as they stood waiting to be formed up. There were six chairs off to the side in front of the formation. The Chaplain, Olk, Andy Walker, Captain Pham, and 'Colonel DaSilva sat in them quietly, waiting for the ceremony to start. There was a strong breeze that day which produced the feeling of being blown all over by a massive hairdryer, and kicked up clouds of dust that whipped across the field.

The Chaplain started the ceremony with the benediction, asking God to bless the ceremony and their efforts to honor their friend and their brother. He asked for comfort for Jonathon's family back home, and that they would know that they did not grieve alone. His prayer was short, and Olk stood up to read a piece of scripture from the bible.

A few days before, Anderson had asked Olk if he would like to speak at the service. Olk had shrugged his shoulders and looked away, mumbling that he didn't know what he would say. Anderson suggested that he could read a bible verse.

"You know how the LT always had his bible with him, even when he wasn't reading it."

Olk smiled faintly, remembering. "Yeah."

"Well, did he ever tell you what verse was his favorite?" Anderson probed.

"No," Olk shook his head.

"Well, what if you read your favorite one? I bet he'd like that."

"You think so?" Olk asked, his voice cracking, barely able to handle the incredible sadness raging inside him.

"Yeah, I really do, Olk," Anderson said. "Why don't you think about what verse you'd like to read, and I'll tell the Chaplain that you may want to read. You can always change your mind if you want, so no pressure, all right?"

"Okay sar'n," Olk had said.

Olk had come back just two days after the attack, the doctors having decided that he was fit to return to duty with just a cut on his forehead from the attack, and Anderson was nervous about how he might react to being back so quickly. Anderson knew that he and Jonathon had gotten close. And while he didn't want to push Olk too fast, he also knew that Olk really did want to say something, and that he would regret it if he didn't.

Olk walked up to the podium, a white bandage on his forehead for his cut, and nervously flipped through the pages until he found the right page. He started to read, but quickly stopped and looked at the formation.

"Lieutenant Garcia always had his bible. I'd see him in the mornings with it before we were all up. I don't know what his favorite verse was, but I bet he had a few," he stopped. "Anyway, Lieutenant Garcia was a good man and I'm gonna miss him." He stopped again—for longer this time—as he collected himself. Finding his place, he forced himself through Psalm 23, and then sat back down.

Andy Walker made his way up to the podium, patting Olk softly on the back as he passed by him. Andy Walker, who would be killed four and a half years later on his third deployment to Iraq, and would similarly have a friend of his eulogize him as he was doing now for Jonathon.

Andy had been surprised when the Chaplain had asked him if he wanted to speak at the ceremony. When he had hesitated, the Chaplain told him that he didn't have to if he didn't want to, but he knew that he and Jonathon had been friends.

"It's not that, Chaplain," Andy shook his head. He hesitated again, looking at the ground. Lifting his head, he asked, "Have you asked Sam Calhoun? I know he and Jon were real close. Don't get me wrong, I'd love to get to say something about Jon, but maybe you should ask Sam first."

The Chaplain smiled patiently and said that he had already spoken with Sam.

When Anderson had come to him earlier that morning and told him about Olk wanting to read a piece of scripture, the Chaplain had asked Anderson whether Jonathon had been particularly close to any of the other officers in the battalion. Anderson had told him that Lieutenant Garcia and Lieutenant Calhoun had become close friends since they had met in An Najaf.

The Chaplain thanked him and asked about how he and the men were doing. Anderson shrugged his shoulders a bit too quickly and looked away and mumbled that they were doing all right.

"Gotta get them back out there, though," he said, trying to hide the sadness in his eyes. "Ain't good for 'em, just sitting around thinking about it. Mac's gonna lose his leg, and every time the men look at Olk, all they see is that big white bandage on his forehead." He shook his head. "It ain't good for 'em. Gotta get 'em back out there," he said again.

"How about you?" the Chaplain probed. "How are you?"

Anderson squinted his eyes and drew himself up just enough to barely notice and said, "I gotta take care of my men, sir."

The Chaplain nodded sympathetically, and asked if maybe he could come by later that afternoon to talk to the platoon about what had happened. Anderson told him that they'd all be there, and to come by anytime he could.

After his conversation with Anderson, the Chaplain had made his way down the street to the building where Charlie Company lived. He knocked on the open door to Sam's room as he walked in, and found Sam sitting shirtless on his cot, flipping through a magazine with a naked woman on the cover.

The Chaplain saw Sam's Saint Jude medallion hanging off his dog tags. "Lost causes, huh?"

Sam didn't even look up, but just offered a distracted, "Yeah."

"You got a minute, Sam?" the Chaplain asked, reaching for a chair nearby.

Sam looked up absently from the magazine, a spark in his eye when he recognized the Chaplain in the soft green light of the room. "Yeah, Chaplain, come on in," he smiled. Sam closed the magazine and offered it to him, a smile on his lips. "Magazine?" he asked as casually as he could manage.

The Chaplain got the joke and laughed. "No thanks, I'm trying to quit."

"Suit yourself," Sam said, and opened it back up and started to flip through the worn-out pages.

After a brief silence, the whir of the pink fan oscillating and blowing hot air around the room, the Chaplain spoke. "How are you doing, Sam?" he asked, his hands folded in his lap and genuine concern in his voice.

Sam continued to flip through the pages, though the Chaplain could tell that he was not paying any attention to the pictures. Sam answered with a quick, "I'm all right, I guess."

After a couple seconds of silence, the Chaplain leaned forward. "Actually, you mind if I look at that?" he asked, indicating the magazine.

Sam was so surprised at the confident tone in the Chaplain's voice that he handed the magazine over without really thinking. The Chaplain rolled up the magazine and held it in his hands against his lap. He smiled, and Sam chuckled as he clapped his hands.

"Can I at least have it back before you leave?" he asked.

"Yeah. Probably wouldn't be a good idea for the Chaplain to be seen walking around with this."

Sam laughed and shook his head. "No, Mel, probably not," using the Chaplain's first name.

The Chaplain smiled and asked again, "So, how are you doing Sam? I know that you were pretty close to Jon—"

"Look," Sam cut him off, "I know that you're here to talk, and I appreciate you thinking of me, but I just don't feel like talking about it to anyone right now."

"Okay," the Chaplain nodded his head slowly. "Well, I wanted to see if you wanted to talk, but I also came by to ask you if you'd like to say something at Jon's ceremony. It's a couple days away, and someone gave me your name as a suggestion for a personal tribute." The Chaplain looked at Sam, who had his hands folded in front of him, his elbows on his knees, looking at the ground. A full minute passed, the room quiet but for the fan, which ticked every time it came to the far left of its oscillation.

"I really don't feel like talking about it right now, Mel. I know you're just doing your job. And I'm not angry or anything, I just don't want to talk," he said, still looking at the ground.

"That's all right, Sam," the Chaplain affirmed. "Losing someone we care about can be hard to deal with."

Sam shook his head and smiled.

"What?" the Chaplain asked, noticing his smile.

"Nothing. That just sounded so cliché, so…"

"Not real?"

Sam raised his dark eyebrows. "Yeah. But it is real. Jon's dead," he shrugged. "He's dead, and everything just keeps on going."

"Yeah," the Chaplain said softly.

A moment of silence one tick long from the fan passed between them. Sam sighed heavily. "Yeah," and nodded his head. "Hey, if you're not going to take that, can I have it back?" he asked, pointing toward the rolled-up magazine in the Chaplain's hands.

The Chaplain leaned forward and handed it back to him while he stood to go. Sam took the magazine and flipped through the pages as the Chaplain turned to go and then stopped at the doorway. "Sam," he said.

"Yeah," Sam raised his eyebrows, not looking up from his page turning.

"If you ever want to talk—"

"Yeah, thanks Mel," he interrupted. "Andy Walker and Jon were friends, too; he may want to say something."

"Thanks Sam," the Chaplain said as he walked out.

"Sure," Sam said to nobody as he continued to flip through the pages, stopping and rotating the magazine every now and then to look at a picture in the faint light.

Andy stepped up to the podium and looked at the battalion in formation, the men standing with their hands behind their backs, their caps pulled down low against the fierce sunlight.

"Lieutenant Jonathon Garcia was a good leader, a good man, and a good friend of mine," Andy started. "But there was something different about him. In all of the conversations that we had, there was always something different about the way he approached whatever the subject was. For the longest time I couldn't understand it. His paradigm for looking at the world was so different from my own that I could barely recognize it. Now I know. Jon was a believer. In people, in our world. He believed in the potential and power of good. There are people who can't not believe in those things because they are afraid of what that might mean, but Jon Garcia was neither naïve nor weak. He knew that people, and especially our world, were far from perfect, but he made a conscious decision to believe in their goodness anyway. It takes something truly extraordinary to look around at our world sometimes and still choose to believe. The son of immigrants, he was proud to serve his country, but his patriotism was not some shallow, self-conceited display of bravado. He believed in serving his country because he believed in the idea and the potential of free people. That if you give a man a choice, he will do what is right. And Jon believed that that choice was worth his life."

Andy paused, looking back down at his notes before he looked up again. "We have a tendency, after a man dies, to canonize him, to make him out to be more than he was. I think that Jon would ask that we not do that to him. He was as imperfect as the rest of us, but he knew that it's our imperfection that allows us to see what we may still become. That men should be free, and that we can be good."

Andy paused again and looked down for a brief minute at the podium.

"Jon, you were a good man and a good soldier. Our prayers are with your family. Rest in peace, brother." Andy turned and quickly walked away from the podium, brushing past Captain Pham as he walked up.

Captain Pham talked about the first impression he had of Jonathon when he had reported to the company. He talked about his dedication, his sense of service, and his desire to always do his best in everything. He said that Jonathon was a great leader in the company, and that his absence would be felt for a long time. When he talked about how well-liked Jonathon had been, he saw Sam, standing in the back left behind the formation, look down to the ground. He finished quickly by challenging the battalion to remember Jonathon's service, and to honor him with theirs.

'Colonel DaSilva stepped up to the podium after shaking hands with Captain Pham. He had sat up late the night before trying to figure out what he was going to say the next day. He had learned long ago that unit memorial ceremonies are not really for the deceased, but rather that they serve as a vehicle to heal the unit, bring it together, and move it forward again. He struggled with wanting to eulogize Jonathon and knowing that what he needed to talk about was something less personal than he wanted. He needed to encourage the battalion, to speak to the men about their fears in the face of the loss, to remind them of their sense of duty, and to instill in them the sense that what they were doing was worth sacrifice. That freedom was worth sacrifice. That is the role of the commander in the midst of a loss to his unit: his task is to lead them through it, to help them heal, and to imbue and remind them of their calling. It seems a little cold, but the leader who truly loves his men sets aside his selfish desire to share his pain and sense of personal loss—for the loss of a man under his command is personal—and reminds them of the virtues of a life devoted to honor and courage and sacrifice.

Those are the things that 'Colonel DaSilva spoke to his men about.

When 'Colonel DaSilva was finished, the Chaplain rose and spoke to the men about fear and God's promise to deliver men from fear and death. He alluded to what Olk had read and said that those who hope in God will have a table prepared for them, and that their cups will overflow.

In the middle of his message, the Chaplain saw Sam turn and walk away.

When the Chaplain had finished, Sergeant Major Plowman called the formation to attention, and the men snapped smartly into rigid position.

First Sergeant Allen, standing in front of Delta Company, executed an about face and faced his company. In a loud, clear voice that punctuated distinctly in the hot air, he called the role.

"Staff Sergeant Hoover!" he barked.

"Here, First Sergeant!" Hoover answered loudly, though his voice cracked just a bit.

"Sergeant First Class Anderson!" Allen called.

"Here, First Sergeant!" Anderson answered, swallowing hard afterwards.

"Lieutenant Garcia!" Allen barked.

There was no answer from among the formation, only the sound of the wind scraping along the ground.

"First Lieutenant Garcia!" Allen barked again, this time more forcibly, as if he could will him back into formation with his brothers. But still there was no answer.

"First Lieutenant Jonathon Garcia!" he called, more somberly now, and the silence that answered him was deafening and tears flooded into the eyes of even the hardest man there.

Allen nodded his head, as if to affirm the absence, and then turned back around to the sergeant major, shaking his head once.

a novel

"Pree-sent arms!" Sergeant Major Plowman ordered in a loud and sharp voice, and the men's arms slowly rose in unison to a salute.

Rifle shots split the air three times, and a bugle sounded from somewhere behind them. The sun beat on the formation of men standing in dirty uniforms as the shrill notes of "Taps" echoed through the air, its unsung words ricocheting through their bones.

Day is done, gone the sun
From the lakes, from the hills, from the sky
All is well, safely rest, God is nigh.

END OF BOOK I

195

END OF BOOK I

BOOK II

BOOK II

CHAPTER 4

It was late September now, and the sting had been taken out of the heat of the days, though summer stubbornly clung to its hold on the weather. Though it was no longer as hot as it had been in July and August, it was obvious that fall had not yet come, and it felt as if the earth itself was tired of the relentless beating of the sun, and had yielded every last drop of moisture it had left, only to find itself to have been cheated of the expected return. The men could feel it too. Summer ought to be over, the heat ought to be subsiding. It should rain.

Then finally, at the end of the month, when the men had forgotten what the feel of frozen air in their throats felt like, when winter was a fairy tale, when the ground itself had long been stripped of any remembrance of water and seemed to be blowing away beneath them, Fall arrived.

It came over two days, in the form of a sandstorm borne of a wind from the north that brought the chill of cooler climates with it. For two days the world was brown. And then, on the third day, the wind stopped and the particles of dust and sand fell to the ground and covered everything—no matter how well-protected—in an inch-thick layer of fine powder.

When they walked outside that third morning, they were met with the welcome warmth of the sun against the chilly morning air. Faint wisps of breath escaped their mouths, barely discernable, but there. And something inside all of them relaxed; summer's long sabotage was over.

Sam stepped out of his small room through his homemade door into the warm sunshine of that first fall morning. The chill of the air, though only mild in reality, caused goose bumps to race over his bare skin. It was cooler now than it had been since the beginning of May, and for the first time since then, instead of shrinking away from the sun like its rays were arrows that pierced the skin with their heat, he stood absorbing its welcomed warmth.

He was unshaven, and not just from the previous day; it had been several days since he had last shaved. Jonathon's memorial ceremony had been two weeks ago, and since then he had taken to shaving only when his five o'clock shadow—as he called it—started to more resemble a full-grown beard. His dark hair was long even for normal standards, and was badly tussled from the night before, sticking out in every direction. He ran his hand through it thoughtfully as he scratched his stomach and yawned. He walked over to the side of the building where three long metal tubes had been driven into the ground to serve as urinals and relieved himself.

As he walked back around the corner, Amber Gibson had just stepped out of his room, her uniform having been hastily thrown on. She was quickly trying to throw her hair into a ponytail to get it out of her puffy and red eyes.

"Morning," Sam said with a playful smile. "Have I ever told you how beautiful you are in the mornings?"

Obviously not appreciating his joke, she threw a scowl at him which quickly changed into a painful smile. The brightness of the sun stung her eyes, and she shielded them with her hand. "I am definitely not beautiful right now," she said. "I gotta get going."

"How about a cup of coffee before you leave?" he asked and then wished he hadn't.

"I'd love to, Sam, but I really need to get going," she smiled. Sam was right, she was beautiful, even when hung over in the morning.

"All right," he nodded. "I'll see you later."

"Bye Sam. Thanks." She smiled at him and then turned toward the building on the far side of the field from where Sam lived with Charlie Company.

Sam ran his fingers through his hair again as he watched her walk away, and then went back inside to the welcome dim light of his room. There was a half-inch of dust over everything from the storm. He sighed heavily and picked the bed sheets up off the floor and took them outside to shake the dust off them. Walking back inside, he reached for the light-blue broom he had bought from a local and started to sweep the dust off the shelves and out the door. There was so much dirt in the room that the flimsy fibers of the broom couldn't push all of it. Once he was satisfied that he had the room as clean as he was capable of at the moment, he flopped down on his chair with his hands crossed behind his head, staring at the ceiling. The pot of coffee he had started when he woke up caught his eye, and he was just pouring himself a cup into a mug that said "OPERATION IRAQI FREEDOM" with a jet coming out of the 'Q", when he heard a light rap on his open door and saw the Chaplain stick his head in.

"Morning Sam," the Chaplain said in his consistently friendly voice.

"Hey Mel," Sam returned, turning back around to his pot of coffee. "Can I get you a cup?" He smiled at the thought of what the Chaplain would have seen had he arrived just a half hour ago.

"That'd be great, thanks," Mel said, a surprised look on his face.

"Well, don't get too excited about it; I figure the way you keep coming around, you either have something to say, or I'm about to become another victim of the Church's affinity for young men," Sam said as he offered Mel the chair and a cup, and sat down carefully on his cot. Mel laughed quietly to himself and shook his head.

"We prefer women in the Episcopalian Church, Sam," Mel said smiling and blowing on the steam rising from his coffee. Sam just grunted and sipped on his coffee. Mel looked around the small room and noticed the almost-empty bottle of Jack Daniels lying on its side on the table next to Sam's cot. "You know, you could get in a lot of real trouble if you got caught with that by the wrong person," he said, indicating the bottle.

Sam managed an "Oh well," as he picked up the bottle and slid it underneath his cot, the top still visible from where Mel sat. Sam sat still, both hands cupped around his mug, sipping and blowing on the hot liquid, his slightly red eyes on the wall in front of him. Mel sat there quietly for a few minutes, his sharp clear eyes studying Sam's posture and appearance. Mel finally broke the silence.

"You know, you look pretty... terrible," he said. "Awful, actually," he added, raising his eyebrows and nodding his head.

"Thanks Mel," Sam replied quickly without looking at him. He took a sip of his coffee and asked, "You always so honest?"

Mel shrugged his shoulders casually and said, "It's what I do."

Sam turned his head and saw a slight smile on Mel's lips. About to say something, Sam changed his mind, and went back to sipping his coffee. Another few minutes passed with nothing but the sounds of the two men sipping lazily from their mugs.

Having finished his first cup, Mel got up to pour himself another. Sitting back down, he looked at Sam again. Sam's dark hair was tussled, his face unshaven, there were slight bags under his eyes, and the shirt he wore was obviously not clean. He looked quickly around the room: the messy piles of paper, the coffee stains on the handmade desk, socks stiff with sweat, and dirty clothes spread all over the floor. Mel smelled a stiff musty odor of unwashed sheets and dirty clothes. And he was pretty sure he smelled something else as he shook his head and laughed quietly to himself.

Sam looked up from his coffee when he heard the soft laugh. "What's that?" he asked.

"Nothing," the Chaplain shook his head, the laughter starting to fade from his throat. Then, gathering himself, he said, "You know, I've always liked bells." Sam just raised his eyes and braced himself for the inevitable sermon. A brief silence followed. "Of course, the bells on horses and that you hear in the bell choir are nice, but that's not the kind I'm talking about. I like those big, beautiful, brass bells that you find in the old churches. I've always wondered what it is about those old bells. They have that deep, solid sound to them, as if their sound actually had substance, you know what I mean?"

"Bells, huh?" was Sam's curt reply.

"Yeah," Mel laughed to himself, "bells."

"No bells here Mel."

Mel sighed. "Yeah," he said, sorrow in his voice. Another brief silence followed. "What do you think it is about bells, Sam?"

Sam swallowed a sip of coffee. "Why, I don't know, Mel, what do you think it is about bells?"

If Mel recognized the patronization, he didn't betray it. Instead, he only sat there for a few more silent sips of coffee. Then suddenly, "I think it's the challenge that they seem to send out. The sound of a big brass bell is so strikingly different from any other sound, isn't it? Penetrating, like it can go right through you, almost break you up inside, you know? Growing up in Illinois, the church we went to had a bell up in the tower, and our pastor would ring it on Sunday mornings before the service. Such a sound it made, Sam," he said, as if the recollection was almost too much to believe. "The way it shot through the air, through the buildings, like a challenge. As if it were saying in every ring that the last note in our lives is not one of despair, that hope can conquer our darkest moments and transform them into glory."

"If you're here to talk to me about Jon, or why he died, save your breath," Sam said firmly, his eyes looking up from his coffee cup and into Mel's.

The levity and wonder vanished from Mel's face, replaced with a severe sadness that surprised Sam. "No Sam," he shook his head, "I'm not here to tell you why Jon died. That's a role I'm all too ill-suited for; it's beyond me, and I wouldn't dare attempt to cheapen that loss with abstractions. Any attempt to explain death, though it may satisfy the intellect, does precious little to comfort the soul. Do you really think I would come to a grieving friend and try to comfort him with words like 'God's will?'" He paused, shaking his head slowly, the sadness still in his eyes. He said softly as the sadness slowly melted, "But you know, Sam, I'll tell you what God's will is.

God's will for us is life. He is the author of life, not of death, and his will for us is life to the fullest."

"Was that God's will for Jon, Mel?" Sam interjected, a thin veil of sarcasm trying to hide the honesty behind the question. "Life to the fullest?"

Mel sighed. "You and I must believe that Jon is no longer suffering, Sam. So the point is not to fixate on Jon's suffering and try to work that out for him. It's already been worked out, and neither of us were consulted at any point along the way. What is left for us, however, is to work out our own suffering in the wake of his death. To sit and ask ourselves why Jon died is a subtle trap that may distract us from what God really desires for us: to allow our suffering and loss to sanctify us."

Sam started slightly at the last part. "So what? Ying and yang and everything balances out in the end, like some kind of fucked up metaphysical equation?" Sam said calmly. "And that good can come out of Jon's death, and that maybe even he died so that good would come out of it?"

Mel frowned and shook his head. "You know better than that, Sam." He paused. "No, I'm not saying at all that the reason Jon died is so we could benefit from it. Not at all. What I am saying is that Jon died, and he didn't die because God killed him or even because God allowed him to—" Sam made a movement as if to speak. "—No, listen to me, Sam. Jon died because a man set off a bomb on the side of a road. That is why Jon died. And now the only response that's been left to us is what we will do with that for ourselves. No. You and I must remember that God's capacity for mercy is greater than our capacity for destruction. We must remember that."

He paused, looking down at his coffee mug. "Sam, what I really wanted to tell you today is that there is in fact an enormous difference between merely suffering, and suffering with grace and dignity. Too often we yield to our suffering because it's so much easier than fighting it, and we content ourselves with the thought that simply to suffer is enough. But it's not, Sam! To suffer with grace, to confront our questions and challenges head-on, on our knees when necessary, that is what we must do. The pain that we encounter in this life is not an abstract solution to the human condition, or a metaphysical variable meant to explain our existence, but a personal exercise in growth. To merely suffer, Sam, animals do that. But you and I have the divine spark, we are made in the image of God, and we are called beyond that. And that is why I love the sound of a bell ringing through the morning air: because it breaks up that animal instinct inside me to simply survive and reminds me that I am more than just a reaction to the things in this world. That, in fact, we have the capacity to be a force of nature, that all of us are kings if we are only willing to bear the weight of the crown."

Sam had watched as Mel had talked, and had noticed that all the while, it had been as if a fever were raging inside him. Now, apparently exhausted with the effort, Mel slumped in his chair, his eyes toward the cooling cup of coffee he held in both hands. Sam ran his fingers through his hair in the slightly awkward silence that seemed to hang in the room. He was just about to break it when Mel stood up suddenly.

"You want another cup, Mel?" Sam asked, a little unsure.

"No. Thanks, though." Mel smiled rather weakly. "I hope you'll think about what I said," he offered as he set his cup down and stood in the doorway.

Sam nodded, "I will Mel, thanks. Say hi to your wife for me, huh?"

Mel smiled sadly. "Yeah, yesterday she told me she was leaving me," he said as he stepped out the door, leaving Sam stunned and alone in the small room.

* * *

All religions depend upon an essential myth and gain the passion and faith of their followers by convincing them to place their trust in its historical occurrence and its relevance to their lives. The role that the essential myth plays in any religion's theology is to paint a premise for the human condition, and set up the solution that its theology will propose. Therefore, God created the earth in 168 hours, dried up the Red Sea, the Son of God was born to a virgin girl... the list goes on. The role that the essential myth plays in man's various faiths is an important one, and should not be dismissed out of hand. The myth could prove true, after all.

The point that too many miss, however, is the purpose behind the essential myth: to instill and sustain faith. Men get so wrapped up in debating the legitimacy of God creating the world in seven days, that they forget the entire point of the story: that after God was finished creating, he said that it was "good," man and all creation lived in peace with each other and with him. The purpose of the myth, therefore, is not to breed some kind of arrogant and destructively narrow-minded hold on something that simply cannot be proven, but rather to remind men that their original vocation in the world was one of peace. It helps to explain what the major monotheistic traditions all claim, that man has fallen from his original role as God intended for him, with each proposing a slightly different path toward mankind reclaiming that station. But men get so intent upon killing and silencing all who would dare question the historicity of their essential myth, that they forget its true purpose. And that is when their faith ceases to be a vehicle of healing and redemption, and begins to be a road that leads to their destruction.

Ramadan is the ninth month of the Islamic Calendar, and is considered one of the most holy months of the year. Muslims believe that Muhammad received the revelations from God that later became the Quran, Islam's holy book, during the month of Ramadan in the year 610 A.D. "The night of determination" is celebrated on the twenty-sixth day of Ramadan, and is the night where Muslims generally agree the revelations were provided to Muhammad.

The month begins when the first crescent moon is sighted on the evening following the new moon and can last for twenty-nine or thirty days, depending on the lunar cycle. The holy month of Ramadan is celebrated by a month long fast, where food is only taken twice each day, once before the sun rises (the *souhoor*), and once after the sun sets (the *aftar*). For the two meals, sweet dishes such as dates, olives, and cheeses are all enjoyed. During the day, however, Muslims abstain from food and drink. The apparent dichotomy between enjoying sweets while at the same time abstaining from food for such a long period serves the function of practicing gratitude: we are to celebrate God's gifts by not indulging in excess.

Eid al Fitr is the celebration that marks the end of Ramadan, and is celebrated on the first day of the new moon in Shawwal, the month following Ramadan. *Eid al Fitr* is a day to be with family and friends, to worship and to give alms to the poor, and is the Islamic equivalent to Christmas.

Ramadan began on October twenty-seventh, lasted through most of November, and was accompanied by a consistent increase in attacks and IEDs. During Ramadan, the battalion was dealt another blow by the death of one of its former officers. Lieutenant Jason Haley had served as the engineer platoon leader throughout most of the battalion's deployment, and had just recently been transferred up to brigade headquarters up in Mosul. He was killed by an IED on a back road outside the base there on Halloween day. The feeling by all was that the tide was changing; there was a swell from somewhere down below them that was gaining force. The battalion had not suffered one death throughout the invasion and subsequent fight in An Najaf. And now that the actual "war" was over, they had lost five men in as many months. The tide was changing, and the men started to count the days until they would be home. Rumor was that they would be home in February. That was three more months. Three more men.

With the exception of the relatively slight increase in the enemy threat, life moved on as normal for Sam for the next several weeks. He developed a strict routine that he found made the days and weeks go by quickly. His liaisons with Amber even became predictable: Wednesday and Saturday nights. The regular supply of Jack Daniels that he had ensured through an interpreter out in Qayyarah provided him with enough entertainment at night to pass the time. On Thursday and Sunday afternoons, after Amber had left and he had had his meeting with Captain Daniels and his supply clerk, Sam would walk into his room, close the door, and drink until he passed out. Like clockwork. Like a cycle that turned inexorably toward some unknown, and unthought-of (and uncared-for) end.

The letters from Rachel kept coming. He got one at least once every two weeks. In her letters she talked about her job as a waitress at the Outback in town. She talked about the news, about the upcoming season, and—Sam's favorite part—she told him how Claire was growing and the new things she was learning. Rachel sent pictures of the two of them at the riverwalk downtown, at the Nashville Zoo, and random pictures of Claire around their apartment. He put the pictures of Claire up on his wall, and when someone would come in and ask about the beautiful, smiling little girl in the pictures, the only answer they got was, "That's Claire." Each time he received one of Rachel's letters, he would open up the bottle of Jack Daniels, and take out a pen and paper and begin a letter that inevitably only lasted through the first paragraph and always ended with "I'm sorry." Every time he got to that point, he would tear up the paper and throw it in the trash, and focus on the bottle, which he found much easier than writing her.

Once, he received a letter from her on a Wednesday, and got so drunk, that by the time Amber came over he could barely speak, let alone get undressed. Which, needless to say, did not make her very happy. When she saw the open letter from Rachel on his desk, and put two and two together, she was even less happy, and proceeded to call him many unflattering names, some of which Sam, in his drunken stupor, thought were quite funny. Unable to handle the apparent insult of the man she was sleeping with getting drunk after reading a letter from his old girlfriend, compounded with him having the insensitivity to laugh when she was so mad she wanted to cry, she reached out and slapped him hard across the face and stormed out before she had to suffer the further indignity of letting him see her cry.

They did not see each other for two weeks after that. Then one day at dinner, Sam saw her sitting with a couple of the girls from her company in the dining facility, and walked over and sat down, smiling and saying hi. The girls scowled at him, and picked up their plates and left the two of them alone.

Amber was intent upon her peas, and was not looking at him.

"Look," Sam started. When Amber still didn't look at him, he said, "Amber, look, I'm sorry." That got her to look at him.

"Do you still love her, Sam?" she asked him, her eyes cold and accusatory.

He shook his head and lied. "No, but you have to understand that we were together for a long time before we deployed. Something like that just isn't that easy to walk away from, you know?" He paused. "I know I hurt you, and I'm sorry."

Her eyes softened and Sam thought that he had done rather well.

Their liaisons became frequent again, as the days got shorter and shorter and the rains came more and more often. New green grass was starting to grow from the fertile ground, long dormant through the heat of the summer, but coming to life with the deluge of water, and the landscape changed dramatically. The brown hills were carpeted with new grass and wildflowers bloomed. Shepherds led their flocks across fields of green, and the sheeps' wool lost the ugly brown they had carried through the dry months. Their wool coats shone with a white that was picturesque as they grazed the fields among the wildflowers. At times, it could have been described as beautiful, if the men had the capacity in the midst of their circumstances to call anything beautiful.

Sam sat outside company headquarters in Qayyarah one day when the sun was shining and warm against the cool air, looking up at the surrounding hills around the oil refinery where the battalion had made their base for the area. Captain Daniels, his company commander, was inside talking with 'Colonel DaSilva and the battalion's intelligence officer, Captain Steve Taylor. Sam had the impression that he didn't need to be present for the meeting, so he had stepped outside, found a chair in the sunshine, and was getting some sun on his bare chest. When they walked back out, 'Colonel DaSilva smiled patiently at Sam's lounging in the sun.

"Sam," 'Colonel DaSilva said as he climbed into his truck.

"Mornin', sir," Sam replied. "How's it going?"

"All right, except that it's two in the afternoon," 'Colonel DaSilva replied with a smile.

Sam looked at his watch. "Hmm. Time flies when you're having fun, sir."

Captain Taylor walked by and let out a condescending "hmmph" at the young officer sunbathing in the open while there were bad guys all around that could just pick him off. Sam thought that Captain Taylor was kind of an asshole but had decided that he liked him anyway—or perhaps because of it. He enjoyed the flagrantly morbid spin he would put on his enemy analysis in his briefs. Captain Taylor had made himself famous when he had put together a spreadsheet that he labeled "Your Likelihood of Surviving Your Year in Iraq" at one of the pre-deployment briefings before the battalion had left. His projections had not been promising, but they did make everyone laugh. And so far, the battalion was doing much better than he had predicted.

Sam gave 'Colonel DaSilva a casual two-fingered salute as they drove away, and returned his focus on the sunshine and the hills outside the camp. Captain Daniels walked out a few minutes after they left, and called out to Sam to come see him.

Sam came in a minute later, still without a shirt, his dog tags with the Saint Jude medallion catching slightly on the bulk of black hair on his chest.

"Sam," Captain Daniels began when Sam had sat down. "The commander and the S-2 were in here talking about a target that Charlie Company is going to go after here in a few weeks."

Sam raised his eyebrows. "A few weeks from now? Why are they telling us now?" Usually, as soon as a target was positively identified, the battalion would kick out an order for one of the company's to go do a "snatch 'n grab," as they were called, as soon as they could execute, usually within twenty-four hours. "Must be somebody important?" Sam asked.

"Well, yeah, he is, and the S-2 still wants some time to collect a little more before we execute. Look, Sam, I'm gonna tell you this because I know that you and Lieutenant Garcia were friends, and I know his death has hit you pretty hard." Sam's eyebrows lowered and his eyes shifted around the room, thinking.

"This guy we're gonna go after had something to do with Jon?" he asked.

"Sam, listen to me. I'm gonna tell you who it is, but this is absolutely top secret, you understand?"

"Yessir."

"The man we're going after is Abdul Yousif Mahmoud."

"Who's that, sir?"

"You may know him better as Marie."

"Marie?" Sam asked. He thought back to a conversation he had had with Jonathon after one of their meetings, how Jonathon had always seemed so enlivened after he had met with the man. His heart started pounding in his chest and his breathing got a little more shallow.

"Yeah. Sam, listen to me, I know that you have a personal interest in this, and that's why I told you. I thought it might do you some good to know that we're going after the guy behind the attack that killed Lieutenant Garcia. So I shouldn't need to remind you how absolutely vital it is that we don't talk about this at all until, and even if, Battalion gives us the order."

Sam nodded his head slowly, his eyes still darting around the room. "Yeah sir, I got it. When do you think we'll do it?" he asked.

Captain Daniels sat back in his chair. "I would say in a few weeks. After Thanksgiving. Sam, do not talk to anyone about this, you got it?"

"Yessir." Sam stood to leave and Captain Daniels pulled a map over on his desk. When he got to the door, Sam turned back. "Hey sir?"

"Yeah Sam?" Captain Daniels looked up from his map.

"Thanks for telling me, sir,"

"Okay." Captain Daniels nodded.

Sam walked out of the room back into the sunshine, his mind racing.

* * *

The holiday season approached the men like a thunderstorm crawling across the desert, a huge, dark cloud that flashed streaks of lightning against their world. They could see it coming for a long time, but unlike the holiday season at home, where people lengthen each holiday with decorations and lights and trees, this holiday season for them would reduce those days back to their most elemental. The day itself would matter, but not much else, and would blow over in a day like the storm, leaving only the short memory, like the little drops of water that drip off the roof onto the ground. All it really meant to each of them was that this time next year they would hopefully be home.

Spending the holiday season in a war away from home provided ample opportunity for the men to sink into what may be the sorriest of conditions and the hardest to climb out of. Not only does self-pity, by its unrelenting negativity, steal that sense of purpose and optimism that fuels men as human beings, but it goes even further by robbing them of a sense of hope that things will ever improve. Mankind was not meant to wallow in the dirt; they were meant to rise up and to overcome, but self-pity puts them back on all fours with the minks and muskrats.

The dining facility celebrated in style on Thanksgiving Day. The long rows of tables that lined the floor were covered with white and orange and red table cloths. Paper carve-outs of turkeys and pumpkins were spread out over the tables. Huge signs hung on the enormous walls reading "Happy Thanksgiving" and "Happy Holidays." Men bowed their heads over plates stacked high with slices of turkey, ham, roast beef, yams, potatoes, green beans, and pie. One young soldier actually cried when a first sergeant from another company in another battalion smiled and told him that yes, he could have two pieces of pumpkin pie if he wanted; he could even have three. Those officers throughout the brigade who were not out on a mission stood behind the serving line and served out huge spoonfuls of food with a laugh and a joke.

Most of Bravo Company was still out on the pipeline. When two of his trucks full of thanksgiving chow sank up to their doors in the quicksand-like mud, the Charlie Company XO, Carter Olearnick, told those with him to shoulder the containers and move out. He said it'd be a cold day in hell before his boys didn't get to eat Thanksgiving dinner. Lieutenant Olearnick was a very big man—everyone in the company called him "Ox"—so no one argued. And when the men in the company, sitting in their positions that they'd been in now for two months, saw him and his gang slugging their way through the mud with their thanksgiving dinner being drug and carried on their backs, Lieutenant Olearnick became a certifiable hero. Those men, cold and wet and filthy, huddling in holes dug into the muddy ground, could have sworn in that moment that it was the best Thanksgiving they had ever had. And years later, when they were old men, and their grandchildren sat on their laps after Thanksgiving dinner, they would tell the story about that Thanksgiving with a satisfied smile and soft inner sigh as they reflected back on the path their lives had taken, and something would come to rest inside them.

The whole planning process for the raid to snatch Mahmoud had begun a week before Thanksgiving. Intelligence from different sources, informants, and agencies was all being sifted through to determine when he would be in a location suitable for a quick, non-lethal abduction.

The non-lethal part was what made the whole planning process so painful. Going into an operation with the intent to destroy everything in sight was always much easier, but when the intent behind the operation was a specific individual who held key information, or a key piece of infrastructure that would require extensive sensitive sight exploitation, then the operation had to become more surgical in nature, and therefore required much more careful and deliberate planning. The intelligence officers at Division and Brigade were literally drooling over the chance to interrogate the man who had been given the dubious honor of being labeled as the Division's High Value Individual Number Three, meaning that Mahmoud was the third most important person to the enemy's ability to threaten the division's mission to provide a safe and stable environment for the people of Iraq.

The entire targeting process had started months ago, long before Captain Pham had told Jonathon and his platoon to patrol the region around the town of Al Sharqi. The only indication, up to that point, that there was anything of specific importance in Al Sharqi was when the Brigade Commander had told 'Colonel DaSilva to make sure that the town of Al Sharqi and the surrounding area had a unit assigned specifically to it. 'Colonel DaSilva was able to read from that that there was something important there, and had simply suggested to Captain Pham that Lieutenant Garcia would be a good choice for the area. Captain Pham was not about to contradict his commander's very clear suggestion, and besides, Peter Pham was one of those rare men who did not insist on his prerogative as commander to make a decision simply because he could. If the Battalion Commander thought that Jonathon should be in Al Sharqi, then that was the end of the story.

One of Jonathon's reports, in which he described a well-dressed, well-spoken man who had been educated in France, had brought the full attention of the intelligence officers at Brigade and Division to the tiny town of Al Sharqi. Once they had decided that the man with the sparkling eyes and white *dish-dasha* was in fact the man they were looking for, two men from 1st Battalion, 5th Special Forces Group, dressed in arab garb, approached a small, toothless man from the village with an offer one day when he was in Makhmur.

Gently coming from behind, they ushered him into a small store that had been vacated and secured by the rest of their unseen team. The two men were brief and intense, with very little exchange of pleasantries. In exchange for information about HVI #3, including accomplices, meeting habits, and modes of transportation, they would offer the man one thousand dollars a month in Iraqi dinar, including twenty-five thousand dollars if the information he provided led to the capture of HVI #3. When the man hesitated only a moment at the offer, one of the men shot back immediately, doubling the offer to two thousand a month, and fifty thousand if he were captured. The villager, missing ten teeth and dressed in an old, dirty-blue *dish-dasha* was stunned. The two men glanced at each other and took his silence as accepting their offer. One of them nodded to the other, who reached out and handed the toothless man a roll of different and varying-sized bills, from one hundred to five hundred dinar notes. Offering a quick, *"Ma'salaama,"* they turned and left the man alone in the building and were gone.

Over the next several months, though the man never knew where they came from, or how they always knew where he would be, he was intercepted and pried for information, which, after he had received the second roll of two thousand dollars, and been assured that he himself was not the target, he gave freely. The unpredictable pattern of his meetings with the two men served its purpose well: it communicated to him that though in fact he was not the target, he was being watched very closely, and was therefore forced to assume that he could be killed all too easily if he double-crossed them.

The truth was that he had no allegiance to HVI #3. Jassim Khalil, as he knew the man by, had simply appeared in Al Sharqi with a few other men one day in April and made himself at home as if he had always lived there. Khalil and the others with him had instantly inserted themselves into the daily life of the village, though they never spoke of where they came from. The men from the village assumed, of course, that they were somehow associated with the Ba'ath Party, and were simply looking for a place to hide from the Americans. And given that the men seemed to have plenty of money and were very generous to the people in Al Sharqi, they had accepted them rather quickly as part of their village. Baghdad and the Ba'ath Party and "Shock and Awe" were a long way from Al Sharqi.

It took the Special Forces team weeks to coordinate the signal plan with the informant. After analyzing HVI #3's habits for a couple of months, they determined that he could be counted on to be in his house in Al Sharqi on Wednesday nights after ten pm. The operation was then set in motion.

Sam, Captain Daniels, and the platoon leaders sat in the dimly lit Tactical Operations Center. The taste of dust rose lazily from the ground as they shifted in their seats while 'Colonel DaSilva and Captain Taylor briefed them all on their piece of the plan. Captain Taylor spent a lot of time specifically covering the importance of HVI

#3 being taken alive and his direct and unquestionable contribution to the enemy mission.

The insurgent chain of command was completely unlike the American one, in that there was no chain of command, but rather a network of individual cells of operators. HVI #3 was the head of the insurgency in North-Eastern Iraq, charged with planning, coordinating, arming, and financing the insurgency in that area. The way it worked was relatively simple, and very effective in ensuring the anonymity of the men themselves. There were only a handful of men who knew who Mahmoud was, let alone that he even existed. He had three lieutenants who worked specifically for him, each with their own areas, which were determined by the presence or absence of American forces, and who could easily be shifted somewhere else. These three men each had an operator, a financier, and an armorer, none of whom knew any of the others. Each of those men had specific men that they in turn would go to in order to either finance, arm, or execute an attack. The actual fighters themselves were simply groups of one to five men who would receive orders to conduct a specific attack, or to simply start executing small attacks at their own discretion, then another man would come pay them, and another would tell them where to get the materiel they would need. The men who carried out the attacks did not know the men who they found themselves working for, or where they came from, or who they were getting their orders from. Nor did they know of the other cell that was active just down the road. The American military was just starting to dissect the way the enemy was organized and operating, and it was starting to get nervous. Here was an enemy that was very well organized, financed, and armed, and in order to be destroyed, would have to be fought at each cell level. Or, if they were lucky, they could find a key player like HVI #3, and interrupt the process.

After Captain Taylor was done with his briefing, Sam raised his hand and asked whether HVI #3 had had anything to do with the attack that had killed Jonathon.

Captain Taylor paused briefly before answering, and shot a quick look toward 'Colonel DaSilva, who nodded his head just slightly in assent. "Indirectly," answered Captain Taylor. "You see, Mahmoud had told one of his lieutenants—who we are also tracking, by the way—in charge of the area around Qayyarah to start conducting attacks on convoys using IEDs. His lieutenant, in turn, contacted his operator and told him to tell the cells operating in that area to begin attacks. He told his financier to start paying these men, and his armorer to ensure they had access to the materiel they would need. So, no, Mahmoud is not the man who killed Lieutenant Garcia, but he is the man ultimately responsible for the IED that hit his truck."

"Why?" asked Sam.

"Why? Well, we believe that it's part of a larger operation meant to distract us from the location of the head of Al Qaeda in Iraq, or AQIZ, who is Corps' HVI #1. If they can cause enough of our focus to be shifted to specific areas, then we'll have to shift focus away from other areas where he may be hiding and running his operations."

"Holy shit," one of the platoon leaders sitting behind Captain Daniels muttered.

Captain Taylor beamed. "Yeah, the enemy is smart. But catching HVI #3 is going to be huge. Of course, we'd all like to see him dead, but the information he can provide will literally be invaluable. That's why it's so important that we don't kill him. Understand?"

Most of the men seated in front of him nodded their agreement.

Charlie Company had David Carver's platoon from Delta Company attached to them for the operation. Captain Pham had thought it wise not to send Jonathon's old platoon to support Charlie on the mission, and David had volunteered anyway. He and Jonathon had gone to West Point together, and though they were never real close friends, they had known each other for over six years, and he was glad to be involved in catching the guy that had had something to do with Jonathon's death.

There would be three CH-47 Chinook helicopters, holding forty-two men each, used to move the bulk of Charlie Company, and four UH-60 Blackhawks which would be used to move David's platoon and sling-load his four guntrucks underneath. Additionally, Captain Daniels had two OH-45 Kiowa helicopters that would serve as a scout weapons team in order to help seal off and observe the town from above.

The operation was a relatively simple one: David's platoon would fly in first and have a Blackhawk drop each of his trucks at one of the four roads that led out of the town, creating a cordon, in effect sealing it off. David and his men had been training for a few days after they had received the warning about the mission, and could now get their trucks and guns up and functional in less than two minutes after being dropped off. During that time, the two Kiowas would fly overhead to track anyone fleeing the town. The Chinooks would be one minute behind the Blackhawks, and would touch down in a field to the east of Al Sharqi.

The town had been separated into three east-west running sectors, one for each of Captain Daniels' three platoons. Using satellite imagery, every road had been given a name to help control the platoons as they moved, and each building had been numbered. They expected HVI #3 to be in building number twelve, located in the middle of town and therefore in the middle of Second Platoon's sector. The platoons would all advance west along their sectors, clearing each house as they went and ensuring that one platoon did not get ahead of another. Captain Daniels would travel with Second Platoon, the first sergeant would move with Third Platoon in the southern sector, and Sam would be with First Platoon to the north. The Chinooks and Blackhawks would remain on station, circling to the south for one hour before they would have to return to base for fuel. But they belonged to Captain Daniels until the operation was over, and would return as soon as he needed them.

A virtual encyclopedia of imagery, maps, and sketches were handed out, along with several different pictures of HVI #3 and his five known aliases. Sam thumbed through the pages and was impressed with the amount of effort that had gone into the plan. He had been around long enough, however, to know that a good plan was just that: a good plan. Inevitably, something would go wrong that would throw a wrench into all those products, and the operation would take on a life of its own. Sam and the men in Charlie Company all knew that they had the best commander in the brigade though, and they knew that whenever whatever was going to go wrong went wrong, that Brent Daniels would get things going right again.

The briefing over, they all walked back down the road to their building. The company order would be put out the following day at noon. Captain Daniels had already pretty much solidified the plan from information that had been given to him earlier, and he only needed to go back and make sure there was nothing new that would affect what he already had. Sam, the first sergeant, and he stayed up until past one that night talking the plan over, going over contingencies, rations, ammo, extraction scenarios, and a multitude of other issues that could appear at the worst time. When the three felt they had thought of everything they were going to think of that night, they turned in. Sam, exhausted from talking and scrutinizing maps, crawled into bed without a drink. It was the first day he hadn't had a drink in over nine weeks.

After Captain Daniels issued his operations order at noon the next day, the company jumped into action. Wheels up for David's lift was 2145 on Wednesday night, and the Chinooks would lift off only ten minutes later. That meant that there was just under thirty-four hours to make sure that everything would go perfectly. They built a model that took up the floor of an entire room, depicting the different houses, buildings, and roads in Al Sharqi. Each platoon walked over at designated times and talked through their piece while Captain Daniels watched and asked probing questions to see if the men were thinking. Every man in the company carried with him a picture of HVI #3. Sergeants checked, rechecked, and rechecked their soldier's equipment. They test-fired every weapon, tested every pair of night vision goggles, zeroed and re-zeroed every laser, inspected every scope.

David and his platoon rehearsed de-rigging their trucks and getting the guns mounted on each so many times that some of the men, as a joke and to make it interesting, were doing most of it with their eyes closed. His platoon would remain until all of Charlie had departed the objective, and then they would drive back to Q-West with the two Kiowas supporting their movement. David knew that the drive back to Q-West could be the most dangerous, as it would be late and they would be susceptible to any reciprocation from the abduction of Mahmoud. The scout weapons team did ease his mind a bit, but the truth was that helicopters were finicky machines out in the desert.

So after a day and a half checking and rehearsing and talking and preparing, the men found themselves sprawled on the asphalt on the airstrip at Q-West, counting down the time until the mission. Some of the men dozed, some chewed on some food, others joked and told stories. All were nervous. Captain Daniels, feeling the tension in his men, grabbed Sam and made a point to walk around and talk a bit to each of them. He didn't grill them with questions about the mission, or HVI #3's five aliases, or the battalion's radio frequency, but rather said hi to each of them by their first name and asked how things were in Twin Falls, Idaho or in Fairfield, Ohio. Captain Daniels made a point to know his men's first names and where they were from. If they were married or had kids, he made sure he knew their names as well, in case he ever ran into them at the Post Exchange or in town. He had always believed that if you wanted your men to know that you really loved them, you would ask about their families by their names. He even took pride in knowing the names of their girlfriends, if he could keep up.

His tour had the desired effect, and the men relaxed a bit when they saw their commander making the rounds telling one of the two jokes he knew. One was about an Irishman who had built a bridge, a ship, and a barn, but still couldn't get any respect because he had once screwed a goat, and the other was about a birch tree, a beech tree, an ash sapling, and a woodpecker. The men, chuckling to themselves and swearing amicably at each other, forgot their fear. Instead, inside them grew that silent urge that exists within soldiers, whispering that there is a part of them that desires the fight, longs for that struggle where men are tested and deep bonds are formed with the men who pass that test. It sets them apart, makes them into something other, joins them with a breed of men that are few and far between. Men who have chosen a life on that edge of glory, and who know, even if they should die, that they have at least died in good company.

With only a few minutes before they would load up and the helicopters would lift off, David made a few last minute checks to ensure that everything was rigged and secured properly, and that the men had the equipment they were supposed to. When Captain Daniels found him, he was re-counting the links of chain on one of the slinglegs that attached to the front of one of the trucks, ensuring that they had the right count to keep the truck flying level beneath the helicopter. Captain Daniels walked over to the young man intently counting links, and placed a large hand on his shoulder.

"Dave," he said, smiling. "How's it going? Everything look all right?"

David turned to see the faint outline of Captain Daniels in the darkness, and stood up, suddenly embarrassed by his concern. "Yeah, sir… I was just checking one more time to make sure…"

Captain Daniels smiled, his white teeth showing in the night. "Good for you," he nodded. "But I'm sure that you all have done everything right." Deciding to get David's attention off the minutia surrounding them, he asked whether he had any questions about the timing or placement of his trucks.

"No, sir. All that sounds pretty simple. We should have all four trucks up and the cordon set right as you touch down."

Captain Daniels nodded. "Good, I'm sure you will. Just remember that I'll be back up on the net as soon as I step off. Until then, you have control of those birds. If something is going on, and they shouldn't land, it's your call, understand?"

"Yessir," David nodded.

"All right, brother," Captain Daniels said warmly, patting him hard on the shoulder and offering his hand. "I'll see you on the objective."

"See you there, sir." David shook the offered hand as his platoon sergeant walked up to tell him it was time to get in the birds.

birdmen

The first thing Sam thought when he stepped off the ramp of the Chinook was how much dust was in the air. Being in a brown-out at night when looking through night vision was much like being in the middle of a bright green cloud. He couldn't see anything, and just kept moving until he felt he had traveled about fifteen meters away from the helicopter, and then laid down on the ground in the prone, his rifle pointing haphazardly into the green cloud he was surrounded by. The red headdress he had bought in An Najaf from a man for five dollars was tied around his face. If anyone had been able to see him, he would have looked like some kind of soldier from the future: with his helmet and goggles on, and the headdress over his nose and face and the night vision monocle over his left eye, he didn't look much like a man at all. The helicopters took off, blowing hard, hot air that lifted the grains of sand from the ground and sent them stinging any skin that was not covered.

He felt movement around him, and stood back up, shouldering his assault pack which carried a wide variety of extra batteries, an infrared strobe light, a bright orange and red VS-17 panel, an MRE, a bottle of water, extra ammo, a radio, and a light long-sleeve shirt in case they were there a long time and it got cold. He emerged from the green cloud of sand, and began to pick out the advancing units moving in front of him. He found First Platoon and their platoon sergeant, and tapped the man on the shoulder to let him know he was there, and then took a knee to keep out of his way, facing back toward where the helicopters had landed and watching men slowly start to fill in the perimeter. He recognized the silhouettes of squad leaders and team leaders running around quietly in the dark, whispering harsh words through clenched teeth to men who had gotten turned around in the landing and the ensuing dust cloud.

When not two minutes had gone by, each squad leader had called in over the radio to the platoon leader, Paul Batsakis, that they had all their men and equipment, and were ready to move out. Sam heard Paul call up Captain Daniels, who told him they were still waiting on Third Platoon, and to wait until he told them to move forward. Everything was to be very deliberate; David's platoon had landed almost four minutes ago now and had the entire village cordoned off. The element of surprise had now passed them, and there was no sense in rushing. Now what mattered most was a controlled and thorough movement through the village. If one platoon got in front of another, or got too spread out, or went into a building that belonged to another platoon's sector, and a fight broke out, then they could commit fratricide. Sam knew that if Marie were still there, it was because David and his men had been able to seal off the exits from the town quickly enough. Over his radio, through the handset he had jammed between his cheek and his helmet's chinstrap, Sam heard David confirm to Captain Daniels that no one had left the village once they had landed. When Captain Daniels asked about any activity in town, David reported that there were only a few men walking around, obviously woken up by the arrival of helicopters thundering over their rooftops on an otherwise silent night.

So far so good, thought Sam, thinking that if there were people walking around, then there was less of a chance of a firefight. This could just turn out to be another normal snatch and grab.

Captain Daniels called to the platoon leaders to start moving into town, and report all phase lines and buildings.

Paul's platoon started to move out, his squads broken into four man teams that formed succeeding inverted V's. Sam waited until the second-to-last team was passing him before he stood up and started moving. There were a total of eight buildings spread throughout their northern sector, and Paul had planned to clear one building after another, leapfrogging his squads as they moved across.

Paul had spent some time thinking about how to invade someone's house in the middle of the night who may be, but probably was not, someone who was either the target he was looking for or who knew where he was. How to walk that line between, 'I'm sorry, but I have to come into your house with these men and check everything, even though you are probably innocent' and 'the guy I'm looking for may very well be in here and may be waiting behind some door with a gun to kill the first American that comes through'? This was the constant dilemma of the American soldier in Iraq, and they had developed a kind of detachment in their execution. The Iraqis could shout and scream and spit all they wanted, but the bottom line was that they were going to get out of the way and the Americans were going to come in.

Invading a person's home seemed to go against one of the fundamental principles of American society, the rights to private property and against unlawful search and seizure. And something inside the men revolted at the idea of just barging into someone's home. But, after the hundredth time of dragging some woman out of the way, or tying some man's hands behind his back so that they could go into his house, even though he had done nothing wrong, the men succumbed to their role as agents, as actors in a drama whose script and rules they had no control over. The Iraqis, too, had apparently gotten used to it also, the constant and seemingly haphazard and unjustified intrusion into their homes by men who were supposed to represent the country that was a beacon of freedom in a dark world. And both realized the stark truth that this was not America, and those principles taught in fifth grade textbooks in Glendora, California, did not exist here. That despite the high rhetoric of the justification for the invasion and subsequent occupation, that neither of them were free. One man found himself bound by his orders, and the other bound by the weight of the circumstances around him.

Using all three of his squads for each building, Paul would have one get in a position to overwatch, another would create a cordon around the building, being careful to see whether anyone snuck out the back, and the other would enter to clear it. Paul had told his two machine gun teams to stay with whatever squad was in overwatch, as walking through those small mud buildings carrying heavy machine guns never worked out very well. Sam also hung back with whatever squad was in overwatch, therefore more disengaged from the activity. His role in the operation was to run the landing zone to bring the helicopters back, run any resupply operations as needed, assist with casualty evacuation and detainee collection, and take over the operation in case Captain Daniels was wounded or killed.

They had already crossed the first phase line, and were in the middle of their sector. Sam listened intently to the talk on the radio, keeping track of the locations and status of the three platoons. He heard Captain Daniels tell Third Platoon to hold up where they were until the two other platoons reported crossing the second phase line. The company had detained four men already, guilty of either belligerence or looking too much like the pictures of Mahmoud in the faint light.

As Sam peered over his right shoulder to the north through his night vision monocle, trying to make anything out in the hazy world of green and black, he thought he saw something. Off to their north and slightly behind them, about twenty-five meters away, was a small structure no bigger than a shed that was used to hold straw for the animals.

He recognized the small mud building and knew that David's men had been tasked with clearing and securing it as part of their outer cordon, as it lay well outside Paul's corridor, and would have held them up significantly and possibly could have put their direction of fire toward the other platoons. He wasn't even sure what he had seen, or whether it had merely been a glitch in his night vision that had caught his eye. He sat still for several seconds, staring intently at the open doorway in the building to see if he saw anything again.

He focused his attention on trying to see whatever it was he had seen brought the rest of his senses into collusion. His ears picked up the heavy breathing of men with too much weight on their backs moving and stopping, moving and stopping, over and over again. His nose picked up the scent of dry earth and sheep dung kicked up by their boots in the still night. Turning his head, he felt the inside of his collar scrape like sandpaper against the back of his neck from when he had stepped off the helicopter. Suddenly he felt the oppression of the warm night and the claustrophobic sensation of the helmet and goggles and gloves and body armor, with the straps from his pack digging into the outside of his shoulders. He took a long, quiet, deep breath in an effort to relax, and shifted from one knee to the other when he saw it again: a slight flicker of light, not even light, but something of a different color, barely discernable in the various shades of green. And again. Something was definitely moving over there, but it was so small it could have been a chicken.

Paul had just cleared the building in front of Sam, and had called them all forward to leapfrog to the next. Sam stood up, his eyes still on the dark opening. He heard Second Platoon call in Building 14, and the sound of metal and plastic scraping as the men stood up and hurried forward. There again, in the opening, had that been a heel? Someone's heel sticking up from the ground and being drug into the small building? He grabbed the man next to him, a sergeant whose name he couldn't remember at the moment, and said, "I'll be right back." The sergeant gave a quick nod in the green light that said, You're the XO, go wherever the hell you want, why're you telling me?

With his rifle at the low ready, Sam walked quietly, but quickly, toward the small mud building, the cracks between the mud bricks starting to show themselves. The doorway was on the right side of the long wall facing him. Suddenly, everything got significantly brighter. He turned his head over his left shoulder and saw that the moon, now waning and the most slender of crescents, had just risen over the small range that separated this valley from the Tigris River. Turning his head back toward the building, now only a few meters away, he raised his rifle carefully. He felt the high of adrenaline buzz through his body. His breathing grew faster and more shallow. Sliding his left hand down, he fingered the tactical light attached to the underside of his barrel. Stopping for only a moment, he took a long, quiet breath, and stepped through the opening into the small building.

His mind assessed multiple details instantly. The cover on his tactical light cast an infrared light into the small room that only his night vision could pick up. The building was what he had thought it to be: a shed where hay was kept. Just over six feet high, he had to duck just slightly to keep his helmet from scraping the roof. Having entered, he took a quick turn to the left, and saw that the inside was only about eight to ten feet wide and roughly six feet deep. Strewn on the floor were bits of hay. In the far corner lay what remained from the last harvest, a pile of hay that stacked against the corner to the ceiling in a tilted triangle. And there, wide-eyed and covered in dirt, lying back into the wheat, was a man.

Sam saw the AK-47 laying on the ground, just beyond the man's reach, and the pile of hay cascading down over him. The man's front covered in dirt, Sam now realized that this man had crawled on his belly in one of the various ditches of sewage in the town, and had made his way into this hayshed to bury himself in the pile of hay to avoid capture. Sam raised his rifle when he realized all of that could only mean one thing.

"Marie," Sam half-whispered, half-accused, over the barrel of his rifle. The man's dark eyes sparkled at the name, the left half of his face covered in mud hiding what the right side showed to be cleanly shaven and smooth brown skin. The man smiled and his dark eyes flashed, realizing that he was caught. He made an effort to get up out of the pile of hay when Sam flicked his rifle just barely, and said very calmly and quietly, "Don't move."

The smile disappeared and the fire was squelched at the tone coming from this shadow of a man who stood between him and the door, where more shadows were running through the village, looking for him. There was something that made the man nervous, made his heart beat faster in fear. This shadow was alone, where were the others? He could hear them outside, running from house to house. Why was this one alone? The shadow had called him "Marie," spat the name out as if it were bitter poison. The air was suddenly stifling inside the small room, made even smaller by the presence of the rifle pointed calmly at his chest, the silver light coming through the door glinting off the black metal. The man's eyes shot down to his weapon, just barely out of reach. The shadow must have seen his eyes move, because he heard the sharp metallic click of the rifle's selector lever switch from safe to semi, as if in invitation.

And the man knew.

"Mercy?" the man asked, almost rhetorically. Because there was no mercy here, in this place, in this small dark room that wreaked of sheep wool and dry hay.

The shadow shook his head slowly, as if in acknowledgement. No. No mercy here. Not for either of them. And the huge shoulders of the shadow rose in a slow and inaudible breath.

Time slowed. For the man who knew that he would soon be dead, every second contained infinite possibilities, every second seemed a lifetime. The man made a half-conscious attempt to clean off some of the mud that clung to his *dish-dasha*, and then realizing the absurdity, abruptly stopped. Mirroring the shadow, he too took a long slow breath, and said, "*In'sha*—"

All the movement outside suddenly stopped at the two sharp cracks that split the night air. Some of those who were more nervous dove on the ground, or got behind some wall or other cover. Most just turned in the direction of the sound. It was a sound they all knew well, the sound of countless rifle ranges and live-fire exercises through the tenure of their service. That sound could not scare them because it was a part of them, a piece of their will exercised on their world. The real fear was in the following explosion of gunfire from foreign barrels, which thankfully never came.

Captain Daniels had been one of the ones who had simply stopped and waited for some kind of indication that would explain the shots. One shot by itself generally meant that someone had negligently discharged their weapon, which always made him angry, but admittedly was far better than getting into a firefight. But two shots, fired in rapid succession the way they were, sounded like the technique of firing a controlled pair. When nothing came over the radio, he called up the platoon leader.

"Paul, Six. Report."

Paul came back on the radio immediately, the breathy sound of his voice indicating that he was moving quickly. "Don't know, sir. Came from the mud hut in the northwest corner. Standby."

Captain Daniels took a long breath and pulled out his map. He told his other two platoons to hold up where they were until Paul could report back. When Paul finally did call back, his voice carried with it a gravity that was sensed by every man who heard it.

"Cobra Six, you need to come up here, sir."

* * *

Captain Steve Taylor was on the edge of losing control. His face flushed a bright red that traveled up and over his bald scalp and disappeared again under his collar. His gesticulations were becoming more and more wild, and at the height of his diatribe, wildly pacing back and forth, Colonel DaSilva had had to tell him to stand still for Christ's sake. Sam, Paul, and Captain Daniels stood at attention off to the side in the small room that served as the battalion commander's office. It was seven o'clock in the morning, and it had been a very long night. All of them carried shadows of various hues on their faces, their eyelids all heavy.

After Captain Daniels had come up to the building in Al Sharqi, he had found Sam standing outside with his rifle slung to his side. When he went in, he found Paul and one of his soldiers getting ready to pull the body out into the moonlight to get positive identification that the body was in fact HVI #3. Captain Daniels saw the two small holes, or rather saw where they had entered and had soaked through with dark blood against the man's *dish-dasha*. One of the bullets had entered right dead center mass of the chest, sending splinters of bone and cartilage ripping through the heart muscle, shredding it to pieces. Sam being right handed, the other bullet had punctured the man's left lung, and then gone tumbling through his body and had left a massive exit wound on his lower left side, above the pelvis bone. The man had breathed his last just as Paul had arrived, his eyes wide open, as if trying to help his gaping mouth suck in more air. After Captain Daniels saw the wounds, he noticed the AK-47 lying on the ground next to the body, and breathed a sigh of relief as he stepped out of the sticky-sweet air of the small room into the cool night. He looked intently at Sam, whose eyes were on the ground, flitting back and forth.

Without waiting for the question, raising his eyes to look at his commander, Sam had said, "He went for his weapon, sir. I shot him." He held the gaze just a moment, and then lowered them back down to the ground again.

When Captain Daniels had called in to Battalion that HVI #3 had been killed, he was told to standby for the commander. Their conversation had been quick. Captain Daniels related the pertinent details over the radio, reporting that HVI #3 had been killed through self defense when he had been caught alone in a building. 'Colonel DaSilva was obviously angry at the report, and had told him to bring in HVI #3 and the two men who had been identified by the toothless villager as Mahmoud's accomplices.

"And Brent," 'Colonel DaSilva added, "there'd better be a damn good reason for this."

"Yessir," he answered, casting a worried look at Sam.

Taylor was about to reiterate for the third time the value of bringing Mahmoud back alive, when 'Colonel DaSilva waved his hand, signaling that enough was enough, he didn't need to be lectured on HVI #3's potential intelligence value. Looking at the men standing to the side at attention, a large wad of chaw shoved into his cheek and protruding like a tumor, he leaned forward on his desk and asked with deliberate articulation, "What in the fuck happened in that building?"

"Sir—" started Captain Daniels, though it was obvious toward whom the question had been directed at.

Good ole' Brent Daniels, Sam thought, always ready to step into the breach.

"Sam," 'Colonel DaSilva said, cutting Captain Daniels off and pointing and looking Sam hard in the face, "what the fuck happened?"

Still standing at the position of attention, Sam related what had happened in concise terms, his eyes shooting back and forth from the wall in front of him to 'Colonel DaSilva. He said how he had seen something, and thought he would just go check it out.

"By yourself? Why would you go *by yourself*?" asked 'Colonel DaSilva incredulously. It was a valid question.

Sam turned his head slightly to look at him. "Yessir. Sir, I really don't... I don't know, sir. I thought it was probably nothing. I didn't wanna... I don't know what I was thinking, sir," he stammered out. That part was true, he honestly didn't know what had made him go off by himself to check on what he had seen. And the knowledge that this part, at least, wasn't a lie, calmed him a bit.

"So what happened when you got to the building?" asked 'Colonel DaSilva, leaning back and settling in for the details of the story.

The truth part was coming to an end now, Sam realized, and he gathered himself for the lie, recalling details that he had invented and would have to remember for a very long time with absolute precision.

"I turned the corner, sir, I had turned on my tac light, and saw a man kind of burrowing himself into the pile of hay in the back corner. He was trying to kind of sit back into it, and then cover himself up. There was an AK on the ground right next to him."

"Did you know it was Mahmoud?" 'Colonel DaSilva's eyes were hard on his.

Sam shook his head thoughtfully. Still all true, no lies yet. "No sir, not immediately. But I figured it out pretty quick."

"How?"

"Well sir, I guess I kind of just figured that it must be, based on the way he was trying to hide. Then I saw his face, and thought he looked like the pictures we had." He paused briefly. "Then I knew it was him, sir."

"So what happened?"

"I said his name…"

"His name?" asked 'Colonel DaSilva.

"Well, no sir, not his real name. I called him 'Marie'." 'Colonel DaSilva's eyes softened a bit, remembering in an instant Jonathon's report where he had first read that name, and a warm night in Makhmur as a young man went running by him with a smile in the dark. Anticipating the next question, Sam continued, "I don't know why, sir, it just came right out."

"Okay…" 'Colonel DaSilva nodded, as in his mind he watched the young man disappear around the corner into the darkness.

"Well, sir, then he gave a look at his AK on the ground, and that's when I raised my weapon on him and told him not to move." Still no lies, he thought with a degree of relief.

"But you said in your report that he went for his weapon?" 'Colonel DaSilva prodded.

"Yessir… he did, sir. After I told him not to move, he paused and smiled and kind of went to raise his hands like he was going to surrender, and then he made a quick grab for the AK. I shot him."

"Bullshit!" spat Taylor.

"Steve," chastised 'Colonel DaSilva, casting a weary look at him. 'Colonel DaSilva spat into an empty red soda can, the ball of tobacco bouncing up and down his cheek as he compressed it for more juice, and leaned all the way back in his chair, folding his hands behind his head.

"He went for his weapon, sir," answered Sam, looking at Taylor, as if to say, What else was I supposed to do? The weapon was real, it had Mahmoud's fingerprints all over it, and—more importantly—did not have Sam's. Sam rested with the knowledge that as bad as it all looked, the bottom line was that it was a totally believable story. That AK was going to keep him out of trouble. And, deep inside so the others would not see, he thanked the man for dragging that AK through the mud with him into the building.

"It's a drop, sir! He brought the AK in!" pleaded Taylor, as if the truth were so obvious that it pained him that only he could see it.

Sam lunged at the exposed flesh of his argument with all the confidence that a man has when the truth is behind him. "It *wasn't* a drop, sir," Sam said firmly, letting the simplicity of those few words hang in the air.

Paul jumped in at this point to support his friend. "Sir," he stammered, as if he were as surprised as the rest of them that he was speaking. "I don't think there is much of a chance that Sam could've brought that AK in with him. He was in the back with the trail squad the whole time. He never came up into the houses that we were searching, and all the weapons that we confiscated and recorded from the houses were accounted for. And Sam didn't bring an AK with him on the bird, sir," he added as he shook his head. "I don't see how he could have had a weapon to drop, sir." Paul finished, and then receded back to a fixture in the room.

But it was enough. They all felt it. Taylor obviously still believed that Sam had killed Mahmoud without provocation, but there was nothing available for him to mount an attack against. They all saw it, Sam especially. The weapon was there, had been there in the small building when Sam had walked in. On that sole fact he rested his entire faith that he would be believed; the lie that he built on that firm foundation would not fall, because there were no means to attack it. The weapon had been in the building, and the only man left alive to say what had happened said that the dead man had gone for his weapon. They all saw it, as plain and simple as the sun. What could anyone do?

And Sam buried this new truth deep inside himself, carving this rearrangement of fact into the walls of his memory so that it would replace that which could not have—and now no longer had—happened.

Not that it was all now over. Mahmoud had been Division's HVI #3, and nobody was happy that he was dead. Well, not *nobody*. Anyone who could see the value in HVI #3 being taken alive. Anyone who had the sobriety of judgment to understand that his capture and resulting interrogation would produce intelligence that would ultimately save American lives, could only furrow their eyebrows with the disappointment in the loss. Those who saw the man not as HVI #3, but merely as Abdul Yousif Mahmoud, the man responsible for the attacks against their unit, could not help but feel that justice had been served, and that the "staff weenies" who had wanted him alive were detached from the situation on the ground.

The brigade commander, Colonel Smith, was keen to have a very pointed conversation about Mahmoud's death. The Division Commander, Major General Stevenson, was breathing pretty heavy down his neck as to just what kind of an organization he was running down there in Qayyarah anyway, where Company XO's were killing Division HVI's. So, later that day, Sam found himself once again standing at the position of attention—clean shaven this time—in another commander's office. Paul, Captain Daniels, Taylor, and 'Colonel DaSilva were all there as well, each standing at attention in front of the brigade commander's desk as courtesy to rank prescribed with Paul on the left and 'Colonel DaSilva on the right.

'Colonel DaSilva did most of the talking, having accepted that what Sam had said had indeed been what had happened, and besides, it was his place to speak for his men in front of the brigade commander. If Colonel Smith had a specific question for any of the other men, he would ask them. But he only asked one question, directed at Sam.

"The AK was lying next to him when you came into the building?" the man peered from behind half-rimmed reading glasses that perched on the end of a long nose.

Sam nodded, "Yessir." Not a lie, he thought.

The man shook his head, accepting what he had no choice but to accept at this point with what the preponderance of the evidence spoke so clearly. He did take the opportunity presented him, however, to communicate his sincere displeasure at the loss of HVI #3, and threw a particularly sharp glance at Captain Daniels when he questioned the control that Captain Daniels had over his company. Hearing this, and feeling the sting of that insult radiate off the man whom he admired and had learned so much from, Sam whispered an apology to him deep in his heart, but of course would not say out loud.

Before Colonel Smith dismissed them, Taylor was able to get in a couple licks about the loss in intelligence that Mahmoud's death would yield before Colonel Smith shot him a look that communicated that he was well aware and need not be lectured by a captain on the operational and intelligence value that captured HVI's could provide. The session ended with Sam being ordered to be debriefed by the brigade's tactical human intelligence team, as well as the military police. He also ordered his S-2, Major Midkiff, to conduct a thorough investigation into the reports and events of that night, to ensure that there were no discrepancies.

'Colonel DaSilva stayed behind after the others were dismissed. Colonel Smith's tone changed almost instantly as he asked him to take a seat. "You want a chew, Marc?" he asked.

"No sir, thank you."

"Hell of a mess, Marc, this is just a hell of a mess," Colonel Smith began.

"Yes sir, it sure is."

Colonel Smith leaned back in his chair and folded his hands over his stomach. "Look, as far as I'm concerned the whole damn thing is a loss. I learned in Panama, and again in Desert Storm, that in a war unfortunate things happen, and that a leader must recognize that fact, and not expend too much energy in worrying about what could have been done differently. Sometimes in war the wrong people die: that's just the nature of war." He paused. "Mahmoud is dead, and the Army has lost a significant source of intel. But that's over and done with now, and I personally see no point in getting all bowed up about something that can't be changed." He paused again. "My only concern at this point is over young Calhoun there. If Calhoun did indeed unjustifiably kill Mahmoud, well, then I want to know because he will, of course, have to be tried by Courts Martial, which makes me sad as hell to think of. But Marc, I also believe passionately that the American military does not just summarily execute people, to do so violates not only the nation's values, but also is out of step with the essential role that honor plays in our profession."

"I absolutely agree sir."

"And let's not even talk about what the headlines would read if some jackass reporter got his dick-beaters on this thing," he added. "But on the other hand, if he did kill Mahmoud in self-defense, then I want to make damn good and sure that there is no way anyone will be able to dig this up and try to hang it around his neck later on down the road. I want to know—*know*, you understand?—that the facts are as solid and undeniable as the cold, dead body of that sonofabitch Mahmoud."

"Yes sir."

*   *   *

The twenty-fifth of December was just another day on a calendar already filled with patrol schedules, resupply missions, and guard shift changes. It was just an ordinary day, except that it had the word "Christmas" typed over it. But as far as having any tangible affect on the rhythm of the day itself, there was none. There would be no relief for the men out on the pipeline, nor for those pulling their two-week rotation out at the oil refinery in Qayyarah; the sun would rise and travel across the sky just as slowly as it always had. There was no relaxation in the patrol schedule to accommodate the holiday: soldiers cursed and swore as they slipped into their body armor vests to go out on a patrol, sniping that they were going to "get clipped on Christmas, what a treat for Mom."

One of the soldiers in Alpha Company had used up an entire roll of duct tape, which he would have gotten in trouble for if the first sergeant hadn't thought that what he had done with it was so funny. In big, three-foot letters across one of the main rooms where the cots were lined up against either wall, he had written, "Merry Fucking Christmas."

"Lopez," the first sergeant had said, shaking his head, "you got it. That's it, right there. You got it, all right," and passed on, shaking his head and laughing to himself while Lopez and his buddies nearby basked in self-satisfaction.

In the attempt to transplant the trappings of the Christmas season, the soldiers had put up Christmas lights around bunkers, decorated their rooms, and hung up cards from home. Some had families that had sent miniature plastic trees that had been decorated with pictures of family and friends from home. As if in reminder that this was all really a cheap mimicry, and that they were a long way from the innocence of home, one of the men had cut out a picture from Playboy and put it at the top of his tree in place of a star. Her name was Amber, and he called her his angel. Of course, when he took a picture of himself in front of the tree to send home to his folks back in Iowa, he had taken his angel down.

There was a small contingent from the Fijian Army on the base, tasked with providing security for the new Iraqi money being printed and distributed through the local banks. A small group of about twenty of these big, dark men with the smell of the sea and their skin glowing with the oils of tropical plants and flowers from their islands led a chorus at eleven-thirty Christmas Eve night.

To those few who went—and there were only a few—it was a treat they would never forget. Sitting in the large, stark-white metallic dining facility, under the blank phosphorescent lights, they treated their audience to a rapture of joy and celebration that embarrassed the somber choirs draped in deep robes singing Handel's Hallelujah Chorus in churches back home, decorated with rich mahogany crosses and over-sized poinsettias. The men could not sing, or at least those few who could hold a tune were drowned out by the almost deafening timbre of those who could not, but they did not care. These were their songs from home, songs that resonated in their blood, mingled with their bone marrow, and their passion was fueled by visions and smells of their childhood and dreams of their families in a land that seemed barely capable of occupying the same planet that they now inhabited. Unchoreographed, and for the most part undirected, their singing was a mixture of song and bellow and laughter and clapping. And it was absolutely beautiful.

The contingent of Pakistanis who were cleaning up the dining facility late that night had to wonder, here in this dark, foreign place, what the source of such apparent celebration could be. Songs that the Fijians' small audience had never heard before, and would never hear again, would echo inside them every time they remembered the unshakable joy that came pouring out of those men's souls like a cataract, and landed with a deafening, thundering crash on their sense of isolation. The torrent of unadulterated joy that came careening out of them was enough to shatter the thin mortar of pessimism that may have calcified around any hearts there that night. In the light of that chorus, their long deployment from home, only compounded by being away during the holiday season, seemed but a light and momentary thing, and their depression momentarily dissipated like the mist on an early Spring morning.

It was Christmas morning as Sam walked down the paved road with its missing chunks of concrete that had been ripped up by tank treads, the holes left behind filled with water from the rains and capped with a fragile layer of ice that had formed overnight. The air was a biting cold, his breath blanketed his face as he walked with his hands shoved into his pockets. His black watch cap pulled tight over his head, his feet still cold from having been hastily shoved into his boots, he thought how it actually felt like Christmas as he walked toward the chapel, aware that he was about a half hour late. But even though his breath still carried the hint of whiskey that even he could detect, and Amber had shot him a look that was both stunned and accusatory when he had nearly jumped out of bed that morning, he could not understand not going to church on Christmas. Having convinced himself to hurry up and get dressed to get to the service in time, he wondered now to himself why he was even bothering. He would look like a fool walking in so late, whiskey on his breath, the tang of sex still on him, the man who had committed murder.

Word about Mahmoud's death had spread like wildfire, and Sam found himself enjoying a celebrity-like status from the men on the base, who almost to a man believed that he was a hero. Sam shrugged off their affections with a twinge of shame that he whitewashed in humility, which of course only turned him into the reluctant hero.

The truth was that the past several weeks had been difficult ones. He had been questioned and re-questioned at least a dozen times by different people who somehow or other had an interest in Mahmoud's death. He had had to write and rewrite sworn statements over and over again, telling in as much detail as he could remember the circumstances of that night. His last interview had been several days ago now, and when he had left, he had the feeling that it was almost over, it didn't seem as if they had found anything incongruous in all the interviews and statements. The stress had taken its toll, though. He had lost several pounds from lack of appetite, restless nights, and the whiskey. His neck had thinned just a bit, and his brown t-shirts that usually clung tight around the base of his neck in a healthy, robust way, now hung just a tad loosely around his frame. He had even had trouble performing. The first time it had happened, Amber was initially upset, but then he saw her anger melt quickly into a softening that made him nervous. Something in the way she had kissed him on the forehead and told him it was all right, they could just sleep next to each other that night, made him anxious and filled him with a sense of impending guilt.

When he walked into the small, green tent that served as the chapel and stank of mildew, he knew they would all look at him and think, There is the man who killed Mahmoud. Which made him a killer of men. And something inside him, on this Christmas morning, revolted at that status, and almost turned him around. But he had been brought up going to church, sitting in hard wooden pews while old men and women sang songs that all sounded the same and which he didn't even begin to understand until he was about thirteen. And every Christmas morning he could remember, after the presents had been torn apart, and the tree stood void and naked, and they had all had pancakes from a sourdough recipe that his dad said went back to *his* granddaddy, they had piled into the family station wagon and headed to First Baptist Church down on River Road. In his mind he could not divorce Christmas from church, something inside him revolted at the idea of a day that meant nothing more than the apogee of capitalism and the triumph of relativism, which was all that was left when there was no baby in a manger.

Stepping over a large puddle of water with shattered sheets of ice floating on top, he quietly slid through the flap into the room. Mel was up front speaking, his velvet-red stole with gold embroidered crosses on the ends draped over his shoulders and resting against his tan uniform. If he was glad to see Sam at the service, the Chaplain did not betray it, not skipping a beat as he proceeded through his sermon. As Sam slipped into a cold metal chair in the back and nearest the door, he saw that no one else had noticed him walk in. And a weight that was at the same time admiration and judgment slid off of his shoulders as he reached into his cargo pocket and pulled out the small, bright green New Testament that he had been given, he thought, at one of the stations the morning they had deployed. It was immediately warmer in the small enclosure. The humidity of the trapped air combined with the warmth of the portable heaters and dank mildew did not allow for much pretense: they were still in Iraq, and this was unlike any Christmas service they had ever been to.

Mel was speaking about something that Sam was not yet able to pay attention to, so he flipped through the thin little sheets of paper to the book of Luke and slowly read the part about the shepherds and the angels. When he finished, his mind had calmed enough to listen to the sermon, now almost half over.

"And so," Mel was finishing a point, "just as the rockets last night disturbed a night that should be full of peace, that should be silent and holy, so we are reminded of our own broken condition, of the condition of our world, and the hopeless futility of a pursuit of peace—both in our own lives, and in our world—outside of God, until we stand in the dawn of that perpetual Christmas and are bathed in the song of the angels as the chorus sings 'War is over, war is over! Thank God Almighty, war is over!'"

Sam shifted in his seat, sitting up a bit, his index finger still stuck in the small bible, marking what he had just read. His rifle lay at his feet, the muzzle pointed toward the back, with only the black of the butt stock and lower receiver visible.

Mel continued with his second point.

"You know, I've been thinking about Christmas a lot this past month, trying to take this time away from everything that is usually associated with the season to try to learn what Christmas is really about. And it's given me an opportunity to see what maybe that first Christmas was like. No family. No home. Cold. Foreign.

"So Christmas can't really be about being home surrounded by our families and loved ones. We all know—or pretend to know— that it's not about presents and such. It isn't about being warm and comfortable and feeling secure in a familiar place. Christmas is simply and wonderfully about God initiating this extraordinary story about the redemption of mankind. Have you ever thought about just how amazing, how wonderful, that story is? Have you?"

Mel looked around the room at the dozen young faces around him, some of them nodding slightly. Sam found himself captured by the tone in Mel's voice.

"It is the single most amazing story ever created, ever told. Creator becomes his creation. Hands that with a gesture flung stars and galaxies into place are now grasping at the air and for mother's milk. A voice that spoke all creation into existence, now cries from a bed of hay. In a barn. Divinity meets impotence. The ageless unites with the corporeal. He who had no beginning and knows no end, who exists outside of time in the way that you exist independent from a letter, endures his own birth and the effects that time will have on his body.

"Willingly. Creator becomes creation, not through compulsion, but willingly. And if he was compelled, it was his own love that compelled him. How amazing is that? Like Shakespeare becoming Romeo! What, then, can our response be when we find ourselves operating inside this story? There is only one response worthy, because it is the only one that he has demanded: receive. And he says to us, 'Receive my gift. Let me work this story, and its implications, into your soul until you reach the point where you understand that you cannot repay me, you cannot give me anything that is worthy of who I am, and then live in joy and peace and awe in what I have done. The story that sprung from my creative genius when I became a man in order to redeem you.'

"That is Christmas! And that is Christmas with presents and Christmas trees or without, with family or without, whether we are in Iraq or sitting by the fireside at home.

"They tried to stop this story at the beginning, in the introductory chapter, though really it is more of the climax, isn't it? The watershed moment in the story? The powers of this world saw—more clearly than we do and definitely with more understanding of the eternal ramifications—and did everything in their power to stop the story there at that chapter. Now, am I trying to reintroduce our old friend the devil, pitchfork and horns? Well, you can keep the pitchfork, but otherwise, yes, absolutely. The disbelief in powers, in the objective existence of good and evil, is a poison from the relativism that has infected our world, and anesthetized us to our own potential. But their power was and is weak, a cheap imitation of the source of all power, and they could not touch the story that sprang forth from the mind of God, because it is his story. It is his story of redemption and sanctification and reconciliation. And we celebrate the culmination of that beautiful story at Christmas."

Mel looked around the room again, and walked from behind the homemade pulpit that had the battalion crest painted onto it.

"But, you say, didn't those powers win after all? Didn't the story end with Jesus nailed to a cross?" He smiled and shook his head. "No. Because the story does not stop, does it? It keeps going. And if we keep reading, we hear the voice that giggled at the silly outfits of those men who brought incense and myrrh, cry from a torn and beaten body, 'Eloi, Eloi, lama sabachthani!' My God, my God, why have you forsaken me?" Was it chance, the haphazard process of

looking around the room while he spoke, or did Mel intentionally lock eyes with Sam at that moment?

Mel paused. This time, Sam thought and was immediately ashamed of it, for dramatic flair. "Christmas never happens without a Good Friday. They are inseparable, and God knew that when he started the story, way back at the beginning, when he formed man from the earth. Eden and a stable and a hill in the shape of a skull are all part of the same storyline. That is what he intended from the moment we chose to disobey when we bit into the apple. Bethlehem is devoid of meaning without Golgotha. There is no empty tomb without there first being a manger that held a baby boy.

"And as such, our lives ought to be lived with a severe kind of joy. He died so that our joy could be complete, and so our lives would be full, but that is not to say that we ought not to remember with what cost those gifts have been given us. We ought to live our lives simultaneously in the light of that star that shone over a stable, and in the shadow of the cross on a hill.

"Let's remember that this is still Christmas morning—Iraq and mortars and war and all—this is still Christmas."

After the sermon, Mel led them all, acappella, in a couple Christmas hymns, both of which Sam was pleased to find he remembered the words to.

When the service was over, Sam hurried out the flap that led back into the crisp, bright morning, and walked back to his room with no real sense of urgency, enjoying the warm sunshine on his face against the bite of the air, and the sense of satisfaction that the service had created inside him. His thoughts traveled back, as he walked along the torn-up road, to Christmases at home as a boy. If he had had the presence of mind or of perspective, he would have noticed the slight upward curve in his mouth that betrayed the honest, good thoughts stirring inside him.

When he got back to his room, he saw that Amber had gone, and knew that she was upset before he read her quick note scribbled on a piece of scratch paper on his desk. The note said simply, "Sam, Merry Christmas. Love, Amber."

"Shit," he muttered to himself as the smile that had been playing on his face disappeared.

Eight thousand miles away, Rachel lay sleeping in her room at her parents' house. It was not yet Christmas morning, and she was sleeping hard from the combination of the stress of the past few days and the wine from dinner that night. Claire lay sleeping in the little bed that Rachel's parents had bought for her, turning and making the small, guttural noises and squeaks that toddlers make in their sleep. She had had trouble sleeping the first night in the house, the newness of the room and the unfamiliar scent of the sheets and stuffed animals that crowded her bed had made her anxious, and she had kept Rachel up most the night, herself unable to sleep well, but for different reasons. The past couple nights, though, Claire had slept soundly, probably due to the overwhelming attention that she was receiving from Grandmother and Grandpa, who didn't seem capable of letting her alone for more than five minutes. Rachel would sigh in frustration at their insistence on waking Claire up in the middle of her nap during the day.

"Well, she just looked so cute, lying there," her mom would say, a little short of apologetically.

The truth was, ever since Stephen and Fort Campbell and Claire, Rachel did not enjoy coming home to Clinton, South Carolina to see her parents. But Claire would be two years old in February, old enough to enjoy Christmas, and Rachel knew that Christmas with Grandmother and Grandpa would be more fun, and would have more presents, than Christmas in their small apartment on Trenton Road. It had been easy for her to get a week off, as business in Clarksville had been slow since the division had deployed and promised to be even slower over the Christmas holidays, as those families that had stayed were most likely to travel away from the town that screamed of the absence of daddies and husbands. Plenty of mommies and wives were missing as well, but the overall effect on the division's deployment had been a practical erasure of men from the town.

So Rachel had loaded up her old Mazda sedan, and brought Claire to her folks' for Christmas. The vacation had started out pleasantly enough, as they always did. Her family, especially her mom, was from the Old South, her family name being Roberts, the same Roberts who had been instrumental in the settling of northern Georgia and what became South Carolina before the revolutionary war. She made no apologies for her pride that on her family tree could be found such names as General James Longstreet. By marriage of course, but even so. Rachel's dad's side, the Carlisle's, were not as old nor as genteel as the Roberts, but had been around South Carolina since before the civil war. The Carlisle's had initially become wealthy through tobacco, then continued to accumulate wealth and status through various businesses and manufacturing enterprises. Rachel's dad, John Robert, had decided to attend law school at 'Ole Miss, and had gone on to be quite a successful property lawyer until he ran for mayor back in 1998 and had won. Rachel was their only child, and as such, Claire their only grandchild.

During Christmas Eve dinner, the trip home had taken the nasty turn that they all inevitably did. With presents piled three and four high under the tree, virtually all for Claire, Rachel had commented, not without a little shame, that her parents were going to spoil the little girl. She had also noticed, resting peacefully on one of the boughs, an envelope with her name written on it. Guessing—correctly—that the envelope was the only gift for her, she could only imagine the amount that would be written on the check inside. Perhaps it was the pile of presents for Claire, perhaps it was the single check for herself, or perhaps it was all of that combined with the pain of the past and the dryness of the wine with dinner, but as she lay in bed afterwards, with one foot on the floor waiting for the room to stop spinning, she could not understand the argument that had ensued between her and her parents, though it was the same argument, essentially, as it had always been.

She had tried before, and attempted again, to convince herself that her parents were only upset for her, a single mom who worked shifts at the local Outback, who had followed her high school sweetheart—against their better judgment, of course—to Fort

Campbell, walking away from an art scholarship at the local private college, only to have him leave her when she became pregnant. And when she had told Stephen, praying that he would throw his arms around her and tell her how great it was that they were going to have a baby, and how he loved her, and how they would get married, he had instead looked at her with eyes that said far more than the simple, cruel sentence he had spoken to her: no baby, not now. She had cried then, sobbed with a self-pity that threatened to kill her and the life inside her. And when she had resolved to keep the baby, and Stephen had left her, and she had gone home and told her parents and they had responded in a silence meant to mask the anger and disappointment and judgment that their eyes betrayed, she found she could not cry anymore. So then, she had thought, she was alone. And the world was cruel.

But, with the failure of her world, she had discovered a new love inside her that grew more each day, and found an old love that had been covered over with the cobwebs of religion and the musty smell of fear. And these two loves, that grew like wisteria vines that support an old house and suspend it above the turbulence of the earth, taught her to forgive the world for its cruelty, and love it in spite of its ugliness.

She woke up Christmas morning with the dull aching of a hangover, her eyes red and heavy with the pain that pulsed against her temples. The truth was that she had only had a couple glasses of wine, but what with her small frame and the fact that she hardly ever drank, it might as well have been an entire bottle for how she felt. She looked over and saw that Claire was not in her bed, and she assumed that her mother had come and taken her while she was still asleep. She sat up slowly, craving the hot cup of coffee that she knew her dad was waiting to pour for her when she emerged from her room. He would kiss her on the forehead and say good morning and hand her the steaming cup, and last night's argument would be behind them. Even the argument last night, assisted with the wine, had the air of a passive aggression, with the kind of stab-and-retreat rhetoric that frustrated her more than an out and out fight would have.

She opened her door quietly, and tip-toed across the cold, hardwood floor to the bathroom, where she splashed cold water on her face. Crossing back to put on her slippers, she emerged into the living room and saw her mother playing with Claire on the floor. Bing Crosby was on the stereo, singing "White Christmas." The shredded wrapping paper scattered around told her that her mother had let Claire open one of her presents early. Her mother gave her a look that said, I'm sorry, I couldn't help it. Rachel figured that it was her prerogative as a grandmother, and only smiled and said good morning, and walked into the kitchen where her dad had just put down a knife and was pouring her coffee. The kitchen was full of the scent of freshly-chopped onion and bell pepper, the spicy-sweet odor of sausage slowly simmering on the stove, the faintest hint of pitch from the tree in the next room. Bing's crooning floated in through the door and completed the scene.

"Good morning, sweetheart. Merry Christmas." Her dad smiled and kissed her softly on her forehead.

"Merry Christmas, Daddy," she smiled back through her headache. She cupped the coffee in both hands and held it close to her face, breathing in the spicy aroma, grateful for onions and sausage and Christmas trees and coffee and little baby girls.

He noticed her careful movements and asked playfully, "Have a little too much fun last night?"

Fun? she thought, though she smiled and nodded her head, playing up to his amnesia.

He gave a deep, contented, self-satisfied laugh, and patted her softly on the back in the way that communicated, You go on and sit in the living room with your mother and little girl and enjoy the morning. She obliged, leaving him whistling softly to himself as he gently rolled up the flat dough that was covered in brown sugar and butter and almonds that made his Christmas almond swirl, which he had been making every Christmas morning since she could remember.

As she walked into the living room, she smiled warmly at her mother sitting on the floor, helping little Claire with her new present and showing her how to put the shaped blocks into the right holes.

"Merry Christmas, Rachel," her mother smiled warmly, obviously pleased beyond words that she had been able to spend the morning with her granddaughter.

"Good morning, Mom. Merry Christmas," Rachel responded just as warmly as she squatted on the couch and tucked her feet underneath her contentedly. Claire, seeing her mom, walked over with a yellow square in her hand, offering it to her. Rachel took it from her and looked at it, smiling at her daughter. "Is this for you?" she asked playfully, though still aware of the throbbing in her head.

Claire squealed in delight, displaying a big open smile full of little white teeth. When Rachel offered the block back to her, she grasped it with both hands and waddled back to the board with the different shaped holes, where she tried to push the square block through the round hole until her grandmother reached over and guided her hand to the right one. Claire let out another squeal as she spun around on her bottom and beamed at her mom, triumphant.

Breakfast first, then the presents. That's the way it had always been growing up. The conversation at breakfast danced around last night's argument, her mother and father refusing to allow any significant length of silence to build that might force the subject up again. Piling the dishes in the sink, rubbing their stomachs and complaining that they had eaten too much, they went into the living room to open the presents. Claire was the center of attention, and it seemed as if the entire day were meant only for her, the three adults were so enraptured in watching her try to undo ribbon and rip open the fragile paper. Rachel's mother must have taken over a hundred pictures of her granddaughter that morning, searching for that priceless pose that would find its way onto the mantel over the fireplace. When Claire had opened all of her presents, they suddenly seemed to remember that there were gifts for them as well under the tree, and the adults got to grow-down for a while.

When Rachel opened her card from the bough of the tree and saw the amount of the check—five thousand dollars—her eyes popped open and she could not speak. The tears that welled in the recesses of her eyelids made her parents smile happily, glad that their gift could mean so much to her. But Rachel was crying because she did not want five thousand dollars. And though she was not sure what she did want from them, she knew enough to know it was not this check that she held in her hand. Understanding that her parents were trying to show her that they loved her and wanted to help take care of her and Claire, she forced a smile that translated her tears into gratitude, and made herself be thankful for their generosity.

The presents all opened, the ladies got ready for church while her dad finished up the dishes in the kitchen. Then they all piled into their Lexus and headed to First Presbyterian Church for the Christmas service. The sanctuary was warm against the biting cold of the outside air, with the deep reds and browns of the cherry and mahogany furniture, punctuated by poinsettias bigger than Rachel thought she had ever seen. The Reverend delivered a sermon on the merits of Christmas, on peace and goodwill toward men, while the choir sang Handel's Hallelujah Chorus and Silent Night and other standards.

"It was such a beautiful service!" her mother exclaimed as they walked back out into the bright sunshine, Claire between her and Rachel.

Rachel's dad grunted softly in affirmation, still hearing the chorus echo in his head, and Rachel agreed out loud as well as in her heart. It really was a beautiful service, she thought, and reprimanded herself for criticizing what she had thought might be excessive attention to the decorations in the sanctuary. Walking out in the bright sunshine toward the black, shiny car whose chrome accents flashed in the crisp air, her thoughts turned to Sam. Being almost noon her time, it should be eleven—or midnight?—at night in Iraq. She wondered what his day had been like, who he had spent it with, what he had done that day, was it cold? raining? She could not imagine the details of his life as she sat in the sun-warmed soft tan leather seats of her parents' car, Claire waving one of her new Christmas blocks in the air as she stared out the window at her safe world that flew by faster than she could absorb.

Rachel wondered whether the package she had sent Sam for Christmas had arrived in time. She had not heard from him for months now, not since his letter in June. The package had not been much, some small food items she knew he liked, and a few candy canes for the season. She had enclosed some recent pictures of Claire at the pumpkin patch for Halloween at the place just north of Interstate 24, where they had a maze carved into a corn field, and one at Thanksgiving when it had been just the two of them and a small turkey on the table.

When she sent the package with the pictures, she asked herself if she was using her daughter to stay close to Sam. She knew that he loved Claire, that something sparkled in his eyes whenever he saw or talked with her. But she was also convinced that he loved her as well, with a calmness and quiet faith that assured her it was not just arrogance. She simply knew he would enjoy the pictures, maybe put them up on his wall, and thought that he might need the reminder that there was still a kind of fetal innocence left in the world.

Some think that some people are born with the gift of selflessness. But they are not born with it; it is not a birth, but rather a death. A kind of execution.

*   *   *

Sam sat at his desk in his room, huddled over the small portable heater that he had bought at the haji-shop on base. He had just come back from a logistics run, bringing food, water, mail, and batteries out to the company at the oil refinery. With the doors off the Humvee as per the brigade's standard operating procedures, he had been soaked with a rain that came at him at a forty-five degree angle in a freezing wind. The rain and the wind had given him quite a chill by the time they had traveled the short distance and back. His blouse now lay open and draped over a chair, hanging dangerously close to the small heater, the steam rising in lazy whiffs as it dried. He had bought a silver travel mug, and was sipping carefully at a hot chocolate and whiskey drink that he had invented a couple weeks ago. He had thought about trying to find some schnapps or rum or vodka to spice up his hot chocolate, but had decided that it probably wasn't worth the risk or the effort to find a new supplier. Though at first the whiskey contrasted sharply with the sweet cocoa, the concoction had eventually settled in his taste buds. He had come to enjoy the heat of the cocoa complimented by the warmth of the whiskey that spread through his body. Amber had tried his hot chocolate a week ago, and had nearly gagged.

"Jesus, Sam," she had said after she had managed to swallow, her pretty face twisting into an ugly grimace. "What the hell is wrong with you? You can't actually enjoy that."

"Actually, I've learned to enjoy some things that are bad for me."

She cocked her head with a smile and bit her lower lip, painted bright red. Her long blonde hair draped over her shoulders. "Are you saying that I'm bad for you?" she teased as she walked toward him, placing her hands on his knees and leaning into him.

Sitting in his chair, he leaned over and glanced behind her to make sure his door was locked. "Oh, I don't know…" he started, before she kissed him full on the mouth.

That had been a short week ago, and the time which used to pass with a redundancy and monotony had started to accelerate. After Christmas, the battalion had begun the process of packing up the non-essentials for shipment back home. With the talk of home, and of their relieving unit now arriving in Kuwait, the air was practically electric. The sourness that had seemed to taint every laugh started to fade. Thoughts of home, which had always occupied a place in their minds, now consumed their thoughts and their energies. Attendance at the small gym had picked up considerably.

Sam's thoughts, too, had started to turn toward home. The Christmas package from Rachel had made an indelible impression on him that he had not been able to shake. The picture she had sent of her and Claire at Thanksgiving had made him cry, and as he wiped away the tears that flooded his eyes, he realized with an ironic little laugh that he was worse off than he had thought, sitting in his room alone, drunk and blubbering like a child over a picture.

Now, sitting before him on his desk, the steam from his drying blouse rising lazily into the air, carrying with it the subtle stink of body odor and sweat, sat a nearly-blank sheet of paper.

Several weeks ago, before Christmas, and when he was still being constantly grilled over the shooting with Marie, the Chaplain had approached him and spoken to him about a letter from Mrs. Garcia, Jonathon's mother.

Mel explained, "Jon's mom has written me a couple times, as well as the boss." Sam's eyes subconsciously roamed around, trying to find an escape from a conversation that revolved around his dead friend's grieving mother. He shifted uncomfortably on his feet, and adjusted the sling that suddenly dug into the flesh between his shoulder and neck.

Mel continued, noting his apparent discomfort. "She asked me in one of her recent letters if I knew any of the men here who had been close to Jon. I gave her your name." Sam let out a long, quiet sigh. A patrol of Humvees rushed by them, the unmistakable high roar of the engines ascending and then descending as they passed. Coming back to their conversation, Sam looked long and hard into the Chaplain's eyes, as if he were silently cursing him. Mel continued, "She wrote a letter to you and asked if I would get it to you. Sam," he paused, choosing his words carefully, "I know that Jon's death has not been easy for you." Sam drew a short breath as if he were about to say something, but Mel continued before he could. "But this is your friend's mother, and she is trying to find comfort in her son's death. I think… this would be a good thing for you to do… for Jon. Maybe good for you, too," he added, laying a hand on Sam's solid shoulder and drawing the letter from his cargo pocket and handing it to him. Sam had taken the letter as if he were being handed a snake.

Holding the letter in both hands, he looked down at it. Her handwriting was not neat, and she had misspelled his last name. Hastily, he had shoved the letter into his cargo pocket. The Chaplain, sensing the time had come for a change of subject, asked him how things were going with the investigation.

"Oh, they're fine," Sam had said, obviously as uncomfortable with the new subject as he was with the old one. The Chaplain nodded his head and looked at him knowingly. Sam, nearly desperate to get from under that gaze, offered up a quick apology and said, "Hey Mel, I really gotta get going. I got a meeting."

"Sure, sure," Mel had nodded. "Just think about that letter, Sam," he said as Sam began to walk away. "Oh, and congratulations on the promotion, Captain."

"Thanks," Sam answered despite himself, turning back to the man. "I will." He was upset with himself; the letter from Mrs. Garcia had completely unnerved him. Mel had seen right through him, with the Marie thing. He was sure that he knew the truth, but he told himself that even if the Chaplain did know anything, he wasn't going to tell anybody based on nothing more than a hunch, which Sam was sure was all he had, if he even had that.

Now, huddled over the heater, sipping his brew of chocolate and whiskey, so far all he had gotten on paper was the greeting, "Dear Mr. and Mrs. Garcia."

He had been staring at that sheet of paper for over an hour now, sifting through all the things that he wanted to say, what he didn't want to say, and what he should say. He was on his third drink, and the pen felt loose in his fingers. Finally, cursing to himself, he began:

> My name is Sam Calhoun. I served with your son Jon here in Iraq. The chaplain gave me your letter, and I will do my best to answer your questions.
>
> Jon and I first met in Najaf. I was the Scout Platoon Leader and he was, as you know, a Platoon Leader in Delta Company. To spare you the details, me and two of my teams got in a little scrap and needed to be reinforced. Jon's platoon was the one sent to extract us. A lot of things went wrong that night, some things happened that I'm not sure Jon ever got over…

He wasn't thinking now, the filter that normally kept him from saying the wrong thing in the wrong way to the wrong people— which never really worked all that well to begin with—had stopped working entirely. He tried to check himself and make a point to be

252

more diplomatic, but eventually he started to write more quickly, gripping his pen so tight that his hand was threatening to cramp.

Afterwards, when we were back at base, I made a point to thank him, deciding that he and I should become close friends. He smiled and offered me his hand. He always introduced himself as Jonathon, but no one here ever called him that. He was always called Jon, which I think kind of bothered him a little.

He and I became fast friends that night. My first impression of him was calm, quiet. I'd often see him sitting by himself in the morning, with his bible next to him. He was well-liked and well-respected in the battalion, especially for being one of the younger platoon leaders. People thought highly of him, and my Company Commander even personally requested his platoon several times for specific missions. Jon was always honest with you in what he thought: he had a way of telling you that you were wrong without making you feel stupid, which is something I've never learned how to do. He and I would often grab chow together and talk about the day or what was going on.

We always seemed to find each other whenever something bad happened that we needed to talk about. Sometimes, when I remember him and our conversations, I'm struck by how odd it is to find a man like Jon in the middle of a war. Where most of us are crass, unbridled, even outright mean, he was almost gentle. He wasn't here out of anger, or a lust for glory, or out of pride. His was a deliberate and simple patriotism. Sometimes, hanging out with him, I'd be ashamed at my own pessimism, though Jon certainly never did or said anything judgmental.

He paused and read quickly back over what he had written. He sighed heavily and took a long swallow from his mug, the whiskey burning all the way down his throat. Running his hand through his dark hair, he continued. He knew what he was supposed to say now, knew that the thing that Jonathon's parents wanted to hear from their son's friend was that he had died for a great cause, that his life was not wasted. But Sam could not find the words to make those sentences. When he picked up his pen again, his writing was feverish, even desperate.

It's tragic that men like him have to die in wars like these. What did Jon offer in his death, what service did it ultimately provide? I can't help but think how much more our world needed him alive, than killed in some God-forsaken place like this. And for what? Nothing, really. But Jon believed in things like honor, and right and wrong. He believed he was here defending his country. Is that the truth? I don't know. It all just seems like such a waste in the end. And all that is left is the fact that he is dead, and I can't begin to understand why. We comfort ourselves by calling him our hero, and we try to convince ourselves that he died for some abstract concept like freedom, but is that really the truth? Try as hard as I can, I can't make the logical connection between his dying in Iraq and the protection of our freedom or the "American Way of Life." Maybe I'm just standing too close. I don't know.

You asked me in your letter if I knew anything more about his death. I don't know what you've been told, but I've spoken with his old Platoon Sergeant, SFC Kevin Anderson, who was there and tried to save him after he'd been hit. As far as I can tell, in real war, people don't die like they do in the movies. All that's left inside the body when life is fading is the determined struggle to keep on living. All efforts are driven toward that end, we realize how insignificant our lives are, and the world becomes cruel and unfair that it will go on without us. Jon didn't die quickly, no matter what you were told, there was no great and dramatic ending to his life. He didn't whisper anything poignant with his last breath. He couldn't. He suffocated to death, drowned in his own blood—

No. Enough, he thought. Too far.

Sam shook his head violently and then scooped up the two pages of his letter, crumpled them up and threw them in the trash with a curse. Throwing his pen down on his desk, he flexed the fingers in his right hand as he leaned back in his chair. His cup of hot chocolate near cold, he grabbed it and emptied it in several, full gulps, as he felt his heart start to slow back down. He laughed and swore to himself, shaking his head as he wiped the tears that pooled in his eyes. "I'm a goddamn train wreck," he said quietly to himself, pouring himself another drink.

Lying on his cot later that night, as he rolled over on his side in the dark, he felt a prayer rise up in him. He knew he could ask for forgiveness, say he was sorry, that he was sad and he needed help, and that maybe the prayer would be answered. How, he didn't know, but he knew that it could be. But he reminded himself that he didn't pray anymore, and he went to sleep.

"Hello?" a tired voice came over the phone, thick with sleep.

"Hi."

"Sam!?"

"Hi Rachel... how are you?" he managed to spit out, convinced he sounded nowhere near as relaxed as he wanted to.

"Fine, how are *you*? Where are you? Ohmygod are you—" came the confused reply through the cracked phone he held in his hand.

"No, no, I'm fine," he answered and heard her breathe a sigh of relief. "How are you?" he asked again, then shook his head in frustration.

"I'm fine," she answered again, and then paused. "What time is it over there?"

"Oh, yeah, I'm sorry to call so early—"

"No, no, that's fine—" she interrupted. He could hear her get out of bed and start moving around.

"—but I wanted to catch you... I thought you might still be teaching aerobics early in the morning."

birdmen

"No," she answered, "I had to stop doing that. It wasn't paying enough, and it was too hard with Claire."

Sam smiled at just the sound of the little girl's name come from her voice. "How is she?" he asked, and hoped that she hadn't heard the slight crack in his voice.

"Oh, she's doing fine," he could hear her smile through the phone, her voice carrying the thick and slow drawl of her accent. "Getting big, talkin' up a storm. Of course, you can't understand any of it, but she's saying something."

"Are you working somewhere else?" Sam asked. He had prepared a list of questions in his head in case the conversation had turned into one of those that has to be driven along. But as soon as he had heard her voice, he was swept up in the moment, and had forgotten all of them. The phone reeked of cigarette smoke from the hundreds of mouths that had spoken into it. On all sides, in the little cubicle built of plywood, various graphic cartoon-like pornographic images had been drawn by men too far away, too angry, or too bored. The smoke and the images were a stark contrast to the simple joy that her voice breathed into him.

"Yeah," she answered, "I got a job at the Outback in town," and continued to tell him about the people she was working with, Claire's preschool, and her neighbors next to her who loved to stay up all night watching TV, laughing and yelling until the sun came up, it seemed. When she realized that she had been talking for the past ten straight minutes, with only Sam's soft grunts and "Uh-huh's" confirming that he was still listening, she stopped suddenly. "I'm sorry I talk so much," she apologized.

Sam smiled so big he could hardly say, "No, no, it's great Rachel." And he meant it. "I could just sit here and listen to you talk for forever."

"Oh," she blushed through the phone. After a pause, her shy, "Hi," came back.

"Hi Rachel," he answered back. He was in ecstasy, tingling all over with the thrill of speaking with her, of hearing her voice, of saying her name. And he cursed himself and thought of the dozens of times that he could have called before this.

"Sam," she started, her voice soft.

"Yeah?" he asked.

"It's just…" she began, and he knew what she was going to say. "I haven't heard from you in so long. Have you been getting my letters?" Of course he had been getting them; she knew that.

"Yeah," was all he could say, then forced himself to vocalize the guilt that rose inside of him. "I'm sorry, Rachel."

It was sincere, and it was enough. He had never understood her capacity for forgiveness, had never been able to appreciate what allowed her to move past peoples' sins against her, but now he fell into the depths of her mercy and let those cool waters surround him. "It's all right, Sam, I just want you to know that I'm here, if you ever need to talk…"

He was silent, did not know what to say, did not have a response for her. "I know," he finally managed to spit out.

She let it drop, feeling the silence weigh heavy over the phone. Searching for a change in subject, she asked, "What's it like over there? What do you do all day? What about your friend Jon? How is he? Do you get to see him much?"

Sam paused before he spoke, trying to figure out how one says what he was about to say. "Jon died, Rachel," she heard him say. "He was killed. Back in September."

"Oh Sam… I'm so sorry," and she ran out of clichés, giving up quickly before she sounded glib.

He sighed quietly over the phone, "Yeah." Then, pretending that he had to go, but in reality recognizing they wouldn't be able to talk about anything else now, and finding himself refusing to talk more about it over the stinking phone, with the soldier two feet from him able to hear all that he would say, he said, "Hey, I gotta go."

"Okay," she answered, forgiving his flight. "It was really nice to hear from you Sam," she said, articulating the words deliberately.

"Yeah, you too, Rachel," he offered back with no less sincerity. "Can I call you again in a couple days?"

"Yeah!" her voice ascended an octave, and he laughed as he heard her blush on the other end of the phone. "I'd really like that," she half whispered.

"Great… well, take care, Rachel, it was good to talk to you."

"You too, Sam," she repeated.

"Yeah, I'll talk to you soon," and he tore the receiver away from his ear and hung up.

Sam sat in the middle of one of the long white tables that lined the dining facility and waited for her. He had seen her, standing in the long line for trays and plastic ware, as he had just filled his tray with food and was looking for a seat. They had made eye contact, and she had mouthed "save me a seat" to him. His heart beat faster in anticipation of the meeting. It was January twentieth, and the base had been virtually overrun by the relieving unit, the new—and clean— digital camouflage uniforms of the 25th Infantry Division from Hawaii a sharp contrast to the brown desert pattern that the soldiers in the 101st had deployed with almost a year ago now. It was as if strangers—aliens—had broken in upon their miserable, static world. Time—real time—had indeed passed; their long, hard deployment was coming to an end. Every day, long flatbed trucks driven by baggy-eyed Pakistanis and Arabs hauled their containers of decreasing essential equipment south to Kuwait. The lines at the chow hall had become almost unbearably long, and would have been so, had not the reason for the long lines been the appearance of their relief. In just one short week, the brigade would leave Forward Operating Base Q-West, and travel south down Highway 1 to Kuwait, where they would wait for a plane to take them home. Home.

Home had been on everyone's mind lately, and Sam and Amber were certainly no exceptions. The last time she had visited him had been just over a week ago. Their time together had been strained recently, as if each would have rather not been with the other, but felt compelled by obligation or habit to meet that way, in the night. After they were through that night, they had both stayed awake for over an hour. Finally, unable to sleep, or to speak the words that might bring sleep, she had gotten dressed in the dark and left him. He had pretended to sleep as she left, and she had pretended that she thought he was asleep.

Now, sitting in the chow hall, waiting and watching her get her food and come closer to him, he knew that the time had come. As she walked toward him, her face lacked the usual warmth, the sparkling blue eyes, the bright red lipstick smile with the flash of ivory teeth.

"Hey," he said as warmly as he could as she sat down opposite him.

"Hi Sam," she said, giving him a quick, but forced, smile, before returning her eyes to her tray.

They sat quietly for a couple minutes, each pretending to enjoy their food in such a way that did not facilitate discussion. The truth was that neither of them really wanted the relationship to last. Amber had a fiancée who was an Apache pilot down in Baghdad, who would be returning home just a few weeks after her, and Sam himself had never gotten too emotionally attached to her, to the idea of them together. Their relationship had been one of convenience based on simple lust and the need for companionship. They had both fulfilled that need in the other, but now that their deployment was ending, it was time to end it. The thing that kept them both silent was the guilt in voicing what they both felt and each knew: that they had used the other. That had been the unspoken agreement between the two of them, and now the terms of that agreement were coming to an end, and it was time to pay the moral debt.

Sam's guilt was compounded by the surge of feelings his recent phone calls with Rachel had produced. Since they had first spoken over ten days ago, he had called every other morning. The change in him produced by those phone calls had manifested itself physically. His shirts no longer hung on him, but wrapped around him in a way that displayed that his health and strength were returning. He had started drinking less as well. Though he did not have the perspective yet to realize it, his drinking habit had morphed from a kind of forced-binge to the casual nip at night before bed, which was still not entirely healthy, but a far cry from the self-destruction and internal flogging that he had been partaking in.

Now, sitting across from each other, their trays both near empty and not ten words having passed between the two of them, Sam decided to begin.

"Amber," he began, deciding that he would be the bad guy on this one, "I don't think that this is going to keep working. I mean," he said, looking at her, "this has been great, but it's not something that I want to keep up at home. I'm sorry, it's just me. I've been talking to Rachel lately, and I think that she and I may have a shot. I'm sorry. You're a great girl, and Kevin is a lucky man to have you. But I just don't think that you and I are gonna work out."

Amber looked at him across the table with soft, warm eyes. Cliché? Sure. Mostly a lie? Sure. "Yeah, Sam," she said, with a sadness in her voice, "you're right. This has been a lot of fun," she reached across the table and laid a hand on his, her red-painted fingernails and fair skin a contrast to the dark, rough skin with flecks of black hair on his. "And I think that maybe we both needed each other through this. You're a great guy, Sam, and I hope that we can remain friends."

Sam shuddered at the thought.

They looked at each other silently for a moment, each wanting to run away from the horribly awkward tension that hung around them, but not wanting to leave on such bad terms. Sam decided that he would wait until she left; he didn't want to leave her sitting by herself, knowing that people were watching and would see him leave her. No, he would let her be the one to walk away, then wait long enough until he was sure they would not meet outside by the trash can or in the mud-saturated parking lot. When he didn't make a move to leave, she squeezed his hand and then walked away, carrying her tray with both hands.

He sat there alone for a couple minutes, finishing the cup of orange drink in front of him, buying the space he needed before he could leave. Feeling the sudden, irresistible urge to talk to Rachel, he glanced at his watch. It was eight at night, the phone line may not be too long, it only being noon at Fort Campbell and only seven in the morning at Schofield Barracks.

He waited in line for almost an hour. Even though the time for each call had been reduced to a strict ten minutes to facilitate the increase in callers, by the time he got to the new and improved internet café, run by a Kurd from Irbil (who was making an absolute killing, by the way, charging a dollar a minute), there was quite a line. Evidently, with one unit so close to coming home, and the other having just left their loved ones, the norms of when was appropriate to call did not apply. Finally finding himself in one of the small cubicles separated by a thin piece of plywood that was thus far barren of the graffiti that had decorated all the other phone and internet cafés, he picked up the phone and dialed her number. He smiled reflexively when he heard her voice.

"Hello?"

"Hey Rachel, it's me…."

Ten days later, he was playing a tackle football game—the second that day—in the hot sand of Camp Victory, Kuwait. After the game, he was going to walk over to the pizza hut in the square of little restaurants and tables in the middle of camp, and buy a large pepperoni pizza, and then head back to his cot in the tent that his company had been crammed into. He had borrowed two movies with Angelina Jolie in spandex, and he was looking forward to enjoying them and the pizza after a long, hot shower.

With virtually nothing to do except attend the nightly update meetings which were always the same ("No, we still don't know when the planes are coming."), the soldiers in the battalion found that they had nothing but time on their hands. Basking in the glory and triumph of their deployment, they laughed arrogantly at the imposed care and wariness with which the soldiers permanently stationed at Camp Victory carried themselves. Finding themselves at the end of their tour, they fell into that easy trap of feeling as if they had cheated death, that they were somehow immortal, and they swaggered and strutted through camp and laughed loudly and carelessly at the small chow hall. Their days were full of sleeping in, eating pizza and hamburgers and ice cream, playing tackle football until the heat—in February—became too much to bear, and watching movies they had already seen a dozen times.

The shadow of death had left them, the specter of despair had departed their spirits, and each of them drew an easy breath as they stepped back from that abyss and reclaimed their hopes for a long and full life. The tents rang with laughter and amicable cursing. Even when their flights had been delayed for the third time, they were still able to relish in the fact that they were almost home.

Sam called his folks the day before he left Kuwait, though he didn't know it would be. He had made a point to call home at least once a month, even if he sometimes waited to call when he knew they would both be at work. His dad told him that they would be there when he landed, but that they were not there to spoil any plans he might have with friends, indicating that it was his mother's insistence that she get to see her baby boy when he got home. His mother told him that they had talked to Rachel—she and Rachel had struck up a kind of friendship when Sam had brought her home to meet his folks before he had deployed—and that they would all be there when he landed. When Sam voiced concern over how they would know in time when he was going to land, she surprised him by telling him that she had known about the previous three delays even before he had.

Home. The traveler, who has been far away from the familiar sights, sounds, and smells of their usual surroundings, knows the quiet urge that beckons him back to the proverbial. To the astronaut, floating in the sea of space, even the cold Pacific is his home when his capsule comes plummeting back to earth. When the sailor, having resided on a floating, pitching world surrounded in unsubstantial blue, finally feels his foot hit firm ground, he knows he is home, even if he cannot speak the language of the natives of that land. So when the expeditionary soldier, gone for so long in some foreign land, with foreign tongues and foreign courtesies, trods the ground that rests in the shade of his home standard, he finds himself at home. When he looks around and sees his native flag flying freely, not on uniforms or flying in the face of mortars and rockets and fear, but flying freely as if it were the only natural thing it could ever do, something comes to rest inside him, and his flag becomes something beautiful to him; something sacred. And the land that before may have seemed so diverse, so spread out, and so large, suddenly telescopes; and he becomes equally at home in the gray cities as in the open farmlands, in the deserts as in the swamps, or in the emerald mountains as in the rolling hills. It is all home to him now, all of it, every single magnificent and insignificant corner, and he finds that he is finally and truly a son of his fatherland.

Sam landed, with just over three hundred other soldiers from his battalion, on a cold morning in February. The crowd, gathered under banners and waving little flags, had been standing in the bitter wind since three that morning. To add to the tension, the plane had had to circle overhead twice in order to buy time for a general to arrive in order to welcome the soldiers home as they stepped off the plane.

Inside the plane, one of the stewardesses had put up drawings that her son's kindergarten class had drawn. Full of peculiarities, and absent of any sense of diplomacy, there were pictures ranging from American flags to tanks driving toward what were supposed to be Arabs waving American flags. American flags and freedom and truth and justice everywhere. As if it were that easy. As if anything was. Thank God we start out so naïve, Sam thought as he pulled down one of the pictures with the tanks. Otherwise we wouldn't stand a chance.

When the plane landed, he stayed in his seat a while, and watched as the men from Charlie Company slowly filed past him out of the plane and into the early morning frost. Seized with a sudden appreciation for the scale of what they had accomplished in the past year, and what this year would come to mean for him through his lifetime, he found himself, strangely, in no hurry to get off the plane. His thoughts flashed to Jonathon, and he held that overwhelming emotion inside him like a child holds a firefly in the palm of his hand, knowing that he'll have to let it go soon but savoring the moment that he holds a great mystery of God.

Gathering his things, he swallowed the thought down and fell into line and stepped outside.

Walking across the tarmac, he heard his mother before he saw her. Always calling him by his full name, with her heavy, slow Cajun drawl, he heard his name up ahead in the crowd and saw a small woman with big, dark hair bundled in a gray overcoat jumping up and down.

"Samyul! Samyul!" he heard her cry, and as he drew nearer, he could see that she was crying through her glasses that fought to stay on her face. He saw his dad, older than he'd last seen him, more creases around the eyes, the light gray on his head starting to overwhelm what used to be dark red, one arm around his bouncing wife, and the other shoved deep into a pocket. Behind the two of them, peeking between the gaps that formed every time his mother left the ground, were a pair of big, round eyes that smiled sheepishly up at him through long eyelashes.

He winked playfully at the brown eyes while he leaned over the low fence that contained the crowd and hugged his mother. The smell of his mother's hair and her perfume drifted through his memory, and he was suddenly seven years old again, holding his mom after he had broken his arm falling out of a tree, tears streaming down his eyes. The urge was not strong, and easily fought, but he wanted to cry. His dad clapped him hard on the back with both hands, and when Sam's mother had let him go, he stretched out a warm hand—the one that had been in the pocket—and said, "Welcome home, Son," in the same tone that he had used when they had dropped him off at Tulane, saying, "Be good, Son." Sam knew, that it was the same thing that his granddaddy had said to his dad, with the same warm handshake, when his granddaddy had picked up his dad at the airport when his dad had come home from Vietnam. It was an acknowledgement of some kind, an indication that they now shared something, some secret knowledge about their world. A thought flew through his mind that maybe that handshake and the warm tone were in his blood somehow, handed down from father to son, for how many generations? How many wars and homecomings?

Letting his dad's hand go, he saw Rachel. Both of them aware that his parents could not help but watch their reunion, they smiled at each other shyly, neither of them moving toward the other. She was wearing a gray ski cap pulled down low over her forehead, hiding her eyebrows. Just below the reach of the cap, the bite of the cold air had painted her cheekbones a rosy red. She wore a blue ski jacket, zipped all the way up so that she could tuck her mouth and nose in against the cold. Her clear eyes, dark-hazel spheres suspended in a sea of sharp white, shone out, and seemed to rise up like a wave and come crashing down on him. He stood there hypnotized, stunned, completely overrun. She seemed to him like the ocean; her eyes pulled him in and held him there suspended in a sea of unadulterated, unpolluted happiness, and for one moment there was no Iraq, no war, or Marie, or even Jonathon. She blinked the cold away, and he returned to himself.

"Hi," was all he could muster before he cautiously wrapped his arms around her small frame. And though he towered over her by almost a full foot, there was no question of who was holding who. As she wrapped her arms around him, he had a vision of towering peaks covered with snow. Being held by her was like being held by a mountain.

"Hi," she whispered into his chest as she held him, her head resting in the crevice formed by his pectorals, the musky scent of aftershave and man wafting into her sinuses.

Letting go first, for a reason that he could not explain, he tore his eyes away from her, and let his mother wrap her arms around him again, her arms around his stomach, her head tilted back and analyzing his face, inspecting him for injuries. He smiled, slightly embarrassed but enjoying the affection at the same time, and in an effort to mask his self-consciousness he asked the first thing that came to mind. "Where's Claire?" he asked into that infinite ocean again, those unending swells that rose up and came crashing over him, leaving him naked and numb.

Rachel answered him with a warm smile, it was not yet six o'clock in the morning, the temperature was hovering around 20 degrees, no place for a toddler. In another inexplicable flash, he thought that, were he the girl's father, she would have been here, and how much he would have liked that, to have walked off the plane to his bouncing mother, the warm hand of his father, those oceanic eyes and that granite embrace, and a little girl's squeal of "Daddy!" It was not a thought born out of need or of disappointment; nevertheless, it surprised him, and he looked at his dad who, he noticed with another rush of self-consciousness was watching him—studying him—as his mother held him around the waist.

Realizing that he had to get inside to the warehouse—there was to be a ceremony—he smiled again and said, "I'll see you inside," and began to walk away, turning once with a wave and a smile at the three sets of eyes glued to him.

The ceremony was brief, some general spoke about something while everyone sighed and looked impatiently at their watches. The soldiers sang the Army Song and the Division Song with less than total enthusiasm. Sam's dad, and several other men in the bleachers, veterans of another war who had come home to empty airports and furtive, suspicious glances, accusing them of a crime they had thought to be an honor, nodded their heads in approval at the general's words and the band and the songs. Perhaps, they thought thankfully, their country was on the road to repenting for its past sins. When the songs were finished, the crowd was allowed to come down into the formation and see their loved ones.

Daddies scooped up little boys waving little American flags and little girls with big signs like, "My Daddy is a Hero," while mothers wiped away a year's worth of tears. Husbands kissed wives gently, and whispered into their ears soft flirtations that made them smile and blush. Soldiers without anyone there to welcome them home found comfort in their isolation with other singles. With nothing to say, they stood around and watched the reunions all around them.

The conversations were fabricated with the kind of awkwardness of having too much to say that cannot be said just yet. Parents asked about the flight. "Fine, fine," their soldier would nod, remembering the delicious scent of perfume on the stewardesses and the clean, comfortable seats. Soldiers asked visitors where they were staying. "In the such-and-such hotel" or "In the extra room... no, no, there's plenty of room..." their loved ones answered. Their soldiers introduced them to strange men with a tone in their voices that communicated the deep bond that had formed between the two. "Honey, this is the guy I told you about with the..." the soldier and his buddy would laugh, remembering, while the family smiled politely, more enjoying the scene than the content of their story. A soldier would introduce his buddy to his girlfriend, with the pride of a little boy showing off his baseball trophy. "This is Brooke," he would beam, and his buddy would try to hide from his eyes and his smile the fact that he had read that personal and sensitive-in-nature letter that she had written her boyfriend to give him something to think about through the long, lonely nights.

He had the feeling of being driven by a great wave, unable and unwilling to try to direct his course. Rolling down the highway into Nashville, his dad driving, his mother in the front seat chattering excitedly, Rachel next to him, answering her and stealing glances toward him, he had the sensation of being driven by a force outside himself. Gazing out the window as the bare trees rushed by him, he had disengaged from the conversation with his mother a while ago, exhausted with the effort, and had taken an interest in the world that passed by his window. He smiled to himself when he caught himself scanning the roadside, a habit that he had developed in Iraq, trying to pick out possible ambush sites or roadside bombs. A box had happened to be lying off to the side of the road, probably having blown out of the back of a pickup roaring down the highway, and he had had the fleeting thought Wait! as his heart skipped a beat. He smiled to himself, realizing right then that there were no more bombs hidden in piles of trash, or enemy positions in the hills around him. He was home, in a place where the roads did not blow up underneath you, where the sky did not rain rockets or mortars in the middle of the night, or where every corner and crowded street did not hide a potential threat.

Rachel had seen the smile sneak onto his face, and she had leaned over and rested her hand on his. Feeling the cool skin of her palm on his hand, he pulled himself out of Iraq, and turned and smiled warmly at her, his eyes still reflecting the depth that his mind had been immersed in. Suddenly aware of their discreet physical contact, and uncertain if they should be touching like that, secretly in the back of his parent's car like love-struck teenagers, she patted the top of his hand gently and then quietly slid her small hand off his.

The restaurant where they were going, the Stock Yard, was a place his dad had looked up and was supposed to have delicious steak along with an excellent wine and liquor menu. His dad, a wine enthusiast, had also read that it had the oldest unopened bottle of wine, worth around a half million dollars, and wanted to see it for himself. The story was that it had been, at one point, in the knapsack of a revolutionary war soldier from the colonies. In the car, when Sam questioned the value of what was essentially a bottle full of vinegar, his dad had entertained his question with a smile that seemed to say, It's not about that, don't you see? Sam had just shaken his head and laughed.

When they had been getting dressed for dinner back at the motel his parents were staying at, Sam had told his dad that they didn't need to go out to some big dinner. His dad had given him the same look he would give him when Sam commented on the two hundred year old bottle of wine. His dad had patted him on the shoulders with a laugh, saying, "Of course we do! This is a night to celebrate."

"Okay," Sam had answered, succumbing to what he recognized again as familial tradition, "but don't count on me being able to drive home."

His dad guffawed, pleased as he could be at the promise of revelry and his role as host for the night. He had acquired Cuban cigars, big, thick tubes that reeked of warm tobacco and damp soil, and he had displayed them proudly to Sam earlier, with a mischievous sparkle in his eye, as if he were showing him a dime bag of marijuana.

Now, as he sat in the car, Sam was too detached from all that was happening around him to appreciate what was going on, what his dad and mother and Rachel were doing, what his homecoming and this night really meant to all of them. He was still just riding the wave of a force against which he had no power to resist or deflect. The reality was that if his parents and Rachel were not there to make him take a long, hot shower, and put a beer in his hand, and make reservations at a nice chop house in Nashville, and drive him there, he would more than likely have ended up on a couch, flipping through the channels, imprisoned and overwhelmed by the sudden and drastic change of his world, unable to move, unable to do anything until something moved him in a particular direction.

Dinner started with snifters of an old scotch that his dad, in his overly-excitable state, kept exclaiming he could not believe the restaurant carried. He ordered one for himself and for Sam—without asking—and then lifted his eyebrows to the two ladies, asking whether they wanted any. Sam laughed. "Dad, do you know what a glass of scotch would do to Rachel?"

Rachel giggled while his mom ordered a cosmopolitan. Rachel, feeling the pressure to join them in their revelry, ordered a mango martini.

Sam sighed audibly when their waiter, a handsome young man with a thin face and long, dark, but neatly groomed, sideburns, asked them what they were celebrating. Sam's mom could not help herself, and exclaimed, "My son." She reached over and patted her palm softly on his cheek while he shook his head, utterly embarrassed. "He just got home from Iraq."

"So don't be too long with those drinks, huh?" his dad said, playing up to the moment.

The waiter raised his eyebrows and nodded his head. When Sam looked up, the waiter was looking him in the eye, and said, "Welcome home, sir." Sam thought how the waiter looked to be a couple years older than himself, and offered a "Thanks" in as clear a voice as he could muster with the tingling sense of self-consciousness that flooded him.

When the waiter brought the drinks, placing each carefully on a white square napkin, he said they were on the house, again looking at Sam and saying that the restaurant was grateful for his service.

"Well, shoot," his dad chimed in, "if this round's free, why don't you get us another couple?"

The waiter nodded his head with a smile, while Sam said with a laugh, "Jesus Christ, dad."

"Samyul Calhoun," his mother's voice came back at him, soft, but sharp, the four syllables slicing through the air. Realizing her tone was sharper than she meant it, she added, reaching over again, this time patting him on his arm, "I know you've been away at war," she stole a glance at her husband, who looked into his glass, "but let's try to remember not to be irreverent."

Pictures of Amber naked, empty bottles of Jack Daniels on the floor, and a man lying against a pile of hay with two holes in his chest, the slight hissing of the cauterized flesh whispering in the air, rumbled through his mind as he looked at his mother, sitting at this linen-covered table in Nashville, Tennessee, her hair having just been cut, a dress that she had bought especially for this day draped over her shoulders, an innocent yet insistent smile on her face. Sam blinked as they locked eyes—could she see those images that had flashed in his mind, projected through his eyes?—and said with a sincerity that surprised him, "I'm sorry, Mom, it won't happen again."

She smiled warmly, glad to dismiss any tension around the table, and reached for her glass, raising the drink in a toast. "To our boy," she offered. "Thank God he is home."

"Amen, and amen," his dad said.

They all clinked glasses in the center of the table. When Sam touched the rim of his glass to Rachel's, their eyes met for a moment before he looked away, afraid of what she may see.

What was that there, she saw? Some cloud, some shadow that seemed to pass between his pupil and the back wall of his retina? And though she smiled, and sipped thankfully from her glass with the others, a fear settled in her, a kind of sorrow at what she thought she had seen.

CHAPTER 5

The hard wood of the pew was unforgiving as he sat up straight, flexing his lower back and shifting his shoulders to stretch parts of him that were growing stiff. Rachel, sitting next to him, felt his restlessness and she glanced his way with a gentle smile. He flashed her a kind of smile back, half an apology for his animated discomfort, and settled back against the rigid wood.

He had been home now for nine days—he had been subconsciously keeping count since his return home, comparing the way time now seemed to pass against its passing in Iraq. It was Sunday morning, and Rachel had convinced him to come with her to the ten-thirty service at her church, a little, modest brick building just down the street from her apartment complex. The sanctuary was very baptist: a strict adherence to simplicity, the hard-wood pews, whitewashed walls, a few stained-glass windows that were there almost as a regrettable acquiescence, filtering in the warm sunlight with a kaleidoscope of colors that danced against the north wall like a living collage of color. Sam had been watching it crawl across the bottom of the wall, slowly creeping closer to the front of the church, where a large, slightly round man stood behind a dark mahogany pulpit with a cross carved into the front of it. There was no subtlety in the carving: the crucifix seemed to lurch out of the wood, hard and exacting, absent of any decorum. Part of the reason Sam had fixated his attention on the stained-glass reflection was that he had been unable to hold the threatening stare of that pulpit, with the large, sweating man in the dark suit, gesticulating with his left hand while his right held down his bible and notes.

Sam had been reflecting about just how she had convinced him to join her this morning; she hadn't tried to coerce him into coming, that was certainly not her way. So how was it that he now found himself sitting in this hard pew, in this stifling room, sitting next to her, the pews and warm air obviously not bothering her in the least? He didn't know, couldn't make sense of the string of events that had somehow led him here. He was reflecting on her capacity to get him to do things without actually asking him to, remembering finally that she had simply told him the night before that she was going to church. His response to her had been simple, and escaped him before he had had time to withhold it.

"I'd like to go with you," he had said, immediately wishing he hadn't. What he had meant, he now realized, was that he had an unexplainable and irresistible desire to stay near her, to be with her; so when she had said that she was going somewhere, his natural response was that he wanted to go there as well. It was simply an unfortunate circumstance that she was going to church.

"Pastor Bob" was what she and the rest of the congregation called the chubby man behind the pulpit; and though he could not understand it, Rachel had become very attached to his sermons—or "talks" as she called them. She had fixed herself a cup of coffee, which she had in hand when he had shown up that morning to walk with her the short two blocks to church. He had noticed that she received more than a few strange looks when she came walking in the door, a cup of coffee in her hand, little Claire holding the other, no ring on her hand, and a strange man beside her. No ring on his hand, either, do you see? the self-designated accountants of the church had whispered. She didn't really know anybody, though there had been a rather fat man with suspenders and a white shirt through which you could see his undershirt, who had leaned back when they sat behind him and asked how Claire was doing. Sam wondered—perhaps with a defensiveness he had not earned a right to—why this man was so interested in Claire. But Rachel had only smiled and said that they had dropped her off at Sunday school with Miss Annette. Then the man, noticing Sam's slightly familiar face and putting two and two together, had smiled and reached out a hand.

"You're Sam, right?"

"Umm," Sam answered, taking the offered hand, then caught himself, "Yessir. Sam Calhoun."

"Well, Sam," smiled the man with the suspenders, gripping his hand and pulling him closer with a smile, "we've all been praying you. Rachel here has kept us up to speed on you for the past year."

Sam glanced at Rachel, embarrassed, touched, and ashamed all at the same time.

"Thank you," he said, still looking at Rachel, then remembering to shift his gaze at the man. "I appreciate that, sir," he said, meaning it.

The man looked hard at him for a moment, saying, "It's good to have you back, son. Welcome home," he said with a hard, single nod, and then turned back in his seat.

As Sam had watched the light from the stained-glass window creep slowly across the wall, his mind wandered through the unconnected stream of consciousness that the mind does when left on its own. He thought of Valentine's night the week before, when he and Rachel had spent the evening eating macaroni and cheese with hotdogs on the floor of her living room.

His parents had, in a deliberate attempt not to make a nuisance of themselves and also facilitate his and Rachel's relationship, made dinner and hotel reservations in Nashville, and had left the two of them on their own for the night. Sam and his parents had spent the day moving his sparse belongings out of storage into his new apartment. After only a few hours, they had moved his things inside the building, and his parents had dismissed themselves. He had spent a few hours by himself, unpacking boxes of dishes and random items that he remembered with a touch of nostalgia packing over a year ago, wondering then whether he would ever see the items he now held in his hands again. It was a surreal moment for him, and one which he felt needed to be augmented with a few beers. On his third, he had reached a box that had a picture in a frame of Rachel and Claire which he held in his hands for several long minutes while a flood of emotions coursed through him. Putting the picture carefully on an end table next to the TV, he had picked up the phone and called Rachel.

"Hey," she said, recognizing his voice, "how are you?"

"Fine, you just get home from work?" he asked.

"Yeah," she answered.

"Well, I was wondering… do you have any plans tonight? It's Valentine's, and I was wondering if you wanted to do something?"

"Yeah, I'd love to!" she answered.

"Well, I'll call a few places and see if we can get in anywhere."

"Actually, Sam—"

"Yeah?" he asked.

"Well, would it be all right with you if we just did something here? It's just that it's gonna be hard for me to find a sitter for Claire with this late notice."

Sam smiled. "Oh yeah, that sounds great. Sorry, I didn't think—"

"No, don't worry about it. So what time are you thinking?" she asked.

"I don't know, I'm just unpacking here, but could get ready and be over in a couple hours."

"About six then?"

"Yeah, that sounds great. I'll see you then," he said, and hung up with a sudden nervousness that surprised him. He tried to get back to unpacking, but found that he wasn't really getting anything more done, and was just aimlessly moving from box to box. Finally, his third beer done, he reached into the refrigerator, which, thanks to his mom and the Wal-Mart just down the street, actually had food, and grabbed another beer and headed for the shower.

When he had jumped into his Jeep, he thought of getting Rachel some flowers and swinging by the liquor store to get a bottle of wine or champagne. Singing to himself and tapping his fingers on the steering wheel to the rhythm of the radio, he was filled with a sense of excitement that surprised him.

Swinging into the local floral shop on the way, he realized with embarrassment that the best he would be able to get were some picked-over carnations. He asked the little old lady behind the counter for all of the red and white ones that she had left, which came to about twenty. Obviously pitying the young man who had not properly planned for Valentine's Day, she threw in a few extra flowers to accent the bouquet, and gave him a discount because of the shape that some of the flowers were in.

Sam, genuinely grateful to her for the flowers, had thanked her and jumped back in his jeep, the engine roaring to life as he lurched back onto the road. Passing by the liquor store, he got there just ten minutes before they were closing, the manager giving him a warm "Afternoon" as he walked in. Finding the champagne section, he quickly perused the prices listed beneath each row. Finding the most expensive, a bottle of Dom Perignon, he walked up to the cashier and handed her his credit card. The cashier raised her eyebrows at the purchase, and gave Sam a quizzical look and a smile. "Must be for somebody special," she said.

"Yeah," Sam said, his face coloring just a little. The truth was that he couldn't tell the difference between this bottle and a ten dollar one, but he had about forty thousand dollars burning a hole in his pocket, and was eager to see the look on Rachel's face when he showed up at her door with picked-over flowers and a bottle of Dom. He hoped that she would appreciate the dichotomy as much as he did.

When he bounded up the stairs to get to her door, taking two at a time, the flowers bouncing in one hand, and holding the neck of the bottle in the other, his heart raced from nerves. It was just past six when he rang her door, the doorbell giving a dull buzz. The door opened, and she emerged behind the screen door with a smile that widened when she saw the flowers. He was dressed in a nice striped sport shirt, with khakis and a new pair of soft brown bicycle loafers. As she pushed the screen door out to let him in, he saw that she was in an old pair of jeans, with rips—which had not been fashionably placed—at the knees and mid-thighs, and a big orange sweatshirt that hung on her small frame and threatened to swallow her.

"Hi," he offered, handing her the flowers, and kissing her carefully on the cheek. As he pulled away from her and saw the slight surprise in her eyes, he realized suddenly that they had not kissed at all since he had left. "I'm sorry…" he stammered, realizing that perhaps he was a little too excited.

"No, no, that's all right," she answered, the surprise in her eyes warming as she looked up at him.

The blood rushed to his face again, as he thrust out the bottle of champagne with more than a little pride. "Happy Valentine's Day."

She took the bottle, her eyes widening when she saw the label. She had never actually seen a bottle of Dom Perignon before, and only recognized the bottle from hearing about it.

"Oh my gosh, Sam, how much was this?" she gushed.

Sam was as pleased as he could be with her reaction and the picture of her there, dressed in her old house clothes, flowers in one hand and a bottle of champagne in the other. "Oh, it's nothing," he said, trying to sound casual. "I got more money than I know what to do with right now, anyway. I figured it was worth it tonight."

She smiled and looked up at him with her big brown eyes, and he felt those waves that had overcome him at the airport rise up around him again. She reached up on her tip toes to kiss him on the cheek, her soft lips grating slightly against his unshaven face. His heart raced when he felt her warm breath against his cheek, and his face flushed slightly.

Turning into the kitchen, which was separated from the small living room by a counter covered in white tile, she said over her shoulder, "I didn't have time to run to the store—"

"That's fine," Sam cut her off. "We'll just throw something together, don't worry about it."

"But you brought flowers and champagne—Dom!" she exclaimed as she found a vase for the flowers.

He was simply beside himself, there with her in her apartment, on Valentine's Day, not in Iraq, getting ready to cook a simple dinner together and spend the evening talking and laughing. Suddenly, he clapped his hands. "Hey, where's Claire?"

"Oh," Rachel answered, "she was acting cranky about a half hour ago, so I put her down for a nap, and she went out like a light.

I'm sure she'll wake up in an hour or so and keep me up all night, but she was driving me crazy."

Sam smiled. "Yeah."

Noticing his smile, Rachel asked, "What is it?"

Looking at her, his smile emanating from him, radiating from his eyes, he shook his head slowly, keeping his eyes on her. "Nothing."

"Oh," she said, shifting shyly under his smile. "Hi."

"Hi Rachel," he said back softly.

She held his stare for another moment. Then, too overrun with the embarrassment of being looked at the way he was looking at her, she turned away and started to look through her cabinets, her refrigerator, her freezer. Sam saddled up to the counter, watching her as she moved. "What're you looking for?" he asked.

"Something for us to eat," she answered, not turning back to look at him.

Sam slid around the counter and opened up a cabinet. "Well," he pronounced, "here's some Mac and Cheese. You got any hotdogs?"

She smiled, embarrassed. "I think so. But Mac and Cheese and hotdogs with Dom?" she asked, incredulous. "And on Valentine's?"

He shrugged. "Sure, why not?"

She laughed out loud with delight.

They were just folding the slices of hotdog into the Mac and Cheese when they heard Claire cry from her room. They had opened the bottle of champagne and were each on their first glass, Rachel carefully taking slow sips. It didn't take much to get her drunk, and she was not sure that she should be drunk tonight. Sam put down his glass and headed around the corner into Claire's small room, where she was standing in her crib, her face red from crying. She resisted him slightly when he bent over and hefted her up, but the faintly familiar smell of his shirt allowed her to rest in his arms. This was the first time that she had seen him since his return, though before he left, he had been a constant presence in her life. Sam let himself believe that perhaps something in her subconscious told her that he was not a stranger, that perhaps somewhere embedded deep in her infant memory resided the smell of his shirts and his skin, and the sound of his heartbeat against his chest as he held her.

277

They emerged back into the kitchen, and Claire, seeing her mother, reached out for her. Rachel took her and spoke to her in soothing words, rubbing the tears off her face. Dinner ready, Sam poured Rachel and himself a fresh glass and set the table as she made their plates, cutting up the pieces of hotdog into small bites for Claire. At just over two years old, Claire had plenty to say, but had not quite mastered the means of saying it. The result was a constant outpour of squeaks and guttural noises that made the two grownups with her constantly laugh.

Between Claire's outbursts, the two of them had a chance to talk for the first time. She asked mostly descriptive questions like what the food had been like, and where he had stayed. When he told her about Makhmur, she became fascinated with the convergence of culture between the Kurds and the Arabs, and the tension between the two. He told her about the three months of MREs that they had had to eat before their first hot meal, and the forty-eight days they had initially gone before their first showers. He described with great, sweeping gesticulations the night of the Camp Pennsylvania bombings in Kuwait, where a young soldier had stolen several grenades and thrown them into the command tent in the middle of the night. That had happened only two nights before the brigade was set to attack into Iraq, and if tensions were not already high enough, that had certainly put everyone on edge. He laughed with amusement at the chaos of that night, of the reports that the enemy had massed just beyond the wire, and that a small team had infiltrated the camp. To compound it all, that was the same night when one of the Patriot batteries had shot down an English fighter jet coming back south from a bombing mission in Baghdad as part of the initial "shock and awe" campaign.

When she had asked him about An Najaf, he had simply shrugged his shoulders and mumbled something about there not being much to say, though she knew that it was very soon after An Najaf that he had been moved out of the battalion's reconnaissance platoon to Charlie Company as the XO. Sensing his aversion to the subject, she let it drop, and asked more questions about the villages and the people he had seen. Obviously happy to stay away from the subject, he dove into the layout of the villages, and how the people dressed. He told stories of AK-47s riding in the cabs of the combines of the farmers as they harvested their wheat crop. She shook her head in amazement. Imagine farmers in America having to carry weapons for both personal defense and to defend their crop as they harvested?

He told her the story of the weapons in the carpet of the bongo truck that he had found. When he remembered the last time he had told that story—and who he had told it to—his eyes grew sad and he rushed into another story. Suddenly realizing that they had been talking for nearly two straight hours—meaning that she had asked perhaps a half dozen questions while he had answered with stories and anecdotes—he stretched and yawned. He had had several glasses of champagne, and had therefore grown more animated with his stories, something that she had noticed with amusement, while she still had not finished the glass that he had topped off before they sat down to eat. They had let Claire out of her chair sometime during the story of the night at Camp Pennsylvania, and she had kept herself entertained with various toys on the floor. But now the back of this throat had become dry from all the talking, and he was ready for a break.

"Sorry I talked so much," he offered as he stood up, clearing the table and walking to the sink.

Rachel looked at him, her eyes dancing, "No! Are you kidding? Sam... what an experience! Thanks so much for telling me about all that." He turned to her, still holding the plates, and smiled softly at her as if to tell her that all he had told her were stories, and there was so much else that he wanted to say to her but could not yet for some reason. Telling stories was a way of saying things without really sharing anything. What he didn't tell her about were the fears and joys, and an incredible sadness that sat like a pile of stones on his chest, even when he was laughing.

His back was to her as he cleaned the plates and loaded the dishwasher. He turned his torso to look at her. He winked playfully, causing her to blush slightly and divert her attention to her baby girl on the floor, gurgling and squealing as she played. After having

888

loaded the dishes into the dishwasher and washed the pots full of congealed cheese, he had opened the fridge and been surprised to see a six-pack of beer. Rachel saw the surprise on his face, and answered, "When you said that you were coming over tonight, I ran down to the corner and bought you your favorite—it is still your favorite, right?" she asked, a sudden look of worry on her face, as though it would have ruined the night if she had not bought the right beer.

He laughed contendedly, looking at her, into her eyes, until she looked away, and he nodded. "Yes, it's still my favorite. Thank you. Can I get you anything?"

She held up her half-glass of champagne. "No, I'm still enjoying my Dom," she gushed.

"Take it easy, now," he teased her as he lay down on the floor behind Claire as she played with a pile of colored blocks. "Make sure that you don't go getting all drunk and making me take care of you again."

She smiled shyly, enjoying the irony. Though it hadn't happened often, if either of the two of them were likely to have too much to drink and need the other to care of them, it certainly was never her.

They sat in silence on the floor as Claire continued playing, little squeals of joy bursting out whenever she had successfully stacked a couple blocks on top of each other. Rachel's mind was full of the images that his stories had painted in her mind, and in wonder at the different perspective that she knew he now had; he was simply tired from talking and full of utter contentment at the scene that he found himself a part of.

There, on the floor, she had asked about what he thought he would do next. With the look she gave him, he understood that it was a loaded question. He sighed as he rubbed his fingers gently through Claire's thin hair. "I don't know, Rachel," he answered, not looking at her.

"You don't want to go back there, do you?" she asked, more incredulously and accusatory than she meant.

He shot her a quick look, letting her know he had heard her tone. He shrugged and rolled over onto his back and crossed his hands behind his head, looking up at the ceiling fan going around, around, above him. In his silence, Rachel said, "I'm sorry, I didn't mean—"

"No, it's okay," he interrupted. Still looking at the ceiling fan silently rotating above him, he heard the repetitive click of the pink oscillating fan that he had had in his room in Makhmur and Q-West. He remembered the oppressive heat, and the memory of a conversation with Jonathon as they sat in his small room in Makhmur after Sergeant Gregson had been killed. He pulled himself back out of that small room, out of Iraq, and back to Rachel's apartment. Rubbing his eyes and sighing, he said, "I don't know, Rachel—I mean, no, I don't want to go back, but…"

She couldn't help herself. "But what?" she asked quietly, carefully.

He sat up, frustrated. "I don't know. It doesn't seem that simple. I don't know how else to—I don't know." He shrugged, then drew in a deep breath and gathered himself as if he were about to confess. His eyes avoided hers and focused on the carpet. "Captain Daniels and I talked about that just the other day," he said.

"About you staying in the army?" she asked.

His eyes shot up toward her, then back to the carpet. "Yeah, sorta. He had asked me when I was going to the Advanced Course, and I told him that I wasn't sure I would go at all."

"What did he say?"

Sam shook his head, his face coloring just a bit. "The gist was that he thought I had a lot of talent as an officer, that there were a lot of soldiers who would benefit from my staying in. He said he couldn't believe I was even considering getting out. Said I was born for this…. On those rare occasions when I manage to keep my head out of my ass. His words." He shrugged his shoulders and smiled sheepishly, and his eyes finally left the carpet and stayed on hers, as if waiting.

But she only shifted herself silently on the floor, obviously unsure of how to respond.

When she said nothing, he shrugged his shoulders and looked at Claire. "I don't know," he said, then sat quietly.

birdmen

"I'm sorry," she offered. "I didn't mean to… there's no rush, right?"

He smiled. No, there was no rush. He had been back just over thirty-six hours, no need to think about all that just yet. He directed his smile at her, and she relaxed.

Claire became cranky as they sat there watching her, and Rachel decided to put her to bed. They both got up, but Rachel said that he should stay in the living room while she put her down. He sat on the couch and sipped at his beer. Looking at his watch, he saw that it was getting late, and an anxiety rose in him. Suddenly, the night transformed from a relaxing meal with a woman he loved with a love that was both confounding and soothing, into the uncertainty of what would happen next.

He heard Claire scream from her room as Rachel emerged, saying softly, "She hates going to bed, but she's tired. Just give her a minute." Sure enough, after a couple minutes of blood-curdling screams, she subsided into quiet and they knew that she was asleep. Rachel stuck her head in shortly to check on her, and came back out with a shy smile. "She's out like a light," she whispered.

Sam shifted uncomfortably on the couch. He had finished the first beer and had grabbed another, which he held in his lap as he watched her. She was beautiful. In her faded, ripped jeans, her small bare feet, her unpainted toenails, her hair up in a ponytail, with no makeup on, and in a simple white t-shirt with a yellow cheese stain from Claire's fingers, she was magnetic, something else entirely.

When she had sat next to him on the couch, embarrassed by his fixed stare, he remained quiet. The apartment, now absent of Claire's chattering, was suddenly silent. He heard that the ceiling fan actually had a very slight tick, only detectable in moments of real quiet. He looked at her sitting next to him on the couch, holding her glass of champagne, now almost gone, sitting on her knees, her bare feet tucked underneath her.

She knew that he was going to kiss her before he made a move. She could see it in his eyes, the way he was looking at her. She knew that look. It was not a lustful one, not one that made her afraid, but nonetheless, she knew that now, this night, was not the right time.

So when he leaned forward, looking into her eyes, she raised her free hand and rested it on his cheek, stopping him.

"Sam," she whispered, "that's not a good idea, not for either of us. Not tonight."

He nodded his head slightly, and his eyes fell to the beer in his hands. He understood what she hoped he would; she was not denying him out of some kind of punishment for his months of silence while he was away. That was simply not her way. He knew that, and a part of him that he barely recognized and did not understand, relaxed with relief at her refusal. He looked up from his beer and smiled at her, her brown eyes fixed on him, pleading for him to understand.

"I understand," he answered. She smiled and he mirrored her as they sat there for several minutes, looking at each other. Finally, she broke the silence with her typical, "Hi," and he tore his eyes away from hers and stood up with a sigh.

"Well, it's late, Rachel, I should be going."

She stood up with him, not wanting him to go, but not wanting him to stay either. She walked him to the door and opened it for him. He turned in the doorway, his hand holding the screen door open. "Thanks for dinner," she said, meaning it.

"Yeah," he said, meaning it as well. "Happy Valentine's Day, Rachel," he said as he bent down. Her heart stopped for a second until she felt his lips rest gently on her forehead, on the thin line where her hair began. Strands of her hair clung to his unshaven stubble as he pulled away.

"Have a good night," he said as he walked out the door, holding the screen so that it wouldn't slam shut, and walked down the stairs to his Jeep.

That had been just over a week ago now, as he sat in the hard wooden pew, watching absently as the stained-glass collage traveled along the north wall. He heard a noise to his right, from Rachel sitting next to him, and looked over to see her discreetly dabbing her eyes with a tissue. Suddenly, he realized that he had not heard a word of the sermon, and was worried about what the pastor had said that had caused her to cry.

Reaching for her hand, a worried look on his face, he mouthed, "Are you okay?" and she nodded her head and smiled at him softly. Keying back into the sermon, near desperate now to learn what could have caused her to cry, he listened as Pastor Bob, standing behind that stark, hard crucifix, finished.

"...and that woman, touched by the presence of God in her life, left that well and became a new creation. Not suddenly perfect, still trapped in her human condition, but changed. The word we use is redeemed. Because only the gospel of Jesus Christ can redeem us from a way of life that slowly kills us. And when we find ourselves impacted by the presence of God in the midst of our sin and of our shame, then like that woman at the well, we too can say, God bless this mess."

Trying to catch up, Sam flipped to the front of his bulletin where the sermon title had been written in large letters: "GBTM: God Bless This Mess."

Pastor Bob finished, and the small choir sang a closing hymn which Sam could not follow because he had been so affected by Rachel's tears. His mind was racing to try to figure out what he had missed, what the pastor had said that had resonated so clearly with her. After the closing hymn and the benediction, they filed past the pastor, shaking his hand, thanking him for the service, wishing him a good day. The two of them stepped out into the bright and crisp sunlight of a bitter-cold February morning. Sam reached for her hand and held it while she finished dabbing her eyes dry.

"Hi," she said meekly when she could no longer bare his stare. Seeing the confusion and concern in his eyes as he watched her, she offered, "I'm all right. Sorry about that, I just really love that story. It's one of my favorites."

"He was talking about the woman at the well, right?" Sam asked and was immediately embarrassed, because obviously, if he had been paying attention, he would have known without a doubt that the story was the one of the woman at the well.

Rachel looked up at him and smiled, and he saw that the sadness, or whatever it was, was passing. She shook her head in wonder as she looked up at him, and he looked away, embarrassed. "I swear Sam," she said, "you crack me up."

He answered her by laughing a little and shrugging his shoulders. "Come on," he said, "let's go get that little girl of yours."

"And then, can we have waffles?" she asked playfully, her smile bright and clear, as if the sadness had somehow purified her joy.

He laughed, more in wonder at the pure delight that now radiated from her in contrast to the sorrow that had been there only minutes ago, and said, "I don't see why not. But we'll have to ask her highness what she would like."

They both laughed happily as they walked down the hall to pick up Claire.

* * *

"So what's it really like in Iraq, man?"

Sam looked up from the papers on the counter, a pen in his hand, and stared in surprise at the pale, young face with an earring and a pathetic goatee peering back at him from behind the counter.

"What?" was all Sam could manage in response, as he felt Rachel's hand, resting in the crook of his bent elbow, give him a slight cautioning squeeze.

"Yeah man, what's the real story? What's it really like over there?" asked the young face again.

Sam blinked several times as he shook his head slowly, his eyes darting from the papers he had been signing to the innocent expression standing in front of him. He, Rachel, and Claire were standing at a rental car counter at the airport in Baton Rouge. It had been a couple weeks since Valentine's Day. The battalion had been given a long weekend, and he had asked her if they would like to come down with him to Denham Springs. His mom and dad, as well as several of his old friends from Denham High and Tulane University, had been insisting on a visit from him. There was going to be a parade. After he had resisted the idea to his mom, he had had to laugh when Rachel brought it up one night over pizza.

"You two in cahoots, huh?" he had asked, shaking his head.

"It'll be nice, Sam," she said. "Lots of people want to thank you." She shrugged between bites. "You're their hometown hero."

birdmen

"I'm no hero," he had said into his pizza, his eyes softening.

But somehow, in that way that she had of getting him to see what was the right thing to do, a week later he found himself standing in the Baton Rouge airport, bewildered by the question being posed to him. He finally managed to ask in return, "Seriously?"

The young man behind the counter was surprised at the sharpness of his question-in-answer, and stuttered, "Well… yeah… yessir… I mean, you were there, and I was just…"

"Do you really think that's what's gonna happen here?" Sam asked, his eyes boring into the young face. "I just wanna rent a car. I'm not interested in having some half-baked conversation with some kid about what's really going on over there."

The young face flinched as if Sam had tried to punch him. Rachel, concern in her face, removed her hand from his elbow, and placed her hand gently on his back in an obvious effort to keep him from saying any more. The old couple standing in line behind them shifted on their feet nervously.

But the hand on his back asking him to calm down only made him more angry. Maybe it was because he was surrounded by people who all wanted to know the same thing, none of whom understood what was happening, and expected him to have the answer; maybe he was angry because he couldn't understand it either.

"I'll tell you what," Sam said, controlling his voice to sound calmer than he felt. The young man had a name tape pinned to his shirt. "How old are you, Derek?"

The young face shook his head, clearly not understanding why he was being asked his age. But he answered, "Twenty-two." Then added, "Sir."

"Twenty-two years old," Sam shook his head as he signed the rental agreement, acknowledging that he did not want insurance, and handed the paper to the young man. "You really want to know what's going on in Iraq, Derek? You look like a healthy young man—you healthy, Derek? Do you have AIDS or a missing leg or anything?" The tension in his voice rose despite his efforts to keep it controlled.

Derek shook his head, oblivious to the purpose of the question. "No."

"So, you're a healthy young man, your country's at war, and you're some kinda fucking rental car jockey. And you think—for some reason that I cannot begin to understand—that you and I have some kind of special bond—like we're boys, right?—and I'm just gonna stand here and bare my soul to you? Because you've obviously earned that, right?" He paused, shaking his head and letting loose a sarcastic chuckle. "What a goddamn joke. You wanna know so bad, Derek, sign up and go find out for yourself. Until then, you can go fuck yourself." The whole time his voice had remained even, though the sharpness of his words had cut through the air so that the people standing around in the adjacent lines could not help but stare. Derek's face was stunned, his mouth half open as if he were trying to say something but could not find the words. Sam heard Rachel shift on her feet next to him.

He took a deep breath. "Just give me my keys."

She didn't say anything as they walked to the car, and neither did he. The rush of adrenaline had made him shaky, and he didn't trust himself to say anything until he had calmed down. That and he knew he had embarrassed her, and was sorry for it, which somehow only helped to keep him angry. Neither of them spoke as he loaded the suitcases into the trunk and she strapped Claire into the child's seat, her tiny hands each holding one of the brightly colored blocks that her grandmother had given her for Christmas. When they were all loaded up, they each got in the car, neither of them saying anything to the other until they were on the highway. It was dark out—they had had to wait until Rachel had finished her shift before they could fly out—and the streets shone with the recent rain. The air was opaque with the heavy humidity, and yellow round clouds of mist hung around the streetlights that ran along the highway.

Claire's little gurgling noises were the only sound in the car when Rachel finally spoke. "Some people don't understand what's happening right now, Sam, and when they hear that you're a captain in the army and that you've served in Iraq, they think that you might be able to answer their questions," she said carefully.

He remained silent, his eyes on the road in front of him, both hands on the wheel.

"Sam," she finally said, frustration in her voice as she spun around on the seat and looked square at his profile. His eyes darted to the right toward her, then shot back to the road.

"Yeah?" he answered, his mind racing for an answer to her he couldn't find. He knew his silence upset her, which was the last thing he wanted at that point.

"You can be angry, Sam," she said to him. "It's okay if you don't have all the answers—"

"Is it?" he shot back at her, finally turning to look at her, their eyes meeting for a moment before he turned back to the glittering road.

She sighed quietly again. "Yeah, Sam, it really is." She nodded her head. "It is. But you can't take it out on people like that, Sam. They just don't know what's going on, they don't understand this war. It's not their fault, they just don't understand." She shook her head.

He was quiet for a minute or two. They had turned off the highway, and were making their way down a dark, winding road. Slowing down, he turned onto a long driveway that climbed up a little hill with a single story brick house resting on the top. The front porch lights were on, and he saw more lights turn on through the windows of the house as he stopped the car. Turning to her, his hands still in the same position on the wheel, her body still rotated in her seat so that she was looking square at him, he said, "I know, Rachel. I'm sorry," and he meant it.

"You don't have to be sorry, Sam," she smiled, forgiving him, and he relaxed. "Let's just try not to swear too much in public like that, okay? Remember that your mom thinks you're her little angel who can do no wrong," she teased him, and he laughed, relieved.

They arrived on a Thursday night. Sam's dad had taken that Friday off, the parade was on Saturday morning, and some good family friends, the Waxes, were throwing Sam a big welcome home party that night after the parade. Mrs. Wax was practically an aunt

a novel

to Sam growing up, as he and her oldest son Michael had been best friends all the way from kindergarten through Tulane. They had even grown up going to Sunday School together. Michael had just graduated from Law School at Tulane the previous year and had started working for a small property law office in New Orleans. Sam and he had started to lose touch when Sam had gone to Park City, though Michael had been Sam's best man at his wedding. After that, though, between the distance and the rapidly-changing life that Sam had begun to lead, they began to grow apart. The last time they had really talked was when Sam had come home from Park City after his divorce, before he had shipped off to Officer Candidate School. Since then, they hadn't talked much at all and had only exchanged a couple quick emails over the past several years. Michael had married a nice girl from New Orleans, Jessie Lee, in September, while Sam was in Iraq. Michael had tried to fix it so that Sam could be home for the wedding, but as the tour-length had inexorably expanded to a full year, it became clear that Sam would not make it. Sam had laughed when he had received the silver and white invitation in August, and had sent Michael an email telling him that, regrettably, he would be otherwise engaged the weekend of July nineteenth.

The party at the Waxes was going to be an event. Miss Sidney—as Sam called Mrs. Wax—and his mom had gone into high gear when he had finally acquiesced to come home. It was only late February and therefore too early for crawfish, so she had ordered one hundred pounds each of gulf shrimp and blue crab. Sam's dad had served on the City Council several years ago, and Mr. Wax—or Mr. Bill—was currently the mayor. It was easy to see, then, how in just over a couple weeks they were able to put together a welcome home parade, replete with a good, old fashioned Louisiana crab-and-shrimp boil. Most of Sam's old friends from Denham High were still around the area, and would be able to be there the weekend of the parade.

That Friday morning, Sam's mom walked him through all of the details about the parade and the party, as he grudgingly tried to listen, though not yet through with his first cup of coffee. After ten minutes of his acknowledging grunts, she finally got the hint that he was in no mood for details just yet. He shot her an apologetic look when she stood up, for she was obviously put off by his lack of interest in the weekend's plans.

"Mom," he had said, looking up at her, his empty coffee cup in his hand, "I'm sorry, we got in late last night. Just give me an hour and we can sit down and go through everything."

She beamed back down at him, her boy, and forgave him immediately. "It's all right, Samyul," she said. "You know your mother. I'm just so excited that you're home, that's all. And that girl Rachel...." She shook her head and smiled at him.

"It's good to be home, Mom." Sam smiled back up at her, letting the subject hang in the air between the two of them for a moment.

She stood there a minute, her eyes glistening as she looked down at him. Sam shifted nervously as he thought she was about to start crying, and said quickly, "I'm gonna get another cup of coffee. Can I get you anything?"

"No, thank you," she said, the moisture in her eyes that had started to build evaporating. She shook her head and bent down to kiss him hard on his head. "I love you, Samyul," she said.

"I love you too, Mom," Sam said as he stood up.

He heard Rachel walking down the hallway from her room as he was getting his second cup, and reached into the cabinet to fix her coffee for her. He shot her a playful look as she slid onto a stool behind the counter in the kitchen.

"Mornin'," he said, smiling. He poured just a drop of cream into the steaming cup, and walked over and placed the cup in front of her. "How'd you sleep?" He looked at her, her eyes heavy, her hair up in a hasty pony tail, wearing her large orange sweatshirt and some flannel pajama pants. He thought how he was always surprised, every time he saw her, at how tiny she was. He resisted the urge to walk around the counter and wrap his arms around her. The early morning light streamed through the windows, warm already against the cool hardwood floors. Sipping on his own cup, he leaned against the far counter, looking at her, bathed in the soft light of the morning in the house he had grown up in, with the familiar smells and sounds of his childhood. She could feel him looking at her the way he did sometimes that made her self-conscious.

"Hi," she said in her nervous habit.

"Hi." He smiled at her.

"Thanks for the coffee."

"Good?" he asked absently, still caught up in the vision.

"Yeah, it is," she answered between sips, holding the cup close to her mouth with both hands, the steam sliding up her face.

Unable to help himself, he walked around the counter and kissed her gently on the side of her forehead, at the hairline on her temple. He didn't say anything and he didn't need to.

The surprise in her face morphed into a warm smile that shone from behind her eyes. She didn't respond back, and didn't need to. He knew that she loved him as well, with a love that at once confounded him and draped over him like the morning sun coming through the windows of his childhood home.

They looked at each other in silence until his mom emerged back from her room.

"Hey sweetheart," his mom said to Rachel. "Did you sleep well?"

Rachel swallowed her coffee and smiled back at her. "Good morning. Yes ma'am, I could've slept all day," she said, still smiling. "That bed is so comfortable, thank you." She was beaming, and Sam let himself believe—rightfully—that it was not just the good night's sleep nor the down pillow-top mattress that had elicited her happy enthusiasm.

The night before the parade, most of Sam's family came over for dinner. Despite his repeated requests throughout the previous week that he did not want a lot of attention, it was clear that they had fallen on deaf ears. Not that he ended up minding it all as much as he thought he would. His mom's mother was his last grandparent still living, and his aunt and uncle, also from her side, were bringing her with them from their home in Vicksburg, Mississippi. His mom had two other sisters, one from Little Rock, Arkansas, and the other from Shreveport, Louisiana. Both were married and had children. His dad was a single child, and both of his parents had passed away several years ago now. Sam had to count whenever he was asked, but all in all, he had seven cousins. Of course, the last he had seen any of them had been almost four years ago. And now, with school and jobs and such, only one of them was going to be able to make it, his youngest cousin Matthew, whose parents were driving in from Vicksburg, and who at the age of sixteen, was no doubt compelled to join his parents and grandmother for the trip to see a cousin he could barely remember.

His dad had bought steaks and several different bottles of scotch for the evening. He even, once again, proudly displayed to Sam his collection of Cuban cigars, saying, "I thought we could break these out with your uncles." The mischievous twinkle in his eye made Sam chuckle.

"That'd be great, Dad," Sam had said, nodding his head.

His aunt and uncle from Shreveport arrived early that afternoon, and his aunt had offered to help Sam's mom in the kitchen while his uncle sat outside with Sam's dad, talking about how they thought the crawfish would run that year. His dad predicted a good year.

The next morning, before he thought the rest of the house was awake, Sam's dad walked outside to the back porch to enjoy a cup of coffee while the sun came up, like he did every morning on the weekends. When he stepped out onto the porch, he was surprised to see Sam already out there, a cup of coffee in his hand.

"Mornin'," his dad offered, taking a seat across the glass-topped table from Sam and turning the chair in the direction of the rising sun.

"Morning, Dad," Sam answered, nodding his head.

Through the live oaks, drops of dew from the night shone on the spanish moss that clung to the high branches. They sat there for several minutes, neither saying anything to the other, only listening to the sound of the beetles and the bugs from the grass and the trees singing their morning song as the two men sipped from their mugs. The heavy morning air was cool and damp and thick with the smell of the earth.

"Today'll be a good day, Sam," his dad said, still facing the east.

Sam nodded, though he was not sure that he agreed. After another few silent minutes, the bugs continuing their undulating song, Sam said, "I'm not a hero, Dad."

Through the corner of his eye, he saw his dad frown and nod his head. "I know that, son," he said almost in a whisper, as if he were keeping a secret.

Sam was surprised; it wasn't the answer he was expecting.

His dad took a long, slow sip from his coffee and swallowed, his Adam's apple bouncing up against his unshaven neck. Looking over at Sam, his dad said to him, "People need to believe in heroes, Sam. We all do."

Sam slowly shook his head, his eyes still on the backyard, and asked, "Why's that?"

His dad looked back toward the sun, toward the glimmering drops of dew hanging from the moss fifty feet off the ground. "Because it forgives us."

Sam furrowed his brow. Damned if I know what the hell that means, he thought.

"Good night, Sam." The large man in the sweater vest thrust out a meaty hand, adorned with two gold rings. "It's good to see you home, son."

Sam took the hand, which swallowed his, and nodded in thanks. "Yessir, thanks for coming Mr. Bondy, it was good to see you."

Sam was a little drunk—he'd been drinking since the parade that morning. Though it had been only eleven in the morning when the fire engine from the Denham Springs Fire Department stopped outside his house to drop them all off after the parade, the idea of being able to get a cold beer whenever he wanted had not lost its novelty. It had been a particularly sultry morning as well, and when he stripped off the coat of his green uniform, he saw that he had sweat through the long-sleeve shirt that was underneath. Wrenching the tie from his neck, he had reached into the fridge and grabbed a green bottle. Popping open the top, he offered one to his dad, whose eyes were raised in amusement.

Sam was quite pleased with himself at the moment. The parade, despite his resistance to the idea, had been a lot of fun. The sheriff's department, and the Denham Springs police and fire departments had been there, their lights and sirens blinking and bleeping at the front of the parade. The high school band had been there, walking down the street lined with people waving flags and signs that said, "Welcome home" and "God Bless America" and "Our Hero." Sam, Rachel, and Claire had ridden in the fire engine at the beginning. Rachel had tried to resist when he first tried to coax her up before the parade had started.

"Hey," he had said with a smile, "this is your fault. Now get on up here." She reluctantly agreed. After the first block though, he had grown tired of standing in the fire engine, waving "like some kind of rose queen," and had jumped down onto the street and walked, giving high fives to kids who ran out to shake his hand, and pausing for the occasional picture.

At one point, he had heard a small girl's voice yell out, "My daddy's a soldier, too!"

He turned toward the voice, and his eyes found a little girl with blonde braids sticking out the side of her head. As he walked over to her, a friendly smile on his face, she backed toward her mom, embarrassed now at her outburst. Reaching her, Sam crouched down and spoke to her. "Your daddy's a soldier, too?" he asked, glancing up at her mom.

Her mom nodded and the little girl said, "Yessir."

Sam stood up. Looking at the mother now, his black beret half covering his right eye, he asked, "Do you know where he is?" asking what base he was on.

The mother smiled and said, "He's in Kuwait, at Camp Victory. He's coming home in a week." Which meant that he was safe, and the long hard sorrow was ending.

Sam looked at her, then down at the little girl. Crouching back down, he said to her, "Will you tell your daddy that I said hello?"

The little girl nodded solemnly. Sam stood back up and looked into the eyes of the mother. Not sure of what to say, he said to her, "Will you tell him I said hi... and thanks?"

a novel

She nodded, looking back at him, the two of them sharing a secret fear as the parade continued past them. He nodded and smiled. "Thank you, ma'am." Turning to walk back to the passing parade, he said to the little girl with braids, "Goodbye, darlin'." The little girl had blushed and waved goodbye.

Now, with most of the guests gone for the night, Sam sat outside on the back porch of the Wax's house with six of his old friends from Denham High. Rachel sat beside him, only half-way through her second beer. Two other girls also sat around the large glass table. Sam had dated the one with red hair, Katie, who now sat on the opposite side of Sam, their junior year. After the breakup, they had become close friends, and Sam had stayed in as close of touch with her over the past few years as he had with any of the others around the table, including Michael. Michael's wife, Jessie, sat beside him, her bobbed blonde hair done up for the night that she would meet her husband's best friend from a life she had not been a part of. The other three men around the table had played football with Michael and Sam. Rachel thought she recognized them from an old picture Sam had always kept in a frame on his TV. They were older now and had put on a little weight, but the faces were the same. The one sitting to the left of Katie, with a close-shaved beard, was Jeffrey. Next to him, with black-rimmed glasses and a thick goatee, was Kevin. Then sat Michael and his wife Jessie, and finally, next to Rachel, Lane.

There were over a dozen empty beer bottles on the table in front of them as Katie told the story of when Sam had first asked her out. Rachel was glad to see Sam laugh easily at a story told mostly at his expense, and for his reluctance to insert his own version of the story in defense. The group all burst into bellowing laughter at the climax of her story, when Sam had first tried to take off her shirt. Sam, his face red, laughed and shook his head as Katie eyed him teasingly.

"For the life of him, he could not figure out how to undo my bra," the redhead said, smiling and reliving the memory. Leaning across Sam, Katie reached out and touched Rachel's hand, saying, "I trust he has learned a few things since then?"

Rachel, playing up to the story, shook her head sadly. "Afraid not," she said, as Sam tilted his head back in mock exasperation as the small band around the table burst into laughter again.

Sam's mom emerged from the sliding glass door that led into the house and walked up behind Sam, placing both hands on the shoulders of her son. Eyeing the empty beer bottles, she obligingly cautioned, "Now you all have a safe way home, right?" She looked around the table at the familiar faces of her son's friends. The shoulders she rested her hands on were the strong, broad shoulders of a grown man, but to her, Sam was still her little boy and these people around the table were still her little boy's childhood friends, still just children themselves.

The faces all around the table nodded their obedience, answering, "Yes ma'am."

She leaned over and kissed Sam on the cheek, which bothered him less than he would have thought it would. "Well, Mr. Calhoun and I are gonna go. You all don't keep Mr. Bill and Miss Sidney up too late tonight."

"Yes ma'am," the group chorused, some of them still smiling from Katie's bra story.

Turning to Rachel, Sam's mom said, "Rachel, can I ask you a question real quick?"

Rachel nodded and stood up from the table and followed his mom into the house. Rachel had put Claire down in an extra room a couple hours ago, and Sam's mom offered to take her home for them. Rachel asked whether the girl's crib was in a room that needed to be used.

"Oh," Sam's mom said, "no honey, not at all. No, she can stay here until y'all leave. I was just offering in case you all decided you were gonna go out."

Rachel smiled at her, thanking the woman for the generous offer. But she had recognized long ago, being on her own with a baby, that she no longer had the luxury of staying out all night. She took her responsibility as a mother seriously, and though Sam's mom's offer was a sincere one, and without allusion to her qualities or abilities as a mother, Rachel instinctively knew that here was a small chance to show the mother of the man whom she loved her qualities as a mother. Though she was not being deliberately tested, she would pass nonetheless. She had also seen, from the small cues that his body language had given, that though Sam was having a good time, this was not going to be one of those nights where he stayed out all night long.

"Thank you," Rachel said to his mom, "but I don't think that we'll be much longer. As long as you don't think that she's in the Wax's way, I'd rather you not have to put her to bed."

"That's fine, honey," Sam's mom answered, gently reaching out and placing a hand on her arm. "And don't you worry about the Wax's. They're like family, and family," here Rachel saw her eyes twinkle just a bit, "is never in the way."

Rachel smiled shyly at the allusion.

"Y'all have a good night," his mom said to her as they stepped back outside. Jeffrey was in the middle of a story from an away game when they were all seniors together, and had traveled to Alexandria. When the door had opened back up, Jeffrey had stopped mid-sentence, and the group's laughter instinctively softened. Sam's mom looked around at those young, familiar faces, and in mock scolding said, "Now what story are you telling now, Jeffrey Bondy?"

The group laughed easily, and Jeffrey knew he didn't have to answer.

"It was good to see you all again," Sam's mom said, her eyes glistening slightly. "Sam, don't forget about church in the morning, now," she warned motherly, eyeing the empty bottles on the table.

Sam forgave her and just said, "We won't be much longer, Mom."

She nodded her head slowly. "Okay sweatheart. Y'all be good," she offered to the crowd.

She was met with a chorus of "Good night" and "Take care" and "Good to see you, too."

Rachel slid back into the chair next to Sam, tucking her feet underneath her.

Sam's mom disappeared back into the house. A couple minutes later, they heard the Calhoun's car back down the driveway, and drive off down the street. The small group had grown quiet, each of them sipping contentedly on the beer in front of them, as the sound of the crickets and beetles pulsed in the night.

Michael's mom emerged shortly after Sam's parents had left and wished them all a good night, saying that she was going to bed. "But you all stay up as long as you want, you ain't gonna bother us any," she said with a smile, seeing the same familiar, young faces Mrs. Calhoun had.

Sam stood up and walked over to her and thanked her for the party. Looking down at her and smiling, he wrapped his arms around the woman who had been like a second mother to him his entire life. "Thank you so much for all of this, Miss Sidney," he said, calling her by the name he had used when he and Michael had been boys playing in her backyard.

She slipped out of his arms, and looked up at him. Rubbing his strong shoulders, she said slowly, "We're all glad to have you back home with us, Sam." She patted him on the cheek. Leaning around him, she called out a "good night" to the crowd around the table, and went back into the house.

With the departures from the older women, the group settled back down into easy stories of their shared youth, and catching up on what each of them were doing. The tone of the conversation transformed from loud jokes and laughter to subdued conversations of substance, as the crickets and beetles continued their night song.

Finally, Michael broached the subject that had been ignored the entire evening. Despite the easy laughter and tales from high school, Iraq had been the eight hundred pound gorilla in the room that everyone wanted to talk about, but was wary of mentioning.

Sam had felt the tension around the table rise, and sighed to himself as he braced for what he knew was inevitably coming. He grew nervous, and took a long pull on his beer, finishing it. He asked Rachel if he could get her anything as he pushed back from the table and walked over to the cooler by the door that had been stocked with beer for the night. Returning to his seat, he twisted off the top to his bottle and sat down.

Finally, he heard Michael across from him bring it up. "Hey Sam, if you don't want to talk about it brother, don't feel like you have to, but I'd really love to hear from you about your time over there." Lane and Jeffrey nodded their heads in agreement, while Katie reached over and placed her hand on his arm. Sam felt Rachel slide her hand onto his leg, and pat it gently, no doubt remembering his tirade in the airport just a few days ago over the same subject. But Sam was not in the mood for a fight tonight, sitting here surrounded by friends from his childhood. No, he thought in response to Rachel's cautioning touch, this would be different.

Feeling the pressure of the quiet that had settled around the table, Michael added, "It's just hard to tell what is really happening over there, the damned media is so jaded. I don't know what to think." He shook his head.

Sam stayed quiet, staring at the label on his beer, trying to collect his thoughts, trying to find an answer to such a broad topic. In his mind flashed images of his small room at Q-West, he could hear the tick of his old pink fan, he saw the hot dry mountain range outside of Makhmur shoot out of the hard brown ground, he saw the familiar light brown, thin face of a dead friend, and the bleeding body of a man in a white *dish-dasha* on a dark night. Where to begin?

"Honestly," he said carefully, "I don't really know what to say." He was fishing, willing to talk to them, even wanting to talk to them, but he needed a starting point. There were simply too many images running through his mind, most of no consequence to them. How to communicate all that he had felt and seen and heard and thought?

Michael must have sensed his friend's need to be channeled in a more specific direction. "Well," he began, "the media are all talking about how we're training the Iraqis to take more responsibility in terms of security and fighting the rising insurgency." Sam nodded his head, and an image painted itself in his mind of dirty men in mismatched uniforms, stacked in the back of an old beat-up pickup with a rusty machine gun mounted to a bracket in the bed of the truck. "Do you think that that's gonna work?"

Sam nodded, a smile playing on his lips. No way in hell, he thought, knowing he couldn't actually say that out loud. He thought about the question and thought about his answer, and thought about how best to answer. "I think it can." He shrugged and equivocated. "I'm not sure," he added. "Fact is that we have to get the Iraqis to the point where they can sustain themselves. Stability has so many facets to it. Water. Electricity. An economy. Education. Rule of law. None of those things—there's no way that foreigners can do that for them'. We simply can't do it for them. And you're talking about a collision of cultures, too. That's big."

Rachel looked away from him and quickly scanned the faces of the six people leaning in on the table, toward Sam, a couple of them nodding. She moved her hand off his leg.

"You're right," agreed Michael, nodding his head. "The only way to get Iraq to the place it needs to be is to incorporate the Iraqi people into the solution."

"We can't expect our army to be able to do that," Kevin chimed in, pushing his dark-rimmed glasses back up his nose. "You guys are great at blowing things up, but you ain't trained to nation build."

"Well let's not forget that the whole reason for the war proved to be a lie in the first place." Jessie spoke for perhaps only the third or fourth time that evening, and Rachel cringed when she heard what she said. Rachel shot a look toward Sam, and saw his body tighten just a bit. It had seemed a harmless jab, but in this dangerous game they were playing, there was a fine line between the conversation being positive and constructive, and pushing Sam into a place where he would grow defensive and accusatory.

Sam did not respond, but averted his eyes back to the label on his beer, and Rachel hoped that he would let the comment slide over him. She waited for someone to bring the conversation back to neutral ground. The tension mounted around the table, as everyone recognized that the conversation had taken a turn for the worse.

Michael, evidently feeling responsible for his wife's comment and acutely aware of the sensitivity of their topic, dropped in with another question that steered the conversation back to safe ground. "So what kind of things did you do in Iraq, Sam?"

Sam looked up across the table and nodded to him, as if in thanks for bailing him out of a potential fight. "Well," he began, feeling with a bit of pride that what he was going to say next was bound to impress them. "In the beginning I led our battalion's sniper and reconnaissance teams." He let the words "sniper" and "reconnaissance" sink into the ears of his audience. The looks on their eager faces as they leaned in on the table made him smile despite himself. From the corner of his eye, he saw Rachel shake her head just slightly at his not-so-subtle attempt to show off to his old friends. Lane asked him what kind of things they had done, and Sam gave them the general answer, avoiding any specifics, not because anything that they had done had either been classified or compromising, but simply because he did not yet feel comfortable talking about specific circumstances and events. So he told them that he was responsible for planning the placement of the teams in an effort to target some kind of known threat, be it caches or bad guys.

"How long did you do that?" Kevin asked him, his round face accentuated by the goatee and square glasses.

Sam thought, remembering places as indicators of time. "Well, we were in Najaf through April, then we pushed up to Makhmur in May," he said, remembering the two large metal silos that had thrust up into the brown sky there. "End of May?" he answered, turning to Rachel, as if she could verify the time and place. He nodded. "End of May... then I moved over to Charlie Company to be their XO."

"What's that?" asked Katie.

"XO stands for Executive Officer. He's second-in-command of a company—"

"How big is a company?" asked Rachel, helping him make sure that he was speaking in a way intelligible to his audience.

He nodded at her, thanking her. "Sorry, a company has about a hundred and twenty men—"

"And you were second-in-command?" asked Katie, impressed.

Rachel shook her head, and Sam saw her. Taking her cue, he confessed, "Yeah, but it's not as sexy as it sounds. Basically, I was— still am—responsible for all the logistical support for the company.

Bullets, food, water, transportation, that kind of thing. Not sexy," he repeated. But now he just sounded humble.

"Did you ever go out on any missions as an XO?" asked Jeffrey. Sam noticed a drop of beer clinging to a few short hairs around his mouth.

Sam nodded, an image of Marie pressing against the pile of hay flashing through his mind. "A few," he said quietly, and let it be at that. The somber look that suddenly came over his face told his audience not to pursue that particular subject.

They were quiet for a minute, a few of them taking pulls on their drinks. Sam's mind kept traveling between a shot-up pickup truck and Marie's limp body as Paul's men had dragged it out of the small mud hut. He was lost in thought when Kevin spoke.

"So no WMD's, huh?"

Sam's eyes shot toward him, unblinking. He could tell by the innocent expression on his old friend's face that he had meant it only as sarcastic rhetoric. Still, Sam could not repress the surge of adrenaline that coursed through him. He sat there silently for a moment, his eyes on his friend in the half-light of the porch.

"Nope," he shook his head, trying to laugh off the subject, "no WMD's." If he had left it at that, the night most likely would not have taken the turn that it did. It's even possible that if he had left it at that, then the rest of his life may have turned out differently. But he didn't—he could not leave it alone. As he stared across the table at his old friend, the man's thin goatee suddenly disgusted him, and he became acutely aware of the distance that now lay between them. And so he added, "But I don't see that that matters much at this point," his eyes still hard on Kevin's face.

His friend scoffed as if Sam had told a joke. But when Sam did not laugh back, Kevin could not help but ask, "Sam, seriously?"

In answer, Sam just took a long pull from the green bottle, finishing the beer. Subconsciously, he was preparing himself for a fight. Rachel's hand found his leg again, acknowledging that she felt the rise in tension as well.

"Sam," Kevin answered in not-so-subtle disbelief at Sam's dismissal, "the whole reason we went to Iraq was a lie, man. There are no weapons of mass destruction." And even though Sam had said the exact same thing to his dead friend Jonathon, he felt that this was something different, the way Kevin was saying it. He hadn't earned the right. Perhaps if he had gone over, been part of the thing, then Sam could forgive him for saying the same thing he had. But not like this. You don't get to sit in the bleachers and do nothing but criticize the men in the arena, or the way the game is fought. Sam seethed inside. No, you have to choose: either you're involved, or you're not. You have to earn the right by being part of it.

Kevin paused and tried to recover. "I mean, I love ya brother, and you know I'm always on your side, but Jessie was right about what she said earlier."

Sam's eyes shot toward Jessie. Michael leaned into her, as if sensing the danger. A very long, silent moment passed before Michael, trying to diffuse the tension that had descended on the little table like a stifling heat, spoke. Speaking carefully, he said, "I think what Kevin is saying—and it's what we all share, Sam—is that it's hard for us to support this war, based on the fact that the whole reason we went has been proven wrong." He paused for emphasis, and articulated very carefully what he said next. "That's not to say that we don't support the troops. We do, all of us do. But it's hard for us to support the war."

Sam had been looking directly at him the entire time he spoke, peeling the paper label off of the empty bottle in front of him. When Michael had finished, Sam remained quiet for a few moments, never taking his eyes off his old friend, whose face now seemed strangely unfamiliar to him. "Hmph. Now just what the fuck is that supposed to mean, exactly?"

Michael started back, and shifted in his seat uncomfortably. He had been deliberate with his wording to avoid just this sort of thing. And he had thought, having graduated from Tulane Law, that he was capable of walking the fine semantic line which he had evidently just fallen off. Looking at Sam, whose eyes were back on the bottle's label as he peeled it off, he thought—hoped—that maybe they could just let the subject drop. He was just about to make an obvious change in subject, reverting back to the time their senior year when they had broken into the high school swimming pool and dumped over one hundred fish into the pool from the pond on Sam's property across River Road, when Sam spoke before he could.

His voice quivered with the effort to control the adrenaline that was surging through him. Rachel had removed her hand from his leg, and had leaned back in her chair, her eyes on him as he spoke. The bugs' nightsong reached a crescendo beyond them in the dark.

"I mean, Jesus Christ Mike, there's a war going on. People are dying. At least have the balls to pick a side."

"I am Sam, we're—"

"No," Sam sharply cut him off, his eyes leaving the label and looking directly at Michael. "Regurgitating carefully calculated bullshit statements that don't mean anything is not picking a side. If you don't have the balls to go fight when your country goes to war, I would hope that you at least have the courage to pick a side and stick to it without all the political rhetoric." Sam shook his head.

But Michael was a good man. He had been a good man his entire life and he knew it, though his knowledge was not an arrogance; and he knew here that his courage was being challenged in such a way that he would not tolerate, that he knew he did not deserve, even from his oldest friend, a man whom he had learned to tie his shoes with. Looking back at Sam, raising his eyes to meet his, he said evenly, "I'm pretty sure I don't deserve to be called a coward." He shook his head. "Not by you or anyone else." The rest of the people around the table had receded away from the table, leaning back in their chairs into the shadows. Like watching a fight between two lovers, they knew when it was best not to interfere.

Sam guffawed, shaking his head. "What else do you call a perfectly healthy man not going to fight when his country goes to war? What're you waiting for? A perfume-scented linen invitation?"

"Not everyone is meant to be a soldier, Sam," Michael shot back.

Sam shook his head. "No, Mike, I guess not. I guess only those of us who feel like we have a responsibility as men to serve our country when she calls are meant to be soldiers. I guess we're only meant to be soldiers if we know that it won't interfere too much with our own plans. We're only meant to be soldiers if we happen to find a war that suits our delicate sensibilities and meets our strict parameters for a just war." Here Sam stopped again, shaking his head. "There are no just wars." He realized that his last sentence was a departure from his theme, and he returned back to his point. "I know a man who knew what it was to be an American—who knew what that meant—even though there are people like you all over this pathetic country of ours who would have deported him and his family." He felt the cool, light metal around his wrist. "You know what happened to him, Mike? He was killed. Killed on some goddamned road in Iraq simply because he could not look himself in the eye and pretend that he was a man when he knew that other men—not to mention eighteen year old girls—were doing his fighting for him."

Sam continued, "While you were sipping martinis. And you know what the real tragedy is, Mike? That patriotism and service are genes, and the more of us that are killed over there, and the more of your kind that continue to stay out, riding that rhetorical fence of uncommitted bullshit, the whole thing just perpetuates itself." He was rambling now—he realized he had had too much to drink, and that he was failing to articulate complex thoughts that he had explored and argued countless times in his own head.

Looking across at Mike, he saw that his old friend had been affected by the introduction of a dead man into the argument. Perhaps it had been unfair, but it was the reality of war, and Sam had flung that ugly reality into his face, sneering at his friend's naïveté.

Michael was quiet a moment before he spoke. "What was his name?" he asked, his eyes softening.

Sam paused a minute, reflecting on the naked bottle in front of him. He shook his head. "Doesn't matter." Jonathon Garcia, he thought to himself. From Fresno. First girl he ever loved was named Rebecca, and he came and helped me out one night in Najaf when I was in a real jam and you were stumbling around Bourbon Street, feeling up your girlfriend like you were some kind of prince and there wasn't a damn thing wrong with the world.

"Sure it matters, Sam—"

"No, Mike, it doesn't." Sam shot back sharply, his voice calm but firm. "Ben, Adam, Josh... don't you see?" He shook his head, his eyes focused on something on the bottle that was far away. "It doesn't matter."

There was a short pause before Michael spoke again, almost in a half-whisper. "Jesus, Sam," Michael shook his head, "you and I have been friends since kindergarten. We learned how to fish together, brother."

Silence hung over the table before Sam spoke. "Yeah... that was a long time ago," he said absently, a trace of sadness in his words.

Michael shook his head and said quietly, "It doesn't seem like so long ago to me."

The next day, sitting in the back of his parents' car with Claire between them, Sam reached over and placed his hand on Rachel's. He was looking out the window into the sunlight shooting through the trees as they drove down Old River Road from the service at First Baptist.

He had apologized to her the night before for getting upset with his friends the way she had thought he would. He apologized to her for saying the things he had said, though he should have said so to them. But as they drove through the night back to his parents' house, she thought she had heard him apologizing for something else. It was the anger that he was sorry for, and he was asking her to forgive him for it.

Rachel had realized where his anger came from. And she knew there was a part of him that did not believe what he had said, but that that part had been covered up with anger and loss. And she had thought he would regret what he had said, not because he didn't believe it, but because it expressed an unfinished thought, an incomplete sentence. The anger was part of it, but it was only part of it; and he was sloshing through the muck trying to figure out the rest, to see where the whole thing laid out in the end. But for now, there was only this part, only this anger and the sadness. And she thought of Jonathon, and his parents, and all the parents and wives and husbands and children and lovers who know their torture, who bear their same burden, and her embarrassment shifted to sorrow.

"I don't know why I reacted like that Rachel," he had said, stealing glances at her as he drove. "I'm sorry." He paused and she waited to see whether he would say anything else.

"It's all right, Sam—"

"No," he cut her off gently, shaking his head. "It's not. Thanks though." He looked at her again. "It's just that there's this thing inside me that I can't seem to shake. I've been home now for a couple weeks and I keep waiting for it to get better, but it's always there. Like I'm chained to something, you know?" he looked at her again, asking her to understand what he was trying to say. "I'm home, I can see that when I look around me, but there's this part of me that's still over there. It's like I haven't really left Iraq yet, even though I look around and... I don't know."

She had only smiled and nodded her head warmly, reaching over and squeezing his hand because she knew exactly what he was trying to say.

Now, when she felt his hand rest on hers, she knew that he was still thinking about that thing that he was carrying around and couldn't get rid of, and she looked at him looking through the window and prayed that he would be given the strength to kill it or walk away from it or to do whatever he needed to do with it.

* * *

A month later, at the end of March, they were walking out of the brick church again, holding hands on their way to pick up Claire from Miss Annette's. The past few weeks had been uneventful, and Sam found he was enjoying the sense of comfort that having a predictable routine provided. Rachel worked the same days every week, with the same hours. On the nights she was home, the three of them would have dinner together, either at her apartment or at Sam's. He had started to develop a talent for new recipes, and they rarely went out to eat anymore. He had spent a couple thousand dollars on new kitchen equipment, and Rachel enjoyed having him prepare dinner for her and Claire, even on nights when they ate at her place.

On Sunday mornings, he would drive over to her place at around ten and sit around while Rachel finished getting Claire ready for church, and then the three of them would walk the few short blocks, cutting over neighbors' lawns which were coming back after the winter. The redbuds and flowering pears were beginning to show bursts of bright green and pink and white on their morning walks. The morning air was cool and damp, and the sun still felt warm and welcome. After church, after they had picked up Claire and walked back to the apartment, the sun's warmth causing them both to sweat just a bit now that it was midday, they would have either waffles or pancakes and then spend the day together. There was a small park down the street where they would take Claire, and they would take turns pushing her on the swing or sliding down the metal slide with her in their laps. Some days they would find a movie on TV and lie on the couch after breakfast and he would always fall asleep and Rachel would try hard to keep Claire from waking him up.

Even in his naps, Rachel could see a struggle inside him. It was the same tension that she felt when they would walk to church in the mornings—his silence was not a peaceful one, and she could tell that for some reason he seemed to sit carefully in the pews each morning, as if he could not quite decide whether or not he wanted to be there. Even some nights when he was cooking them dinner, he would grow suddenly quiet and turn in on himself.

She had noticed within the first few weeks that he seemed to have several drinks every night. It didn't matter whether it was a Monday or a Thursday or a Saturday, she found that he was having five or six drinks a night. But it never seemed like a binge; he would make margaritas or mojitos or mai tais and she would have one with him, and let herself get caught up in the idea of having party drinks on a Tuesday night. But after a few weeks, she grew more cautious, and once when he offered her a margarita and she refused, he simply shrugged his shoulders and said, "Suit yourself," and finished two pitchers that night by himself.

And so she waited. Patiently and full of love and hope, she waited to see some hint that the darkness that he was holding onto was leaving him. She measured his countenance every Sunday on their walk back from church against the previous week's, and she strained and cheated to find some improvement. Not that he was overtly somber or depressed. He would laugh and sing and smile, but even so there was always the shadow there that she could still detect, even when she wanted to believe that it was passing.

The past month had been entirely repetitious, even boring. And though they both knew that neither of them wanted to keep much longer to that kind of absolute predictability, Rachel also knew that Sam needed the sense of normalcy that their routine that month provided. She kept in mind that this was part of his "Reintegration Phase"—as her *Handbook for Those with Loved Ones Returning From Iraq* told her—when she felt frustrated that they were having dinner at his place *again*.

What she could not know, because it was something he could not express to her, was that he was still not over the novelty of being home; how in the mornings when he would shave and he would turn on the hot water, he would pause and watch it come pouring out of the faucet, the steam rising up to his face, and he would think, hot water. Just like that. How every time he would step outside, his adrenaline would pulse just a bit and he would look around, suddenly afraid of being out in the open, until he reminded himself that he was in the United States and that no one was waiting to blow him up down the street; how he would close the blinds at night and avoid the windows, because something inside him still told him that it was not a good idea to have the lights on in the house when it was dark outside: that was just giving someone an easy shot; how, if she had asked him, he would have told her that the reason that he drank a few too many drinks every night was because why not? He was alive and life was good, so why not have a few drinks every night to celebrate that? She knew that that was why he thought he was drinking, but she wondered at the real reason, and knew that we can derive a perverse sort of pleasure in trying to destroy ourselves.

At the end of March, the battalion was given another four day weekend, which was only a slight break from the routine of the past month. Rachel had been scheduled to work the day shift that Monday, and would get home at around six that night. Sam had offered to take Claire for the day, saying that he had nothing special to do. Rachel had thanked him, but told him that she already had a daycare that she paid for by the month whether Claire went or not. "Besides," she had smiled, "maybe it'll give you a chance to finally get everything unpacked. Can we do dinner that night?"

So now Sam found himself alone in his two-bedroom apartment, rifling through the few remaining boxes that he had not yet opened. There was one box he had been avoiding. It was a small package he had mailed back to himself right before he had left Q-West. In it were some of the letters he had received from family and friends, and the pictures Rachel had sent him. But there was something else in that box: the letter from Jonathon's mom that he had never answered. Glancing at the box warily, he walked into the kitchen and opened the refrigerator. Noticing that there was not much there, and finding a run to the grocery store a convenient chore, he decided to restock his fridge.

Two hours later, he began to shuttle the two dozen bags of food he had bought up the stairs to his apartment. After another hour of unloading and organizing, he plopped down on the couch and found the same box still there, sitting on the coffee table where he had left it, staring at him. He looked at his watch out of boredom and turned on the TV. He found a program about the Bengal tigers in Russia, and tried to dive into the narrator's voice. But the box stayed there on the table, and seemed to drown out and muddle the narration so that he couldn't understand it. Finally, running his hand through his hair and sighing, he reached forward and pulled it over onto his lap. He opened up the box carefully with a knife, being cautious not to cut any of the letters or the pictures inside. Looking in, he saw the stack of pictures that he had kept of Claire, some of the corners ripped where the tape that he had used to fix them to his wall had torn them. They were bent and curved from the heat of the shipment, and he was disappointed at how many of them had creases as he slowly flipped through them. He was surprised when he recognized a longing for the familiarity of his old room, with his coffee- and tobacco-stained desk, the pictures of the little girl adorning his wall, with the reassuring tick of his oscillating fan.

With the flood of sentiment for his old room, he stood up and went to the fridge and opened a beer. Taking a healthy pull, he sat back down next to the box, and placing the small pile of pictures on the table, he sorted through the various letters. His hand stopped when it felt something solid and cold. Peering underneath a letter, he saw the metallic black memory bracelet that Jonathon's old platoon sergeant had given him awhile after Jonathon had died, a month before Marie.

He had been in his room, sitting at his desk, a mug of whiskey beside him, and a green soda can in his left hand that he raised periodically to his mouth to spit tobacco juice into. He had heard a knock and a familiar voice call through the thin door, "Captain Calhoun, you in there, sir? It's Sergeant Anderson. From Delta Company," he added. Sam had jumped up and opened the door.

"Hey Sar'n, what can I do for you?" Sam asked, reaching out his hand with a warm handshake.

"Hey sir," Anderson's voice growled, not unfriendly, from beneath his mustache. Sam could tell that he was not comfortable. Looking at his hands, he had seen that he held something in his left. Anderson thrust out the hand, holding the black aluminum bracelet in his fingers, offering it to Sam. "The boys and I thought that you might want this, sir. We got them for the LT." Anderson's eyes were looking beyond Sam, to his wall with the pictures of Claire.

"Yeah... thanks," Sam stuttered, reeling as if he had just been punched.

The two men stood there silently for a minute, neither knowing how to say what men need to say to each other at moments like that, but both wanting to tell the other how much they had loved Jonathon, and that his death had torn a hole in the thin fabric of their lives, had revealed something terrible about themselves and their world which made them want to weep bitterly, openly, and shamelessly. But neither of them understood then that in their profession, grieving was as natural as fighting.

Anderson looked at Sam with eyes so sad that Sam could tell the man's heart was broken. But there was something else there also—another sadness, a kind of quiet rage. Betrayal. The sadness of a man who had devoted his life to something, only to find that he had been cheated in the end.

"What do you think you'll do after this?" Sam asked, not knowing why he had.

"Oh, I think I'm out, sir," Anderson shook his head. Then, as if in confession, he blurted, "Maybe if it was for the country—" and caught himself, but then added anyway, "but not this."

Sam stood, completely unsure of what to say next. "He used to have these nightmares," Anderson continued. "Sometimes when he'd be sleeping, I'd hear him moaning and see him shaking his head, like he was trying to get away from something."

Sam stood there, paralyzed with the fear of revealing his emotions openly. He looked down at his feet. "Yeah," was all he could offer, and was immediately ashamed of it.

Quickly collecting himself, he added, "I appreciate this, Sar'n," catching Anderson's gaze for a moment. There was a brief, uncomfortable pause while the two men stood there in the small doorway, neither looking at the other. "Hey," Sam finally said, "can I pay you for this?" Not waiting for an answer, he had spun on his heels and grabbed his wallet, thrusting a twenty dollar bill at the man.

"Thanks, sir… no, don't worry about it, they weren't that much," Anderson refused.

Sam insisted, almost pleading with his eyes. "No Sar'n, take it. We officers are paid too much anyway." It was an old joke, and it wasn't even that funny, but it was meant to be, so Anderson smiled and broke the tension hanging over them.

"All right sir. Thanks," he said, sticking his hand out, obviously not wanting to stay any longer than was necessary.

Sam took the hand and shook it, holding up the bracelet with his other. "I appreciate this, Sar'n, thanks."

"No problem, sir," Anderson mumbled as he turned and left.

Sam had gone back to his desk, holding the bracelet in front of him, reading the inscription: "1LT JONATHON GARCIA 5/ D/ 1-327th INF REGT 11 SEP 03 IRAQ." Sam put the bracelet down on the corner of his desk, under his lamp, where it had remained until he had placed it in the box he now peered into.

Looking at the words inscribed in the black metal, he rotated it in the light from his window. Taking a hard pull on his beer, he slid the bracelet on his left wrist. Turning his wrist, inspecting his new accoutrement, he was satisfied with the fit and with the idea.

Finishing his beer, he went to the kitchen to get another, bringing with him the letter that Jonathon's mother had written him. Opening the bottle, he leaned his elbows against the counter as he read through it. The letter was a few pages long, with many misspellings and grammar errors, and several places where she had drawn a line through entire sentences. Finishing the beer with the letter, he looked at his watch, then reached into the fridge for another as he made his way to the shower. Since it was only four, he decided to go have a drink at one of the little bars on the way to Rachel's for dinner.

When he saddled up to the sticky counter a half-hour later at the Speakeasy Bar, he raised his hand to get the bartender's attention. Rubbing a glass with a white towel, the bartender ambled over, and with raised eyebrows, asked what he would like.

"You got any whiskey?" Sam asked.

"Sure do," the bartender nodded. "Whadya like?"

"Got any Crown?"

"Yep," he nodded again.

"Double. Neat," Sam ordered.

"Be right up."

He was finishing his seventh glass when he felt a light tap on his shoulder from behind. A familiar perfume wafted past him, and when he turned, Amber's piercingly-blue eyes met his. He noticed behind her were a couple other girls, talking to each other and glancing their way.

"Hi," he said, slurring just a little. Then, raising his glass, he motioned to the bartender for another. The man raised his eyebrows and shook his head just slightly, but poured him another. Eyeing

Amber as he slid Sam the drink, she saw that it was the last that Sam was going to get.

Looking at him, she smiled a pretty smile painted bright red, with perfect teeth. He stared at her, too drunk to realize that he was staring.

"You drink like a man who hates himself, you know that?"

"Yes." He nodded once emphatically.

She sighed and looked back at her two friends. "Come on, I'll take you home," she offered.

"I gotta finish this first," he said, raising his glass just a bit too close to her face.

"Here, I'll help." She took the glass from him and drained it, wincing slightly as she set the glass down on the bar.

Sam stared at her, his eyes wide as he watched her. "That was awesome," he said in wonder, a playful smile on his lips. "Could you please do that again?"

Obviously unimpressed, Amber answered, "Yeah, Sam, pretty awesome," she said. "Now come on, settle up with the barkeep, and let's get you home."

"What time is it?" he asked, looking at his watch.

"Just after nine."

"But I was supposed to—" he cut himself off, looking at her to see whether she knew what he was about to say. But the look that she gave him was only a frustrated one, and he shrugged his shoulders and acquiesced to her demands.

When they arrived at her apartment, her friends honking and waving their hands out the window, obviously heading back out on the town for the night, Sam waved back as Amber unlocked her door.

The room was dark when they walked in, and she flipped some lights on to reveal a very well-decorated, spacious, and clean living room. Sam looked around and, impressed, tried to whistle. Failing, he offered, "Nice place."

She turned to him, pulling off her high heels. Glancing over her shoulder, disinterested, she said, "Yeah," and walked toward him.

His heart beat faster at the look in her eyes as she came close to him, looking up at him, her breath warm against his neck. They looked at each other closely for a moment before he leaned forward and kissed her hard, his mouth open. She kissed him back, hard and passionate, as her arms wrapped around him, pulling him close to her. He could feel her breasts against his chest, and placed his hands on the small of her back, pulling her waist close to his. She pulled away slowly, looking at him. "I've missed you, Sam," she said, her eyes warm and inviting.

"Mm hmm," he said, his eyes closed, focused on the warmth that was radiating from her. Taking his hand and turning, she walked him into her room and shut the door behind them.

He was sitting in his Jeep at the base of the stairway that led to her apartment door when she pulled up the next day, having just come off her shift and from picking up Claire at daycare. When he saw her small Mazda pull into the parking lot, he climbed out of his Jeep and walked toward where she had parked. He reached her car in time for him to open the door for her before she had shut the car off.

"I'm sorry about last night," he offered, before she could say anything.

"That's okay," she answered, with eyes that said that it wasn't, but would be.

"Can I help you with anything?" he asked eagerly, trying to bribe her with kindness.

"You could get Claire."

He nodded obediently and opened the rear door, where Claire was strapped into her seat, singing a song to herself that only she knew the words to. "Come on, darlin'," he said, pulling her out of the chair and holding her. Walking up the stairs behind Rachel, she opened the door for him as he walked in and flipped on a couple lights. Setting Claire down, he turned and looked at Rachel. She was tired from her shift, and she moved slowly. Dressed in her outfit for work, a simple white blouse with black pants that were just tight enough to help with tips, she sorted through the day's mail, her back to him.

He sat against the back of the couch, watching her.

"I'm sorry, Rachel, really. I am," he said, meaning it.

She turned toward him, her gaze tired. She shook her head. "What happened? I thought that we..." she trailed off.

"I know," he said, not moving. Her gaze had frozen him to his place. He had to deliberately stop and collect himself under the weight of her eyes. Looking at the floor, he shifted his feet. Stealing a glance back up at her eyes, he saw that she was waiting for an answer. Looking back down, he shrugged. "I started going through some things from Iraq," he answered. "I had a little too much to drink."

"You didn't answer your cell. I was worried," she said, trying not to sound judgmental or demanding.

He raised his eyes back to hers, surprise in his face. The truth was that he had heard her call him while he was at the bar on his fifth drink and already two hours late, but he hadn't answered. But his surprised look was genuine: he honestly didn't remember the phone call. "I must not have heard," he mumbled.

She stared at him a moment before she smiled and shook her head, laughing despite herself while he just stood there, unsure of whether he was safe or not.

When she looked up, he saw that her eyes had softened, and that her laugh was sincere. "You're such a mess," she said, softening the accusation with a warm smile.

He chuckled in response. "Yeah, no argument there."

"I'm gonna go get changed," she said. "Make yourself comfortable. You wanna stay for dinner?" she asked over her shoulder as she walked into her room and shut the door.

"Sure," he called after her. "What do you want?"

"I don't know, surprise me," she called back.

"Okay, okay," he said, looking through the cabinets and the pantry. "How about spaghetti?"

After dinner, where she—smiling—had poured him a glass of milk before he could get himself anything else, they sat on the couch with the TV on while they talked and watched Claire play with her blocks. When it got late, Rachel picked up her daughter in her arms saying, "Time for bed." She walked over and dipped her down so that Sam could kiss her on the forehead goodnight, and then went into her room to put her down for the night.

When she emerged—Claire's screams slowing and losing their fevered pitch—Sam was slouched on the couch, flipping through the channels, obviously not impressed with the options. She plopped down beside him with a tired sigh. "That girl," she said, shaking her head, "she goes down fightin' every night."

Sam turned off the TV in frustration, and put the remote on the coffee table in front of him. He could feel her eyes on him as he sat on the couch, staring at the blank screen. He finally turned his head to look back at her. They looked at each other for a moment before he turned away. She had noticed the black bracelet around his wrist while they had eaten dinner, and had been able to see what it said. Putting two and two together, she began to understand what she thought had happened to him the night before.

"What kind of things were you going through last night?" she asked, seemingly out of nowhere.

"What?" he asked, turning his head back to her.

"Last night, when you started to drink, what things were you going through?"

He saw in her eyes that she was not looking for a way to resurrect his absence from the night before, but simply wanted to know. He also saw a kind of sympathy in her eyes, as if she already understood some of what must have happened. He glanced at his bracelet, then silently held his wrist up for her to see.

"I saw that earlier," she said. "What is it?"

"A memory bracelet," he answered, unsure whether to explain further or not, unsure how to explain further if she asked.

"Oh," she said. "For Jon?"

"Yeah," he nodded, then added. "His mom wrote me a letter several months ago, I found it with this in a box that I had mailed to my folks before we left."

"His mom wrote you a letter?" she asked, her eyes widening in surprise and sympathy.

"Yeah," he shook his head in response to her next question.

"Did you write her back?"

He said nothing, only shook his head. The room fell silent for a few minutes while she looked at him as he stared at the blank TV. Suddenly, he spoke. "I couldn't—I mean, I tried," he looked at her, with eyes that begged forgiveness. He shook his head, "I didn't know what to say... what to tell her," he said, shrugging his heavy shoulders. "Still don't."

Rachel leaned over and placed her hand on his shoulder, rubbing it slowly for a moment before she pulled it away again.

"Sam," she said after another few moments of silence had passed between them, "tell me about Jon."

* * *

Objective Snake East had been an old Iraqi military compound that rested on the southwestern edge of An Najaf. Charlie Company had been ordered to attack it as the first company in the battalion's effort to clear the city of enemy combatants. Jonathon's platoon had been attached to Charlie for the operation, which was supposed to be a raid: attack, clear, and withdraw. Three weeks after the attack, the company having conducted various raids, cordons and search, and presence patrols from the occupied compound, Captain Daniels would shake his head and laugh at how it was supposed to have been a "raid," and not an "attack." He had a penchant for definitions.

The raid he had planned had been textbook. With two tanks, Jonathon's platoon, a reconnaissance and a sniper team from Sam's platoon, and a team of Apache helicopters that Battalion had attached to him, it was the kind of operation that every commander dreams of. Very rarely does a military commander—at any level—find himself in a position where he not only gets a clear mission, but is also provided the resources necessary to be successful: tanks, helicopters, a whole additional platoon, a recon team, and a sniper team, in addition to his full company—military leaders lived for the kind of operation that he had been handed. One of the reasons for all the support was that 'Colonel DaSilva believed strongly that a leader's job was to empower and enable his subordinates, and provide them with the knowledge and resources they needed to be successful. He had learned, through nearly twenty years of service, that too many leaders misunderstand the relationship between subordinate and parent unit, and thought that the subordinate was there solely for the parent's success. One of the many reasons why his battalion proved to be so effective in An Najaf was that he stuck to his philosophy of giving his company commanders what they needed to succeed. And his commanders, understanding his position, paid him back in kind: they loved him and tried not to exasperate him with a constant list of unrealistic demands.

So Captain Daniels found himself in the position that made him the envy of the other company commanders in the battalion: the first company into the city, with what would undoubtedly be the best mission. Captain Daniels had placed the sniper team in a building across the street the night before, with the intent that they would engage any enemy while Paul Batsakis's platoon tried to gain a foothold in the compound. He had pushed the recon team to the west of the compound, in order to screen and engage any enemy as they fled. (The night before, when he had briefed his plan, Sam, as the scout platoon leader, had challenged Captain Daniels' positioning of the sniper and recon teams, arguing that they would be better utilized in other locations. Captain Daniels had cut his argument short with a look that was ice cold and a scowl that said he didn't really give a shit what the scout platoon leader—a lieutenant—thought.) The Apache's would serve as both aerial observers, as they would be able to update him with the best view of the compound, and, with their thirty millimeter cannon and 2.75 inch rockets, would be able to provide plenty of firepower to support the company as it moved through.

The enemy resistance at Snake East was nowhere near as intense as Captain Taylor had estimated. After one of the tanks had blown a hole in the compound's wall, and his first platoon had flowed through, they met only sporadic resistance from a group of a dozen disorganized soldiers. The rest of them had fled into the city the day before, leaving behind their uniforms and weapons. Less than an hour later, the men thrilled and dripping sweat, their heads aching from the exertion and the concussions of rifle fire, grenades, rockets, and tank rounds, Objective Snake East had been secured.

Jonathon's platoon, their pride wounded at having been left out of the fight, brought up the rest of the company's equipment well after the fight. When Captain Daniels had briefed Jonathon on his plan the night before, he had seen the disappointment in his eyes. Looking at Jonathon sincerely, he had said, "Jon, I know you would love to get in this, but the fact is that they may have lots of RPGs, and your trucks... well, they wouldn't hold up too well."

Jonathon had countered, saying, "Sir, we can dismount our guns and provide a base of fire for you."

Captain Daniels had nodded, appreciating the work and strain that would place on Jonathon and his men, and respecting Jonathon's sincere desire to get in the fight. "I don't doubt your courage Jon," he said simply and to the point, "or your men's proficiency with their weapons. But not this time around. Next time."

Next time? Jonathon thought. When in the world was there ever going to be another time like this one? Jonathon knew as well as Captain Daniels did that opportunities for a fight like this one never happened. But there was nothing he could do except to say, "Yessir."

After Charlie Company had secured Snake East, Alpha had attacked an old university, named Snake West, where the battalion ended up making their headquarters. The next day, Bravo had pushed north through the city, seizing an old business complex. Forty-eight hours after Charlie had secured Snake East, the battalion took a breath and a long look around, and found that they were all out of bad guys. Delta Company, minus a couple detached platoons, had been tasked with several "thunder runs" through the unoccupied areas of the southern part of the city in order to locate and identify any pockets of enemy resistance. Minus a few pot shots taken at them as they had sped by, they had met with no contact. An Najaf, it seemed, was secure.

'Colonel DaSilva, appreciating the fact that the battalion needed to maintain the initiative, split his part of the city into areas and assigned each area to a company responsible for defeating any enemy presence and securing the local population. As the soldiers came into more and more contact with the locals through their constant patrols, they started to develop intelligence on cache sites around the city. Action on what was at first believed to be hazy intelligence at best, proved to unearth an incredible amount of arms, ammunition, and explosives hidden in schools, libraries, factories, homes, anywhere and everywhere. Only one week into it, Captain Daniels had a pile of rifles, mortar tubes, and RPGs that was literally staggering to see: over three thousand AK-47s, hundreds of mortar and RPG tubes, tens of thousands of rounds of small arms ammunition and mortars, and hundreds of RPG rockets. And that was just in Charlie Company. Alpha and Bravo had similar numbers, with more coming in on a daily basis.

Jonathon and his platoon, working with Charlie, were conducting around the clock operations, providing much needed transportation and security for presence patrols as well as the missions to seize caches. Every few days, the company would get a mission to clear a certain building or complex, which broke up the monotony of endlessly-boring patrols with exploding walls and doors and the rush of the possibility of a fight that never seemed to come. "The bloody battle for An Najaf," as the young platoon leaders jokingly referred to it, was all but over.

Two weeks into their operations, Sam had appeared with the rest of his platoon at Snake East. Sam was a year senior to Jonathon, and the two had never served in a company together. They knew each other casually, from passing each other on the sidewalks back at Fort Campbell and at the battalion's various functions. Captain Daniels called Jonathon over the radio, asking him to report to the company command post, located in a pock-marked building that sat in the middle of the compound. On his short walk there, he passed cargo Humvees full of the battalion's scouts, their faces unshaven, most of them either swearing or smoking cigarettes. Walking into the CP, he looked to his right and saw Sam sitting on an MRE box, a goatee and sideburns on his face, his long dark hair shiny and messy. He had a brown and greasy *shumagg* wrapped around his neck, the headdress tucked into the opening of his blouse. Jonathon shifted his eyes to Captain Daniels, who looked disapprovingly at Sam's appearance.

"Hey sir," Jonathon said as he sat on an old chair in the corner adjacent to Sam, Captain Daniels and the first sergeant sitting in front of them. Sam had an open map on his lap that he was busy studying. Captain Daniels leaned forward and handed Jonathon a map similar to Sam's.

"Jon," Captain Daniels nodded. "You know Lieutenant Calhoun?" he asked.

Sam looked up from his map, and thrust out a dirty hand with a big smile. His eyes were heavy and red, with dark circles underneath. Jonathon had thought his own pace had been near exhausting, but by the look of him, Sam and his boys had had it much worse. "Sam," he said, introducing himself.

"Hey," Jonathon answered, taking the offered hand and nodding his head.

"Jon," started Captain Daniels, "tomorrow night, Sam here is going to conduct a mission of OPs in our area. There's been some intelligence that indicates enemy activity around a certain area, and Battalion wants to see if Sam and his boys can take them out." Jonathon raised his eyes. He had never heard, throughout the entire fight up to this point, Captain Daniels express anything but positive support for the missions that came down. He had never before heard Captain Daniels issue orders saying "Battalion wants," instead of in his own name. Things like that were a sure sign that he didn't approve of the order. No doubt that at least some of that had to do with the fact that Battalion had not told his company to execute the mission, but had assigned the scouts to operate in his area of operations. "You and your platoon are to serve as QRF while the scouts are out. Sam here has some idea of where his teams will be, and what he's gonna need from you."

"Sir," Jonathon interrupted, "what about our patrols?"

"No patrols for you, Battalion's orders."

There it is again, Jonathon thought. "But how will you—"

"We'll deal with it, Jon, don't worry about it."

Jonathon raised his eyebrows under the terse response, but didn't say anything. He suddenly became aware of a thick tension hanging in the room, and sought to cut through it.

"No problem, sir," Jonathon smiled, then turned to Sam, who was still studying his map. "Sam, you wanna go talk this through? I got some room for you and your guys over with my trucks where we can talk."

Sam looked up from his map and nodded his head. "Sounds good," he said, standing up. "Sir," he said to Captain Daniels, "I'll come brief you on the plan in a couple hours."

Jonathon thought Captain Daniels nodded his head a bit sullenly.

Jonathon and Sam emerged from the room back into the harsh afternoon light, and walked back down the short road to where Jonathon and his platoon stayed. Passing the trucks full of the smoking, swearing scouts, they suddenly became quieter as they walked by. One of them, young and smooth-faced, asked Sam as he walked by, "We gonna go kill some haji's, sir?"

Sam laughed a big laugh and said, "Sure are, Hall, so long as we can keep you from falling off buildings." Jonathon laughed carefully to himself. He had heard, a couple weeks ago, of a scout having fallen off a two-story building into a pile of trash and sewage while on a mission. Evidently it was true.

Getting to the first truck, Sam leaned in and spoke to the man in the front passenger seat. "Hey, Sar'n, let's get the boys outta the sun—" then turned to Jonathon, "You got room for us over where you are?"

Jonathon nodded. "Plenty. Just have him get with Sar'n Anderson."

"Great, thanks," he said, and then turned back. "Jon here says they got room for us," and they continued their short walk to the long, single story barracks where Jonathon and his platoon had taken up residence. All of the windows in the building had been either shot or blown out. At one end, someone had taken a crap on the smooth concrete floor and left the pile there, which was enough to convince Jonathon and his men to sleep outside. In general, things in the compound looked so run-down that it was impossible to know what damage had been the result of the attack, and what had been simply the result of neglect.

Jonathon and Sam talked over their plans with their two platoon sergeants, the two older men sharing their thoughts and making sure that fundamentals were not being overlooked. Sam had his platoon split into three separate elements: each element consisted of one six-man recon team paired up with one three-man sniper team. He would travel with one of the teams, and his platoon sergeant would travel with another. They would all depart Snake East at 0200 the following night, and walk to their separate buildings. Each of the buildings covered a section of the main road that ran north-south through town, where a majority of the attacks were occurring. Their plan was to infiltrate by foot, seize and occupy each respective building, overwatch until 0500 the following day, and extract by foot back to Snake East on separate routes. Jonathon's role was to serve as a Quick Reaction Force, should any of Sam's teams need either to be reinforced or to be extracted. Jonathon spent some time with Sam going over the possible routes and the several different link-up points, given different extraction scenarios. Jon could not help but be impressed: Sam was very thorough in his planning and seemed to be comfortable with executing a mission that relied heavily on tight coordination. Sam talked about things that Jonathon had never thought of before. Terms like "extraction corridors" were new terminology for him, and he found himself getting excited with this fresh knowledge.

Looking at the map, Jonathon noticed that two of the three buildings that the teams were going to occupy were houses. He pointed this out to Sam, who looked at him quite matter-of-factly, and responded, "Yeah, we know. And that middle building, which we think is vacant, may very well have people living in it as well."

"Huh?" Jonathon asked, confused.

Sam smirked. "Yeah. Turns out, in Iraq, where all the evil terrorists are, they let their homeless guard—quote, un-quote—public buildings so they don't have to sleep in the street."

"So what… what're you gonna do with the people inside?" Jonathon asked, curious. It seemed to him, that if people were inside the buildings that the teams were going to occupy, then it would be almost impossible to remain covert. "How're you gonna keep from getting compromised?"

"We're not. If there are people inside the buildings, then we're going to have to detain them."

"Really?" Jonathon was surprised. Busting into people's homes in the middle of the night was one thing, but it seemed holding them prisoner in their own home was quite another.

"Yeah," Sam answered patiently. "It could be difficult, but the boss thinks that it could work. Besides," he added, "we're not going to be there very long. It's only for a day. We're taking extra food, water, and money to compensate them."

Jonathon nodded his head in agreement, though he was not comfortable with the idea. To detain people in their own homes seemed a crime contrary to the very freedoms that they were supposedly there to propagate. Wasn't the right against illegal search and seizure a hallmark of our constitutional values? He thought about asking Sam about this, but looked at him as he was busy scribbling notes and routes on his map, and decided against it. It really didn't matter, he guessed, what either of them thought. And, he was learning, war was not some nice, neat package wrapped up in the pretty paper of "freedom and justice for all" and so forth; whatever it was, it was certainly not pretty or poetic.

Jonathon was awake with Sam several hours before their departure time. He had just come off a patrol with one of the Charlie platoons, bringing in another impressive cache of weapons and munitions. It was late, and he told Sergeants Cline and Hoover to put the boys down at fifty percent rest, which meant half of them up while the other half slept.

Right before they left, Jonathon did some final coordination with Sam, confirming the primary and alternate linkup sites, radio frequencies, and the elements' return routes. He was excited and disappointed at the same time, to be staying back at base while they went out on an operation, only to be called if he was needed. But he had resolved that, if Sam should need their help, then his platoon would be there immediately. He and Anderson had sat down earlier that day and gone over scenarios that could call them up. They had talked about what they would do, who would go where, how they would handle evacuating any casualties, and how and where they would link-up with any of the teams at the alternate link-up sites. For over three hours, they had worked through the various scenarios, and the novelty of the operation was waning for Jonathon as Anderson forced him to talk through as many possibilities as he could think of.

Sam and his teams departed through the south wall of the compound, meaning they would be taking very out-of-the-way routes to their designated buildings. Jonathon saw them off, then sat by the radio in his truck, monitoring Sam's radio frequency for two hours before Anderson came and relieved him. That entire day, the platoon sat and waited, playing cards, sleeping, or reading. It turned out to be like a day off, as Captain Daniels had been told by Battalion that he could not use Jonathon's platoon for his patrols the entire time that the scouts were out.

Jonathon, Anderson, Hoover, and Cline took turns sitting in Jonathon's truck, listening to the radio for any call from the scouts for help. All day none came, and the men's boredom turned to restlessness, as they were stuck in that difficult place of having nothing to do, but also were not able to go do anything, as they had to be ready to go at a moment's notice. Jonathon, too, grew weary of the waiting game. The day passed and the sun began to set, and Jonathon grew more convinced that they would not be called at all, realizing that he was both relieved, because that meant that nothing was going to go wrong, but also disappointed, as he had been excited to get in the fight if there was the opportunity.

Over an hour after dark, Anderson sat by the radio when they all heard two faint explosions from the north, from the direction of Sam's teams. Jonathon had been eating an MRE on the hood of the truck, lost in thought, and he walked over to the door, waiting for any call. The men had heard it also, and Cline and Hoover were already getting the men ready to go, telling them to start the trucks and load up. Suddenly, Sam's voice broke the long silence.

"Devil Five-Six, Viper Six," came Sam's voice, calm but direct.

Jonathon reached inside the truck past Anderson, who moved out of the way, telling the platoon to get ready. A flurry of motion set out around the trucks, as gunners raced up the hoods of their trucks, slinging on their body armor and sliding behind their guns. Trucks roared to life. Hoover and Cline were already conducting radio checks. If Jonathon had had the presence of mind to notice how quickly and efficiently his platoon got ready, he would have been proud. "Viper Six, Devil Five-Six," Jonathon answered.

"Hey Jon," came Sam's voice over the radio, "need you to get your platoon to Bravo." The three observation posts had been oriented along Market Street, the north-south running main road of the town, labeled OP's Alpha, Bravo, and Charlie, from south to north. OP Bravo, then, was the middle position. Sam was at the north OP, Charlie. Olk, Jonathon's driver, had jumped in and started the truck, which caused the two radios to turn off briefly as the engine turned over. Jonathon shot Olk a frustrated look, but caught himself. He had learned that it was important not to get too excited about little things during times like these, as it generally only made things worse. His gunner, MacLimore, had slid behind his gun, and called down through the hatch, "Ready to go, sir."

Jonathon jumped into his seat, listening to Sam's report as he handed Olk the other radio handmike, indicating for him to call up the platoon for radio checks. Olk called up each truck while Jonathon talked to Sam.

"What's going on?" Jonathon asked Sam.

There was no answer. Sam was obviously doing several things at the same time, and Jonathon was immediately sorry he had asked. What was going on was not important right now, Jonathon told himself. Sam had told him that he needed to get to OP Bravo. Jonathon reached back over and took the handmike from Olk, calling up to his platoon, "Okay, we're moving to Bravo. Let's get going. One, take the lead, use the primary route."

"Roger Six," Hoover answered, moving his truck out in front while Jonathon's fell in behind, followed by Cline's two trucks, with Anderson's cargo Humvee in between.

When they had all fallen in line, Jonathon said, "Let's go," and the trucks picked up speed as they wound through the barricades that blocked the entrance to the compound. Picking up the platoon handmike, he called Anderson, "Hey Seven, would you push to Charlie Company's net and tell them what's going on?"

"Already done, sir," Anderson's deep voice answered him. Jonathon smiled. His platoon ran like a clock.

Sam's voice came back over the other radio. "Devil Five-Six, Viper Six."

"Devil Five-Six," Jonathon replied quickly.

"Bravo was hit with a couple grenades," Sam answered his earlier question and then paused. Jonathon could tell that Sam was moving, probably very quickly, as he spoke, his sentences coming in quick bursts. "Two wounded. One sounds bad. No contact. We've abandoned Charlie. Moving to Bravo down Market Street. Alpha will stay put."

"Roger," Jonathon answered, as he felt Olk turn his head quickly when he heard about the wounded.

"They got wounded, sir?" Olk asked, trying to hide the nervousness in his voice.

"Yeah," Jonathon answered quickly, before he called up the platoon. "AT-5, this is Six, Viper has two known friendly wounded at OP Bravo. Sounds like they were compromised and got hit with grenades. Doesn't sound like they're in contact. One, need your truck to push past them a little, and cover to the north. Two, put your trucks on the southern end of the building along Market and cover the south and east. Seven, you'll need to pull right up to the front, and be ready to assist with CASEVAC."

"Roger," Anderson answered.

"Roger Six," Hoover answered.

"Got it," answered Cline.

The narrow streets were dark as the drivers drove them as quickly as they could with no headlights, driving with their night goggles.

Neon lights from shop windows occasionally blinded them, and the drivers had to slow down enough to see. Jonathon could hear Olk swearing to himself in frustration at maneuvering the wide Humvee through the narrow streets. Jonathon turned to Olk, encouraging him, "Okay, Olk, good job, slow is smooth, smooth is fast."

Jonathon's trucks pulled up outside the building just as they saw Sam's team coming around a corner up ahead, moving quickly and heavily under their loads.

"Friendlies to the north," Jonathon called into his platoon radio.

"Got 'em," answered Hoover, as his truck pushed past them to cover their movement.

Jonathon had Olk push just past the main front gate, and turn the truck to face east, across the main street, to allow room for Anderson to bring his cargo truck right up to the gate. Jonathon saw Sam, and stepped out of his truck to talk to him. Sam was issuing quiet, calm orders as Jonathon placed a hand on his shoulder in the dark, being careful not to let their night vision monocles hit each other.

"Sar'n Anderson will pull his cargo right up to the gate to help with your wounded. The rest of my trucks will provide security."

"Thanks Jon," Sam answered quickly, as his RTO handed him a handmike saying, "Battalion, sir."

Jonathon stepped out of the way, and looked around through the green lens of his monocle. Across the four-lane street were two-story buildings with several alleys intersecting with the road. He looked north to Hoover's truck, about twenty-five meters in front of him, then south to Cline's trucks, about fifty meters south of the building. Cline obviously had the same concerns about the multiple alleys across the street, and had told his gunner to watch them. Looking back at his truck, he saw that MacLimore had done the same with his gun. It was dark and quiet out, the past several weeks of near-constant patrols had trained the locals that it was best to stay inside after dark. The trucks all had kept their lights off, using their night vision to scan around the building. Except for their small area where engines idled and men ran around giving and obeying orders, the city was asleep.

Back behind him, Jonathon heard men talking loudly as they carried someone down and placed him in the bed of Anderson's Humvee. He saw quickly that the wounded man, Specialist Ryan Carlson, had a bloody bandage wrapped around his calf, yelling and moaning while the others tried to get him to calm down. Jonathon turned back to his trucks, hoping that he was the one that Sam had said was badly wounded. It turned out later that he was.

He and another man, Daniel Panak, had been lying on the roof, scanning their sector of the road, when two men had emerged from an alley behind them. Even though the team leader, Staff Sergeant Brandon Reynolds, had been as careful as he could be to ensure that he had complete security around their building; it was simply too big of an area for the eight men that he had with him to adequately cover. The two men who had attacked them had happened to come down and trace one of the low walls from the west which had not been covered, to get close enough to toss the two grenades onto the rooftop. It was pure luck on their part that they hadn't been seen, and that the two grenades they had blindly tossed onto the rooftop had happened to find their intended targets. They had disappeared into the web of alleys to the west before the grenades had even exploded.

Carlson had received the worst of it: a piece of steel had torn a large chunk of the back of his calf off. Panak had been luckier, a much smaller piece had just grazed the meat of his shoulder. As the men carried Carlson down, Panak had walked behind them, the right shoulder of his blouse soaked with blood. Jonathon could tell that he was hurt, but he didn't seem to be as hurt as he was mad, spitting and swearing the whole time, while also trying to calm Carlson down. He could hear Sam talking loudly into the radio, reporting to Battalion, who didn't seem to understand what had happened.

"Negative, I have *two* wounded," Sam was saying, slowly and clearly into the radio, obviously growing exasperated. "One routine, one litter-urgent. How copy?"

A pause while he listened, then, "Roger, good copy," and handed the handmike back to his RTO. Two helicopters came flying overhead, reporting to Sam over his net that they had been pushed down to him to help. Sam answered back into his radio, asking them to fly west of their position to keep people out of the streets, and also relaying to them the grid coordinates for OP Alpha, where he still had a third team.

Jonathon looked around. With the darkness, Carlson yelling in pain, the noise of the helicopters overhead, and men in general moving around a lot, Jonathon started to feel like things were getting more chaotic. Just then, a burst of gunfire sounded to the north, neither too close by nor directed at them, but close enough with all that was going on to get everyone's attention.

Immediately after the gunfire, Jonathon heard the high whine of a small engine and saw bright headlights come around a corner in front of Hoover's Humvee. Jonathon instinctively started to run toward Hoover's truck as he heard another burst of gunfire, and noticed that the approaching car was not slowing down as it came closer. He reached Hoover's truck, Hoover standing behind his open door with his weapon pointed at the oncoming vehicle. Out of the corner of his eye, he saw Melton, Hoover's gunner, settle behind his .50 cal, his elbows tucked against his sides, his eyes resting over the barrel of the weapon, aiming at the car. Another burst of gunfire from the north, and the car, not slowing down, swerved a bit and continued to bore down on them, the whine of the engine growing higher. Hoover shot a round over the top as a warning, trying to get it to stop. Jonathon gave it a split second to slow down, then, as he stepped out into the headlights, yelled, "Fire!"

A deafening burst of machine-gun fire split the night apart. Sparks flew off the grill and hood of the car as it slowed and drifted to their right, past Hoover's Humvee, and came to rest right in front of a wide-eyed Olk as he crouched behind his open door, his weapon pointing at the small pickup, a wisp of smoke rising from the end of his barrel.

After the gunfire stopped, there was a muffled ringing in his ears as he walked up to the truck, his weapon at the passenger door. He could begin to hear the sound of a man mumbling in foreign words, then someone moaning, as he signaled for Olk to open the door so that he could see in. Flipping on his tac-light, bathing the side of the truck in white light, Olk opened the door, and Jonathon dropped his weapon at what he saw.

"Medic!" Jonathon yelled over his shoulder.

When Olk had opened the door, a young, feminine face, with large, vacant eyes and a gaping mouth, met Jonathon's eyes. She leaned as if she were about to fall out of the truck, and Jonathon rushed forward to catch her. As he drug her out of the truck and laid her on the ground, the bulge that he saw in her stomach made him nauseous. The young face told him that she couldn't be more than fourteen years old. Fourteen years old and pregnant. And, from the looks of the holes in her chest, and the sound of her gasping breaths, she was dying. Fourteen years old and pregnant and dying. The scout's medic rushed up from behind him, pushing Jonathon gently out of the way as he pulled out bandages and began to try to stop the bleeding from a half-dozen little holes of pulsing blood. Jonathon stepped back out of the way, and saw that Olk had walked around to the other side of the disabled pickup. Several of the scouts had run over, and were both trying to stay out of the way and see the dying girl lying in the road at the same time. Two of them got down immediately and began helping "Doc," as they called him, with the bandages.

As Olk reached the driver's door, he opened it and called to Jonathon over the roaring engine, "Hey, sir, there's another one."

"Another—" began Jonathon before Olk cut him off.

"A man, sir, doesn't look too hurt, his face is all cut up and bleeding," Olk called, dropping his weapon to help the older man who emerged, shaking and obviously stunned. Another faceless scout ran over and helped Olk with the man, sitting him down on the other side of Jonathon's Humvee, with his back to the dying girl. Jonathon walked over and looked at the man. He could see tiny shards of glass lodged in the man's face, dozens of little flecks of red. He breathed heavily as he came out of his shock, and started to mumble in Arabic. Looking around wildly, he peered into the strange faces of the men who were checking him for wounds, and then looked over his shoulder.

When he saw the girl lying on the ground, a pool of blood thick and dark-shiny around her body, the protrusion of her unborn baby jutting up toward the sky, his eyes rolled back in his head, and something between a scream and a wail shot through the air, and ran like razor blades up Jonathon's spine.

Sam jogged over to Jonathon, looking first at the girl and then at the man, who was thrashing wildly about, trying to get away from the Americans, who were now concerned that he might attack one of them in his hysteria if they let him get up. They eventually tied his hands behind his back and rolled him onto the ground on his stomach, his eyes wide, still yelling and screaming, the multiple pockmarks of shiny glass and bright red dotting his face. Sam walked back over to his medic, who was performing CPR, pushing with downward thrusts on the girl's chest. A half dozen tampons were protruding out of the holes in her body, and Doc had run an IV into one arm which one of Sam's men held up the bag for. Jonathon heard him ask, "Doc?" The medic looked up and shook his head.

Sam came back over to Jonathon, who was obviously stunned. Stopping right in front of him, speaking directly into his face, Sam said, "Jon," speaking deliberately, "we're gonna have to get outta here. My guy—"

"Sir," interrupted his RTO, "Battalion." He handed the handmike to him.

"Not now," Sam said curtly, while his RTO turned his back and said, "Bulldog Main, standby," into the radio.

The helicopters flew back overhead. The man was moaning, his mouth open, tears and snot and saliva running down his chin, looking at the girl, dead on the ground, her face turned toward him in a blank stare. All of the Humvee engines were running. Behind them, back at Anderson's Humvee, Jonathon could hear Carlson moaning in pain, as voices tried to calm him. "Jon," Sam articulated again, "my guy is hurt bad. We gotta get him outta here. And we're gonna have to take the girl and the man back too."

Jonathon, his eyes wide, and his mouth slightly open, taking in long, slow breaths, slowly came back and started to nod his head. "Okay," he said, blinking the images out of his mind. "Okay."

"All right," Sam nodded, mirroring Jonathon. "Now, we need to get my wounded and the civilians back as soon as possible to Battalion. Can some of your trucks stay with my guys as we move back?"

"Yeah," nodded Jonathon, and he sprung into action. Stepping over the still-moaning man, he climbed into his truck. "Two, Five-six," he called.

"Two," Cline answered immediately.

"Need you to escort Seven with the wounded to Bulldog Main. One and I will stay behind and cover the scouts as they move back. You got that, One?"

"Roger," Cline answered.

"Roger Six," answered Hoover.

Jonathon set the handmike down on his seat and ran heavily up to Anderson's truck, his equipment jostling and clanking as he ran. Finding him helping with bandages around Carlson's leg, he said over Carlson's subsiding groans, "Cline is gonna take you and the wounded to Bulldog Main. Hoover and I are gonna stay back and cover the scouts as they move back to Snake East."

Anderson nodded his head, agreeing. "Roger, sir. Right now?"

Jonathon nodded back. "As soon as we can get the girl and the man loaded up."

"Sir, we can't put those two in here with Carlson—"

"No where else to put 'em," interrupted Jonathon as he turned and walked away. Two scouts lifted the girl's body and carried her over to the cargo Humvee and slid her body in. Carlson, though in excruciating pain, sat up and got as far from the body as he could, a horrified look on his face. Two others went and picked up the man and escorted him to the truck. When he saw the girl's dead pregnant body, he let loose a fit again such that it took four men to get him in the truck and hold him down. "Throw something over her body," Jonathon said to a face that he did not recognize. Several men jumped into the back of the cargo Humvee with Doc, as it drove off down the street with Cline's two trucks.

Sam was talking on the radio, reporting as clearly as he could who had been hurt, where, how, what had happened, and what was now happening. He was clearly frustrated, but did his best to remain calm over the radio. When Battalion finally correctly repeated back his report, he flung the handmike to his RTO and spat, "Thank fucking God." Then turning to Jonathon, he asked, "Ready to go?"

"Yeah," Jonathon nodded, as he jumped into his truck, and he and Hoover escorted the scouts as they walked south down the dark street, away from the hissing, steaming engine of the empty pickup, as silence and darkness slowly settled back upon the city.

Sam turned to Rachel in the quiet stillness of her small living room. "I don't think Jon ever forgave himself for that night."

* * *

"I was thinking about maybe heading back home for Easter."

It was a week later, and they were at the small park behind Rachel's apartment, watching Claire as she ran from see-saw to see-saw with a young boy about a year older than her. Rachel only looked down over her shoulder at him, stretched out on the grass and propping his head up with his elbow. When she did not answer, he pursued, "Would you want to come with me?"

"Yeah, we'd love to," she smiled and nodded her head. "Do you think your folks would mind?"

He laughed and rolled over onto his back, closing his eyes from the brightness of the Spring sun. "Well, they don't really like you all that much, but I'll see if I can talk 'em into it." She shook her head, slightly embarrassed.

Ever since he had told her about Najaf, he had felt more comfortable around her, as if in sharing he had brought her closer to his world. In holding that back, keeping it inside him, it had kept him there, and telling it to Rachel had forced the realization that that was a story from Iraq, over there, back then, and that he was no longer there, but here, now, with Rachel.

Rachel had noticed a difference, too. The first time she had seen him pour himself a glass of milk for dinner instead of his usual beer, she had let herself believe that it was perhaps more significant than the simplicity of the act itself. And it was. Standing there in the fridge that night, he had made the simple moral decision not to drink anymore during the week. He was surprised at how easy the decision, once made, had been to follow through with, and he could not help but wonder why he had not made it earlier. And they had both noticed that he was having a few less drinks over the weekend as well. Rachel knew that this reintegration could be slow and tedious, and she literally rejoiced for him over these small measures, these simple steps toward fully coming home, and she had thanked God for small victories.

"Great," he said, squinting up at her. "I'll give them a call and see what they think."

As they sat on the grass and Claire played with her new friend, Sam started to think about the sermon from that morning. The title had been "Rules for Holy Living," and Sam had been trying to decide what he thought about what the preacher had said the whole day. He reminded himself, lying there, of his new mantra to share more with Rachel, to be more open and vulnerable with her, that in doing so he knew he was getting better. He asked her what she thought of the sermon.

"I liked it," she offered, surprised. "What did you think?" she asked, turning to him just a bit so that she could look at him and still keep an eye on Claire.

He sat up. He was trying to decide whether this new rule of his really meant all that he felt it ought to mean, and he finally decided that it did. "I don't know," he began. "All these rules. Don't swear. Don't drink. Don't have sex. Seems to me that can't be the point."

"Well, it's not the point," she said.

"Yeah, but all this focus on what not to do and what to do. It's like when you were twenty, and having a drink was this earth-shattering event, like as if you got drunk then the whole world was gonna end, you know? And then, suddenly, you're twenty-one, and you find that having a drink is really not that big of a deal."

Rachel nodded her head.

"Seems like all these rules are pretty arbitrary. If I'm in Germany, I can drink no problem when I'm eighteen, but it's like some kind of mortal sin to have a drink in the U.S. before I'm twenty-one."

Rachel nodded her head again, waiting.

"So is it all relative?" he asked. "Are all these rules really just cultural expectations, and not really anything like, you know, what really matters? Where's the line between what is true and what has merely been manufactured?"

Rachel remained quiet, nodding her head, waiting for him to say what he wanted to say.

He continued, though carefully. "Aren't they just selling a product? I mean, you can't blame them, but a lot of these pastors seem to have lost touch with what the point is in the first place. No one can be perfect, right? So what's the point in trying, why try to get people to some kind of perfect standard when we all know we can't really get there?" He paused. He had not had a serious talk about religion in a very long time, and he was a little uncomfortable. He shrugged. "But maybe I'm just ... maybe I just don't get it because of... whatever."

He was dancing around something, and because of it, she was having trouble understanding what he was really saying. He could see that she was waiting patiently to get to his point, and he looked around to make sure that no one else was near them and that Claire was all right and would not come suddenly bursting in.

Tell her, he told himself. Just tell her. He looked at her, squinting slightly because the sun was up above her. "I love you," he said, looking straight at her. It wasn't news, it was a preface, like checking for the chord of a parachute at the door, waiting to jump.

"I love you too," she nodded, smiling, reaffirming that because of that he could tell her his secret, that he could tell her anything.

"I killed a man."

She sat quietly there as he continued to look at her, and waited for the full meaning of the thing to sink in.

"Well," she began, searching for words. "You were in a war, you had to do things like that, terrible things." Then she made a point to add that it didn't make him a bad man. She reached out and touched his arm and looked him directly in the eyes.

He shook his head. "No. I mean, yes, you're right. But this wasn't like that." He paused. "I killed a man in cold blood. Murdered him." He paused again, wondering whether he should tell her the whole story. No. "And then I lied about it, made it look like I'd done it in self-defense." He shook his head, his eyes still on the grass by his feet. "But it wasn't self-defense, Rachel."

He saw that she then got the whole of the thing. She looked hard at him, and they were both quiet for several minutes.

"Have you asked for forgiveness?"

Sam stared for a few moments at the grass, his eyes boring a hole in the warm earth. Finally, slowly, he shook his head. "He deserved to die," he said quietly, almost to himself. He plucked a blade of grass.

Rachel sat up straight, as if a snake had just crawled out in front of her. "He deserved to die?" She shook her head violently. "Deserved to die?—no, Sam, not at all." She reached out and grabbed his arm and he was surprised at how hard she squeezed it. "Look at me Sam: no one deserves to die. Who are you—who are we to say who deserves to die? Did we give them life? Then what right do we have to take it? What right do we have to that kind of claim? To say when another man no longer deserves to live? No Sam, he did not deserve to die—"

"He killed Jon."

"Sam... do you know that?" She shook her head sadly. "Did you see him kill Jon? Do you have proof of any kind whatsoever?"

Sam shook his head. "No," he said quietly, still playing with the blade of grass.

"No." She paused. Sam glanced up at her out of the corner of his eye. He saw that her face was flushed and her eyes were wide in disbelief. When he saw her eyes soften, his own darted back down to the grass. "I don't understand that Sam. Do not ask me to understand that. I can't."

"Would it make a difference if I were sorry?"

"Are you?"

But he didn't answer because he was ashamed that he was not sorry.

"Have you asked for forgiveness?" she asked again.

But he only shook his head.

She cocked her head, trying to understand. "Why not?" she said almost in a whisper. "Sam, why wouldn't you...."

• Sam shrugged. "I don't know," even though he really did. Then he told her. "I'm not sorry, Rachel." He paused a moment, stealing a glance up from the grass to her, and then back down to the ground. He heard Claire squeal with laughter on the playground, but Rachel did not take her eyes off him. "Maybe I should be," again he shrugged, "but... I don't know. I'm not."

They sat together like that, close, quiet, for a long time. Finally, he spoke again, getting back to his point, as if he had just confessed to stealing cookies out of the cookie jar. "So if I killed a man, if I committed murder, then what does it matter if I swear or drink or even have sex outside of marriage? Doesn't that put all of that stuff in perspective? Make them seem... insignificant?"

And she saw that he didn't understand. "No, you don't understand." She paused. "It's not the act we're forgiven for, Sam. It's we ourselves who are forgiven. God does not redeem the act, or make the sin suddenly not a sin anymore. Sin is sin; murder or theft or lying: it's all sin. What Jesus does is redeem us from our sin. It's what sin does to us—what it can turn us into—that we are saved from. He doesn't erase the sin, he redeems the sinner."

She paused, unsure what to say next. She remembered a time when she would have launched into a full-blown expostulation about the demerits of sin and the process of grace. Back when she didn't really know all that much about it. But since Stephen and Claire, her faith had become more simple, more sublime. She had seen that God truly does work for the good of those who love him—Claire was all the proof she needed of that—and that the accountants who wanted to turn Christianity into a sort of club were a bit too quick to draw a line separating the good from the bad and the black from the white with no room for the staggering amount of gray in between the two.

"But if we don't learn to forgive ourselves," she allowed herself to add, feeling that this last point was important, "if we won't let ourselves first see the sin as what it is, as a wrong that can be separate from ourselves, then it doesn't matter that God forgives us."

Sam nodded his head slightly, plucking at the blades of grass. Finally, he spoke. Still not looking up at her, he said, "I'm just not sure that I can be sorry for that, Rachel. I know it must sound terrible, but with Jon and…." He shook his head. "I don't know. I want to be sorry. I want to feel bad about it, like it was wrong. But I don't, and I can't fake it, right? I mean, that's something you shouldn't fake, right? Being sorry you killed a man?"

"No Sam, you're right. Don't try to fake that; it won't work. Maybe for a little while, but it'll fail you in the end."

She waited to see if he would say more. When he remained quiet, still plucking at the grass, she knew he had said all that he wanted to say. Stooping down so that he could see her face, she said, "Sam. Look at me. I love you."

He looked up at her. "I love you, too."

"Thank you for telling me that."

"Yeah."

A few weeks later, they were back in Denham Springs for the Easter weekend. Sam watched with a great deal of satisfaction the way his dad seemed to interact with Claire, as if she were his granddaughter. Which she soon may be. He had bought a ring, and he found himself in that place that all young lovers do when they are overrun with optimism about all things because of the love they hold for some person which they know is returned in measure. All of the world's ugliness loses its bitterness and the world seems right and good despite the overwhelming evidence to the contrary. Even their own transgressions seem to waste away in the piercing light of their affections, and they make the mistaken assumption that just because time has passed that their misdeeds have lost their effect. That their love really has covered over a multitude of sins.

The ring was burning a hole in his pocket, but he had restrained himself and decided to wait for the right moment, to prepare for the perfect time. He had not thought of what to say to her, or how to ask her. All he could think of at the moment was she herself. All he had to say to her was that he loved her, and he thought a marriage proposal ought to have more to it than that. So he found himself riding a tidal wave of emotion that seemed to override his senses. He was ready to swear off anything to gain assurance of her hand, as if he needed to barter in order to marry her. He had told her his secret, his great secret, and she had not flinched. Instead she had led him away from that darkness he had been holding inside himself all that time, and brought him out into the searing light of the sun. And he saw that not all good was vanity, not all things ended in destruction and perversion, that there was another answer, another hypothesis that suddenly demanded his attention. He remembered his last conversation with Jonathon and what he had said about there not being anything at the end of that long dark road of dismay.

Not that he had wholly accepted the alternative, but still the fact that the option even existed was air fresh enough.

On Easter Sunday, his family, with Rachel and Claire, loaded up into the car and headed down the meandering, tree-canopied road to First Baptist Church. There, Sam felt that the good reverend had cut out so much of the chaff that pastors must inject for the rest of the year to keep the seats filled, and his congregation was blessed by the very simple deliverance of the gospel that is Easter itself. That there is life after a death. And who would dare pervert that beautiful truth with such things as "Rules for Holy Living," or "Consubstantiality?" Who would dare, on that day of all days, add such human constructs to the simple truth of God? Perhaps some time in August, but not then. An empty tomb mocks man's every attempt to capture and define such an unadulterated thing. Sam thought that maybe the reason so many people only go to church twice a year may very well be due to their intolerance for bullshit.

Walking out the doors back into the sunlight, Sam looked up suddenly to see Michael Wax and his wife Jesse Lee walking their way. His first instinct was to run, but the hand that squeezed his told him to stay, and he looked down and smiled weakly to Rachel with a sigh of resignation.

When Michael and Jesse reached them, the two men forced smiles and shook hands awkwardly while the two ladies attempted to help their men by saying hello and asking how they were and commenting on what a lovely sermon it had been. When they had exhausted their short banter, Michael asked Sam how he had been.

Sam nodded his head and said, "Well, Mike," in a way that demonstrated that he had actually thought about how he had been and had answered truly. "You?"

"Things are going well for us," and he looked over to Jesse who smiled and nodded her head just slightly. Rachel knew what they were about to say and her face burst into a beautiful smile. Michael shook his head and beamed. "We're pregnant. Four months."

Sam's mouth opened into an open-mouth smile. "Yeah?" He laughed. Perfect, he thought right then. Everything was perfect. The world was good and you can start again, you can be good even when you think there's no point to it because there is a point, and in the end whether you were good may be all that matters.

Michael nodded his head and smiled back. "Yeah. A boy." He was about to burst, and the four of them stood around awkwardly once again until Rachel saved them and reached over and gave Jesse a hug and said congratulations. Then Sam followed her and gave Michael a big hug that lasted just long enough to make it more than just a hug between strangers, but the kind of hug men give each other when their hearts are full and they cannot say fully what they feel.

Michael and Jesse will be at the wedding, Sam thought. And their baby boy will be there, too. And he could see Jesse seated in the small rows of white chairs while her husband stood beside Sam up near the alter while they waited for Rachel to come down the aisle behind little Claire, who would be scattering flowers. It was all he could do to keep himself from getting down on one knee and asking Rachel to marry him right then and there.

Rachel and Jesse were talking about how the parents had reacted—they were ecstatic, of course—and the two men found themselves looking from each other to the ladies and back at each other.

"Listen," Michael began with a sigh, stuffing his hands into his front pockets. "Sam, about that night, I didn't—"

"No, Mike," Sam cut him off. "I'm sorry about that. I was...." But there was no way for him to say it all. "I'm sorry, brother. I really am."

"That's all right." Michael nodded his head, still beaming as he watched with fascination his wife discuss the young life inside her. Sam smiled as tears welled up in his eyes. What could not be okay? What thing would possibly have the audacity to be anything less than okay at that moment? The two old friends smiled at each other and Sam laughed and Michael shook his head with a huge smile.

"You guys have plans for dinner today?" Michael asked.

"Yeah, we're having dinner at about two."

Michael reached for Jesse's hand and swung it slightly. "Well, why don't y'all come on over after for a drink?"

"Yeah?" Sam asked.

Michael nodded for emphasis. "Yeah."

"I hope y'all will bring Claire, too," Jesse jumped in, looking at Rachel.

And Sam never thought that he would ever be happier than he was at that moment.

Easter dinner was only a few hours after church, and they all laughed and stuffed themselves with ham and green beans and mashed potatoes until they were all worn out from the meal. Claire had been the center of attention and the source of much of the laughter as she squeaked and sang and stuffed food practically everywhere but her mouth. Chuckling and smiling, they cleared the plates and Mrs. Calhoun told everyone to go sit down, that she would do the few remaining dishes.

Sam and his dad hung around the kitchen for a few minutes regardless, scraping the leftovers into tupperware and loading the dishwasher until they were shooed away. Sam's dad reached for the Sunday paper and walked outside to the back table and sat down heavily with a contented sigh. Sam had followed him outside, and when Rachel handed him Claire in the backyard and walked back into the kitchen and offered to help, Sam smiled when he imagined the delight the offer would illicit from his mom.

Sam stayed in the backyard with Claire. Their backyard was an acre of St. Augustine and encroaching clover, broken by several old water oaks that shot up into the sky, practically covering the whole place with patches of dancing shade. There, shielded from the sun and the heat of the humidity, he and Claire searched for grasshoppers, dug for worms, and rested in the cool grass.

At one point, more content than tired, Sam stretched out on the damp grass and crossed his hands behind his head for a nap. Claire chased after butterflies as his dad sat on the back porch watching them as he read the local paper, bifocals perched on the tip of his nose. Down the road, from a small local church, music from a live jazz band came through the shade of the oak trees and floated over the lawn as Sam drifted off to sleep.

From the kitchen, Rachel had seen him playing with Claire, her little dress dancing in the breeze. When she saw Sam lie down, she stuck her head outside. Sam's dad eased her concern, folding his newspaper and assuring her, "I'll watch her." Rachel smiled at him with an affection that betrayed her love for his son. He simply nodded and smiled back at her. After she thanked him and went back inside, he shook his head and watched with wonder as his little boy—a grown man now, home from a war—rested in the cool grass while the little girl started to pick flowers from the lawn and place them on him while he slept.

A few minutes later Rachel emerged, having seen Claire doing the same, concerned that she would wake him. When she walked back outside, his dad waved her off, saying, "Let her be. It's good for him." She stood there and watched from behind him as her daughter placed flowers on his son. And for the first time, the thought occurred to her of the weight that must press on the shoulders of fathers whose sons have gone off to fight in a war, and the peace that this little scene must be bringing to ease the gnawing fear that had poisoned his dreams for so long. She thought that maybe even this little scene was enough to forgive the whole world of all its arbitrary and colossal cruelty; that just maybe the simple weight of even the most insignificant act of charity was sufficient to tip the balance against the staggering sum of human suffering that repeats and multiplies itself through the centuries.

Sam woke up to the feel of something tickling his ear. He listened without moving, and heard the quiet breathing of a small body, and smelled the faint scent of baby powder. With a smile and without opening his eyes, he asked, "What're you doin', huh?" He heard a squeal of high laughter, and opened his eyes to see Claire's face not two inches from his. He smiled and said playfully, "Hey there darlin', what're you doing?" And he lifted his head and saw that he had been adorned in dandelions and yellow grass flowers. He let his head back down and closed his eyes, and could not repress the smile that forced itself up through his face as he let Claire continue dressing him up.

Seeing him wake, Rachel walked over and sat beside him while Claire continued her game. She watched silently and saw— as if it were something physically sliding off—his body relax and something leave him. The smile was gone, but his face still betrayed the joy underneath the man's skin, moving deep inside him. Claire continued her delicate task of finding flowers and placing them gently in his hair, on his neck, on his shirt, his shorts, on his legs. Rachel could tell he was still awake because every now and then Claire would try to stick the stem of one of her flowers into his ear or nose, and he would wrinkle his face from the tickle.

Rachel turned her face from the two of them toward the sound of the music and the sun sifting through the leaves. And even though the music wasn't very good, it was joyful music and it was a beautiful Easter day, and somewhere inside her spirit she thanked God for that day, for Claire and for flowers, and for Sam, and even for Stephen. She smiled when she thought about how joy can work backwards in our lives: go through and find pain we thought could not be healed—which we thought had crippled us—and bind it up, make us whole again. And how we all need an Easter at some point in our lives, something beautiful that resurrects us after a long darkness and pulls us up out of the ground into the light of day.

CHAPTER 6

"Hello?"

"Hi Sam," a woman's voice came through the phone. "It's me, Amber."

`"Oh, hey," he stuttered. "Hi. How are you? What's up?" He fumbled for words.

It had been over a month since his visit home over Easter, and he had finally begun to settle in a little. Since that weekend, strangely, he had felt more relaxed. Over dinner a week ago, in that incapacity of hers to dance around a subject, Rachel had asked him one night how he was feeling. Chewing on a piece of pizza, he had looked at her quizzically, trying to pretend he didn't know what she meant.

"Did you ever write to Jon's parents?" she pursued.

"Oh," he had said, looking toward Claire as she played on the living room floor. "No."

But she spoke on easily enough. He wondered across the table at her. Her question had none of the implication of a judgment; it was not meant to make him feel guilty. It was simply her way of asking.

She had noticed a change in him since their trip to see his parents. She had first noticed it that afternoon when Claire had decorated him in flowers. She knew that sometimes things can build up like a toxin, and that the infection sometimes has to be lanced so the pressure can be relieved. And she had seen that happen in him since they had returned home. So when she asked him over dinner that night how he was feeling, she was asking because she had sensed a positive change in him, and wanted to see whether he would be willing to talk with her about it.

And though there was a part of him that lay awake at night when he had gone back to his apartment, staring at his ceiling fan as it rotated around his bed and rehearsing all the things he would like to tell her, still he found himself unwilling whenever she asked. It was something else that he thought about late at night, his inability to share with her the things he wanted to tell her. However, with a mouthful of pizza, he had told her that he was, in fact, feeling a little better.

"I don't know," he had said answering her question about Jon's parents. "Seems now like that's in the past. I wish I'd done it before, but now it seems like it's too late, like reopening an old wound." He shrugged, taking another bite of pizza. "You know?"

She nodded quietly.

After a minute of silence, the only sounds coming from the clinking of their forks on the plates on the table and Claire's self-dialogue, he had changed the subject, and Rachel had let him.

Now, sitting in his office, hearing this voice from this woman, and there was a tension in her voice, a thick and deep resonance that made him nervous.

"I'm all right, Sam," and she paused. He could hear her breathing heavy over the phone.

He grew more confused, and as a result of his confusion, more nervous. "So... how are things, Amber?" He tried to sound easy and relaxed, as if he were simply talking to an old friend.

"Good," she answered quickly. Then, "Sam, I was wondering, do you think that maybe we could get some lunch, or a cup of coffee?"

Taken aback, he searched for words. "Umm, sure, Amber, lunch could be good." He looked at his watch, just past ten thirty. He was at work, digging through a pile of damage and loss statements for the company's equipment, matching them with work-order numbers. It was tedious work, and he thought that lunch might be a good escape for a while. Besides, he thought, it was the Thursday before Memorial Day, and the battalion was getting a four-day weekend, which meant that in a couple hours, people would start disappearing. "I could do lunch," he said, nodding to himself, as if to convince himself he wanted to do lunch. "Have anywhere in mind?"

She was noncommittal. "No."

He searched in his mind for places to eat, and thought that burgers sounded good. He had skipped breakfast, and his stomach had been growling at him all morning. He suggested the local brewery downtown.

"That sounds good," she said, her voice lacking any real enthusiasm.

"Great," he said back quickly. "How about noon?"

"Sounds good."

"Okay, I'll see you then."

She hung up the phone without saying goodbye. Putting his phone back in his pocket, he thought for a minute about the strangeness of the phone call. The tension in her voice and her quick responses made him uneasy, and though he tried to get back to the stack of papers on his desk, he found it suddenly hard to concentrate.

Finally, throwing his pen down in frustration, he swore and grabbed his keys.

He had finished a pint before she arrived at his table, a little two-seater stuck in the corner of the main dining room. Rich smells of garlic and bread and cheese filled the air, and he was happy to see her because the beer had gone straight to his head and he was hungry. The beer had calmed his nerves a bit from her strange call. Looking up at her, the empty pint to the side, he was struck by how bad she looked. She was still pretty—there was no way for her not to look pretty—but with her hair up in a hasty bun, and dark bags around her red-puffy eyes, Sam could tell that she had just been crying. His mind had raced through the reasons for her wish to meet with him, and he had come to rest on the chance that her fiancée and she had broken up, and she was looking to re-ignite their old romance. His nerves, once he had settled on that reason, were therefore a result of his resolve to resist her approaches at all cost, and his fear that his own capacity to self-destruct would win over his good sense.

He smiled at her weakly as she slid into the chair opposite him. A waiter with dark hair and long sideburns came up to the table and asked whether they wanted anything to drink. Sam put his finger on the empty pint, and gestured toward Amber, asking her if she wanted the same. She looked at him hard shaking her head. She managed to say, "Just water, please," and fake a smile at the waiter before he left with their order.

In an effort to soften the tension that had crashed onto the table like an avalanche, suddenly cold and pressing and frightening, he reached for the menu. Opening it, he asked her, "What do you feel like?"

But he saw that she had no intention of looking at a menu, but just sat across from him, looking at him, studying him. Laying the menu back on the table, he cocked his head in sincere concern. "Amber, everything okay? What's going on?"

At the questions, her eyes shot down to her hands folded in her lap as she shook her head slowly, stray hairs that had escaped the ponytail dangling down. Sam remained quiet, though his uneasiness, coupled with the beer and his hunger, started to turn into frustration. Just when he was finally about to ask her just what the hell was going on, her head shot back up, her eyes freshly moist and reddened.

"Kevin left me," she said, a single tear tracing down the gentle draw between her nose and cheek.

Sam relaxed a bit now that the subject had been revealed to him. He reached across the table in an effort to sound sincere. "I'm so—"

"I'm pregnant, Sam," she spat the words out, cutting him off.

He froze in place, his arms half-way across the table. The waiter reappeared with the fresh pint and a glass of water. Seeing the woman's crying eyes and the man across from her frozen to his place, he simply set the two glasses down and left.

Drawing his hands back, finding his beer, Sam held it with both hands on the table in front of him. There was a group of young men, who were obviously in the army, behind them that burst into laughter. The silence weighed heavy around them and he finally spoke. "You're pregnant and he left you?" he asked quietly, sympathetically.

She offered him one last clue. "I'm about eight weeks."

Her eyes rested on his, and with her look she connected the dots for him. When he realized what she was saying, why she was a mess, why Kevin had left her, why she had only wanted a glass of water, his breathing quickened, whistling through his nose, and his face flushed. His eyes wide, he blinked away his ignorance, and it was his turn to stare down at his hands folded around the frosted mug in front of him. His first thought was of Rachel and Claire, and then only of Rachel, and the night at the Speakeasy, and his mouth was suddenly dry and he took a long pull from the mug, the cold carbonation burning his throat.

Finally forcing himself to speak to the eyes that were nailed to him, obviously resolved to let him speak next, he stammered, "Is it mine?" and immediately wished he had not spoken out loud what he had hoped for inside. It was a desperate question, a lurch for a single pathetic branch that clung to the cliff which the avalanche carried him over, down, down, down, all roaring and stinging and cold and blinding.

She shook her head, in disbelief and anger rather than as an answer. And Sam saw the answer in her eyes, and he tumbled over, falling and reeling and tumbling. The air left his lungs, he could not move his tongue, not even to wet his lips which were suddenly terribly dry.

When he spoke, it was not him, not his voice, not what he wanted to say. It was the fear from this falling which spoke. "Are you sure?"

Her eyes turned into a raging whirl of hatred and rage. "Asshole," she labeled him, branding it onto his forehead with her eyes.

Plummeting between his disbelief and her hate, he stammered, "I just thought…. didn't you… weren't there…." And she just sat across from him, shaking her head. She didn't speak, only sat across from him, moving her head from side to side, over and over again, as if it were the mechanism driving the dialogue of decision in her head.

He saw the cold resolve rise up from inside her and set in her face. Her eyes dried and color returned to her cheeks. Still silent, Sam watched the change with a shudder. Again, he thought of Rachel and little Claire. And as Amber stood up in front of him, hating him with her eyes, leaving him still tumbling down in a blind, freezing fall, he thought of Rachel again, and then he thought of Stephen and Claire, and his stomach lurched inside him. A part of him wanted to speak, even tried to speak, to save that little life, but his fear and his selfishness kept him frozen and silently nailed to his chair, and his silence killed the life inside her. His paralysis, which had initially been a result of his selfish fear, changed into a paralysis of disgust with himself, a seething, loathing recognition of his own failures. His stomach did a somersault inside him.

Without saying a word to him, nor looking at him, Amber stood up and walked out of the restaurant. He barely made it in time to the men's room.

Sam stumbled through the door into the dark room, the woman on the stage awkwardly twirling around a brass pole illuminated by red foot lights. She obviously was not a professional and had not been doing this long, as she danced with a rhythm that was just behind the music. His eyes were already tired from the strain of his heaving and the following six beers he had had at the restaurant before the waiter had refused to serve him anymore.

Taking a quick glance around the room, he noticed a familiar profile at one of the small round tables in front of the stage, sipping carefully from a half-empty glass with eyes that watched the woman on the stage with a kind of amused fixation. His eyes on the man, Sam reached behind him and pulled a metal flask out of his back pocket.

Sitting by himself at the restaurant, whenever he had started to feel that swell of self-disgust rise up in him, he had taken a long pull from the beers in front of him. When the beer had run out, he had decided that he needed a more reliable source of medicine. So, on the way from the restaurant to the strip club, he had gone by his apartment and picked up the metal flask and a bottle of tequila. He was not sure what the throwing up and the beers and the flask and this strip-club all meant; he was still reeling as if in a great fall off some secure place, and the ingredients he reached for in his fall seemed to ease the fear and whisper to him not to fight this falling. If he was going to fall, he figured, he might as well fall all the way.

Sam swore to himself and shook his head, and walked up to the man. Off to the side of him, the man felt a huge shadow standing over him and heard it say, "Well, is this something they teach at seminary? Like research or something?"

The man looked up at Sam, who slid into the empty seat next to him and had raised his hand to the waitress behind the bar to order a drink.

"What are you doing here?" Mel asked, gazing absently into his near-empty glass, the ice cubes coated in an amber sheen.

"I could ask you the same thing," Sam replied as the waitress arrived and waited—impatiently—for him to place his order. Sam raised his eyes to Mel and asked, "What're we drinking?"

"Maker's," Mel offered back, draining the last from his glass and rattling the ice cubes for effect.

"Two doubles," Sam said to the girl in the mini skirt, holding a large round tray.

"All right... I'll be right back," she forced a rehearsed smile.

As she walked away, Sam leaned forward on the table and gazed at Mel, who avoided his eyes by pretending to be absorbed in the awkward woman on the stage. Sam could not suppress the smile that stretched from ear to ear as he took in the scene he had stumbled into.

Finally, unable to play the game anymore, Mel spoke. "You think that it's absurd for me to be here, because I'm a pastor," he said, his eyes still watching the woman.

"Well, Mel," Sam said slowly, "yeah, I was kinda wondering what you were doing here, seeing as how you're a holy man and all."

Mel turned at the words "holy man," and shot Sam a look that for a second wiped the smirk off his face. Sam realized that perhaps he was enjoying this just a bit too much, and checked himself. He asked again, "What *are* you doing here, Mel?"

"The same thing you are," Mel answered, his eyes still on the stage, as the waitress brought their drinks. "Thank you," Mel offered with a warm smile that elicited a surprised and unrehearsed smile from her that said, You're welcome.

Sam dug into his wallet and pulled out a ten dollar bill which he placed on her tray and told her to keep the change.

She didn't even bother with the fake smile as she grabbed the bill and placed it in her pocket, and walked away back behind the bar, where the bartender was busily drying glasses. Sam watched her go, her rear end pressing against the stretched pleather of the mini skirt, which—even if she was a waitress in a strip club—was dangerously close to being too short.

Sam turned back to Mel, who was already working on his fresh glass. Sam started to say something before stopping, trying to remember what they had been talking about. Then he remembered. "Yeah, but—"

"No, no buts, Sam," Mel cut him off, his voice absent any malice. He spoke calmly, slowly twirling his drink in his hand as amber fingers of Kentucky bourbon traced down the inside of his glass. His eyes watched the woman on the stage as she danced back and forth from the edge of the stage to the brass pole. "I'm a pastor and I shouldn't be here," he nodded to himself, "but the truth is that you're a man and you shouldn't have killed another man, not the way you did."

Sam drew a breath to speak, but was so surprised by the comment that Mel was able to keep speaking without being interrupted. "What you did was murder, plain and simple," he said, shaking his head and taking a long sip from his glass. After a pause, during which Sam's mind whirled between disbelief and defense, Mel put down the glass and tore his eyes from the woman on the stage to meet Sam's. "No, you and I may both be cowards, Sam, but my cowardice only leads me to a strip club and a few drinks. Yours led you to kill a man."

Sam wanted to rear up to his challenge, to call attention to the string of evidence that supported his argument that he had actually killed Marie in self-defense. He was able to say, "The AK," before Mel's gaze—a gaze that cut his argument down in mid-air and dismissed any of his proofs as the fallacies that they were—communicated that they were beyond all of that. This was no court, lawyers' arguments held no sway here, and the only two men who mattered at the moment both knew the truth. There was simply no point in going down the same old road. Mel looked at Sam with the confident calm of a man who knows he is right and knows that he doesn't need to waste his time convincing his audience that he is right. Sam fell silent, finally saying, "I don't know about the whole 'coward' thing—"

"No, Sam," Mel cut him off, shaking his head slowly. "You don't understand. It requires courage to show mercy, Sam. When you give a man something that you both know he doesn't deserve, you expose yourself as vulnerable. That's what you don't understand. At the crucial moment, Sam, you failed; your courage floundered; you yielded to your fear of justice. You may have everybody fooled with your large frame and rough exterior and sleeping around, but none of that translates directly into courage. You killed Marie because you don't have the courage to believe in mercy." He looked back at his glass, empty now, and raised his hand toward the waitress for his check.

Sam's eyes were glued to him; he was angry and afraid and angry because he was afraid, and trying to decide how to respond, or even if he should respond at all. Finally, after the waitress had brought Mel his check, and, judging by the smile that she gave him, he had obviously tipped her well beyond what was expected and she had left them alone, Sam spoke. His voice was just a bit shaky despite his best efforts to sound in control of himself, as if Mel's multiple accusations were of no consequence to him.

"You, a pastor, sitting in a strip club at three in the afternoon, drowning your self-pity in whiskey and naked women, are going to lecture me on Christian virtues of courage and mercy? Who the fuck are you, preacher man?" Sam felt himself getting angrier and knew he was about to lose his composure, which only made him more angry because he knew his anger would only validate Mel's accusations. He paused a moment to regain his composure and said, "Seems to me you're a long way off the mark as well, brother."

Mel did not reply, only met his gaze for a moment before he stood up. He took a long, slow breath, and looked down at Sam. Sam saw that the calm resolution that had been in his eyes had been replaced with a deep sadness. "Be careful not to confuse hypocrisy with what may just be the human condition, Sam. There is a difference. It's a fine line between the two, but there is a difference. I make no excuses for being here; I know that what I'm doing is wrong. Problem is, you killed a man and can't seem to see that it was wrong. Because if it was wrong, then that puts you in his place, doesn't it? Puts you with your back against the wall, with death's hollow finger pointed at your chest."

Sam stared at the drink in his hands. "I thought God was supposed to be all about forgiveness."

"What, you mean like mercy?" Mel asked.

"Yeah."

Mel was silent a moment, and looked at Sam with a puzzled look as if he were trying to decide what to say. "Do you really think—do you really believe you deserve that which you denied another?"

Sam shook his head. "No."

"And yet you ask for it anyway? Pretty bold, don't you think?"

"Maybe." Sam shrugged. "I don't know. What do you think?"

Mel drew a long, slow breath and ran his hand over his face, rubbing the stubble around his mouth. He smiled faintly and then laughed and shook his head. "Sam," he said, the smile softening, "I think you're a lot closer than you want to give yourself credit for. That's what I think."

Mel paused a moment and looked down at Sam, studying him. Sam avoided his stare, and kept his eyes on his drink. Mel took a breath as if to say something, to tell him that God would not pull the killing trigger as he had, but decided against it. Better to let the comparison hang in the air. Patting Sam on the shoulder with an affection that caused Sam to start as if he had punched him, Mel turned and walked out the door into the burning sunlight.

The bartender, a big round man with a round face and small eyes and a beard and a shaved head, threw Sam out several hours later when, in his drunkenness, he had reached up and grabbed the waitress's black pleather skirt and called her a whore. For no apparent reason. Sam didn't resist the rough handling, nor being tossed out onto the chewed-up asphalt of the small parking lot, which scraped his left hand with a burning sting. He did not resist it all, he even welcomed it; it was all part of his treatment, part of the falling.

Having sense enough to know that now, at ten o'clock, he was far too drunk to get any reputable bar to serve him anymore, he chose one of the seedier bars he knew of on the south side of town. Climbing into his car, he took a long, slow breath in an effort to clear his mind enough for the drive. He thought of a half-empty prayer before he pulled out onto the highway that ran past the gates of Fort Campbell, not actually praying, but the kind of thought that can masquerade as a prayer; asking only that when he ran off the road and killed himself, that he wouldn't hurt anyone else.

Sam woke up in his Jeep the next morning around nine to his cell phone ringing. The moment he opened his eyes to the burning, heavy sunlight, his self-loathing rose up in him again, recalling his failure, reminding him of his guilt, and he realized with a sincere disappointment that he was still alive. His head felt as if it were being crushed, and the ringing shot through his temples and nearly blinded him with a pulsing, pulsing, pulsing pain. He felt for his phone with his eyes shut, and finally found it on the floor and held it up to his face.

"Rachel," he said to himself. There was a rise of something, something that wanted to resist this falling, this self-flagellating, but the pain in his head swallowed it up, and he silenced the awful ringing and fell back asleep.

He woke up again a couple hours later, the heat from the sun and the humidity causing streams of sweat to run down his face. When he woke, the pounding pain in his head was still there, compounded by the terrible oppression of the stifling heat inside the Jeep. He sat up and squinted his eyes hard against the painful sunlight. He felt damp, and opened his door for some air. His mouth was dry and tacky as he leaned his head back against the headrest, the breeze from outside rolling over him, cooling him.

He sat like that, in the front seat of his Jeep with the door swung all the way open, for over an hour, drifting in and out of sleep, drifting between loathing and nothing. Finally he woke and felt the need to move. He squinted up at his rear-view mirror and saw a gas station across the street with a quickie-mart. He looked around him and finally realized where he was, and shook his head, unsure of how or when he had left the last bar, and how he had ended up in this broken parking lot of a vacant store. Plywood covered the spaces where some of the windows used to be, a few of them had holes shot through them, and some of the holes were bigger.

He shook his head and climbed out, the fierce heaviness of the sun threatening to crush him as he walked across the street.

The old black woman behind the counter looked at him with a look that communicated both pity and amusement. The box of powdered donuts and the quart of whole milk cost him just over four dollars, and he dug into his pocket and pulled out a wad of cash. The woman had to help him count out the change.

She offered him a bag, and he only answered with a weak smile and a slow nod of his puffy face. "You be careful now, honey," she called after him as he walked out the door, the electronic chime sounding his departure.

When he arrived back at his Jeep, he walked over to the side with the shade and sat down on the warm, cracked asphalt and leaned up against a tire, his legs stretched out in front of him. He opened up the quart of milk and took a long, slow drink, the cold, thick liquid sliding down his throat. His eyes closed and he lowered the plastic jug he felt the coolness spread inside him. He grabbed for the box and opened it up and stuffed two of the small white donuts into his mouth, washing them down with another long drink. As he sat there, he began to feel better, but then realized that he didn't want to feel better. But he did want to be able to move, he could not stay here all day, and he certainly could not drive yet. He could barely keep his eyes open long enough to reach for the donuts beside him on the ground.

At one point, his eyes closed and his head leaned back against the hard, warm rubber of the tire, he heard the sound of young voices and their footsteps. He opened his eyes and saw four young black men to his right, their dark jeans hanging around their thighs in a way that seemed to defy physics, walking toward him. Thin and young and lean and black, for a moment a primal fear rose up inside him as they walked close by him, staring in wonder at the messed-up white boy sitting on the ground next to his car, with a quart of milk and a box of donuts beside him. The fear rose in him until he recognized it, until he realized why he was afraid, and then the fear dissolved inside him. He smiled to himself. Let them come. Part of the falling. Part of the treatment.

But they did not come, of course, and he watched through half-open eyes as they walked away.

"Now, you drink like a man who hates himself," a deep, soft voice said from behind him. Sam turned his head toward the sound and saw a thin, old man with a mesh baseball hat that said "Hal's" in red on the front, slide into the stool beside him.

"Seems to be the theme," Sam heard himself say, turning back to the bar and his drink.

"What'll it be Randolph?" the bartender asked, himself an old man, but shorter and more round in the face than the man who sat beside Sam.

"I'll take a Budweiser, Johnny," Randolph answered.

Johnny, Randolph, Sam thought the names. Good old-man names. Whatever happened to names like those? Especially Randolph. I think if I ever have a son again, I'll name him Randolph. Or Montgomery. He smirked to himself. Good, old names. Names with substance, history. Names that have blood running all the way through them. Like Isaac. Or Samuel. He almost laughed.

He almost laughed, but instead took another long pull at the amber bottle in front of him. He was drunk again, though he had never truly sobered up from the night before at the strip club with

Mel. The milk and the donuts that morning had given him enough strength to get back to his apartment, where he had passed out right after taking another two shots of tequila. He had woken up only a couple hours later to the sound of his cell phone ringing. This time, he didn't even bother checking it; something in the sound of the ring told him that it was Rachel. He didn't answer. He knew that he could not answer if he wanted to continue this falling, knew that her voice alone could arrest his fall, and he did not want that.

A few times the impulse would rise in him to stop this self-destruction, but when that happened, he would deliberately bring to mind Marie, repeating the one-worded question that the man had asked him before he had shot him. Mercy? And Sam would shake his head to himself. No. No mercy. Or he would think of Amber's baby boy learning to ride his first bike. What would his name have been? Or he would think of a thousand regrets that he had in his life. He would bring to mind the night that Stephanie had walked in on him and that waitress from the bar going at it in their bed, the look on her face, the sadness and shame in her eyes. He had plenty of material to draw from, and used it liberally, pouring those memories over any spark of repentance, drenching himself in a shame and guilt he had never let go of.

He had crawled off his couch around two that afternoon, had taken another shot of the near-empty bottle of tequila, and gone into the bathroom to splash water on his face, only to come back out for another shot. He grabbed his keys and meant to get to the next bar before the second shot hit him.

He felt the buzzing numbness return just as he had pulled into the small parking lot of the local VFW, where he knew he could get a few more drinks. When he walked into the dark building and handed the old man at the door his military ID, the old man had looked at it and let him pass without even glancing at him. On the televisions that hung suspended in the corners of the smoky bar, various news anchors were recapping the day's headlines. Things were only getting worse in Iraq. Sam had saddled up to the bar and asked for a beer. Being only mid-afternoon, he had decided to pace himself. He was still there six hours later when the old man had come up behind him and had a seat next to him.

He heard Randolph next to him say something, but was lost in a fog of thought and didn't hear.

"Son," came the deep voice, directed at the side of Sam's head. Sam turned to see the old man, his long, pointy nose seeming to almost cascade from underneath the baseball hat.

"I'm sorry sir?" Sam managed to say, feeling a bit uneasy, not trusting his ability to speak at the moment. He looked at his watch. Past eight, he thought. He had spent the past several hours slowly drinking beer, lost in that tangling mess of regret he had buried himself in, and was now left waiting, praying for the air to run out. The old man's voice had yanked him out of that suffocation.

"You just come back from Iraq?" the old man asked, though it was more of an observation than a question.

Sam nodded, "Yessir."

"Pretty rough over there?" the soft hazel eyes asked him. The eyes were a sharp contrast to the sagging, leathery skin on the man's face. Sam saw strands of silver hair climbing out of his large ears. Old men always had big ears, Sam thought, looking at the man. Big ears and big noses. Isn't that because the cartilage keeps on growing?

He thought all of these things while Randolph sat there looking at him, patiently waiting for his answer. Sam was not thinking as quickly as he thought he was, the thoughts in his head occurring in real time. He had lost the ability or the patience or the discipline to think and speak simultaneously, and had to work through his thoughts before he could answer the question. But Randolph just took a sip from the beer in front of him and waited for the young man beside him to decide to answer with all the patience of his eighty-seven years.

Yeah, the cartilage keeps growing. That's why old men always have such big ears. Big ears and big noses and I don't know how to answer your question, old man, he thought. Rough? Yeah, I would say so, but not like jumping out of a plane at Normandy or spending a winter in Bastogne or assaulting a beach on Tarawa. I don't know sir, he thought, then realized that he hadn't spoken.

He shrugged his shoulders. "Yeah, I guess so." Then he thought to add, "But probably not like anything you saw."

The old man chuckled to himself, and Sam saw his old yellow teeth stained but clean looking, and heard the faint wheeze come out from the man's chest. Randolph didn't answer, but rested his elbows on the bar and took a sip, still chuckling to himself. Sam did not understand what he had said to make the old man laugh to himself like that, and he thought for a minute he may have gotten an old kook, all busted up in the head, and he started to look around as if to find a way to get away.

Then the old man's chuckling died off, and only the echo of the laughter shone out in his eyes and the slight upward turn of his mouth. "That's what we all say, son," and said it so calmly, so matter-of-factly, that Sam dismissed his ideas of the man being crazy. "It's what my generation said about the first world war, and what they had said about the civil war, and so on and so on, on and on all the way back to Gaugamela."

But now you're just showing off, Sam thought. Gaugamela, now there was one hell of a fight. Didn't Jon tell me once that they thought that Alexander had fought that battle somewhere up around Makhmur? A picture of the two metal silos thrusting out of the hard brown earth came to his mind. He thought back, trying to remember, but his mind couldn't find the conversation in its library, it kept jumping from one aisle to the next and he couldn't get it to focus on one subject. He closed his eyes tight and shook his head.

"What you boys and girls are facing over there is the same that we all faced: war, just war," the man shook his head, as if war were a suggestion someone had just brought up at a board meeting as a possible course of action, which he rejected. Randolph grew quiet for a minute, his mind running through all the images supporting his distaste for the whole idea. "It's all the same. Oh, I suppose some have it worse than others, but the whole thing, if you ask me, is a mess," and Randolph shook his head to himself again, the eyes sparkling with that internal humor which Sam did not understand.

"Where were you?" Sam asked.

Randolph turned his head, looking for a second at him. "I was in Africa. Then Italy. Then France. Had a hell of a time," he shook his head and smacked his lips. "I was an engineer, and spent a lot of time blowing bridges, and then rebuilding them later on when we wanted to use them." He continued on with a particular story one night when he and his small unit had gone to blow a bridge only to find that the Germans were there also, to blow the same bridge.

He spoke now, not out of any desire to share his story or to show off, or to flaunt his credentials, but to draw the young man who sat beside him out of himself. Randolph had lived through a war where men whom he had known well and had even loved had not. And he knew what happened to men in war, and had seen how it affects all of them differently. There were some, like himself, who had come home and seemed fine for the longest time. Had married the pretty girl down the street, gone back to college, gotten a good job, and had had children, and the war was behind them; a shadow, a breeze, an early grey hair. Only to discover, twenty years later, that suddenly they couldn't sleep at night, or couldn't dream, or couldn't put the bottle down anymore, didn't want to.

After he had finished his story, Randolph turned his head to the young man beside him, who had finished his beer and had not ordered another one yet. Yes, he thought, he looks like you doesn't he? Not the face, but the eyes and the shoulders are familiar, aren't they? Randolph shook his head. You almost didn't come out of that one, did you, old man? It almost had you. We all thought that you were a goner for a while there. All but Kathryn. No, not her. She wrapped her arms around you down in that darkness of yours and she held on and she pulled you out of your hell. Her faith was like a cadence, a beautiful, miraculous sacrament performed day-in, day-out. Just where would you be without her, old man? And his face grew sad, because he remembered that he was without her now, and every now and then, like on days like today, for no apparent reason, that old darkness would start to rise up in him again and threaten to swallow up the echo of her testimony.

They sat quietly for a couple minutes, Sam holding his empty bottle, the images that Randolph's story had put in his mind competing with the jumbled mess that the past twenty-four hours had created, and Randolph thinking simple thoughts of his sweet Kathryn.

Sam was lost in thought, weaving through his tangled and twisted memories, when a man stumbled in through the door behind them. Sam could hear the man murmuring to himself, and wouldn't have turned as unsubtly as he did if he had not been drinking for as long as he had. The man, unshaven, with torn jeans and an old faded flannel shirt buttoned all the way up, with a salt-stained baseball cap cocked up on his head, met his stare for a moment, and then walked to the end of the bar to their left, still murmuring to himself, and sat down. On seeing the strange man walk in, Sam had shifted uncomfortably and quickly ordered another beer.

The old man next to Sam turned toward the strange man and said hello. "Hey there Tom, how are you tonight?"

The man's lips stopped moving when he heard his name and the friendly tone, and popped into a gracious and friendly smile that seemed completely incongruous with his murmuring and attire. "I'm fine, Randy, how are you?"

"Just fine, thanks."

"Good to see you here."

"It's good to see you too, Tom."

Randolph turned back to the bar and his beer and the young man sitting to his right. They were silent for several minutes, the two of them quietly sipping at their beers while Johnny poured Tom a free drink, and the two of them had the same exact conversation that Tom and Randolph had just had, which was the same conversation that every man in that bar had always had with Tom every night that he stumbled in for a drink. Every night the murmuring, every night that same smile that seemed to appear from underneath the man's skin, but just long enough for those few lines, and then it would disappear again behind the twitching face, and the lips would start their involuntary monologue.

At one point, after Tom had had his drink poured and the other two men had been drinking their beers quietly for several minutes, Tom's monologue ascended to a near shriek. "Goddamn it!" Sam could not help the chuckle that escaped him, even though there was a way all these old men in this old bar treated the strange man when he entered, as if he were John the Baptist, coming in from the desert dressed in goatskins and with locust wings in his teeth. He laughed nonetheless, and felt the sharp, disapproving eyes of Randolph bore into the side of his head. Sam turned his head slightly, enough to see the man's eyes and confirm that he was staring at him and not one of the pictures at the end of the bar. When Randolph saw Sam look at him and then go back to his beer, he shook his head sadly and sighed.

"You know," Randolph said softly so just the two of them could hear, "son, I don't know what you're doing in here—a young man on a Friday night—and that's none of my business, I guess. But you shouldn't be laughing at old Tom over there. Ain't nothing funny about old Tom. I suppose he doesn't dress too nice, and he talks to himself, and he drinks too much, but none of that's all that funny."

Sam grew quiet a moment, focusing on the label on his beer. "What happened to him?" he heard himself ask, as if he were asking to be forgiven for laughing at John the Baptist dressed in faded flannel.

Randolph shrugged his thin, old shoulders. "Don't know, really," he said. "Served in Vietnam. Had a name in his old unit, evidently. Called him Birdman. Was wounded twice from what I hear."

Hoping there would be a funny story behind the name that would lead them away from Randolph's lecture, Sam asked, "Why Birdman?"

But Randolph only frowned and shook his head.

"Hmm," Sam nodded his head and took a pull from his beer, finishing it, and then raised it up toward Johnny, asking for another. Johnny came over with a fresh bottle and opened it with a flick of his wrist and took the old one away. Sam could still hear Tom talking to himself at the end of the bar.

Randolph had folded his hands on the bar, and was looking at a spot on his right palm which he rubbed in small circles with his left thumb slowly, thoughtfully. "War's a funny thing, son. Usually all we think about when we think about war are those who are killed. But there are other casualties in war. Having to live afterwards is like having to live with a wound that won't heal up all the way. Something inside all of us dies in a war. Hope... innocence... maybe just naïveté? I don't know, but something goes away. Oh, they give us medals and parades and call us heroes afterwards to cover up our scars and ease their collective conscience, but..." he trailed off and shrugged his tired shoulders, frowning.

He indicated with his head toward Tom. "Tom over there is one kind of casualty. Seems to me like you're another. And me and Johnny and all the rest of us... well, we all have our own wounds that we have to learn to carry, son, if we can. For some of us, those wounds run too deep and we run out of faith, and we end up like Tom over there. But we don't have to. It's a choice we make. Sometimes that choice is harder for some to make than others." He paused a moment, drawing a deep breath with a faint wheeze as he shook his head slowly. "No, there's nothing funny about it."

Sam had been listening, but the man talking to himself at the end of the bar with the torn jeans and the buttoned up flannel had made him nervous. A kind of fear had risen in him when the man walked in, and not that childish fear of the homeless man, not the fear of shame when we look into eyes asking for help which we deny. It was a different kind of fear than Sam had felt before, like a hard cold spreading through his body, running through his veins, and he finished his last beer quickly, deciding that it was time for him to leave.

"Some of us just can't seem to go on with those scars, but the real tragedy is when we won't let ourselves go on." At that last point, Randolph looked knowingly at Sam. Sam saw the look and emptied his beer, the thick coldness wrapping around his neck, and he felt his throat tighten with the effort to breathe. Sam stood up and he stumbled. Randolph reached out a thin, strong hand and caught him above the elbow to steady him. Sam was impressed with the power in that thin old arm. "Easy there, son." Then, "You off?"

"Yeah," Sam said into his wallet as he pulled out enough to cover his drinks and a good tip for Johnny. Johnny and Randolph with the good names that had blood running all the way through them. "I appreciate the company, Randolph. Have a good night." He reached out his hand despite the strangling cold that had found his chest and had wrapped around him like a constrictor.

Randolph took the hand and smiled.

"Never got your name son," he said as Sam reached the door.

Sam turned and forced a smile, "Sam Calhoun."

"Samuel," Randolph repeated and nodded approvingly. "Heard of God."

"I don't know about that." Sam shook his head and forced a smile, and turned back to the door.

"Good night, Sam," he heard a voice call out from behind him. Turning, he saw Tom with the strangely sane smile and thought that he seemed perfectly fine for the moment.

"Good night, Tom."

The next night he found himself back at the Speakeasy, drinking doubles of Crown again from the same bartender who had poured him his last drinks in that dark, smoky and sticky bar when Amber had come in and they had gone back to her place and he had gotten her pregnant and then he had told her that he wanted nothing to do with her or her baby boy learning how to ride a bike.

He had walked into the bar before he had even really thought about it, and was suddenly evaluating his motives. What are you doing here? he asked himself. Are you looking for her? Or are you looking for that young life that you killed? Do you think if you come back here that you can change what you've done? Is that what you're doing here, Samuel, Heard of God? Heard of God my ass. You'd be lucky if he just killed you dead tonight. Of course he won't, you know that even though you wish he would because that would be like rewarding you for your sins, and that's not the way it works, is it? God himself knows that you've had enough to drink over the past three days to drown a fish, and if he wanted to, it wouldn't be hard to snatch the life right out of you tonight. Right here. You'd just lay your head down on this bar in that small pool of stale beer and die right here in this stinking place where you created and killed at the same time. You're a real son of a bitch, Samuel Heard-of-God Calhoun. Un-Samuel. He smiled to himself a drunk, lazy smile that hung on his face long after his appreciation for his own wit waned. He was long past simply drunk now. After the VFW bar with Randolph, he had tried to get into another bar on the south side of town, but had apparently reeked so much of alcohol and body odor and a stale mouth, that even the bouncer there would not let him in. And that had shown him just what kind of shape he was in. So he had climbed back into his Jeep, and whispered the same old thought-masquerading-as-a-prayer as he had the night before, and driven himself home.

He had seen Rachel's note taped to his front door, and he had walked in and torn it down and dropped it, and it floated down sliding from side to side until it came to rest on the floor. He had checked his phone and saw two messages from her also. He reached into his cabinet and pulled out a half-empty bottle of vodka and poured it over some ice and plopped down on his couch. If they wouldn't let him kill himself in public, he thought, then he could just as easily do it in his apartment and no one was going to tell him any different. Nobody. It was a free country after all, and a man had his rights and he had to stick up for them because all everybody else wanted to do was get in a man's business and start telling him his rights and his not-rights. But he had his rights, and he was going to sit there on that couch and drink his vodka until he couldn't see.

He had woken up the next morning and felt awful. Enjoying the pain that pulsed and beat inside his head, he had forced himself to finish the warm, now-diluted vodka left in his glass from the night before. It did not even burn anymore as it slid down his throat, and he thought that he was getting pretty good at this falling. He was hungry and he grabbed a loaf of bread and chewed several pieces of it, and it was sweet and soft and he felt it go down his esophagus and into his stomach. He thought then that some actual food like potatoes with some sausage would be real good, and would even provide some substenance... subsistence... sustenance, but as soon as he heard himself say the word sustenance, he got up and poured himself another glass of vodka and ice. Then, since it was breakfast, he splashed some orange juice on top and thought that even though orange juice had Vitamin C and Vitamin C was good for you, it really wasn't against the rules and was probably okay.

He had passed the morning like that, flipping through the TV, watching infomercials about juicers and special cloths that said they soaked up anything better than anything, and pouring himself vodka over ice. At one point he had reached for the letter from Rachel that was still in the same place it had fallen when he had dropped it the night before. He was starting to feel better and he needed another stab, so he picked it up and read it. And when the pain didn't come as sharp as he thought it would, as sharp as he wanted it to be, he reached over and listened to the two messages on his phone. Ah, there it was, that comforting sting. That beautiful, adoring, delicious pain. Her voice, carrying a gentle Carolinian accent, which was different from the Louisianian accent which was more cajun than southern, stabbed like so many needles into his chest. When those needles lost their sharpness, his mind had wondered through the remaining alternatives. Then the Speakeasy and doubles of whiskey came to mind, and he had stood up uneasily and grabbed his keys.

There was on old song that he loved which had always made him think of Rachel, even when he was in Iraq and wasn't thinking of her, playing on the old jukebox in the little bar. He was on his God-only-knew-what drink and it was near midnight. Drinking was getting more difficult. He kept passing in and out of delirium and a semi-consciousness, never fully conscious though never fully asleep.

Suddenly the door burst open and a group of young men poured into the bar, laughing and swearing and pushing each other. Sam turned slightly to his left when one of the guys bumped into him as he took the stool next to him. Sam thought to himself that it was a little rude to just bump into a guy like that and not offer even a half-hearted apology. "A simple sorry would do fine," he said, though he did not mean to speak and did not know that he had.

The guy next to him, smaller with blonde hair and a young, baby-fat face, looked condescendingly over his shoulder at Sam and smirked. The group had ordered a round of kamakazies; apparently one of the young men was getting married the following day, and they had just come from the local strip club just on the northern side of the Tennessee- Kentucky border of Route 41A. One of them was talking about where they could get their soon-to-be-married friend a hooker. Sam thought that this guy's fiancée must be one lucky woman, but he managed not to say it out loud, though he wanted to because he thought it was particularly funny. He looked over at the small group of young men. One of them looked slightly familiar, and he tried to wade through a pile of jumbled memories to find out who he was and why he felt as if he knew him. After trying to think for several minutes, which felt like several hours, he shrugged his shoulders and dismissed the pursuit.

When Sam was on his next drink, after looking several times over his shoulder at the increasingly annoying group of young men who had taken over the bar with their jokes and laughter and swearing, the young man next to him bumped into him again, this time hitting his arm as he was about to take a sip and causing him to spill part of his drink.

"Okay, hey, you know what man?" Sam said slowly to his neighbor.

The young man turned around, his face still flush with laughter. "What's up?" he asked coolly, aware of the five pairs of eyes that were watching behind him. He possessed all of the arrogance of a man who knows that he is the stronger because he outnumbers his opponent, and therefore feels that it's beneath his dignity to have to apologize or to otherwise adhere to any kind of social norms and decency.

"Would you watch what you're doing?" Sam said slowly, trying to sound friendly and also more sober than he was. The man flinched and blinked his eyes at Sam's breath as he spoke. "I'm just… I'm just trying to have a drink here boys, all right?" Sam postured, only half aware of the six pairs of threatening eyes that were staring at him. He saw the familiar face again, the eyes on him. He was a bit older than the others, though still obviously younger than Sam. He had seen that face before, the way the eyebrows dove down to the nose. In a picture. Where? Rachel. And he was holding little Claire when she was still only a baby. A picture album. He saw Rachel turn a page, and her smile faded as she pointed out a picture of a young man with eyebrows that dove down to his nose. Stephen.

Sam looked past several eyes to the man in the back, bore his eyes into his, and for a moment he was not drunk, he was totally sober and he hated that face and that man and what he had said. Then the moment passed and he was drunk again, and he saw Stephen's face change, and for a split second he saw his own face superimposed on the diving eyebrows and the short nose. And he hated that face. That one that he only saw for a second and the one that was before it, and he lurched out of his chair toward those faces.

"Stephen," Sam said, accusing, hissing his name.

The man raised his eyebrows. "Do I know you?" he asked.

Sam stopped just in front of him, and he felt the presence of five other bodies all close around him, threatening, waiting for an opportunity to pounce him. And Sam said to himself, Let them come. Perhaps God has heard me after all and I will be killed tonight fighting this man I hate, who tried to kill Claire, whom I now see is the same as me, and I hate that man and I want him to fight these men so that they will beat him and maybe kill him and there will be justice again.

"Your name Stephen?" Sam asked, his stinking breath suspended in front of the man's face so that his eyes watered.

"Yeah, do I know you?" he asked again. Sam was a couple inches taller than Stephen, and outweighed him by almost fifty pounds of mostly muscle. If Stephen had found himself confronted with this hulking man at any other time, he would have submitted and saved himself the beating he was sure to get. But he looked around and saw that the tottering man in front of him was barely standing on his own two feet and that he was alone and that he, Stephen, had five friends with him.

It wasn't even a fair fight. They had simply grabbed his arms and his collar and dragged him outside and had taken turns punching and kicking him while the others held him. Sam had been in fights before and had lost fights before, but the combination of his drunkenness and the sounds of their boots on his ribs and his face and their fists colliding with his jaw incapacitated him, and he couldn't even move to protect himself in the parts he knew were important to protect when you are on the ground surrounded by a wild group of men who are trying to kill you.

They had left him out in the dark parking lot. There was no traffic on the road, and he lay there on the ground, barely able to breathe, the blood running down his nose forcing him to breathe through his mouth. His nose hurt like hell, he thought to himself, but was not broken. He stammered up to his feet and then almost fell back down, but caught himself with his left arm which sent a shooting, raging pain up through his elbow to his shoulder. He was barely conscious now and knew that he had to get to his Jeep. His instinct to live had superseded his own hatred of himself, which told him to just stay on the ground so that he may get run over. He made it to his Jeep and his phone rang and he answered without thinking.

"Hello?" he said through gasps of pain.

"Sam! Is that you?" It was Rachel and he smiled at the Carolinian accent her voice lent his name, almost like "Sayum" but quicker. "Where are you?"

"Speakeasy... parking lot..." and he felt himself slipping and dropped the phone.

He woke up to her small, heavy grunts as she drug him out of his Jeep, trying to get him into her car. When he realized what was happening, he put some of his weight on his own legs. Still, at only one hundred and five pounds, it was not easy work to haul his stinking, bloody body into her little car.

He sat in her car with his eyes and mouth open because he still couldn't breathe through his nose. She was mad, he could feel her anger hovering all around him. "Thanks," he said, and he thought how it wasn't true anymore that he wanted to die, not really, now that he was next to her.

She didn't even look at him when she answered. "Don't thank me Sam. What're you doing, huh? Just what the hell are you doing? Where have you been? Have you gotten any of my calls? You son of a bitch, I didn't know where you were…" and her voice choked. Sam tilted his head to the left so that he could look at her and he thought about her profile, her small chin and thin lips and her little nose and those eyes that were like the ocean. Something rose up in him, through all the garbage and filth he had poured on top of it, and he wanted to tell her how beautiful she was. How God-unbelievably beautiful she was, but he didn't because his mouth would not obey the impulse. Instead he just looked at her and marveled.

"I didn't know what had happened to you, Sam… I can't do this," she shook her head. "I love you. God, how I love you. So much it hurts, like I can't breathe when I think about it. You know? Do you know that?" she looked at him, asking him with her swollen eyes and her trembling mouth. He blinked, acknowledging, only thinking that she must be the most beautiful thing he had ever seen. She shook her head again. "But I cannot love this. Do you understand? Because this is not you. This is not what I love and I will not love this because it is a lie and to love a lie is beneath the dignity of my love. Do you hear me? I cannot love this, Sam, I can't." And she started crying.

He blinked his eyes again slowly, hearing her but hearing her tone more than he heard her words. He tilted his head back and closed his eyes against the harsh yellow streetlights as they passed by his window.

Rachel had wrestled him up the stairs to her apartment and let him drop onto the couch before she had gone to her neighbor to retrieve Claire. The look that her neighbor had given her made her furious, a look that was both pity and disapproval, and she had to keep herself from kicking Sam in the head when she got back to her apartment. She kept telling herself that she had done well with what she had; that she was a good mother to her daughter and she worked hard and didn't ask for handouts from her rich parents and that bitch! What the hell was she supposed to do when all Sam said was what he had said? "Just what the hell was I supposed to do?" she blurted out loud and then was embarrassed, both at her anger and at the fact that she was talking to herself. She kissed Claire on her sleepy forehead, asking her daughter to forgive her, and she carried her into her room and laid her down in her crib. She stood there for several quiet dark minutes, watching as her daughter rubbed her eyes and squirmed slowly to find a comfortable position from all the night's annoyances.

When her daughter calmed down and she could tell she had drifted off, Rachel let herself stand there and watch her daughter sleep, and she let the tears and the sadness, which she had restrained until then, come up. She stood there in the dark, her tears running down her face to her chin and dripping into her daughter's crib, sobbing quietly. She knew it was okay to cry like that, and that she needed to let herself bend to the burden of her self-pity, and not be stubborn and foolishly proud and try to pretend that she did not feel sorry for herself or sad or angry or cheated. When the tears stopped, and her breathing softened and lengthened again, she smiled with the feeling that comes after a great pressure has been relieved, though it is a smile that still remembers the pain.

She walked back out to her living room and saw Sam sprawled onto the couch, his jeans ripped and dirty, his face bruised and his nose and upper lip bleeding. She looked at him for several minutes and remembered the great sadness she had just exorcised from herself and she felt sorry for him and a tenderness for him came over her that she did not try to understand. She thought he would sleep for a long while, and was glad that he had a place to sleep and to rest and that the place he could do that was here, in her home. She sighed to herself and then laughed at her own naïveté—was it naïveté, or something else? she didn't know—and then began to haul him into her bedroom. He made several incoherent grunts at the moving, which was far from gentle even though she did not mean it to be. Her anger was gone, and she knew she didn't understand what was happening inside him to make him do this, and in that there was a level of understanding that passed many others'.

She flicked her light off as she finally got him onto her bed, and she proceeded to take his clothes off him. The moon shone through the pin oak outside her window, casting a cool, silver light into her room. His clothes were dirty and he stank, and she thought she might have to throw away her sheets before she slept in them again. Already there were little spots of blood where her hauling him had reopened barely-dried cuts and scrapes.

When she had taken all his clothes off him and he lay there naked, sprawled on his back, she saw his nakedness and a longing rose inside her that surprised her. She walked into the bathroom and to get some warm water and a cloth. She sat next to him in his incoherence and washed the dirt and the blood and the oil off his face and she wondered what he had gone through, what had happened to him to make him do this to himself. On his bare chest lay his ID tags with the medallion of Saint Jude which he never took off, and she wanted to rip that medallion off him but knew that was not hers to do.

As she washed him—his neck and a particularly bad spot on his shoulder where he must have fallen when they first attacked him—and his hands and his knees, she began to pray for him, to herself at first but then out loud to make sure she would be heard because this was an important prayer and she was praying it with all the love and faith that she had. Then in the middle of her prayer, she began to sing "Rock of Ages," an old hymn, the words of which she was surprised she remembered. She sang timidly at first because she had been told that she had not been given a beautiful voice, but then more confidently when she heard her voice alone and soft in the quiet moonlight.

When she had sung the final verse several times and had finished, she draped a sheet over him, and walked out into the kitchen to get him a glass of water. She was not sure what good only a glass would do with all of the poison he had in him, but set it there on her bedside nonetheless, in case he woke up and was thirsty. Checking him over one more time to ensure she had cleaned all of his bad spots as best she could for the moment with him unconscious, she reached over and grabbed the pillow that his head was not on, and her bedspread with lines of purple and green and red and yellow, and walked quietly into her daughter's room and lay on the floor beside her crib.

* * *

He stood in a large open valley, and could see the sun rising behind the mountains in front of him, casting them in a shade of rich purple. Behind the purple mountains, where the sun had already risen on an unseen landscape, the sky was bathed in gold. Around him, in the valley below the mountains hiding the sun, he saw that he stood in a great meadow. There was a copse of trees off to his right, what must be a mile away. He was both impressed and intimidated by the size of the valley he stood in.

All was silent around him with the silence of the outdoors. When he listened carefully, he could hear a slight breeze blowing over the high meadow grass. White and yellow flowers were sprinkled as far as he could see. When he closed his eyes, letting that cool breeze run over his skin, carrying with it the scent of the high places from the mountains, he could feel the fragrance spread out inside him and he heard the faint sound of water rippling and thought that there must be a stream meandering through this meadow.

He thought of the small trout that would be idling in those chilly waters, striking at the surface at the small insects drifting along the top, and he thought how much he wished he had his fly rod with him, even though the trout would be too small to keep. He wished he had remembered to bring his fly rod with him because he would like to stand by that small stream, facing the sun as it climbed up the backside of those beautiful mountains, and feeling the cool breeze run over his face, causing all the little hairs to stand on end. He pictured himself there, gently whipping and manipulating his long line that floated on the cold air to lay just where he wanted, just where he knew the trout were laying on the rocky bottom, looking up through their shattering ceiling as the dark slowly transformed to day.

Then he suddenly remembered that he hadn't forgotten his fly rod, and that it was just there, lying behind him on the ground. He turned and stooped and picked it up, and it was only half the length that it should have been, but he didn't think much about it and thought that it would work just fine anyway. Later, when he woke up, he would realize that this was his first clue that he had been dreaming.

He balanced the rod in his hand and he set off north, keeping the mountains and the golden sky on his right. Many times in his walk toward the sound of the water he would stop and gaze toward the mountains, enjoying—laughing out loud—in the absolute and perfect beauty of that sunrise. Later, as he walked and stopped, he realized that the sun did not seem to be rising anymore, but it seemed to have reached some kind of resting place there behind the mountains, waiting for some cue before it would come bursting from behind. He knew that that would be quite a scene, to see this valley bathed in that perfect light.

He felt as if he had been walking a long time, and had made many stops which he had lost count of in his marveling at the fixed sunrise behind the purple mountains. He stopped to take a look behind him to try to see how far he had walked, and he saw that the copse of trees that had been off to his right when he had set off were now only just a dot on the horizon in this enormous valley, and he thought that this was the biggest valley he'd ever been in.

On his stops to rest and to enjoy the sunrise, he would listen for the sound of the creek, and he could hear its faint sighing as it slid past its banks and the grasses that clung to them. He thought it was a bit strange to be able to hear something so quiet from what had evidently been so far away. But he thought that maybe the crisp morning air had simply made it sound closer than it was, and besides, he did not mind the walk, the brilliant air felt good and cool in his lungs, and he could stop whenever he wanted to marvel at the mountains and the suspended sun hidden behind them.

On one of his stops, while he gazed toward the mountains, Jonathon came up from behind and quietly stood beside him.

"It's really something, isn't it?" Jonathon asked, his eyes on fire from the smoldering light behind the horizon.

Sam cast a warm look at his old friend and smiled. "Sure is," he said. Then, puzzled, he asked, "Where've you been? I've been walking across this valley for what seems like hours."

"I was just over by the stream."

"Is it close? I've been looking for it." He held up his fly rod. "I was thinking that maybe we could spend some time fishing together. Do you have your rod?"

"Yeah, it's just over where I was sitting."

Sam sighed, reluctant to take his eyes off the mountains so far away. "All right," he finally said. "How much further to the stream?"

Jonathon chuckled.

"What's so funny, huh?" Sam asked amicably. He took a good look at his friend for the first time and realized how happy he was to see him.

"You've been walking right next to it the whole time," Jonathon explained, smiling and shaking his head. "You never were too bright, you know that?"

Sam laughed an honest laugh. "I never said I was, brother."

"That's true." And the two old friends shared in a long, honest laugh.

"Well, let's go see what we can catch, huh?" Jonathon said, as he turned away from the sunrise.

"Sounds good to me. You got any flies on you?" Sam said, following him as the two set off to the west, the great valley running out in front of them as if it would never end.

"Yeah, I've got plenty."

"What's working?"

"Drowned tricos and caddis poopahs, mostly. Though I've caught a couple monsters on just the old caddis standby."

Sam nodded his head and was quiet a moment. There was some deep emotion, some profound sadness that suddenly surrounded him and he didn't really understand it. "It's good to see you, Jon," he said, trying to articulate what he was feeling.

"It's good to see you too, Sam. It's been a while."

"It has, hasn't it?" Sam asked, finally understanding why he was so glad to see Jonathon. But he couldn't remember why he hadn't seen Jonathon in so long. As the two slowly walked, he tried to think about when he had last seen Jonathon, but all he could remember was their conversation that night on the hood of the Humvee. "Why is that?" he finally asked.

"Why's what?" Jonathon asked.

"Why haven't I seen you in so long? Where've you been?"

"I died, remember?" Jonathon said, though he smiled when he said it, as if he thought it funny that his good friend would forget something so important.

Sam nodded his head. "Yeah. But—"

"Let's not worry about that right now. The good news is that we're both here right now and there are lots of fish in that stream just waiting for us to catch them."

Sam nodded and smiled. "Sounds great." They walked a moment more, their feet leaving footprints on the damp grass, the little meadow flowers bending to their weight when they passed. "How much further to the stream?" Sam asked, looking at Jonathon.

"We're here," Jonathon announced.

Sam set his rod down on the cool and sparkling grass and knelt beside the stream. He bent over the water, and could see it was only a foot deep there and that it was a very small stream. He turned his head to the left and right, upstream and down respectively, to see whether he could see any of the trout that he knew must live here, but he didn't see any. Cupping his hands carefully, he dipped them into the achingly-cold water, and he held them for a moment just under the surface, watching the water rush surprisingly quickly over them. He saw blood run out of his hands from unseen injuries, swirling in the water off to his right; but when he lifted his hands out to inspect them, they were no longer bleeding and he couldn't see any cuts or scars. He simply shrugged and thought it made sense that his hands should bleed in the stream, and he lowered them back in.

He stooped even lower so not to lose any of the water from his hands, and splashed his cupped hands against his face. He could feel the skin on his face tighten from the sudden cold, and he smiled with the feeling. He reached his hands back into the stream, again with the blood that drifted and swirled away downstream, and he stooped close to the surface and brought his cupped hands to his mouth and he drank that deliciously cold, clear water.

He had the sudden thought that he may get sick from drinking water from a stream like that, and cast a look up at Jonathon.

"Don't worry, you can drink it," Jonathon said, smiling and showing his white teeth.

Sam reached down and drank greedily from his cupped hands again. He splashed his face once more, and smiled at his skin which again constricted with the cold. He fell back on his haunches and sat on the grass beside Jonathon, their backs to the mountains and the sunrise as they watched the valley spread out in front of them for what seemed like forever, the mountains on each side inexorably falling away until they disappeared behind the horizon. The two old friends sat there quietly and enjoyed the crisp air and the breeze that smelled of the grasses and the forests high up in the mountains, and the sound of the water as it slid and gurgled past him.

Off to their right, Sam saw a man working the banks. "Who's that?" he asked.

"That's Abdul—Marie," Jonathon said, casting a look at Sam.

Sam frowned. "What's he doing here?" He made a move to get up, but Jonathon put his hand on his shoulder and told him to sit down.

"Don't worry about it, Sam." Jonathon paused, watching the man. "He likes to come here in the mornings before most people are awake. Usually he doesn't have his rod with him."

"But why is he here? He... didn't he... how can you...?"

Jonathon smiled. "He's here for the same reason you and I are."

But Sam thought that Jonathon had misunderstood his question, and was about to reword it when Jonathon got to his feet.

"I gotta go," he said, gesturing for Sam not to get up.

Sam looked up at him and didn't understand. "Where are you going? I thought we were gonna fish?"

"We can do that later," he said, but he didn't say where he was going, and Sam was about to ask him again when Jonathon spoke before he could.

"It's good to see you, Sam," Jonathon said smiling a big warm smile that showed his gleaming-white teeth. "Don't worry about it. Why don't you just hang out for a while?" Again he flashed a bright smile. "I'll see you soon."

Sam forced a smile, though suddenly he was so sad to see Jonathon go that he thought he might cry. "Yeah. Well, I'll be right here if you want to hang out some more. It sure was good seeing you, Jon."

Jonathon looked down at his friend and nodded his head. "Good to see you too, Sam." And then he turned and walked away.

Sam watched in amazement as Jonathon walked down the bank toward Marie. When he saw Jonathon greet the man and the two exchange a warm handshake, he thought it was the damnedest thing he'd ever seen. He shook his head and laughed to himself, and then lay back on the ground, folding his hands behind his head for a pillow and crossing his feet, wondering where Jonathon had had to run off to. Suddenly he felt the warmth of the sun on his shoulders and he turned toward it.

He awoke in Rachel's room, the sun pouring through the blinds onto where he lay on her bed.

Fuck. He looked around the room, and then let his head back down and covered his eyes with his hands. Fuck.

He thought about what he was going to say to her when she came home. Thank you? I'm sorry? How long have I been here? I hate myself and what I've done to you? But none of that said all of it. He got up gingerly and limped to the bathroom. He was shocked when he looked in the mirror. His left eye was swollen nearly shut, there was a gash on his forehead, and his upper lip was split and swollen. He shook his head in disgust and tried to shower, but became dizzy and threw up.

He swore at himself again and told himself to get the hell out of her apartment, that he was a worthless sack of shit and an utter failure, and he had no business ruining her life.

He staggered back to the bed and reached for his jeans. They had been cleaned and folded and placed on the chair in the corner.

He was so weak that his hands and arms shook, and he had to sit down to get them on.

When he finally got them on, he walked into the kitchen and poured himself a glass of water. But the water dribbled over his lip and down his chin onto the floor. He swore and slowly bent down to wipe it up. He was suddenly starving and reached into her pantry for a slice of bread, the only thing he thought he would be able to get down. He carefully sat down on the kitchen chair and slowly chewed the soft bread. His breathing was shallow and forced and his head ached with an enormous pressure.

Hearing only his wheezy breathing, he realized the heavy silence in the apartment. He looked at the clock on the stove. Almost four. What to do? Get out? Run like hell? Stay? Could you possibly stay? Wouldn't she just throw you out when she came home and found you awake? Of course she would. Better to save you both all of that and just get out before she got home.

He limped back into her room and was pulling his shirt on when he heard the door open. He sat down on the bed, his eyes on the floor.

He was still staring at the floor when she walked in. She stopped in the doorway and looked at him, sitting on the edge of her bed, broken and bleeding, his clothes torn. She stood looking at him for a long time, waiting for him to look up at her. But he never did.

He finally shook his head slowly, his eyes still on the ground in front of him, and mumbled something that she couldn't hear.

She was at his feet before he had finished.

"I'm sorry," he forced himself, still unable to look at her, still unable to stand the thought of her seeing him like this and of what he had done to her.

She bent her head down so that he could see her and he saw that she was crying. Her beautiful eyes were red and full of tears as she looked up at him.

"Rachel, I don't—" he began, but he never got the chance to make any kind of speech.

She kissed him on the forehead, and then gingerly on the cheek. She grabbed his hands with his busted knuckles and kissed them. He felt the softness of her lips against the cracks and it felt delicious. He could smell her hair, that beautiful familiar scent, and he breathed it in with a long, slow draw.

She looked up at him again and kissed him softly on the mouth, contorting her mouth for his bulging upper lip. It hurt like hell but he did not care.

They made love like he never had before in his entire life and like he never would again.

After, as they lay there, he felt her breath blow through his chest hair and the smooth skin of her inner thigh as it rested over his leg. Her tiny hand draped over his dog tags, the Saint Jude medallion slowly rising and falling on his chest.

No.

He felt her hair tickle the bottom of his chin, and he smiled sadly and stored that memory away for one day when he would be an old man without her, sitting on his porch watching the sun set. He grew sad because he knew now that he had messed the whole thing up, and that it would not ever be right like it could have been. But even though he knew all of that, and he knew that the only way to put it right was to go back and tell her everything, and he knew if he did that things could be good—that they would be good—that he could tell her right now, he knew he would not. He knew that she would forgive him but he could not stand the thought of that awful forgiveness.

Not that it never could be right, but that it never would be. Remember that, Sam, he told himself. Remember that it could have been right, but that you chose for it not to be. He leaned forward and kissed her gently on her forehead, blessing the day he met her, blessing the day he fell in love with her, and asking her to forgive him for what would happen. He leaned his head back on the pillow and thought, Not that it could not have been, but that it would not be. That's very important, Sam, remember that.

END OF BOOK II

Epilogue

He left her on a Sunday morning.

When she woke up, the sun's rays danced through the blinds on the window, and cast blurry images on the wall next to her bed.

She knew that something was wrong as soon as she opened her eyes. She could hear Claire crying in her room, and knew he was gone. Knew it even before she realized that today was her birthday, and she was now twenty-four years old. She got out of bed quietly, numbly, and walked across the hall to Claire's room. She opened the door and looked at her daughter standing in her crib, her face bright red from screaming, and her eyes all puffy from crying. She thought how that was how she felt right then, all empty and numb and torn up inside, with no way to find the words to express the storm raging inside her.

She stood in the doorway to her daughter's room, watching her scream and cry, thinking how she had known he would leave, but had hoped she was wrong. She had seen his leaving in his face sometimes when he would watch her and he didn't think that she saw him. It had been in his eyes and in the way he had made love to her. There was something he had held back, something careful and heavy there, some kind of weight. He had pretended well enough for the past two months since he had come home to her, and she had known that he wanted it to be right. But still there was that sadness in his sighing which her perpetual hope had told her would pass.

Now, she walked over to Claire and lifted her out of her bed and wiped her face clean with her hand, the angriness in her face slowly fading. The two walked into the kitchen, where a piece of paper rested on the counter next to the stove. She walked over to it and picked it up. In the middle of the white sheet he had rubbed over his medallion of Saint Jude with a pencil, the blotch of graphite a stark contrast to the white of the paper. On the paper, he had written, "Rachel, God bless this mess. Yours, Sam."

And that was it.

She made herself go to church that morning. Made herself give Claire a bath, even made a point to dress her in the new light-blue dress she had wanted to save for a special day. Then she made herself get dressed and put on the dress that she had worn at his parents' house that day when Claire had decorated him with flowers, and she had sat next to him and thought that she had seen the despair leave him.

They were quite a pair, the two of them, as they walked across the green lawn to the church in the bright sunlight, Rachel stooping just a little to hold little Claire's hand because she wanted to walk. Grasshoppers jumped from beneath their tread. The morning was humid with the heat of June, and the sweat that beaded on their foreheads only added to the radiance of the two of them as they walked out of the bright sunlight into the cool light of the church. Even some of the women who stood around sharing other people's prayer concerns couldn't help but stop their chatter and smile at the picture of the two of them walking through the doors: they were like giants, the both of them, like the last two bright lights in the sky chasing the sun after it has set and everything else is darkness. Their entrance, to some, was all they would remember about the service that morning.

Normally, she would drop Claire off with Miss Annette for Sunday school, but not today. Today she needed her daughter next to her at church to remind her of what she had told him in a letter so long ago: that God works in and through our brokenness, something she still believed, even though right now she didn't want to.

"There is nothing new under the sun..." Pastor Bob was saying in his sermon, but her heart wasn't in it and she couldn't keep up. Everything inside her was fragile, as if it all might shatter at the slightest bump. There was a moment during the sermon when Claire's incessant shifting made her want to grab the hymn book in her hands and fling it at the pulpit, branding them all as a bunch of suckers, that couldn't they see it wasn't worth it, all their hope was a waste, that they believed in something that simply could not be true? All the evidence, all the proof, pointed in the other direction, couldn't they see? Fools, all of them. Especially herself.

She tried to force herself to take communion, but when she placed the flat round wafer in her mouth she thought of the first time they had made love, and her stomach lurched inside her and she wanted to throw up. She passed on the grape juice because she didn't have the faith or the strength to take it.

She did not realize the service was over until she found herself standing and receiving the benediction to go in peace. To go in peace, she thought, and she saw in front of her a road that forked. And to the left she saw him walking away, and it was dark where he was going and she wanted to run after him, to walk through the darkness with him, and who knows? maybe they would come out all right on the other end. But she knew that was not how it would be if she followed after him; she knew that she would be lost too. And so she chose the road to the right, but her heart broke all over again when she did, and instead of walking down that road away from him, she collapsed in a heap.

Tears ran down her cheeks as she watched him disappear into the dark and she heard the congregation say "Amen."

One of the old men who always wore suspenders and loved to say hi to Claire on Sundays reached across the pew and nodded, "Good mornin'," to Rachel, and patted Claire's shoulder with a warm smile, saying, "Good mornin', darlin'," like he did every Sunday. Claire beamed back at him and laughed like she did every Sunday, the light pouring through the stained-glass windows falling on the wall behind her.

They walked back outside into the bright morning light, the two tiny giants hand in hand, Venus and the moon chasing the sun through the night.

As they walked back across the lawn, Rachel's white dress and light brown hair blowing softly in the breeze, she heard Pastor Bob ring the church bell, its reverberations traveling thick in the warm, damp air. She turned and watched, lifting the one hand that was not holding Claire's to shield her eyes from the sun. They both stood there and watched the man grip high on the thick rope and heave down again and again.

Pastor Bob always rang the bell for the ten-thirty service, but never for the nine o'clock. He said that a big bell ringing at nine in the morning just wasn't good manners to folks who may be sleeping off Saturday night, but that come ten-thirty they'd had enough sleep and maybe that bell would remind them that it's best to get up and get to church.

As she stood there, she thought of him, and remembered that it was her birthday and that he had left her on her birthday. It made her sad to think that he thought his leaving was his birthday gift to her. The best he could give her. And that lie made her sad, but she steeled herself against that pity, and told herself that eventually she must pick herself up and start walking again. That it would get easier with every step, but she must not follow him.

And right then, as Pastor Bob made the last hard pull on the old rope, and that last ring echoed through the air and over the trees, she saw him slogging through that darkness all by himself. And as she watched him, she asked God that he would hear that last ring and know that the truth is that none of us are innocent—not entirely; we were not born to be perfect, and no gospel of anything will ever make it happen. That the real tragedy of it all is that we disqualify ourselves long before God has a chance to say one way or the other.

And with that last echo, she prayed that one day he would learn to let his life be what our lives are indeed meant to be: a broken—and beautiful—hallelujah. Then, with her daughter's magnificent, miraculous little hand in hers, they started the walk home.

ACKNOWLEDGMENTS

It was the Summer of 2003 in Mosul, Iraq, when I ran into a very good friend of mine whom I had not seen since we deployed. We hugged each other and slapped the other's shoulder and stood around smiling a lot. I can't remember the bulk of the conversation, but I do remember when John told me he had written a book. I couldn't believe it. You can just write a book? Just like that? Yep. Just like that. Well shoot, I thought, I'm gonna write a book too. *Birdmen* is a direct result of that conversation. So thank you very much, John.

I would be remiss if I did not thank the hundreds of soldiers I have served with, and with whom I have shared the thousand little sights and sounds and smells that form the backdrop for this book. They are truly great Americans whose service honors us as a people, and whom we could not thank enough. *ATR!*

Several people helped edit this book, offering insight and asking me to re-look several portions. Brandon Bennett and Greg Weisler were gracious enough to offer me their critiques, and I am sure the book is better for their suggestions. Lindsay Horne was especially generous with her time—and patience—in smoothing out some of the rough edges in the manuscript. I am both humbled by and extraordinarily thankful for all of their time and energy.

Erik Castellanos painted the cover art, and I am grateful for his thoughtful interpretation, as well as his friendship and talent. I also want to thank Stacey Mieding, who took care of the design for the cover, perhaps putting more thought into the font for the title than I did for the actual title itself.

In case anyone wants to know what the highest measure of love and devotion is, it just may be rereading countless times your husband's successive manuscripts of "his book." My wife Emily generously offered her time and talent to help make the book the best it could be, often challenging me to find the most constructive way to tell this story, and I am thankful for it.

Any errors, of course, are solely my responsibility. Though I have read the manuscript over and over again, I am perpetually confounded by the presence of errors, and have decided to chalk it up as metaphor.

And finally, thank you for buying my book. I hope you enjoy it.

A PARTING SHOT

There are two organizations—both nonprofits—that I am rather passionate about and would like to introduce you to as a parting shot before we go our separate ways.

The Wainwright Foundation is a pending nonprofit whose mission is to support the development of America's future leadership by investing in youth-led, community-based projects, and creating a forum to discuss and share lessons learned. We at the Wainwright Foundation believe that our nation is suffering because we as a people have convinced ourselves that our civic responsibility stops at the ballot box; the Wainwright Foundation is committed to reversing that ethic by exposing our young leaders to the multiple challenges in their communities, and participating with them in their efforts to make a difference. Our investment is in the future leaders of our country; our return on investment is a more engaged citizenry and the perpetuation of our American heritage. We invite you to visit us at www.wainwrightfoundation.org for more.

The US Military Endowment is run by two men I served with in Iraq. The US Military Endowment's mission is to provide resources to our brave men and women who have served in the military, so that they may successfully transition from military to civilian life. Since their inception, they have focused on building vital every day skills for our veterans, and raising awareness about the challenges they face upon their return from combat. Some quick facts:

- over 1.5 million American service members have served in Iraq and Afghanistan since the Global War on Terror began;
- 30 to 40% of those veterans will face psychological wounds upon coming home;
- the VA estimates that one third of the adult homeless population are veterans, and that about 131,000 vets are homeless on any given night. (See www.mentalhealth.va.gov/homelessness for more.)

To say the least, those numbers are staggering. We at the US Military Endowment simply find them unacceptable, and are committed to doing something about it. As my good friend Pete Kyriakoulis, one of the founders, once said to me over a cup of coffee, the idea is that "maybe one day, when we're old men, we'll be able to look back and say that we made the world a little better for the next generation of soldiers." Please visit the US Military Endowment's website at www.usmilitaryendowment.org to learn how we can all help thank our veterans in a tangible and meaningful way.

For those of us who have experienced the profound privilege of leading our service members and serving our country, we must insist that our responsibility does not end when we hang up the uniform. The fact is that we all took oaths that bind us in perpetuity to our country and her people. To those of us who do not know the great pleasure of serving in uniform, we must remember that these men and women are our neighbors and our countrymen, and that the worst kind of betrayal would be to deny them in their hour of need, when they did not do so while we were in ours.

All over the country there are centers where our homeless veterans are taken off the street and taught the skills they need to turn their lives around. Please find one of the centers near you, and express your gratitude with your time and money.

I know that things are tough right now. They will get better. Thank you for donating your hard-earned money to these very worthy causes.